Sinful Secrets

These passionate lovers hide sizzling secrets…

Three passionate novels!

By
Request™

*In February 2007 Mills & Boon bring
back two of their classic collections,
each featuring three favourite
romances by our bestselling authors…*

SINFUL SECRETS

A Secret Vengeance by Miranda Lee
Sarah's Secret by Catherine George
Morgan's Secret Son by Sara Wood

ITALIAN PROPOSALS

The Venetian's Proposal
by Lee Wilkinson
The Italian Doctor's Wife
by Sarah Morgan
The Italian Doctor's Proposal
by Kate Hardy

Sinful Secrets

A SECRET VENGEANCE
by
Miranda Lee

SARAH'S SECRET
by
Catherine George

MORGAN'S SECRET SON
by
Sara Wood

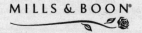
MILLS & BOON®

*MILLS & BOON and MILLS & BOON with the Rose Device
are registered trademarks of the publisher.*
Harlequin Mills & Boon Limited,
Eton House, 18-24 Paradise Road, Richmond, Surrey, TW9 1SR

SINFUL SECRETS © by Harlequin Enterprises II B.V. 2007

A Secret Vengeance, Sarah's Secret and *Morgan's Secret Son* were
first published in Great Britain by Harlequin Mills & Boon
Limited in separate, single volumes.

A Secret Vengeance © Miranda Lee 2001
Sarah's Secret © Catherine George 2002
Morgan's Secret Son © Sara Wood 2001

ISBN 10: 0 263 85510 4
ISBN 13: 978 0 263 85510 4

05-0207

*Printed and bound in Spain
by Litografia Rosés S.A., Barcelona*

A SECRET VENGEANCE

by

Miranda Lee

Miranda Lee is Australian, living near Sydney. Born and raised in the bush, she was boarding-school educated and briefly pursued a career in classical music, before moving to Sydney and embracing the world of computers. Happily married, with three daughters, she began writing when family commitments kept her at home. She likes to create stories that are believable, modern, fast-paced and sexy. Her interests include meaty sagas, doing word puzzles, gambling and going to the movies.

PROLOGUE

CELIA was still half asleep when the phone rang. Lifting one eyelid, she glanced at her bedside clock radio.

Ten past eight. Not all that early, she supposed, but it was Sunday. Celia liked to sleep in on a Sunday. Everyone who knew her well, *knew* she liked to sleep in on a Sunday.

Which meant whoever was ringing her at this ungodly hour must have a good reason for doing so.

"Probably Mum," Celia muttered as she threw back her duvet and reached for the receiver.

"Hello," she said.

"He's dead," came a woman's voice, sounding spaced out.

Celia sucked in sharply and sat up. It *was* her mother. And Celia didn't have to ask who *he* was.

There was only one *he* in her mother's life. Lionel Freeman. Sydney's most awarded architect. Fifty-four years old. Married, with one grown-up son, named Luke.

Celia's mother had been Lionel Freeman's mistress for more years than her daughter liked to think about.

"What...what happened?" Celia asked, her thoughts whirling.

"He's dead," her mother repeated like a stuck record.

Celia took a deep breath and tried not to panic. "Is Lionel there with you now?"

"What?"

"Did Lionel come to visit you at Pretty Point this weekend?" Celia was thinking heart attack or stroke. The idea that they might have been actually *doing it* at the time brought a degree of revulsion. But it had to be faced. That was why Lionel Freeman visited his mistress after all. To have sex. And plenty of it, no doubt.

"No. No, he was going to, but then he couldn't make it."

Celia was torn between relief and anger. Her mother had wasted nearly half of her life waiting for her married lover to show up.

Well, now her waiting for Lionel was over. For good. But at what price?

"It was on the radio."

"What was on the radio, Mum?"

"They said it wasn't his fault. The other driver was drunk."

Celia nodded. Sounded like an accident of some kind. A car crash. And Lionel Freeman had been killed.

There was little pity in her heart for the man, only for her mother, her poor deluded mother who'd sacrificed everything for the illicit moments she'd spent with him. She'd loved Lionel Freeman more than life itself.

Now he was dead, and his distraught mistress was all alone in the secret love nest where the selfish Lionel had installed her a few years back.

Celia was terrified that, once the reality of her beloved's death sank in, her mum might very well do something stupid. Celia wasn't going to let that happen. Her mother had wasted twenty years of her life on Lionel Freeman. Celia wasn't going to let him take her with him in death.

"Mum, go and make yourself a cup of tea," she said firmly. "And put plenty of sugar in it. I'll be with you very soon."

Celia lived not all that far away, in Swansea. She also drove a zappy little hatchback which could move when she wanted it to.

Celia reached Pretty Point in twenty-three minutes flat. A record, considering it usually took her over half an hour. Of course, there'd hardly been a car on the road. The Sunday day-trippers from Sydney didn't swarm up in their droves till the seriously warm weather arrived, and summer was still a couple of months off.

"Mum?" she called out as she knocked frantically on the locked back door. "Mum, where are you? Let me in."

No answer. Celia's chest tightened like a vice as she raced round to the front of the house which faced the lake. She began imagining all kinds of horror scenarios.

But there her mother was, sitting at a table on the deck which overlooked the lake. The rising sun was behind her, outlining her perfect profile and glinting on her softly curled red-gold hair. She was wearing a silky lemon robe, sashed tightly around her still tiny waist. From a distance, she looked very young and very beautiful.

And, thankfully, very alive.

Celia heaved a great sigh of relief and hurried up the wooden steps which led onto the deck.

Her mother glanced up at her, her usually expressive green eyes worryingly vacant. She'd made the cup of tea, as ordered, but it sat in front of her, untouched.

She was still in deep shock, Celia realised.

"Mum," she chided gently as she sat down opposite her. "You haven't drunk your tea."

"What?"

"Your tea…"

"Oh… Yes… The tea. I'm sorry. I made it but I forgot to drink it."

"So I see." Celia decided against making another. Far better to get her mother away from here as soon as possible to a place where someone could watch her twenty-four hours a day for a while.

As much as Celia would have liked that person to be herself, she had a clinic to run and appointments that she simply had to keep this coming week. And the next week too. Maybe, by the end of that week, she could clear her diary somewhat and have some time off.

Meanwhile, Aunt Helen would have to come to the party, whether she wanted to or not.

"Mum," she said firmly, "you do know you can't stay here, don't you? This place belonged to Lionel. No doubt he kept it a secret from his family, but there will be a deed somewhere. Sooner or later, someone will show up and if you're still here, questions will be asked. You always told me Lionel didn't want his wife and son to know about you, so…"

"She's dead too," her mother broke in. "His wife. Kath. In the accident. They were both killed instantly."

"Dear heaven. How dreadful." Celia sagged back against her chair. She'd often wished Lionel Freeman would go take a running jump from one of his tallest buildings, but she'd never wished any harm on his unfortunate wife.

Poor woman, Celia thought.

"Poor Luke," her mother choked out. "He's going to be shattered."

Celia frowned. She didn't often think of the son, especially nowadays. He was a grown man after all, and not living at home. But now that her mother had mentioned him, she did feel sorry for the man. How awful to lose both his parents so tragically, especially his mother. Still, there was nothing she could do for him. She had her own shattered mother to worry about.

Her mum suddenly looked up, her eyes troubled. "You're right," she said in panicky tones. "I can't stay here. Luke might come. Lionel would die if Luke found out about me."

Once she realised what she'd just said, her face paled and a strangled sob escaped her throat.

"I doubt Lionel's son would come here personally, Mum," Celia reassured her. "But even if he does, you won't be here. I'm taking you to stay at Aunt Helen's for a while till I can organise something more permanent for you."

Her mother shook her head from side to side, tears flooding her eyes. "No. No, I couldn't go there. Helen didn't approve of my relationship with Lionel. She hated him.''

Didn't we all? Celia thought ruefully.

But this was hardly the time to say so.

''She hated what he did to you, Mum,'' Celia said gently. ''Which is another thing entirely. And the situation's changed now, isn't it?''

''But she never understood,'' her mother cried, the tears spilling over. ''You didn't either, did you, Celia? You thought I was wicked. And a fool.''

''I never thought you were wicked, Mum.''

''But you thought me a fool. And maybe I was. But love makes fools of all of us.''

Not me, Celia vowed privately. Never! When and if she fell in love, it wouldn't be with a man like Lionel Freeman.

''I know you think Lionel didn't really love me,'' her mother said brokenly. ''But he did.''

''If you say so, Mum,'' was all Celia could say to that.

''You don't believe me.''

Celia neither denied, nor confirmed this truth.

''There are things you don't know…things I've never told you…''

''And please don't go telling me now, Mum,'' Celia begged. The last thing she wanted to listen to was all the lies Lionel had fed his mistress to excuse and explain his two decades of adultery. She'd refused to discuss Lionel with her mother for some years now.

Her mother sighed a long shuddering sigh and, as the air left her lungs, so, it seemed, did her spirit. Her shoulders sagged. Her eyes dulled. Perhaps it was only the sun going behind a cloud, but so did her hair.

Suddenly, the eternally youthful and sensual creature that Lionel Freeman had lusted after so obsessively faded to nothing but a shadow of her former self. Till a moment before, she could have passed for thirty. Now, she looked every second of her forty-two years. And more.

"You're right," she said with a weariness that worried Celia more than her earlier shocked state. "What does anything matter any more? He's dead. Lionel is dead. It's over."

Celia gazed anxiously at her mother. This was what she'd been afraid of, her thinking there was nothing left to live for without the man she adored.

People said she was just like her mother, and she was, in looks. But, there, any similarities ended.

Her mother was a romantic, Celia, a realist. Especially when it came to men. Impossible for her to be otherwise after twenty years of watching her mother being so ruthlessly used by Lionel Freeman.

Perversely, there'd been a time when Celia had thought Lionel was wonderful. He'd entered her life when she'd been six, a lonely, fatherless little girl. What lonely little six-year-old wouldn't have adored the handsome man who'd made her mummy so happy when he'd visited, and had brought such marvellous toys?

It hadn't been till Celia had reached puberty that she'd taken off her rose-coloured glasses where her mummy's friend had been concerned. Once she'd realised exactly what Lionel came to visit for, and that he made her mother cry much more than smile, Celia's love for him had turned to hate overnight.

Outraged as only a disillusioned and disgusted teenager was able, she'd confronted Lionel and had torn strips off him, appalled when her mother had then torn strips off her in return for being out of line. But, after that, the lovers had met elsewhere other than at her mother's flat. Celia's mum had still cried a lot in the dead of night, and a distraught Celia had vowed never to grow up and fall in love with any man who wasn't a genuine Mr Wonderful. Her dream man wouldn't be afraid of commitment and fatherhood. And he certainly wouldn't be already married to someone else, like Lionel. He would be decent and honest, brave and reliable, loyal and loving.

Oh, and of course he'd be terribly good-looking and a really good kisser. She'd been only thirteen when she'd conjured up this vision of masculine perfection, after all.

Celia hadn't found him yet. In fact, she was pretty sure her Mr Wonderful didn't exist. She'd had quite a few boyfriends since leaving school, but hadn't found a single one who didn't eventually disappoint her, both in bed and out.

Maybe she had impossibly high standards. Her girlfriends always said she did. Whatever, her relationships never worked out.

The last one had been a couple of months ago. He'd been a footballer she'd treated for a knee injury, and he had pursued her to death after his treatments had finished, telling her he was simply crazy about her, promising her the world if she would just go out with him.

She had in the end, because she'd actually found him very attractive. She liked tall, well-built men. He was also surprisingly intelligent and seemingly sincere. Naturally, she'd made him wait for sex. She never went to bed with a guy on a first date. Nor a second. Nor even a third. When she finally had, she'd wished she hadn't. For it had been such an anticlimax.

He'd seemed pretty satisfied, however, which was always the case with men, she'd found. They really weren't too worried about their girlfriends' lack of orgasms, provided the girlfriend was coming across. They always blamed the woman, never themselves. And they invariably promised things would get better.

Sometimes, if the guy was nice, Celia hung in there, hoping things *would* improve. But when the footballer had sensitively informed her during his second go that his previous girlfriend would have come three times by then, Celia had decided Mr Wonderful he wasn't. Nor ever would be.

She'd dumped him the next morning.

Pity her mother hadn't dumped Lionel Freeman the morning after all those years ago when she'd found out he was married. But then, Lionel, in bed at least, *had been* her mother's Mr Wonderful. Apparently, she did refuse to see him for a little while. But the manipulative devil had wormed his way back into her bed with all those excuses and lies Celia didn't want to hear about, and he'd been there on a regular basis ever since.

Celia didn't doubt it was a case of true love on her

mum's part, but she would put a million dollars on it being nothing but lust on darling Lionel's.

Celia wanted to be angry with her mother for being such a romantic fool all these years but, somehow, she couldn't. Not today. Not when the poor woman's heart was already breaking apart.

"Why don't you go shower and dress while I ring Aunt Helen?" she suggested gently.

Fortunately, Celia's aunt lived less than ten miles away, over at Dora Creek. Her husband, John, worked at the local power station. Their two sons had long grown up and left home, so they had plenty of spare bedrooms.

Her mother shrugged listlessly. "Whatever."

"We'll just pack you a small case of essentials for now. I can come back at a later date and get the rest of your things." There was no real hurry. Under the circumstances, Celia couldn't see anyone turning up here for ages. She doubted Lionel's son ever would personally. Seriously rich people had lackeys to attend to such matters. And Luke Freeman was now a seriously rich man.

She stood up, her car keys still in her hand.

Her mother levered herself up slowly before glancing around with sad eyes. "Lionel really loved this place," she said wanly. "He designed and built it, especially for us."

Celia didn't doubt it. The A-framed cabin with its glass façade and large wooden decks overlooking the lake made the perfect love nest. Remote and beautiful in setting, the open-plan interior was filled with all the romantic accoutrements lovers would appreciate. A huge sandstone fireplace, complete with deep squashy sofas flanking a plushly piled cream rug. Upstairs, the loft bedroom was dominated by a king-sized bed, with the adjoining bathroom sporting a spa bath which could easily accommodate two.

No guest room, of course. Lionel had never wanted his mistress to have guests.

Celia had never stayed here overnight. Neither did she drop in on a weekend, unless her mother gave her the all clear. Running into Lionel had been something to be avoided at all costs since she'd grown up, because Celia had known she would have been vicious to him if the occasion had arisen.

But she visited her mother at least once during most weeks. And regardless of the day, she always knew if Lionel had visited the previous weekend. He'd had this distinctive cologne that he'd always worn, and that had lingered long after he'd been gone. She could remember smelling it in her mother's bedroom as a child, especially when she'd climbed into her mother's bed in the morning. It always disturbed her to remember how much she'd liked the smell back then. And how much she'd liked Lionel.

''Mum, let's go,'' Celia said brusquely, and took her mother's arm.

Jessica went quietly, because she knew it was for the best. There were too many memories of Lionel at Pretty Point. Too many ghosts to haunt her at night. Too many bad thoughts waiting to assail her.

She'd always believed Lionel had genuinely loved her, that his passion for her had been more than sexual.

Now, Jessica wasn't so sure. Often, in the past, when she hadn't seen Lionel for some time, she'd begin having these terrible doubts. But once he'd arrived and had taken her in his arms again, all her doubts would vanish.

But he would never take her in his arms again. Never make love to her again. Never tell her how much she meant to him again.

Which meant her doubts would never be put to rest. They would fester and grow like some dreadful disease.

Jessica's heart seemed to disintegrate in her chest under the weight of this appalling prospect. For if she didn't believe Lionel had loved her as much as she'd loved him, then what had been the point of all the sacrifices she'd made? Never to write to him, nor send him cards. Never to spend Christmas or birthdays with him. Never to go anywhere in public with him.

Never to have his child.

Had it all been a waste of time? Had his love for her been a horrible illusion? Had he really been a deeply sensitive man...or a wickedly selfish liar?

She couldn't bear to think such thoughts. Couldn't bear it.

Suddenly, she began to sob, great heaving sobs which racked her whole body.

"Oh, Mum," her daughter cried and hugged her close. "You'll be all right. You'll see. We just have to get you away from here."

CHAPTER ONE

"IS THAT everything, Harvey?" Luke asked, putting his pen away in his jacket pocket and pushing the papers back across the desk.

"Yes. For now," the solicitor answered, stacking up all the forms and sliding them into a file.

Luke went to rise from his chair.

"No, wait. There is another small matter concerning your father's estate which I need your advice upon."

Luke sat back down and glanced at his watch. It was a quarter to one. He was to meet Isabel downstairs at one for lunch, after which they were going shopping for their wedding rings. "What is it?"

"The Friday before the accident, your father came to see me about a waterfront property he owned on Lake Macquarie."

Luke frowned. "You wouldn't be talking about a place on Pretty Point, would you?"

"Yes. That's the place. Pretty Point. It's a ten-acre holding, plus a single-bedroomed residence."

Luke's frown deepened. "I thought Dad had sold that old place years ago. He'd said he didn't use it any more because the fishing in the lake wasn't what it used to be."

His father had been mad about fishing. He'd taken Luke fishing with him as soon as he'd been old enough to hold a line. By the time Luke was six or seven, father and son would often go away for the weekend together, mostly to the cabin at Pretty Point which had a jetty and a small runabout moored there permanently. Luke's mother had always stayed home on these occasions. She'd hated everything to do with fish. The smell. The feel. Even the taste.

Luke had loved those weekends, but not because of the fishing. It was his dad's company and attention he'd loved. In all honesty, Luke found fishing about as fascinating as watching grass grow.

Luke's discovering basketball in a big way around twelve had finally forced him to confess that he didn't want to go away fishing any more. He'd wanted to spend his weekends at the local youth club, practising his basketball skills and competing in tournaments.

His dad had been very understanding, as he'd always been understanding. He'd been a great dad. And a great husband too.

Of course, his mum had been a wonderful wife as well, one of the old-fashioned kind who hadn't worked, and had devoted herself entirely to her husband and son, a woman who'd taken pride in keeping her home spotless and doing all the cooking and cleaning herself, even though they could well have afforded paid help.

Yet she hadn't been the strongest of women, healthwise, suffering from terrible migraines. Luke could remember as a boy having to be extra quiet around the house when she was having one of her attacks. His father would often come home from work to sit with his wife in her darkened bedroom.

Such a devoted couple.

And now they were both dead, victims of some stoned individual in a four-wheel drive who'd crossed over to the wrong side of the road and had collected his dad's car, head on.

Come tomorrow, the accident would have happened two weeks ago. It had been on a Saturday night, just this side of midnight. It had happened on the Mona Vale road. They'd been returning from a dinner party at Narrabeen.

They'd only been in their mid-fifties. Hardly old. Talk about life being unfair.

Luke shifted in his seat and cleared his throat. What had Harvey been asking him? Oh, yes…about the week-ender at Pretty Point.

"I guess Dad didn't get round to selling the old place after all," he said. "He could be sentimental at times. So what did he want to do with it?"

"He wanted to gift it over to a lady friend of his."

Luke was taken aback. "*Who*?" he demanded to know.

"A Ms Jessica Gilbert."

Luke frowned. Who on earth was Ms Jessica Gilbert?

"I don't recognise the name," he ground out, trying not to think the impossible, but thinking it all the same.

"Don't jump to conclusions, Luke," Harvey advised. "You and I both know your father wasn't that kind of man."

Luke certainly hadn't thought so. Till now. He'd hero-worshipped his father, and had always wanted to be just like him, in every way.

"Did Dad tell you anything about this Ms Gilbert?" he asked, his gut tightening.

"Not all that much. He said she was a lovely lady, to whom life hadn't been very kind, and whom he wanted to help. Apparently, she doesn't own a home of her own and he'd been letting her live in the place at Pretty Point for the last few years, rent free. He thought it best if he gifted the property over to her and then she'd have a secure roof over her head for life."

Luke's inner tension began to ease. His father was well-known for his charitable gestures. But, for a moment there…

"Your father was worried that if he died suddenly and the present rent-free arrangement came to light, your mother might do exactly what you just did: jump to all the wrong conclusions."

"I feel terrible for thinking the worst," Luke confessed, "even for a moment."

"Don't be too hard on yourself. I had a few doubts myself when Lionel first told me, especially when he asked me to be very discreet and not mention it to a soul. But I only had to think of how totally devoted he was to your mother to know I couldn't be more wrong. So, shall I go ahead then," Harvey asked, "and gift the property over to this Ms Gilbert?"

"Yes, yes, draw up the necessary papers and I'll come back and sign them when they're ready."

"I thought you'd say that. Your father would be proud of you, Luke. After all, waterfront properties of that size on Lake Macquarie, regardless of how remote, are worth a bundle these days."

"I'm only doing what Dad wanted. And it's not as though I haven't inherited enough property." As well as the family home in St Ives, Luke now owned several investment units all over Sydney, some right in the CBD. It seemed every time his father had designed a large block of units, part of his fee had been to keep one of them.

"I must go, Harvey," Luke said. "I'm meeting Isabel downstairs at one."

"Ah. The lovely Isabel. What a glorious bride she's going to make. It's such a tragedy to have this dreadful thing happen so close to your marriage."

"Yes. I was going to postpone the ceremony, but things are a bit too far along for that. Isabel's parents have already spent a small fortune, and they're not wealthy people."

"Your own parents wouldn't have wanted you to postpone a single thing, Luke. Your father was especially delighted you were settling down to family life here in Australia. He missed you a lot when you went overseas to work. He was worried you might marry some foreign girl and never come back."

"He should have known I would never do that," Luke said swiftly, and stood up. "I'll see you and your wife at the wedding, then?"

Harvey stood up as well. "Looking forward to it."

Both men shook hands across the desk and Luke left, grateful to have at least temporarily finished with the legal and practical problems that had followed his parents' deaths. There'd been so much to do, so many arrangements, so many decisions to be made. Too many, really.

But being an only child, there'd been no one else. The buck stopped with him.

He hoped he'd done everything well, and properly. He hoped his father *was* proud of him.

Luke's mind returned to Ms Jessica Gilbert on the ride down in the lift and he wondered who she was and how his father had come to know her. Had she been an ex-employee? A loyal secretary who'd worked for him during his early days as a struggling architect? Maybe the cleaning lady who'd looked after the place at Pretty Point all those years ago? Luke recalled some local woman had come in to clean up after them.

Or was she some poor unfortunate whose hard-luck story had come to his dad's attention through one of the various charities he'd given money to? Some elderly spinster who'd never had much, and never would.

Luke thought this last scenario a likely one. His father liked to help little old ladies.

Even so, it was only a guess. He wished Harvey had known more. It was irritating, not knowing the full circumstances behind such a substantial bequest. The weekender at Pretty Point, though small and a bit ramshackle, *was* sitting on a parcel of valuable land.

Maybe, when the time came, he'd take the gifted deed up to the woman personally. That way his curiosity would be well and truly satisfied, and this tiny but nagging doubt that his father might not have been so perfect after all would be safely banished.

Luke still hadn't made up his mind on the issue when

the lift doors opened and there, straight ahead, stood Isabel, looking classy and coolly beautiful, as usual. She was wearing a simple black dress and her long blonde hair was sleekly up, showing off her elegant neck, and the diamond earrings he'd given her recently for her birthday.

She smiled at him, one of those serene smiles that had a soothing effect on Luke, no matter how stressed out he was. He smiled back as he walked towards her, thinking how lucky he was to have found a woman like Isabel to marry. Not only beautiful, but so sensible and level-headed.

He never had to put up with jealous scenes or possessive demands with her as he had with previous girlfriends. On top of that, Isabel could cook like a cordon bleu chef and actually considered being a wife and mother a career in itself. Just like his mum.

She'd already quit her job as receptionist at the large architectural firm Luke was currently contracted to and where they'd met at last year's Christmas party. She had no plans to go back to work after their marriage. They were going to start trying for a baby straight away.

Of course, Isabel *was* thirty, with a whole lifetime of experiences behind her, so she was ripe and ready for settling down, as Luke was himself at thirty-two. Like him, she'd travelled extensively, *and* admitted to several lovers, something that didn't bother Luke one little bit.

He liked the fact Isabel was experienced in bed. He liked it that she wasn't insecure with him. He especially liked the fact she wanted the same things he wanted: a marriage that would last, and a family of at least two children.

Okay, so he wasn't in love with her, and vice versa. But darn it all, he'd fallen in love a few times in the past, and he hadn't really liked the feel of it. It wasn't stable for starters. And it never lasted.

By the time Luke had decided it was time to settle down, he'd concluded romantic love was not a sound basis for marriage. Isabel had reached the same conclusion after a few disastrous love affairs of her own.

Which meant they were perfectly in tune with each other. They had the same goals, and they never ever argued, which was something Luke valued very highly.

Arguments and disagreements always upset him. Quite a lot. He wanted none of that in his marriage. He wanted peace, and harmony. He wanted what his father had had with his mother.

"All finished?" Isabel asked, reaching up to kiss him on the cheek.

"For the time being," he returned, his thoughts sliding once again back to the mysterious Ms Gilbert. Frustrating, really. Why couldn't he forget about her? He opened his mouth to tell Isabel about the woman, then he closed it again. Why, he wasn't sure. Perhaps because he didn't want to see that awful doubt about his father in *her* eyes as well.

Ms Gilbert was just a charity case, Luke reassured himself, some poor little old lady who didn't have the wherewithal to help herself. To think anything else was untenable.

But the more Luke tried to picture Ms Jessica Gilbert

as some poor little old lady, the less he was convinced. His father wouldn't have been worried about his mother jumping to the wrong conclusions if the woman was elderly. He would only have worried about jealousy if the woman was young. And attractive.

"Is there something wrong, Luke?"

"Would you mind very much if I took a rain check on lunch, plus the ring-buying expedition?" he said on the spur of the moment. "There's something I simply must do which can't wait."

"What, for heaven's sake?" She wasn't angry, just puzzled.

"I need to drive up to Lake Macquarie."

Isabel blinked her surprise. "Lake Macquarie! But *why*?"

Why, indeed?

"There's a property up there, an old fishing cabin where Dad used to take me when I was a boy. I haven't been there for years. I just found out that he didn't sell it like I thought he had. I know it sounds crazy but I have this compulsion to see it again."

"And you have to go see it this very day, this very afternoon?"

"Yes."

He expected her to ask more questions but she just smiled a wry smile. "You're a lot more sentimental than you think you are, Luke Freeman. Look, why don't you drive up there and stay the weekend? Have a rest. It'll do you the world of good. These last two weeks must have been dreadful for you."

Yes, he *could* stay the night at least, if he wanted to.

He knew where his father had always hidden the key and he doubted that would have changed.

"You wouldn't mind?" he said.

Isabel shrugged. "Why should I mind? In just over two weeks' time, I'll have you for the rest of my life. I think I can spare you for a couple of days' R and R. But, Luke, I don't want to put off buying the rings. They might need to be resized. Would you trust me to choose them without you?"

Luke couldn't think of any other female he'd ever known who was so blessedly lacking in being a drama queen about things. "You are one incredible woman, do you know that? Here. Take this credit card and put the rings on that. And put lunch on it too."

"If you insist," she said, smiling saucily as she whipped the card out of his fingers.

"I insist," he said, and smiled warmly back at her.

Another thing about Isabel that Luke appreciated was the fact she didn't pretend she didn't like money. She did. Even before the tragedy, which had turned him into a multimillionaire overnight, Isabel had openly appreciated the fact that he was earning a high six-figure salary, owned a town house in Turramurra, drove a recent-model BMW, and could afford to take her to Dream Island on their honeymoon.

Now, of course, he could afford a whole lot more.

"I'll call you later," he promised.

"You'd better."

"And you're right. I might stay up there for a day or two." Depending on what he found once he got there, of course.

"I've already told you to."

"I'll miss you," he said, and kissed her on the cheek.

"You call that a kiss?"

He laughed, then kissed her on the mouth. Her tongue touched his and Luke momentarily regretted not making love with Isabel the night before. But, at the time, he hadn't wanted to. He hadn't wanted sex in any way, shape or form since the funerals.

"Mmm." His lips lifted and he smiled wryly down at her. "I might come back tonight after all."

"Waste of time, handsome. I'm taking Rachel out to dinner and the theatre tonight, remember? I can't put it off. I've already arranged everything."

"I wouldn't want you to put it off," he told her. Rachel was an old school friend of Isabel's from her boarding school days. She'd once been a top secretary at the Australian Broadcasting Corporation, but she hadn't worked for some years. Nowadays, she spent twenty-four hours a day, seven days a week, looking after her foster mother who had Alzheimer's.

Luke could well imagine how much Rachel looked forward to the one night a month off Isabel organised for her. He'd met her once briefly, and had thought how tired and old she'd looked. Yet she was only a year older than Isabel.

"It'll keep, won't it?" Isabel added.

"Sure." Luke shrugged, the need already fading. They'd never gone through one of those lust-driven stages where they'd just had to have each other, regardless of where they were, or what was going on around them. They'd become friends before they'd become lovers. Some engaged couples Luke knew couldn't keep their hands off each other, even in public. He and Isabel were never like that.

Which perhaps explained why his father had taken Luke aside at his engagement party and had questioned him on whether he was completely happy with Isabel in bed. Luke had been taken aback at the time by his father's grilling over their sex life, but he had assured him that everything was fine in the bedroom department.

Thinking of this instance, however, suddenly made Luke wonder if his father had been totally happy with *his* sex life. To all intents and purposes, Luke's parents had *seemed* happy with each other. They were openly affectionate with each other. Always holding hands and hugging. But who knew what happened behind closed doors?

Luke imagined that a man dissatisfied with his sex life might be tempted to stray…

"I think you'd better get going, Luke," Isabel said drily. "You've drifted off somewhere again."

"Sorry."

"You were thinking of your father, weren't you?"

Luke stared at her.

"You don't have to look at me like that. I know what he meant to you. And I know how much you'll miss him. Much more than your mother. Oh, I know you loved your mother too. How could you not? She was the nicest, sweetest lady. But your father was more to you than a parent. He was your best friend. And your hero. So go and talk to him for a while up at that old place on Lake Macquarie. He'll be there, I'm sure. And he'll listen to you, as he always did.''

Luke now wished he'd told Isabel the complete truth about Pretty Point. He hadn't realised she had such sensitivity. She always seemed so pragmatic about things.

But it was too late now. She'd wonder why he hadn't been honest with her right from the start. And their relationship might suffer.

But it was a valuable lesson learned. He vowed to always tell his fiancée the truth in future, no matter what.

CHAPTER TWO

WHEN the idea to go to Pretty Point for the weekend first popped into Celia's head, she'd immediately rejected it. But the more she'd thought about it, the more she'd realised that Lionel's love nest was the perfect getaway.

And, brother, did she need to get away.

The last two weeks had left her totally and utterly drained. She'd spent every evening and all the previous weekend over at Aunt Helen's, either sitting with her almost catatonic mother, or arguing with her aunt over what should be done about her.

Celia wanted her mother to see a psychiatrist, and to get onto some medication for depression, but her sister disagreed.

''Jessica isn't crazy,'' Helen had stated firmly last night. ''Just broken-hearted. All she needs is time, and some tender loving care and she'll come good. You'll be the one needing medication shortly if you keep worrying about her the way you are. Now, I don't want to see hide nor hair of you this weekend, Celia. Go out with your friends. Or better still, go away somewhere. *Anywhere.*''

Celia lent back in the deck chair with a sigh and thought *anywhere* had never looked so good. What was it about a water view that relaxed nerves and soothed even the weariest soul?

She had to give to Lionel. He'd built his love nest on one superb spot.

He'd also had great taste in wine.

Celia took another sip of the excellent Chablis she'd found chilling in the fridge door and thought how lucky it was that her last appointment had cancelled that afternoon. She always tried to finish up early on a Friday but it was a real stroke of luck to finish at lunch-time. By two o'clock, she'd been packed and on her way to Pretty Point, with only a small detour necessary for some groceries.

And now here she was, mid-afternoon, with a lovely glass of wine in her hands, a million-dollar view to enjoy, and two days of blissful peace and solitude to look forward.

Celia kept on sipping the wine and gradually, the tension melted out of her knotted neck and shoulder muscles till she was leaning back, feeling deliciously mellow. Alcohol, she decided, was proving much more relaxing than all the head rotating exercises she'd been trying on herself every night this week. And infinitely more relaxing than Joanne's solution.

"What you need, honey," Celia's fellow physio at the clinic had said yesterday, "is to get laid."

Pig's ear, she did.

Sex never relaxed Celia. Her only feelings afterwards were disappointment, disillusionment and dismay.

But that was just her, she'd finally accepted. Sex *was* widely accepted as a very pleasurable activity, as well as being touted as mother nature's sleeping pill. *She* was the abnormal one.

Her mother had obviously been very partial to sex. With Lionel, anyway.

More than partial. She'd been possessed by it.

Celia wondered what it would be like to experience the sort of uncontrollable passion that turned an otherwise intelligent, independent woman into some kind of mindless sex slave. Had the pleasure of the moments spent with Lionel compensated for her mother's pain afterwards? Had a weekend of sex and excitement with him been worth weeks of subsequent depression?

Celia had to assume her mother thought it had. Otherwise, why keep on doing it?

Maybe if *she* was ever swept up in a *grande* passion—or even a *petite* passion—Celia might understand her mother's masochistic behaviour. As it was, from an objective, outsider's point of view, such an all-consuming passion seemed nothing better than a slow-acting poison. One of those corrosive substances that ate away at one's insides till there was nothing left but a dying shell.

Her mother had been well on the way to being reduced to such a shell long before Lionel had died. Hopefully, his death had come just in time and Aunt Helen was right: with a bit of tender loving care Celia's mother might not end up having a complete nervous breakdown, nor going stark raving mad.

On the other hand…

Celia scowled at herself. She really didn't want to

think about her mother's ill-fated relationship with Lionel Freeman this weekend.

Difficult not to, however, considering where she was. The place still reeked of the illicit lovers. Celia might have cleared all the rooms of her mother's things, but Jessica's highly individual decorating touch remained, as did loads of Lionel's personal possessions. Clothes. Stacks of CDs. Shelves full of books. And bottles and bottles of wine.

Celia sighed. It had been a mistake to come here. She'd been right to reject the idea when it had first occurred to her. What on earth had she been thinking of?

But she was stuck here for now. She'd had too much to drink on an empty stomach to drive anywhere at the moment. Maybe later on this evening, she would go home.

And maybe not.

The bitter truth was she'd end up thinking of her mother at the moment, no matter where she was. Might as well stay here, Celia decided wearily.

Might as well have another glass of wine, too.

Luke was lost. Hopelessly lost. He'd thought he knew the way. But it had been nearly twenty years since he'd been to Pretty Point and, even then, he'd only been a child passenger, not the adult driver.

The relatively new freeway showed no turn-offs to Pretty Point, nor to any other place names he recognised. He realised after sailing past the turn-off to Morisset and Cooranbong that he probably should have taken it. He'd been driving north way too long. Nearly two hours from Sydney. He took the next turn-off to Toronto, drove into the town and bought a local map at a newsagent's.

After studying it for a while, he made his way back onto the expressway, took the correct turn-off, and fifteen minutes later began to finally see some familiarity in the roads.

Even so, the area had changed dramatically.

Bush had been cleared and housing estates had popped up all over the place, even on Pretty Point. It was certainly no longer a backwater. As he drove down the now tarred road which led to the far end of the Point—and his father's property—Luke began to appreciate how much ten acres of waterfront land was worth here in the present climate.

Ms Jessica Gilbert, whoever she was, had done very well for herself out of his father's generosity.

Luke's tension grew as he drew closer, his eyes narrowing as he glimpsed a building through the trees, a triangular-shaped house with a sloping green roof. He slowed, then braked, then scratched his head. Had his memory played him false? The area looked right, but the house was all wrong.

He drove on slowly, looking for a sign that this was the right place. And there it was, on the big white gum tree with the gnarled branches. His childish message, carved into the trunk all those years ago. LF was here.

Luke's stomach contracted. The place was right. But the house was definitely wrong. He stared at it again.

It looked almost new, built on exactly the same spot where the old cabin had stood.

If his father had built a new weekender up here, then why hadn't he ever mentioned it to him?

Don't jump to conclusions, he warned himself. All will be explained once you meet its occupier in the flesh.

Meanwhile, Luke clung to the hope that the new place had originally been built as an investment property—possibly when he'd been living in England. Maybe his father had intended to sell it, but then had generously allowed this Ms Gilbert to live there, once he'd heard her hard-luck story.

Luke directed his car down the gravel driveway which wound a gentle path through the tall trees and up towards the back porch of the A-framed dwelling.

A sporty white hatchback was parked next to the steps.

Not a car that an elderly spinster would drive.

Luke tried not to keep jumping to a not-very-nice conclusion, but it was increasingly hard.

He climbed out from behind the wheel and rather reluctantly mounted the long back porch, all the while frowning down at the pine decking, then up at the pine logs which made up the entire back wall of the house.

One of his father's favourite woods had been pine.

Luke knew then that his father had not just had this place built, he'd designed it himself. Had designed and had built it without telling him. Without telling his wife as well, Luke warranted.

Clenching a fist, he rapped on the door. There was

no doorbell, of course. His father had hated doorbells. He'd hated phones as well. He'd hated anything that made irritating interrupting noises.

Luke knocked again. Louder this time.

Twenty more seconds ticked by. Twenty more silent tension-twisting seconds.

Why didn't the woman answer? Was she deaf?

Suddenly, Luke hoped she was just that. Deaf. Elderly people were often deaf.

The door was reefed open and she stood before him. In the flesh.

She wasn't old. *Nor deaf.*

She was young. And beautiful. With full lips, slanting green eyes and glorious red-gold hair.

It was up. But not like Isabel wore hers up, all neat and smooth and confined. This hair defied order, rebellious curls easily escaping their loose prison to kiss the skin on her slender neck and rest lightly against her smooth, pale-skinned face.

''Ms Gilbert?'' he demanded to know, his voice curt, his stomach churning. Maybe it wasn't her. Maybe she was a friend. A welfare officer. A community nurse, even.

And maybe he was the next winner of the Nobel prize for architecture. If there was one.

''Yes,'' she admitted, and Luke finally knew the answers to every question he'd been asking himself since he'd first heard her name.

CHAPTER THREE

CELIA stared up at the dark haired and very handsome man standing in the doorway, her memory trying to place him. His face was familiar, and so were his eyes. Almost black, they were. Long lashed and very deeply set.

She was frowning into their inky depths when recognition struck.

"Dear heaven," she said, her hand tightening on the door knob. "You must be Luke. Lionel's son." She kept on staring at him. Impossible not to. It was like seeing Lionel, twenty years ago.

"Right in one, Ms Gilbert."

The fact that he knew *her* name took a moment or two to register. As did his simmering anger.

Clearly, Luke Freeman hadn't come to claim or inspect an inheritance. Somehow, he'd found out about his father's extramarital affair with her mother, and had come charging up here, far from happy.

But what did he want? To hear first hand all of the sordid details? To confront his father's mistress personally? To tear strips off her for corrupting his precious parent?

Over my dead body, Celia vowed. Her mother had suffered enough at the hands of one Freeman man. She

37

wasn't about to let the son finish off what the father had started.

She crossed her arms and gathered herself to do battle. "I don't how you found out," she said through gritted teeth, "but I presume you know everything."

"About your affair with my father, you mean?" he returned in a voice that would have cut diamonds. "Oh, yes, I know. *Now*. But I suspected the truth as soon as you opened the door. To give my father credit, he had taste. You are one beautiful woman, Ms Jessica Gilbert."

Celia was too shocked to be even mildly flattered by this back-handed compliment. My goodness! He thought *she* was his father's mistress!

She opened her mouth to tear strips off *him*, but then slowly closed it again, her mind racing to put this puzzle together. If he thought *she* was his father's bit on the side, then he actually knew very little. Just a name. Not the woman in question's age. Nor anything else about her. He certainly had no idea Ms Jessica Gilbert was a forty-two-year-old single mother with a twenty-six-year-old daughter. He definitely had no idea how long the affair had been going on.

Celia could say anything she liked and Lionel's son would probably believe it.

She thought of her mother and knew what she had to do.

Celia sighed, uncrossed her arms and stepped back out of the doorway. "I suppose you'd better come in," she said with a wave of her hand, all the while wondering what approach she should take for the part of Lionel's secret mistress.

His son was no fool, so best stick to the truth as much as possible so that she didn't slip up. She would simply bring the affair forward twenty years and put herself in her mother's place.

It would be difficult to pretend she'd loved the ruthless Lionel, let alone made love with him.

But she'd manage.

Somehow.

Luke tried to get a grip on his anger as he accepted her reluctant invitation and stepped into his father's secret love nest.

He failed wretchedly. But who, exactly, was he angry with? His father, for not living up to his hero status? Or this creature, this incredibly sensual creature of the captivating and cat-like green eyes?

Luke strode across the large open-plan living room, his eyes taking in at a glance the simple yet elegant beauty of the place. The extensive use of wood had his father's hand stamped all over it, though not everything was made of pine inside, only the kitchen and the walls. The polished wooden floors were boxwood and the high panelled ceiling looked like various types of cedar. The dining room table was made in a rich walnut, the finely carved chairs fashioned in the same wood, with dark green velvet cushions. The huge sofa facing the sandstone fireplace was also covered in the same dark green velvet.

As Luke walked past it, he couldn't help thinking

about what might have transpired on that sofa between his father and his mistress. And on the plush-pile cream rug stretched out on the floor in front of the fireplace. He could see her red-gold hair now, spread out and glowing in the fire light. He could almost feel the warmth of the flames on her pale skin, and practically taste the siren sweetness of her lips, drawing her married lover down, down into the hell-fires where lust ruled and faithfulness was totally forgotten.

Luke wrenched out one of the dining chairs and plonked himself down sideways in it, one elbow on the table, his other on the back of the chair. No way was he going to sit on the sofa. Nor make himself too comfortable. This was going to be a very brief visit.

"Would you like a drink?" she asked politely after shutting the door. "Tea? Coffee? A glass of wine?"

"No, thanks." No politeness in *his* voice. It was rough and gruff.

"I think, perhaps," she murmured in her sweet siren's voice, "I could do with one."

He watched her walk over to the galley-style kitchen, his gaze sweeping down her body then up again.

She was mistress material all right, with curves in all the right places. And she dressed for the part. Long, floaty wraparound skirt in a deep burgundy colour. A black knitted cardigan top with a deep scooped neckline and easy-to-undo buttons. No bra. Bare feet.

Luke estimated it would take a man less than twenty seconds to strip her naked, if she made no objections.

The image of his father sweeping through that door and immediately doing just that brought a flood of fierce feelings within Luke. More anger. A degree of disgust. And a perturbing amount of jealousy!

She poured herself a glass of white wine from a bottle in the fridge and came round to slide up on one of three pine stools which faced the kitchen counter. But she didn't face the kitchen counter. She faced him, her green eyes thoughtful.

"What *do* you want, then?" she said as she crossed her legs and lifted the glass to her lips.

When her skirt fell slightly apart to show more than a tantalising glimpse of shapely leg, Luke struggled to banish the X-rated images that zoomed into his mind.

"I just want to talk to you," he replied, pleased that his tone was a bit more businesslike and less angry.

Her delicate eyebrows arched cynically, and Luke wondered if his father had told her he only wanted to talk to her when they'd first met.

The image of his father as a ruthless womaniser didn't sit any better with Luke than the image of him as a seduced fool.

He'd thought he'd known all the answers when she'd opened the door, but that wasn't true. The physical reality of Ms Jessica Gilbert now raised a hundred more tantalising questions. But one stood out amongst all the others?

"Did you love him?" he asked abruptly, and watched her reactions.

Her lovely eyes rounded, her nostrils flaring in and out as she sucked in sharply. "I don't think that's any of your business," she bit out.

"I think it is, Ms Gilbert. My father visited his solicitor the day before he died,'' he went on. ''His intention was to gift this place over to you. But he was killed before he could see to the transfer. He revealed that he'd been letting you live here rent-free for the past few years, but that he wanted you to have security for life.''

''I see…''

Her green eyes glittered with contempt. But for whom? Luke puzzled.

''You think I was sleeping with your father for what I could get out of him,'' she stated coldly.

''It did cross my mind,'' he admitted.

''I'm sure it did. I presume *you* won't be signing this place over to me, then, will you?'' she added drily.

''That depends,'' he said, and watched a speculative interest replace the contempt in her eyes.

''On what?'' she asked carefully.

The moment she asked that question in that fashion, Luke at least knew one of the answers he'd been looking for. She *hadn't* been in love with his father. She *had* been in it for the material gain all along.

It made brutal sense. Why else would a girl as young as this be having an affair with a man as old as his father?

Luke wondered how much she'd already gleaned from him in cash during their liaison. Not to mention presents, the sort of presents rich older men gave their beautiful young mistresses. Clothes. Jewelry. Perfume. Lingerie.

She'd look incredibly sexy in black lace…

''On *what* does it depend?'' she demanded to know

and, immediately, another X-rated image raised its ugly head, rattling Luke with the power this female had to both arouse and tempt him without seemingly doing a thing.

Luke stared at her and tried to imagine what she would say if he offered her this place in exchange for one weekend being *his* mistress, giving him everything she'd given his father. And more.

Oh, yes, he'd want more. He was only thirty-two years old, a man in his sexual prime, a man who hadn't made love to his fiancée in…

Guilt consumed him as his train of thought ended with Isabel: the woman he was going to marry in a fortnight's time, the woman he'd vowed always to be truthful with in future.

What was happening to him here?

Not that he'd actually *done* anything. A man could not be hung for his thoughts, especially when in the presence of the temptation sitting before him. Did she have any idea how sexy she looked, swinging her prettily painted toes in front of him, that slit in her skirt falling further and further apart till he could practically see the entire side of her left leg? And all the while she was sipping her wine and watching him over the rim of the glass like a hunter quietly watching its prey.

Luke began to understand why his father had fallen victim to her wiles. She was the devil in disguise.

At the back of his mind, Luke knew he should get the hell out of there. But his curiosity far overrode his common sense.

"It depends on your telling me all about your affair with my father," he said brusquely.

Her left leg slipped off her right knee, bringing her skirt back to a more modest arrangement. When she put her glass back down, Luke saw that her hand was shaking slightly. "*All?* What do you mean by...*all*?"

Luke liked seeing her agitated. He wasn't sure why. Perhaps because he didn't really want her to be a cold-blooded money-grubbing bitch. Luke was afraid that if she was, he might find himself in deep trouble here. For if she'd sleep with a man old enough to be her father, strictly for material gain, then what would she be capable of with *him*?

Never in Luke's life had he felt the pulling power of his dark side this much. Sure, during his years at uni, he'd sometimes acted foolishly in the sexual sense. Even recklessly. He'd been a bit of a lad over in London too, perhaps because he'd been away from his father's supposedly good influence for the first time.

But ever since he'd come back to Australia two years ago, he hadn't wanted wild sexual thrills any more. He'd wanted a more safe, secure and settled life. He'd wanted what his father had had.

Luke stared at his father's sexy young mistress and realised ruefully his dark side still wanted what his father had had. The nice little woman at home, and *this*, waiting for him at weekends.

His heart raced just thinking about it.

But they were still only just thoughts, he told himself firmly. He couldn't, he just *couldn't* act on them, no matter how tempting. He would hate himself for ever if he did.

But he still wanted to know everything about his father's affair, to try to make sense of it all.

''Exactly that,'' he bit out. ''I want to know how and when you met my father? Who made the first move and why? How often you met and where? I want to know if he truly loved you, or just wanted you for sex. Tell me the whole rotten truth, Ms Gilbert, and this place is yours.''

CHAPTER FOUR

FOR a split second Celia wanted to lash out at him. But then she saw the pain behind Luke's anger, and sympathy for him washed into her heart.

It was never nice, being confronted with a parent's fallibility, especially in matters of the flesh. Even more upsetting, at this time in his life, so soon after both his parents' tragic deaths.

"You're very angry with your father, aren't you?" she said softly.

He didn't move a muscle, except for the one twitching in his jaw.

He was more than angry. He was in a state of extreme distress. She'd sensed it the moment he'd stalked inside. His body language had been telling: the way he'd dragged out that chair, the way he'd sat down, the way he'd stared at her.

Celia picked up her glass again and drank the rest of the wine. He still didn't say a word, just kept on looking at her with those glittering black eyes. She began to feel self-conscious. No, that was a lie. She'd begun to feel self-conscious some time back, which was why she'd crossed her legs and had nervously swung her foot.

"You're very angry with me too, aren't you?" she blurted out.

"What do *you* think?" he threw back at her. "He was a married man. You didn't even love him."

Celia wished she hadn't started this, wished she'd told him the truth right from the start.

But it was too late. There was more at stake now than just protecting her mother from the pain of being grilled by Lionel's son. There was this place, which her mother deserved. She didn't have to live here. She could sell it. It would be security for her old age. Payment, for services rendered. Retribution, for want of a better word.

And if there was a measure of secret vengeance against Lionel in her decision to pretend to be his mistress, Celia didn't deny it. At the same time, she wasn't going to take the part of a callous gold-digger. Her mother hadn't been anything of the kind!

"You're wrong," Celia refuted, putting her mother's words into her own mouth. "I did love Lionel. I loved him very much."

Celia was amazed at how convincing she sounded. But then…she'd heard her mother say it often enough over the years, and had seen the way she'd looked when she said it. Celia adopted what she hoped was the same dreamy-eyed expression and waited for Luke's reaction.

Luke was amazed at how convincing she'd sounded. And how soft and warm her eyes had suddenly gone.

Was it an act? Or the truth?

"You expect me to believe that?" he said sharply.

Her green eyes cooled somewhat. "No. But you wanted the truth. That's the truth."

"If you say so. When did you first meet my father? How long ago?"

She seemed to have to think about that. "I...I was twenty-two at the time."

God, only twenty-two. And his father had been... what? Fifty!

"How old are you now?" he asked, all the while trying not to think about her at twenty-two sleeping with his fifty-year-old father.

"Twenty-six."

"Four years ago, then," he growled.

"I see your maths is excellent. But, then, you're an architect too, aren't you? Like Lionel."

"I'm my father's son," he said with an edge of irony in his voice.

"In every way," she agreed.

"What do you mean by that crack?" he snapped, and she looked genuinely taken aback. Which meant it was his own guilty mind jumping to conclusions.

"I...I only meant that you look a lot like him," she said.

Perversely, Luke began thinking that if she'd liked his father's looks, then she'd like his. And if she'd liked his father's money, then she'd like his as well. Because he had all his father's money now, as well as his own.

"How did you meet?" he asked, desperate for distraction from the darkness of his thoughts.

"At one of the wine resorts in the Hunter Valley," she answered. "Your father was there for a two-day architectural conference. I was working as a massage therapist in a few of those places at the time. Lionel booked me for a massage in his room after dinner. And the rest…as they say…is history.''

Luke struggled with the images and conclusions her curt story conjured up. He didn't want to understand his father. Nor forgive him. But what red-blooded man wouldn't have been turned on by her hands on his near naked flesh?

"Had he been drinking?'' he asked brusquely.

"He'd probably had some wine over dinner. Lionel liked his wine.''

"When did you find out he was married?''

"He confessed the next morning.''

"What did you think about that?''

"I was very upset. But I—'' She broke off, as though searching for the right words. Or was it an excuse she was looking for?

"But you *what*?'' he persisted.

"But by then I was madly in love with him,'' she finished with a sigh.

Luke snorted. "Love doesn't happen as quickly as that.''

"Maybe not to you,'' she threw at him, "but it did to me.''

This time, she wasn't nearly so convincing. Her eyes wouldn't quite meet his.

"And then what?''

Now her eyes did meet his, defiant and challenging. "I told him I could never see him again. But he wouldn't let me go.''

"What do you mean…*wouldn't*?''

"He pursued me, and he…he seduced me again.''

"Oh, for pity's sake! I don't believe he seduced you in the first place. I think *you* were the one who did the seducing."

She stared at him, startled by his accusation. "Why on earth would you think that?"

"Back at the beginning, you were only twenty-two. I know girls of twenty-two. I've dated plenty. They aren't attracted to men of fifty, even rich, relatively handsome ones. Not unless they're on the make."

She was on her feet in a shot, green eyes blazing. "Now, that's enough!" she spat out. "I won't listen to any more of your insults or answer any more of your rude questions. This place isn't worth it. So *you* keep it, and believe whatever you like. I don't give a damn. I'm out of here!"

She started marching towards the door.

He jumped to his feet, his blood all fired up as well. But for different reasons than hers. "You can't drive anywhere. You've been drinking."

She whirled, her face flushed, her eyes bright. "Then *you* get out," she demanded. "Because one of us is leaving here, or I won't be responsible for what I'll say next."

"Meaning?"

"Look," she said, clearly struggling for control, "I don't want to hurt you any more than you've been hurt by this. Believe it or not, I know what you're feeling right now."

He laughed. "You have no idea what I'm feeling right now. No idea at all! I used to hero-worship my father. I thought he was perfect. Yet here you are, telling me he was not only unfaithful to my mother, but he was a callous seducer of young girls, a sexual predator of the worst kind.''

''Close,'' she bit out. ''You want the truth? Well, here's the truth. Your father was a bastard. A ruthless, selfish, rotten bastard. And you're right. I didn't love him. I hated him. I hated him so much I wasn't at all sorry when he died. Because it wasn't me he…he… oh…oh…oh, no!''

He watched the horror of what she'd just said register in her eyes. Her face crumpled, tears flooding into her eyes.

''I'm sorry.'' She sobbed. ''Sorry…''

Spinning, she ran, not towards the door this time, but towards the staircase which led up to what looked like a loft bedroom. His shocked gaze followed her flight upwards till she disappeared from view, a banging door signalling that she'd sought refuge where weeping women often sought refuge.

In a bathroom.

Luke ran both his hands through his hair. They were shaking. No point in going after her. He would have to wait till she came back down.

But then…then he would *force* her to tell him the total truth!

The sound of a phone ringing startled Luke. It was not a loud ring. More of a musical one. A mobile. Not his. His was still out in his car.

Luke's eyes scanned the room and there it was, sitting on the kitchen counter. He waited impatiently for its owner to emerge from the bathroom to come down and answer it, but she didn't. She probably didn't even hear it. Luke tried to ignore the sound but he couldn't. In the end he strode over, picked the darned thing up, pressed the blue button and put it to his ear. "Yes?"

"Oh! Er...could I speak to Celia please?" A woman's voice, obviously taken aback at a man answering.

"I'm sorry," he said curtly. "There's no Celia here."

"What? Are you sure?"

"Positive. This is a Ms Gilbert's phone. Ms Jessica Gilbert. You must have rung the wrong number."

"No, I didn't," the woman refuted crisply. "I rang the right number. I have it programmed into my phone. That's Celia Gilbert's mobile you've answered, not Jessica's."

Luke frowned. Jessica must have a sister, named Celia. "Then Jessica must have borrowed Celia's mobile because the only lady in this house at the moment is a Ms *Jessica* Gilbert, not Celia."

"But that's impossible! Jessica's here with me. Right now. She's the reason I'm ringing Celia, to tell her her mother might need her to drop in some time this weekend after all. She's been asking after her."

"Her *mother*?" Luke repeated, feeling totally confused.

"Yes, her mother. I'm Helen, Jessica's older sister. And who, pray tell, are you? Some tradesman or other? Is that why you thought Celia was Jessica, because she's staying at her mother's place this weekend?"

Finally, some of the pieces of the puzzle of his father's affair slotted into place. Jessica upstairs wasn't

Jessica at all. She was Celia, Jessica's daughter. His father's mistress *hadn't* been a sexy young thing but a mature woman.

Whilst Luke preferred this picture to the one that had been troubling him severely, the fact he'd been lied to raised another very big question. *Why*, for goodness' sake?

"No," he ground out. "No, I'm not a tradesman. My name is Luke Freeman."

A horrified gasp wafted down the line, telling Luke that the woman named Helen knew exactly who he was.

"The reason I thought Celia was Jessica," he ground out, "was because she's been pretending to be Ms Jessica Gilbert ever since I arrived here a short time back."

"Oh, dear," the woman said.

"Don't hang up!" Luke ordered.

A sigh this time. "Not much point, is there? If Celia's been pretending to be Jessica then you already know my sister and your father were having an affair."

"I had my suspicions," he grated out, "which Celia more or less confirmed once she realised who I was. What I'd like to know is *why* she lied to me? Why the farce? Do you have any idea the thoughts I've had about my father, having it off with a girl young enough to be his daughter? Bad enough that he was having an affair at all!"

"Don't be angry with Celia," Helen pleaded with him. "She's very protective of her mother. Poor Jessica has had a nervous breakdown since your father died so, naturally, Celia wouldn't have wanted you coming to see her and asking her horrible questions.''

Well, yes, Luke thought grudgingly. He could understand that.

A nervous breakdown? Dad, what kind of a man *were* you? Did I ever really know you at *all*?

Luke shook his head. There was only one way to find out. He had to meet the real Ms Jessica Gilbert. ''You said this Jessica was staying with you at the moment?''

''Yes. She needs a lot of looking after. Can't do much for herself. Hardly says a word. Mostly, she just sits and stares. Or cries.''

''So where do you live, Helen? How far from Pretty Point? Can't be all that far if Celia could just drop in.''

''I'm not sure I should say. I don't want you barging in here all hot under the collar and upsetting my sister.''

''I wouldn't do that.''

''Really? You barged in there, I'll bet. Otherwise Celia would have told you the truth. There was no love lost between her and your father, I can tell you.''

''Yes. I gathered that.''

''If you don't mind my asking, what made you think your father had been having an affair in the first place? I wasn't privy to too much detail about Jessica and Lionel's relationship, but I do know he went to a lot of trouble so that his family never found out about her.''

Luke told her what had transpired at the solicitors' that day.

''I see,'' Helen murmured. ''So you're under the impression this affair has only been going on for a few years, is that it?''

"Well, yes. Of course. What…what are you trying to say?" His heart began to race in anticipation of more startling revelations.

"I hate to disillusion you further, Luke, but my sister was your father's mistress for the past twenty years."

CHAPTER FIVE

CELIA finally stopped crying and faced not only her reflection in the bathroom mirror but the fact she'd made a total mess of things downstairs.

Her blotchy cheeks and puffy eyes she could fix. Sort of. But what could she possibly tell Lionel's son to explain her outburst of hatred against his father, the man she'd supposedly loved?

Perhaps that her love had finally turned to hate because Lionel wouldn't leave his wife and marry her; that she'd realised in the end that Lionel hadn't loved her as she'd loved him. He'd just used her for sex.

Yes. Yes, maybe that would do it.

Celia would have preferred to go down there and tell the man the truth. She hated having to pretend she'd been Lionel's lover. The idea was gross. She could understand why Luke kept looking at her as he did. But on the other hand, she had to do what she could to protect her mother, and to get her this house.

Celia decided not to bother trying to fix her face other than to splash a little cold water across it. Better she went downstairs, still looking upset, with puffy eyes and dishevelled hair. After all, her lover had only died a fortnight ago. She would not be expected to be cool, calm and collected. A few hysterics were perfectly understandable.

56

Steeling herself, Celia opened the bathroom door, crossed the loft bedroom and slowly descended the wooden steps, glancing around with increasingly worried eyes as she did so.

Because Luke was not where she'd left him.

He was out on the deck, she soon discovered, not sitting but standing at the pine railing and staring out at the lake. His feet were apart and his hands were in his trousers pockets, the sides of his sleek suit jacket bunched up over his hips. His shoulders were slumped slightly, his body language no longer betraying anger but a type of weariness, or defeat.

A wave of sympathy washed through Celia. She'd felt sorry for him before, but not like this. Suddenly, she couldn't lie to him any more. He didn't deserve it. It wasn't right.

Nerves fluttered in her stomach as she walked over and slid back the glass door. Telling Luke she'd lied to him was going to be even harder than lying in the first place.

He spun round at the sound of the door sliding back, and stared at her again, just as intensely but not quite so angrily. Celia stared right back, for the first time seeing Luke Freeman, the man, and not just Lionel's son.

He was more handsome than his father, she realised, his face finer, his mouth softer, his dark eyes more heavily lashed. But he had his father's stubbornly squared chin, complete with dimple. And his father's hair. Thick and black and straight.

The body, too, was pure Lionel. Tall and impressive,

with broad shoulders and low slung, very slim hips. He looked a million dollars in that grey business suit, white shirt and dark red tie. But a man of his looks and build would look great in anything.

When a shiver ran down her spine, Celia frowned and crossed her arms. "It's getting chilly out there," she said from the open doorway. "Would you mind coming back inside? I have something I have to say to you."

He shrugged and withdrew his hands from his trouser pockets, the elegant grey jacket flapping shut again. "If you insist," he said, and began walking towards her. She stepped back just in time, but his right arm still brushed against hers as he entered the room, sending an electric current right down to her fingertips.

Celia smothered the gasp that rose to her lips, standing there frozen for a few seconds while she watched him walk over and settle himself on the sofa in front of the fireplace.

Not cold, she realised. Chemistry. Sexual chemistry.

Celia shouldn't have been shocked. Luke Freeman was a very handsome man, the sort who would have female hearts a-thumping whenever he walked into a room. But good grief, the last man on earth she wanted to be attracted to was Lionel's son! Mother nature had a very peculiar and extremely perverse sense of humour.

With a blackly frustrated sigh, she shut the door and walked over to stand on the rug, facing him, her back to the fireplace.

Be businesslike, she told herself. And firm. Don't waffle. Or make excuses. Just tell him the truth.

* * *

Luke looked up at her and wondered what lies she was going to feed him now.

He wasn't angry with her any more. He understood full well why she'd done what she'd done. But he was curious as to how far she would go to protect her mother.

"I have to apologise," she began, surprising him.

"For what, exactly?"

"I lied to you," she stated, impressing him now. It took courage to admit to lying.

"What about?"

"I'm not your father's mistress," she stated boldly and rather bravely, he thought. "And my name's not Jessica. It's Celia. If you recall, when you first arrived you asked me if I was a Ms Gilbert and I said yes, because I am. But I'm *Celia* Gilbert. Jessica Gilbert is my mother."

Any idea he had to string her along went out the window.

"I know," he said.

She blinked her shock. "Huh?"

Time for *him* to be honest. "While you were upstairs in the bathroom, your Aunt Helen rang. I answered your phone. She asked for Celia. I told her there was no Celia here, only a Jessica. She told me that was impossible because Jessica was there, with her. I think you can fill in the rest, don't you?"

"Oh…" Stunned, she stumbled over and sank down on the other end of the sofa. "How…how much did she tell you?"

"Enough," he said. "Yet not enough."

She gnawed at her bottom lip, bringing his attention to how full it was, how full *both* her lips were. Her not being his father's mistress hadn't stopped the X-rated thoughts at all.

He'd thought... He'd hoped...

Luke shook his head. He'd been wrong, blast it.

"What *did* Aunt Helen tell you?" she asked, her lovely eyes worried.

Luke recalled her aunt's bitter relaying of the facts over the phone.

"Jessica was twenty-two when she met your father. She was a single mum with a six-year-old-girl at the time, struggling to make ends meet by giving massages at resorts in the Hunter Valley to wealthy businessmen and tourists. She was living in a pokey two-room flat in Maitland and drove a car which should have been condemned. Despite all that, she was the most beautiful girl, both inside and out.

"But that's still no excuse for your father. He knew he was married with a son when he first met Jessica. But she didn't know that till after she'd spent the night with him and, by then, she was deeply in love. She tried to give him up but simply couldn't. He wouldn't let her. He kept coming back and coming back, bringing little Celia gifts and telling Jessica how much he loved her, as well as other lies. In the end, Jessica was so besotted with him that she did whatever he wanted. And what he wanted was her at his beck and call, but with total secrecy and discretion. They managed that at Jessica's place till Celia grew up enough to know what was going on. I gather the poor child made quite a scene one day.

But did they have the decency to stop then? Good heavens, no. After that, Jessica was always running all over the countryside, meeting up with your father in remote motels for a few wretched hours. Then there was this grotty little fishing cabin they spent weekends in sometimes. I don't know where. Lionel finally built the place you're in at this moment and set her up there. A love nest, Jessica called it. A lust nest more like it!''

There'd been more of the same. Clearly, Lionel hadn't been a favourite with Aunt Helen. Her sister's behaviour hadn't been too popular, either.

Luke decided a briefer, less venomous version was called for.

''I know how long the affair's been going on,'' he admitted. ''I know your mother's circumstances when they met. I know she loved my father a lot.''

''Did Aunt Helen say that?'' She looked amazed.

''No,'' he confessed drily. ''When I questioned her about that, she used words such as sexual obsession and infatuation. But why else would your mother have a breakdown, if her caring hadn't been very real, and very deep?''

Celia threw him a grateful look. ''It was,'' she said, sighing. ''Too deep.''

''Is that why you pretended to be your mother? Because of her fragile emotional state?''

''Yes.''

''You didn't want me talking to her.''

''That's right.''

''But you still wanted me to leave her this house.''

She grimaced, then shot him a pleading glance. ''I

thought she deserved...something. When he was alive, she never took anything from your father. Not anything of any value, anyway,'' she added. ''She always supported herself. Lionel bought her some little gifts over the years and, more recently, he let her live here rent-free. He might have slipped her a few dollars every now and then, but only for food or wine or whatever other creature comforts he himself enjoyed during the time he spent here. But that's not much in exchange for almost a lifetime of loving and sacrifice. Not that Mum ever asked for anything from Lionel. The only thing she ever wanted from your father was his love.''

''I gather you and your Aunt Helen don't think she ever really got that.''

Her spine stiffened. ''That's right,'' she said tartly. ''We don't.''

''What about your mother herself? What did she think?''

''She thought he loved her. Apparently, he used to say he did. But men often say that to get sex, don't they?'' she added bitterly.

''Do they?'' He looked deep into her eyes and wondered if that had been *her* experience, men telling her they loved her to have sex with her. If they did, he could well understand it.

She glanced away from his probing gaze and stood up. ''I think I could do with some coffee. Would you like some? Or tea? There's still some white wine left in the bottle, if you'd prefer. It's Chablis.''

If he started drinking, things could go from bad to

worse. He might do something really dreadful, rather than just think about it.

"Coffee would be great, thanks. White. No sugar."

She hurried over to the kitchen, relieved, he thought, to put some distance between them. Maybe she was aware of the rampant desire that smouldered within him every time he looked at her. And it frightened her. It frightened him. He'd never felt anything like it.

He watched her silently make the coffee, never glancing over his way. Deliberately, he wondered? Or was she just lost in thought?

He wished he could stop himself looking at her but he couldn't. He swivelled round in the corner of the sofa to keep her in view, his eyes following her every movement.

"Are you a dancer?" he asked at last.

Her head jerked up, her green eyes startled. "No. Why? What made you think that?"

"The way you look. The way you move."

She laughed, as women do when they're both embarrassed and pleased at the same time. "Sorry. No, I'm not a dancer, though I do like dancing. I'm a physiotherapist. It's what my mother always wanted to be but she never had the proper training. She's a darned good masseuse, though."

"And you? Are you a darned good masseuse?"

She shrugged. "I'm an efficient one."

He wallowed for a few moments in the idea of her hands on his naked flesh.

Big mistake! He shifted uncomfortably on the sofa. "Er...where do you practise your physiotherapy?"

"I'm managing a sports injury clinic over at Swansea at the moment. The owner's away on maternity leave."

"You like your job?"

"Most days. Though it's not quite as rewarding as my previous one. I used to work with accident victims in various hospitals around the Central Coast, but it got me down in the end, especially when children were involved and things didn't go right. Still, I might go back to that kind of work when I'm older. And tougher."

"You could never be tough," he said and she smiled a wry little smile.

"I'm tougher than I look. Trust me. Would you like something with your coffee?"

You, he thought.

His teeth clenched hard in his jaw. Stop it, Luke, he ordered himself.

But how *did* one stop your mind from thinking things?

"There's not much here at the moment," she added, whilst he did his best to look innocent, and not like the closet lech he'd suddenly become. "No cake, just some biscuits. I didn't realise the cupboards were so bare."

"I don't want anything else for now. Just the coffee."

She brought his mug of coffee over and set it on the side table next to his left arm. Unfortunately, this required her leaning over. Far too close to him for comfort.

The sight of her braless breasts swinging away from her chest wall and forming a temporary but most tantalising cleavage barely inches from his face did things to Luke's body that could only be described as sadistic. He immediately sat up straighter, and when she turned to walk away he swept up the mug and cradled it in his hands over his lap.

She sat back down at the other end of the sofa and sipped her coffee, not looking his way, thank goodness. She was, instead, staring blankly ahead into the dead hearth of the fireplace.

"By the way," he said, "your Aunt Helen said to tell you your mother's been asking for you, so you might have to drop in on her this weekend after all."

She nodded slowly, sadly.

"How bad is she?" he asked, happy to be feeling sympathy for her rather than desire.

She shook her head. "Not good. She hardly speaks. She's very depressed. She has nightmares. Sometimes, in her sleep, she'll cry and call out Lionel's name."

"Ah…" Luke still found it hard to see his father as the kind of man who could ruthlessly and selfishly destroy another woman's life. But that was what he'd done, whether he'd meant to or not. Luke could understand his father being overcome by a moment's passion when he'd been away from home—especially if Celia's mother was half as beautiful as Celia—but he should have walked away after that first night. He should never have come back. The emotional damage he'd done to that innocent mother and child over the years must have been horrendous.

He thought of what Celia's Aunt Helen had told him about his father's coming back time after time, showering gifts on Celia as a child, playing at being her father for a day then disappearing again, possibly for weeks on end. No wonder Celia hated him with a passion. She'd probably loved him once, as lonely needy children loved grown-ups who were kind to them.

But once she'd started to grow up herself and had seen the situation for what it was, she'd recognised the hypocrisy of the man, and her love had turned to hate.

"I'm so sorry, Celia," he said softly. "So very, very sorry. My father has a lot to answer for. I have no excuses for him. What he did was very wrong. But your mother's not the only person he hurt over the past twenty years, is she?"

Their eyes met across the length of the sofa. "What...what do you mean? Your mother didn't know. *Did* she?"

Luke was taken aback by Celia's question, raising sudden doubts of his own.

Till now he'd clung to the fact that his mother had not known about her husband's affair, and would now never know. It would have broken her heart if she'd discovered her beloved Lionel had been unfaithful to her.

But what if she *had* known? Perhaps that was why he'd caught her looking so sad sometimes for no apparent reason, why she'd suffered those dreadful migraines.

No, no, that didn't make sense. His father hadn't met Jessica till Luke had been twelve and his mother had had migraines for as far back as he could remember. As for her looking sad sometimes, everyone suffered some small bouts of depression. It wasn't possible to be happy all the time.

He was imagining things.

"For what it's worth," Celia said swiftly, "Mum's very sure your mother didn't know about them. I didn't mean to imply differently. It was just that you said my mother was not the only one Lionel hurt and I thought...I mean..." She shrugged, clearly a bit confused.

Luke nodded. "It's all right. I'm sure she didn't know too. I was talking about you, Celia. My father hurt you as well."

Celia stared at him, her green eyes wide with surprise.

"Dad's not here to apologise for his reprehensible behaviour," Luke went on, "so I'd like to do so on his behalf. I'm sure he didn't mean to hurt you, Celia. He loved children. But he did hurt you, all the same, and I feel really rotten about it."

"Oh..." She looked stricken by his sympathetic words. Her chin began to wobble and so did her hands, a couple of spots of hot coffee spilling into her lap.

"Oh!" she cried, then burst into tears.

Luke didn't stop to think. He acted, hurriedly putting down his mug of coffee and sliding down the sofa to pry hers out of her suddenly shaking hands before more coffee was spilt. He had to lean over her to put her mug down on the other side table, but there was no sexual intent in the physical contact. Luke was just being what he basically was: a gentleman.

When he straightened, however, he was sitting right

beside her, their sides jammed up against each other. Before he could safely retreat, she swivelled and buried her face into his chest, clutching the lapels of his jacket and sobbing piteously.

Panic—and possibly something else—set Luke's heart pounding. What was a man to do?

Run, came the common-sense command.

But how could he? She needed comforting. And there was no one else.

Luke squeezed his eyes shut, prayed for salvation, and put his arms around her.

CHAPTER SIX

CELIA soon stopped clutching his lapels and sank into the warmth of his solid embrace, the side of her head pressed against the wall of his chest, her arms sliding underneath his suit jacket and around his back where she hugged him tightly, never wanting to let him go.

How good it felt to be held like this, she thought even as she wept. How good for someone to finally understand how angry and frustrated she'd been over the years, watching her mother throwing her life away on a married man.

Her mother had never understood, especially not once Celia had left home. She'd told her to go and make her own life and to stop worrying about hers.

That Lionel Freeman's son would understand was amazing.

How nice he was. How kind. How...*strong*, she suddenly realised when his arms tightened around her.

He must work out, she began thinking as her fingertips moved across his back, feeling the bunched muscles beneath them, admiring their shape and their power.

He moaned, a startlingly tormented sound which brought her head up, her eyes searching his in bewilderment.

They glittered back down at her.

"You shouldn't have touched me like that," he

growled, one hand coming up to cup her chin. "I'm only human, Celia. Only human..." And he held her face captive while his mouth crashed down on hers.

Celia's first instinct was to struggle. Because this was Lionel's son kissing her. *Lionel's* son!

But then his tongue slipped past her startled lips and Celia's heart stopped beating.

Dear heaven, she thought dazedly.

When her heart finally kicked back to life there was no further thought of struggling. There was nothing but surrender.

She melted against him, wallowing in the warm, wet pleasure of his tongue dancing with hers. When his mouth lifted momentarily, she groaned in protest. He muttered something unintelligible then tipped her head back over his arm and clamped his lips to the soft skin at the base of her throat, sucking on it like some ravenous beast.

Celia finally understood why some women found vampire films erotic. Her moans carried no pain. Just pleasure. Primitive primal pleasure.

When his free hand found a breast, her senses reeled further, her nipple peaking hard against the heat of his palm. When his hand splayed wide and he rubbed the surface of his taut skin over the rock-like peak, the sensations were exquisite.

Too soon, his hand fell away, and she groaned in dismay. Not so when it slid inside her skirt and sought to stroke her between her thighs. Now she gasped, her knees instinctively parting to give him better access to the molten fire that already awaited him there. At first he caressed her over her panties, but finally his fingers slipped underneath the elastic.

Celia had never felt anything like it. She cried out, her back arching as her body raced towards a climax. Never, with any other man, had this happened to her so quickly.

His hand suddenly stilled, his head lifting from her throat. Their eyes met and, whilst his looked pained, Celia knew hers had to be reflecting sheer desperation.

''Don't stop,'' she pleaded breathlessly.

He laughed an odd sort of laugh, scooping her up with him as he stood up. ''Your wish is my command, beautiful. But not here. If I'm going to do this, and it seems I am,'' he added ruefully as he carried her towards the stairs, ''then I might as well be hung for a sheep as a lamb.''

He mounted the wooden steps two at a time, bringing them swiftly to the loft bedroom where her mother and his father must have made love hundreds of times.

It was spacious but sparsely furnished, with a huge bed in the middle of the polished floor, and colourfully woven rugs on three sides. The foot of the bed faced a wall of sliding glass doors that led out onto another deck overlooking the lake. There was a walk-in wardrobe built into one sloping side wall and a bathroom set into the other.

Celia had stripped the bed and had put her own sheets and duvet on when she'd arrived that afternoon, not feeling comfortable with the remnants of Lionel's distinctive cologne pervading the bedclothes.

If anyone had told her then, that in a couple of hours

she would be about to make love with Lionel Freeman's son on that same bed, she would have called them insane. Yet here she was, in Luke's arms, breathless with anticipation, excited beyond all words, feverish in her desire to be naked on that bed with him.

Talk about ironic!

At least she now had more understanding of why her mother had acted as she had. If Lionel had made her feel anything like this, it would have been very difficult to send him away, married or not?

This last thought brought a jab of panic.

"You're not married, are you?" she asked him anxiously as he approached the bed.

He ground to a halt and stared down at her for a few excruciatingly long moments. "No," he said at last. "Are you?"

"Of course not!"

He smiled, a darkly enigmatic smile. "Of course not," he repeated, and laid her down across the bed.

He straightened to stare down at her for several seconds, then bent to slide his hands up her legs under her skirt and pull down her black cotton panties.

Celia's eyes had grown very round by the time they slipped off her feet.

He tossed her panties aside then began to take off his own clothes, starting with his jacket and tie. She just lay there, watching him with wide eyes, her heart beating like jungle drums, her face flushed with excitement. He walked over to the one and only chair in the room, draping his jacket and tie over the back before sitting down to remove his shoes and socks.

This done, he stood up again and walked back over to stand by the bed, looking down at her.

''Undo the buttons on your top,'' he said as he began undoing *his* shirt buttons.

There was no thought of refusing him, though her hands did fumble a bit as she worked her way down the six black buttons. When she'd undone the last one, she hesitated. He'd undone his last button as well but hadn't removed his shirt. His hands had dropped back to his sides and his focus was all on her.

''Open it,'' he commanded.

She took a breath and opened the cardigan, baring her braless breasts to his avid eyes.

He stared, and her already erect nipples tightened further.

''Now your skirt,'' he ordered. ''Don't take it off. Open it. Wide.''

Celia sucked in sharply. She'd never known anything so wickedly thrilling. Yet he was only looking at her.

She parted her skirt and pulled the sides back, exposing all her legs plus the triangle of dark curls between them.

''And now...your legs,'' he said, his voice as thick as syrup.

Celia's head spun. Her legs... He wanted her to open her legs... Wanted to see where she was wet with desire for him...

She couldn't. Surely not. She'd die of embarrassment.

She opened her legs, and didn't die of embarrassment. She felt shockingly alive and incredibly turned on.

His eyes glittered wildly and heat washed all through her. As did a fierce longing. Looking at her there wasn't nearly enough. She wanted his hands there. His mouth. His tongue. Just the thought of such things made her light-headed. Her thighs quivered and her heartbeat quickened.

"Luke, please," she choked out.

"I won't be long," he promised and reefed open his shirt, tossing it aside.

Celia stared at the beauty of him and was besieged by even more needs. Not just to be touched but to do the touching herself. She was dying to run her hands over his magnificent chest and shoulders, to tangle her fingers in the thatch of dark curls that covered the centre of his chest, following them down to where they disappeared beyond his waistband, that waistband that Luke was at that very moment snapping undone.

She watched, mouth drying, as he unzipped his fly and dragged his trousers off, revealing snug black briefs that were straining to encompass the evidence of *his* desire. Celia tried to imagine how it would feel when he entered her and her insides clenched down hard at the thought. He was big, she could see. Bigger than any other man she'd been with.

Would that make a difference? she wondered breathlessly. Did size *really* matter?

Celia was wallowing in the thought that she would soon know when Luke bent to pull his wallet from his discarded trousers and, from there, a condom.

"I've only got the one with me," he muttered, dropping the wallet on the floor. "That'll have to do."

Celia stared at him for a moment, doing her best to find excuses for herself for not even thinking about protection before this. Normally, she was so insistent about practising safe sex. Making sure a condom was going to be used was usually her number one priority before going to bed with any of her previous boyfriends.

But the truth was she'd have let Luke have her down there on the sofa, without protection. She'd have probably let him have her up here as well. Okay, so perhaps, at the back of her mind, she already knew that the odds of her conceiving today were less than zero. Her period was due early next week.

But still…pregnancy was not the only problem associated with having sex these days.

Thank goodness Luke wasn't quite as carried away as she was.

Or was he? His hands were shaking as he tossed his wallet aside, then he dropped his underpants.

Celia blinked, then swallowed. He *was* big. She hoped the condom would fit.

In the past, she'd never actually watched any man putting on protection. But she watched Luke, her awed eyes feasting on his flesh, anticipating the pleasure of his possession. If this man didn't satisfy her, then no man ever could.

Because no man had. Not once. Not properly.

But when he finally stepped up to the bed between her spread knees, Celia had one last depressing thought. Maybe Luke's size or abilities as a lover weren't going to make a blind bit of difference. Maybe her coming or not coming during sex *was* all her fault. Maybe she just wasn't capable of coming that way. End of story.

His hands scooped under her bare buttocks and pulled her abruptly towards him. No more foreplay, she realised with a degree of shock as he angled himself into her. Just him, driving home to the hilt, then pumping powerfully, each stroke of his swollen flesh twisting her insides tighter and tighter like a coiled spring. This is it, she thought elatedly. But when several minutes passed with no orgasm happening, her ecstasy turned to agony.

She moaned, her head thrashing from side to side, her eyes squeezing tightly shut, her face grimacing in eternal frustration. She was never going to come. Never!

His pulling out brought a startled cry of dismay.

''Trust me,'' he told her and flipped her over, pushing her skirt up out of the way and hoisting her up onto her knees. Her face flamed momentarily with a fierce embarrassment. How must she look to him like that? But he was inside her again in no time, and any qualms were soon obliterated by the heat of the moment.

It felt fantastic his doing it to her like that. Wickedly wantonly fantastic!

She began to moan quite loudly, muffling the mortifying sounds by pressing her face into the mattress. Her hands clutched the duvet on either side of her head and everything spun way, way out of control. No thoughts of failure now. No thoughts at all. Just heat and sex. Raw animal sounds. His. Hers.

Their bodies exploded together, his hips shuddering

to a halt whilst hers rocked wildly back and forth against him.

"More," she muttered through clenched teeth when the spasms of blinding pleasure began to fade. "More."

But soon, there was no more. There was nothing but an emotion-charged stillness. She could still hear his ragged breathing. And her own. But he wasn't moving a muscle, and neither was she.

His withdrawal from her body was so abrupt she cried out.

"No more," he ground out. "*Definitely* no more. This was a mistake. A big mistake."

Celia remained frozen where she was.

"Hell," he muttered, forcefully pressing her flat on the bed and yanking her skirt down over her naked bottom. "I'm sorry, Celia. Sorry…"

By the time a stunned Celia rolled over, he was already disappearing into the bathroom and banging the door shut behind him.

For a few moments, she just lay there, staring at the bathroom door. It was almost impossible to think straight when her body was still thrumming with the aftermath of their torrid lovemaking and that nerve-numbing climax. But eventually, the reality of what she'd just done with Luke sank in.

Celia rolled back over and buried her face into the bed. What must he think of her?

And what did she think of herself, going to bed with him so soon after meeting him?

It wasn't like her to do that. It wasn't like her to feel

what she'd felt with him, either. Or to make love in such a flagrantly provocative position.

But, oh, it had been wonderful with Luke, hadn't it? As for that orgasm...talk about mind-blowing! Despite feeling shock at her boldness, Celia couldn't help being thrilled that her never coming before hadn't been her fault after all. It seemed all she'd needed was the right man, with the right moves.

Still, the fact that Lionel Freeman's son should be that right man was shocking in itself. Fate really did have a perverse sense of humour.

The sound of the toilet flushing sent Celia rolling back over to stare at the bathroom door. Her heart started to pound as she waited for Luke to emerge again. But he didn't. Instead, she heard the shower being snapped on.

Celia had to confess to being relieved. She needed a few more minutes to think before facing Luke again. Above all, she wanted to work out just why he thought making love to her was such a big mistake?

Was it because of the speed and impulsiveness of their encounter? Or simply because of who she was? His father's mistress's daughter.

Perhaps. He might also think, for the very same reason, that their exploring a further relationship was out of the question.

But how could he turn his back on the incredible sex they'd just shared? The passion! The pleasure!

Celia knew she couldn't. She wanted Luke to come back to this bed and make more wonderful love to her. Yet it seemed he wasn't going to do that. Strange, when most men would have jumped at the chance. What was the real problem here? It had to be more than just who they were. There had to be something else...

"Oh!" Celia gasped, her heart lurching. "Oh, no."

How stupid of her not to realise! A man like Luke. Handsome. Rich. Clever. Eligible. There was no way there wouldn't be some woman in his life. Maybe not a wife. But certainly a girlfriend of some kind.

That was why he'd called their making love a big mistake. Because he was already involved with someone else!

She stared at the door that separated them and tried to be angry with him. But she wasn't. How strange. She should have been angry. She should have been furious!

Yet all she felt was despair...

The sounds of the shower gushing on and on gradually began to get under her skin, as did his washing himself totally clean of her before returning to Sydney.

The thought of his going back to another woman's bed tonight finally brought anger. Plus the bleakest, blackest jealousy.

She couldn't let him get away with that, not without being made to face her and tell her the truth!

Celia scrambled off the bed and headed for the bathroom door, hurriedly fixing her clothes as she went.

CHAPTER SEVEN

LUKE leant with his hands and head against the shower wall and groaned. He was no better than his father, really, was he? Making love to a girl without telling her the truth about himself.

When she'd asked him if he was married, he shouldn't have said no. He should have said shortly.

But of course saying shortly would have dashed it for him, wouldn't it? And he hadn't wanted that. Not right at that precise moment. He'd wanted her, how he'd wanted her.

He still wanted her, he conceded, glancing downwards. Once hadn't been nearly enough.

Gritting his teeth, he reached to snap off the hot tap. But, even as the water turned cold and the icy spray painfully pummelled his body, he kept thinking about her. The way she'd done everything he'd asked. The way she'd trusted him when he'd turned her over.

She shouldn't have. He wasn't worthy of her trust.

The shower door sliding back frightened the life out of him. He jerked around and there she stood, his nemesis, her beautiful green eyes blazing, her arms crossed over her chest, her lovely hair falling down around her very angry face.

The buttons on her top, he noted, had been refastened, but into the wrong slots. And her skirt was still askew. There was a purplish love bite at the base of her neck, only partially covered by her hair.

"You have a girlfriend back in Sydney, don't you?" she threw at him. "That's why you're sorry. That's why you said making love to me was a big mistake."

Luke turned off the shower and did his best to look dignified. Difficult when he was naked and freezing, and not nearly limp enough.

"Hand me a towel, will you?" he asked in what he hoped was a coolly commanding tone.

She glowered at him. "Here." She snatched one of the white towels off the towel rail and shoved it into his stomach.

He grunted, then wrapped the towel very firmly around his hips because the last thing he wanted was the darned thing to fall off. "Shall we go back out into the bedroom?" he suggested with seeming calm.

"Oh, by all means," she snapped. "Let's return to the scene of the crime."

"I haven't committed a crime, Celia. A mistake, yes. But not a crime."

"That's just semantics, and you know it." She whirled and marched back out into the bedroom, with him following. Once he got there, however, Luke wished he'd stayed in the bathroom. Just looking at that bed reminded him of how she'd looked, lying spread-eagled for him, so turned on she simply *couldn't* have said no to him.

Suddenly, he felt afraid, afraid of what he might say to turn her on like that again so that he could make her do all those other things a man wants a woman to do when he desires her this much.

But if he ever set about seducing her again, ruthlessly and without regard to her feelings, he really would be no better than his father.

He had to tell her the truth. And quickly. For his own sake as well as hers.

"Yes," he admitted. "I have a girlfriend."

She made a tiny whimpering sound of distress that stung his conscience.

"I'm sorry, Celia," he said sincerely. "All I can say in my defence is that I didn't mean any of this to happen. I was only trying to comfort you when I took you in my arms. As I said before, you're a very beautiful girl, and I'm only human."

She sank down on the side of the bed as though dazed, her hurt eyes still on him. "What's her name?"

"Isabel."

"Isabel," she repeated, and just kept staring at him. "Do...do you live with her?"

"No."

"Do you have a date with her tonight?"

"No."

He saw the flicker of relief in her eyes and realised with a degree of self-disgust that she'd been worried he would go straight from her bed to Isabel's. Obviously, after the way his father had treated her mother, Celia expected men to behave badly. Guilt consumed Luke when he recalled the comment she'd made about how men often lied to get sex. He hadn't lied directly, but he had by omission.

"Are you serious about each other?" she asked, and he stiffened. He didn't want to hurt her any more than necessary. Surely it would serve no purpose for her to know he was engaged.

"We've been dating for quite a while," he hedged. "I met her at work late last year."

"I see…" She fell silent then, her shoulders sagging, her head drooping. Luke had never felt so rotten in his entire life. He dared not go to her and touch her in any way, but he felt compelled to let her know how special he thought she was.

"What we shared, Celia," he said gently, "it was…amazing. I'll always remember you. Always."

Her head lifted, and a sad little smile played on her lips. "And I you, Luke Freeman. Do you know that was the first time I've ever come during sex?"

He stared at her. Did she have to tell him that?

"You don't believe me?"

"I…I'm surprised, that's all."

She stood up abruptly. "You'd better get dressed. I'll go downstairs and leave you to it."

Celia somehow made it downstairs before dissolving into tears. She cried quietly, afraid that if she surrendered to sobbing, he would hear it up in the loft. Finally, she fled out onto the deck, tears streaming down her face, her thoughts as tormenting as her emotions.

He had a girlfriend. Named Isabel. Probably an architect, like him. Some superintelligent, stunningly sophisticated creature who would never admit to him that she'd never climaxed during sex before.

Celia knew, without being told, that she simply could

not compete—or compare—with this Isabel. Even her name was superior. Celia was such an old-fashioned name. Isabel sounded coolly stylish and elegant, like its owner, no doubt.

Celia looked down at herself and groaned. How could Luke possibly call her beautiful? She was a mess. Her hair. Her clothes. Her face.

Flattery, she supposed. Men were such good liars.

She dashed the tears from her cheeks with the back of her hands then pulled the remaining pins from her hair, letting it tumble around her shoulders. She fixed the buttons on her top then yanked her skirt around straight. Not a good move, the action reminding her she was still naked underneath.

Her face flamed when she thought of how obedient she'd been. How…willing.

"Now your skirt… Open it," he'd said. "Wide.

"And now…your legs…"

Her mouth dried at the memory and her legs shifted slightly apart. She gripped the railing and thought of how it would feel if he were inside her now.

"Celia?"

She spun round at the sound of his voice, her face flushing guiltily as though she'd been caught doing something indecent.

Luke tried not to ogle her. But she was a tempting sight with that glorious hair of hers down on her shoulders. He ached to reach out and touch it, to wind it through his fingers and pull her head back, baring her neck to him again. He couldn't see the mark on her throat any more but he knew it was there.

His mark. *His* brand. *His* woman.

The fierce possessiveness of his thoughts shook him.

He really wished she hadn't told him he'd been the first man to satisfy her. That kind of thing was bound to stroke a man's ego, and tempt his dark side.

Such knowledge would make it so very easy to seduce her again. He only had to step forward and take her into his arms, tell her he'd break up with Isabel, then start kissing her. She wouldn't stand a chance.

Luke cleared his throat. Definitely time to go.

"I'll have the solicitor mail the deed of this property to your mother as soon as possible," he said. "If you could just give me her current address?"

"I'll write it down for you."

Celia walked towards where he was standing in the doorway and waited for him to turn and go back inside. But he didn't, and for one ghastly moment she thought he was going to reach out and pull her into his arms once more. It wasn't that he made a move, but there was something in his eyes. A sudden predatory gleam.

She sucked in sharply and glared at him.

"Don't you dare touch me!"

"I wasn't going to," he denied.

"Then, step back," she ordered, and he did.

Celia hurried past him and headed straight for the drawer in the kitchen where she knew there was a pen and a note pad. She was leaning on the counter and writing down Aunt Helen's address when her mobile phone began to ring. It was barely inches from her hands but she kept on writing and the phone kept on ringing.

"Shouldn't you answer it?" Luke said, an edge in his voice. "It might be *your* boyfriend."

Celia blinked up at him. "*My* boyfriend?"

"It came to me just now that there has to be one. A girl like you wouldn't be wanting for admirers. Or dates."

"There is no current boyfriend," she returned brusquely. "I gave up on them some time back. In fact, I gave on the whole male species. Pity I made an exception for you today. The trouble was I thought you were different. But you aren't different at all. You just have better moves than most. Now, if you'll excuse me?"

Celia banged down the pen and snatched up the mobile. "Yes?"

"Celia, it's Aunt Helen."

"Oh, yes, Aunt Helen. I got your message. I was going to come over later night, after you've had dinner. I didn't want to put you to any trouble. Is that all right?"

"Is Lionel's son still there?"

"What? Well…er…yes. But he was just leaving," she added, glowering over at him.

"Could I talk to him first please?"

"What about?" Celia was instantly wary.

"I have this idea."

"What idea?"

"It's about your mother. Look, I didn't want to worry you but her depression is much worse today. She's finally come to the conclusion that Lionel didn't love her at all. Pity she didn't realise that twenty years ago but there's nothing we can do about that now.''

True, Celia thought bitterly.

''I was wondering if it wouldn't do her some good to see and talk to Lionel's son. I know he wanted to talk to her and, having talked to him myself, I'm sure he won't say anything nasty. I think he's just curious to meet her, and you can understand that. Anyway, perhaps he could tell her about his father wanting to leave her their little love nest at the same time. Maybe that will reassure her that his dad did care for her in more than a sexual sense. She needs *some* kind of reassurance, believe me. And neither of us can give it to her.''

Celia knew what her aunt was saying made sense, but the thought of spending more time with Luke made her very tense. ''Luke didn't mention to you that he's intending to gift this place over to Mum himself?'' she said.

''No! Oh, how marvellous! That's even better. Jessica really loves that place, you know. In that case, why don't the two of you come over for dinner? John's working the early nightshift at the plant and won't be here. It'll just be the four of us, though I'm not sure your mother will come down from her room. She's taken to having a meal on a tray all by herself. What time is it now? Sixish. I'll make dinner for seven-thirty. Come any time after seven.''

''I'll have to ask Luke first, Aunt Helen.''

''Oh, yes. Yes, of course.''

Celia covered the phone with her hand and turned to him.

"Ask me what?" he said with a worried frown on his far too handsome face.

Celia told him her aunt's suggestion.

"So what do you think?" she asked when he stayed silent and frowning.

"I'll do it on one condition."

"What's that?"

"We take our own cars, so I can drive back to Sydney straight afterwards."

She stared at his grim expression and realised he was afraid to be alone with her. *Afraid.*

It was a telling revelation. And a terribly tempting one. Luke had already confessed that he found her beautiful, and that he was only human.

Well…she was only human too…

"Unfortunately, that's not possible," she said. "You'll have to drive me. When you were getting dressed just now I had another glass of wine. My nerves were rather shot at the time."

It was a lie. Her first of many, she imagined. Now *she* was afraid, afraid of what she was prepared to do to get this man into bed with her again. No wonder there was a saying that all was fair in love and war, she thought. Because when you were in love, you…

Celia managed not to gasp in shock, nor to look too taken aback. But she was rattled all the same. This *couldn't* be love she felt for Luke. It was just sex. No one fell in love as quickly as that. Except perhaps romantic fools like her mother.

But if that was the case, why did the idea of his

leaving her and going back to Isabel bother her so much?

It didn't just bother her. It made her go crazy inside. This had to be love. Had to be!

You *are* just like your mother, came the shattering realisation. When the right man came along, you fell hard and fast and you'll do anything to keep him. Anything at all!

As Celia looked at Luke with her newly opened eyes, her initial shock swiftly changing to a stubborn resolve. She might be like her mother in some ways, but she wasn't going to end up like her mother. No way!

But she would have to be bold to get what she wanted. Luke wasn't married yet. He wasn't even engaged. And he didn't love this Isabel. If he did, he would have said so. He also wouldn't have fallen into bed with her so fast, if he'd been really in love with someone else.

As much as Celia was a bit cynical about men and sex, she felt sure Luke wasn't that type of man. His horror at his father's behaviour had been genuine. No, Luke was basically a straight shooter, not a deceiver.

She figured he had to be fiercely attracted to her to have done what he'd done this afternoon. If he fancied her that much in old clothes and with no make-up on, then wait till he saw her tonight!

She'd brought one decent outfit with her. She *always* took one decent outfit with her whenever she went away anywhere for a couple of days. On top of that, there was so much more she could do with her face and hair.

Add some jewelry and a dash of perfume, and she would knock him for six!

"All right?" she said, cool on the outside but feverishly determined on the inside. She wasn't going to spend the rest of her life with a broken heart. She was going to win this man. He *was* different, she believed. Different from his father. Different from every man she'd ever known.

"I suppose so," he replied reluctantly. "It's not far, is it?"

"Only ten minutes or so. He said that's fine," she told her Aunt Helen crisply. "Expect us there between seven and seven-thirty. I have to shower and change first. I'm a bit of a mess."

Luke looked more worried than ever.

"Should I tell Jessica in advance who you're bringing?" Aunt Helen asked.

"No," Celia returned swiftly. "She'll panic. The reason I was able to get her out of this place so quickly was because she was afraid Luke might turn up and jump to all the right conclusions. Lionel did a good job of brainwashing her that secrecy was their number one priority."

She saw Luke wince and knew he felt guilty over keeping Isabel a secret today. Good, she thought. It showed he had a conscience. Nothing like his father.

"Don't tell her I'm bringing anyone at all," Celia warned her aunt. "I'll go up to her room when I first get there and explain. I don't want her answering the door or seeing Luke till I do that, all right?"

"If you say so, but it seems a bit cloak-and-daggerish."

"Maybe so, but it's a necessary precaution because when Mum meets Luke she's in for a real shock."

"In what way?"

"He's the dead spit of Lionel, twenty years ago."

CHAPTER EIGHT

"WHICH way now?" Luke asked brusquely as they approached a roundabout.

"Turn right," Celia directed. "Then just follow that road. It'll take you through Morisset and over the railway line then straight to Dora Creek. It's not far. Just a few kilometres."

Luke followed her directions in a grim silence, not at all happy with the situation. As much as he *did* want to see and talk to the woman who'd obviously held his father in thrall for an amazing twenty years, his need to flee the presence of her equally seductive daughter had become far greater during the last fifteen minutes.

Celia had disappeared up into the loft after the phone call from her Aunt Helen, claiming she was only going to freshen up. But she had swanned down a full hour later, looking—and smelling—far too enticing for words.

Green was undoubtedly her colour. Especially this green. Not bright or lime, but a soft, smoky green which complimented her natural colouring. She was wearing another skirt and top, obviously a fashion favourite with her. The skirt was darker than her top and was made of a floaty material. Softly gathered at the waist, it fell to her ankles and swished a little when she walked. The top had tight, three-quarter sleeves and a low crossover neckline which would have been criminal without a bra, yet still provocative with one. Her red-gold hair was back up, with lots of curls kissing her face and neck. The love bite he'd given her, he noted, seemed to have disappeared.

Make-up, he supposed.

Her make-up was, indeed, perfect, enhancing her already lovely complexion, eyes and mouth. Everything about her was perfect, including the sexy bronze slip-on sandals she was wearing, which had no backs and three-inch heels.

But the *coup de grâce* was her earrings.

Talk about exotic! Gold and dangling, they had a large heart covering each lobe from which fell gold chains of various lengths supporting either a gold star or a gold heart on the ends. They swung and tinkled together when she moved, a perversely erotic sight and sound.

Luke had watched her long slow walk down the stairs with almost hypnotised eyes. By the time she'd reached the bottom, his far from sated flesh had been in a right state.

Now, as he sat in his car, gripping the wheel tightly, he began to wonder if she'd deliberately made herself look extra sexy tonight. Though for what reason? A secret sadistic form of vengeance, or an outright attempt at seducing him? Had she really had that glass of wine she'd said she'd had? Or was that a ploy to be alone with him again at the end of the night?

To give her credit, she wasn't acting flirtatiously, but he doubted that would ever be Celia's way. Not that she needed to flirt. She just had to be breathing to affect a man.

Luke sucked in a deep breath himself, then wished he hadn't. Because the perfume she was wearing was as tantalising as the rest of her, especially in the confines of the car. It smelt of vanilla, and he'd always been partial to vanilla.

Frankly, Luke could not recall being this turned on in years. It was difficult to function, or focus on any other subject but sex. Was that what it had been like when his father had been with her mother? Had he found her so sexually irresistible that he'd forgotten everything else? His wife? His marriage vows? His normal sense of decency and honour?

Luke shook his head over the horrible thought that he was living some sort of ghastly replay of the past.

''Do you look much like your mother?'' he asked abruptly.

She turned her head to face him but he kept *his* eyes on the road ahead.

''Quite a lot, I'm told,'' she said. ''But I think she's much better looking than me. I'm a size larger. I'm also taller. And tougher,'' she added firmly.

Was that some kind of hint, her being tougher? Or was she just warning him to be gentle with her mother?

''We must be nearly there,'' he said.

''Turn right as soon as you get over this bridge. Then hard right again. The road follows the creek. Aunt Helen's house is a few hundred metres along it on the left. It's two-storeyed with a double garage out the front and a large porch. But I'll tell you when to stop.''

"Do that."

"Stop," she commanded a couple of minutes later, and he pulled over in front of a cream brick house which was exactly as she'd described. A project home, he noted, but one with a sense of style, especially in the gabled roof.

Luke was not an architectural snob. He thought project-built homes had come a long way since the uninspiring three-bedroom boxes of the sixties. Not everyone, he appreciated, could afford individually designed homes.

"Aunt Helen's husband works for the local power station," Celia explained as they walked together towards the front porch. "He's working the four till midnight shift tonight so he won't be here. Aunt Helen does have three sons as well, but they're all grown-up and living away from home."

"Why are you telling me all this?" Luke asked warily, still not sure what she was up to.

"No reason. Just thought you might like to know the lie of the land," she added with a smile. A sweet smile. Almost a flirtatious one.

The only lie of the land Luke wanted to know at that moment, he decided ruefully, was hers. She was playing at something here and he didn't like the feel of it. Nor the smell of it, for that matter. That was a provocative perfume! He could almost taste it, the thought conjuring up visions of his doing just that. Tasting it. And tasting *her*. All over.

He sighed as he stepped up onto the front porch. It was going to be a long evening.

Concentrate on the mother and forget the daughter!

Yeah, right. As if that's going to help, he thought irritably. Dear old Dad did exactly the same to the mother as I want to do to the daughter. And he did it for twenty years!

Luke sighed again.

"Why are you sighing like that?" Celia said, pouncing, the sweet smile fading. "I thought this was what you wanted. To meet my mother."

"I do. Or I did. But the situation is a little different now. It's become awkward."

"I don't see how. It's not as though my mother knows anything about our relationship."

Warning bells went off in Luke's brain. "We don't *have* a relationship, Celia," he pointed out firmly. "We had sex together. Once. And there will be no repeat performance. You have my word on that."

When her pale cheeks went a guilty shade of pink, Luke knew the truth. She *had* been planning on seducing him.

Luke wasn't sure if the realisation aroused or angered him. Because if she was prepared to go to bed with him again, *knowing* he had a steady girlfriend back in Sydney, then she was just doing it for the sex. And he'd thought more of her than that.

Okay, so it must be tempting for her, wanting to experience what she'd experienced with him one more time. Orgasms had a way of being very addictive. And coinciding orgasms during sex were as rare as hen's teeth.

He'd never had a coinciding one with Isabel. If he

allowed for the fact that a lot of women faked them in order to flatter their lovers, then he had possibly never had one. And yes, it had been out of this world, pleasurewise.

But that was still no excuse, in Luke's opinion. If he could resist temptation, then she could as well.

"I would have thought you'd be the last girl on earth who would tolerate a two-timing lover," he said harshly.

"I don't know what you're talking about," she said, and pushed the front doorbell.

"Oh, yes, you do, sweetheart," he hissed under his breath. "You know exactly what I'm talking about. Don't try to play me for a fool. I suspected the moment you sashayed downstairs in that sexy outfit that you had a hidden agenda for tonight. That, and that pathetic excuse about the wine. You didn't have any extra glass. You just wanted me to drive you here and then drive you home. Alone. You want another sample of what I gave you this afternoon. Why don't you admit it, instead of pulling this innocent act?"

Celia could feel her face going red.

"And to think I believed all that holier than thou crap about you not wanting me to touch you again!" he raged on. "The truth is you *do* want me to touch you again. You want me to touch you again one hell of a lot!"

Celia had never felt such shame, nor such outrage. He was right, but he was so wrong. She didn't want just what he'd given her this afternoon. She wanted so much more. She wanted what he'd said they didn't have: a real relationship. Or the chance of one.

She was trying to find the words to tell him exactly that when the front door opened and there stood Aunt Helen, looking her usual smart self in black trousers and an embroidered red top. Her once long auburn tresses—now worn short and died blond—showed evidence of her regular Friday trip to the hairdresser with not a hair out of place. She was not as striking as her kid sister, but still very attractive for her fifty-three years.

"Hello, Auntie," Celia said, struggling to find a smile through her emotional distress. "Sorry we're a bit late. This is Luke. Luke, my Aunt Helen."

He didn't seem to have any trouble smiling, nor in charming her aunt with a kiss on the cheek and a few well chosen words.

"Oh, my," her aunt said, looking a bit shell-shocked as she led them both inside and straight into the open-plan lounge. The house had no hallway as such, with the stairs leading to the upper floor on the left of the front door. "Celia was right. You do look a lot like your father. Not that I ever met him. But I've seen a couple of photos. Now, why don't you sit down in here with me, Luke, while Celia runs upstairs and talks to her mother. I popped a casserole in the oven for dinner, so we can have that any time you're ready, Celia. I'm not sure Jessica will join us for the meal," she said, directing her words at Luke. "She's not eating much at the moment. Hopefully, your visit might perk her up. Meanwhile, I've prepared a plate of nibbles for us and opened a nice bottle of Hunter Valley red. You like red wine, Luke?''

''Love it,'' he said as he sat down on the floral sofa. ''But I'm driving, so I can only have a glass or two, then I'll have to swap to water.''

Aunt Helen beamed approval at him as she settled into one of the matching armchairs. ''Sensible man. Nothing worse than people who drink and drive. So irresponsible. They cause so many accidents.''

Celia winced. ''Aunt Helen,'' she said in sharp warning and her aunt glanced her way, her expression bewildered.

''Luke's parents,'' Celia said softly.

Her aunt looked stricken. ''Oh, dear. Oh, how stupid of me. Luke, I'm so sorry. I just didn't think.''

''It's all right, Helen. Truly. I know you meant no harm. Besides, better to talk about something out in the open than to pretend it never happened. Which is one of the reasons I've come here tonight. To find some answers for what happened between my father and your sister.''

''What kind of answers? The simple truth is your father had an extramarital affair with my sister. For twenty years. I'm afraid there are no mysteries about it, Luke.''

''That may be, but the thing is, Helen, I always believed my father was the perfect family man. Other people did too. Of course, I know no one's perfect. I'm not that naive. But I can't accept the image of my father as a heartless womaniser. It doesn't ring true. Since I can't ask him for some answers in person, I was hoping your sister could shed some more light on the subject, so I too can come to terms with what he did. My mother, thank goodness, will never now know what happened. But I do. And I—''

Luke suddenly broke off and stared, not at Celia, who was still standing, but at something just over her shoulder. Celia knew instinctively what he'd seen. Oh, dear, she thought, her heart sinking as she turned.

Her mother was coming slowly down the stairs, her eyes wide, one hand at her throat, the other clutching the banisters. She was wearing a dusky pink dressing-gown, sashed at the waist, pink satin slippers and not a scrap of make-up.

But for all that, in the soft evening light, she looked so exquisitely beautiful, it was heart-breaking. There was a light hanging high above her head, casting a golden glow over her hair which was fluffed out over her very slender shoulders. She'd lost considerable weight since her lover's death, making her already large green eyes look larger. The dark rings underneath them were not unattractive, only adding to her haunting beauty. She looked like a character from one of those old melodramatic movies: the beautiful but mad bride who'd been locked up in a tower for years but who sometimes escaped in the dead of night.

''It's Luke,'' Celia said straight away before her mother got the wrong idea over whom she was seeing. ''Lionel's son. He's come to visit and he has some good news for you.''

Her mother's bewildered eyes briefly shifted to Celia before returning to Luke.

"I...I heard Lionel's voice," she choked out. "And I thought...I thought I was going insane." Tears filled her eyes but she didn't cry. She descended the last few steps very slowly, as though sleep-walking, then equally slowly came forward, staring at Luke all the while. "You're so like him," she murmured dazedly. "You sound like him. Look like him."

Luke rose and took her hands in his, drawing her over to the lounge. "So I'm told, ma'am," he said gently as they sat down together. "And your daughter, if I might say so, is startlingly like you."

"What? Oh, yes, people say that all the time. But close family don't always see the similarities, do they?"

"True."

Celia exchanged glances with her aunt who suggested with her eyes that they leave the room. But Celia was reluctant to do so. What if her mother got upset? What if Luke said the wrong thing?

She frowned and shook her head, so they remained, standing guard over their fragile charge. Celia began to worry that she hadn't thought this meeting through properly. All she'd been thinking about, in the end, was herself.

When Jessica reached out to touch Luke's arm Celia stiffened. Her mother was a toucher, but not everyone liked that kind of thing. But Luke didn't pull away, for which Celia was grateful.

"How did you find out about me?" Jessica asked in puzzled tones.

Celia tensed up again. What would Luke tell her? Not

the whole truth, surely. She tried to catch his eye but he seemed determined not to look at her.

"Dad went to see his solicitor the day before he died," he began, "and told him about you in confidence. You see, he wanted to gift over the house at Pretty Point to you. Unfortunately, the accident happened before he could do that, so the solicitor referred the matter to me. Your relationship wasn't spelt out in black and white but I suspected you had to be more than good friends for Dad to want to give you such an expensive property. So I drove up here today and, by coincidence, Celia was at the house when I arrived."

Celia flinched when her mother threw her a questioning glance.

"I needed a place to spend a quiet weekend," she said. "Somewhere I could just rest and read."

Luke finally looked at her—his eyes wry—and Celia struggled not to blush.

"But I still wanted to be close to you," she added. "I didn't think anyone would mind. No one was living there and it needed a dust through, anyway."

"But I thought you hated the place," her mother said, frowning.

Celia sighed. "Not the house itself, Mum," she muttered. Just what went on in it.

Luke shot her a sharp glance as if reading her mind and warning her to remain discreetly silent.

"As I was saying," he said, jumping in, "when Celia answered the door, I thought at first that she was the Ms Gilbert the solicitor told me about."

Celia flinched and closed her eyes. Oh, no. Don't tell

her what I did. Oh, please, don't do that! That would be much worse than anything I might have said just now.

"Celia quickly explained she wasn't my fa- ther's…er…friend," he continued rather delicately. "Her mother was. By then, I knew you and he had to have been lovers. Seeing the house was very telling. I know his personal style well. He built that place espe- cially for you two, didn't he?"

She nodded, her eyes flooding anew. "You…you must hate me," she choked out, two big tears running down her cheeks.

Luke covered her hands with his own in what Celia thought was an awfully kind gesture. A lump formed in her throat, tears of her own threatening. He really was a very nice man.

Luke shook his head. "No," he said. "What point would there be in my hating you? I can see you're not some kind of ruthless home-wrecker or money-grubbing gold digger. You're a very nice lady. And I'm sure my father cared for you very much."

It was heart-breaking, the look of desperate hope that filled her mother's face. Celia understood that kind of desperation now.

"You…you really think so?" Jessica said shakily.

Celia held her breath as she awaited Luke's reply.

"I'm sure of it," he pronounced, and she almost burst into tears of relief and gratitude. "My father was a good man. A decent man. The only thing which would make him be unfaithful to my mother for twenty years was the deepest of affections. I just want to know why, if he wasn't happy with my mother—and he clearly couldn't have been—why he didn't divorce her and marry you?''

Jessica glanced worriedly at her sister and daughter before looking back at her lover's son. ''Your father...he...he told me things in confidence. Things about your mother, Luke. Things he didn't really want other people to know.''

''I see. But my father's gone now, and so is my mother. I really need to know this, ma'am. I need some answers. My mother...was she...frigid?'' Luke asked reluctantly. ''Was that it?''

''In a fashion,'' Jessica hedged, then sighed. ''I guess there's no point in not telling you. It's not as though anyone in this room will tell anyone else, will they?''

''Of course not,'' both Celia and Aunt Helen murmured in unison.

''Tell me,'' Luke prodded softly. ''Please.''

''Your mother was attacked as a young girl.''

Luke sucked in sharply. ''Raped, you mean?''

''Yes. By a gang of louts. She was thirteen at the time.''

Celia was horrified. The poor girl. And poor Luke. He was looking poleaxed.

''She never told anyone,'' her mother went on. ''She kept it a secret. She pretended it never happened. But of course, you can't do that, can you, and stay mentally and emotionally healthy?''

''I wouldn't think so,'' Luke murmured sadly.

''Lionel thought she was a virgin when he married her because she wouldn't let him touch her before the wedding. As you can imagine, the wedding night wasn't a huge success. Neither was the honeymoon. Lionel said she tried so hard to please him yet was obviously hating everything about sex. He said he loved her but nothing he did made things better. He was actually thinking about divorce when she fell pregnant with you, Luke. Naturally, he couldn't leave her then.

"After you were born, she went into a deep postnatal depression which lasted over a year and eventually she became quite manic. Some days she'd be angry and argumentative, on others withdrawn and silent. Sex was a minefield best left totally alone. When Lionel came home one day and found her screaming at you in your cot for being a boy, and that all boys grew up to be bad, he took her straight to a psychiatrist. Under hypnotherapy, the truth finally came out. After extensive counselling and medication, she surprised Lionel by becoming an almost perfect wife and mother, although she never did get any pleasure from sex. Yet if Lionel didn't regularly sleep with her she'd become tearful and suspicious. Lionel said it nearly killed him to see how relieved she'd be when he had to go away, for whatever reason, because that meant no sex for a while."

Celia could see Luke was struggling with the impact of these appalling revelations, his face mirroring both distress and disbelief. On her part, she wasn't sure what to believe. Surely Lionel couldn't have invented this horror story to excuse his actions in his mistress's eyes. That would have been really evil.

"I still don't understand why he didn't divorce Mum after meeting you," Luke said, frowning. "I mean, from the sounds of things, my mother would probably have been relieved.''

Jessica gave him an odd look. ''You mean you haven't figured that out yet?''

''Sorry. I'm not sure what you mean.''

''The reason Lionel didn't leave your mother for me was because of you, Luke.''

''*Me?*''

''Yes, you. Believe me when I say your father loved you far more than he loved either your mother or me. Far, far more! Your happiness and security were his number one priorities. Everything was to be sacrificed for you, Luke. And it was.''

CHAPTER NINE

LUKE was stunned.

Jessica reached out and patted his arm. "Did your father ever tell you that his own father left his mother for another woman when he was just a boy?"

"No! He...he said his father died of a heart attack when he was ten and his mother when he was twenty. Of some kind of liver failure. He said she'd been ill for years. She'd caught some kind of virus."

"His father did die of a heart attack, but only recently. Your grandfather had contacted your father when he became ill, but Lionel would have nothing to do with him. He said to me that his father had been dead in his mind for over forty years. His mother—your grandmother—did die when Lionel was twenty. That wasn't a lie. And yes, of liver failure. But not because of a virus. She became an alcoholic after her husband left and eventually drank herself to death."

Luke shook his head, shocked, not only by these new revelations but the extent of this woman's knowledge.

"Why didn't Dad tell *me* any of this?" he demanded, feeling frustrated and almost angry that he'd been kept so much in the dark about his family history. He could understand why he hadn't been told about his mother's wretched past, but why keep his grandfather's actions—

and existence—a secret? And why lie over how his grandmother had died?

Just how many lies *had* his father fed him over the years?

"Lionel wouldn't have wanted you to know because he was ashamed," his mistress confessed. "Of both his parents. His father's desertion had hurt him terribly. That was why he couldn't leave your mother after you were born. Because he could never do to his son what his father had done to him. He explained that to me right from the beginning and I understood. I really did."

Maybe she did. But Luke didn't. Yes, he could understand his father making such a sacrifice for him during his vulnerable growing-up years. But what about after he'd grown up and left home? What about during the years he'd spent overseas? What was his father's excuse then?

No, no, Luke hated to admit it but this poor woman was the victim of male selfishness. She'd become a convenience by then. A beautiful, sexy, soft-hearted woman who was prepared to give his dad what his poor emotionally damaged mother hadn't been capable of.

In short, she'd been used.

Luke was more ashamed of his father at that moment than he'd been since finding out about his extramarital affair. To have a bit of sex on the side was forgiveable under the circumstances of his marriage. To put his son first whilst he'd been a mere boy was also forgiveable. But to string this lovely lady along for twenty years was *not* forgiveable.

Something of what he was feeling must have shown on his face because Celia's mother suddenly looked sad.

"I know what you're thinking," she said. "Why didn't he leave your mother after you finished university and went overseas to live? It wouldn't have affected you that badly by then."

"That thought did occur to me," Luke confessed reluctantly.

She shrugged her terribly thin shoulders. "Not as often as it's occurred to me, but by then I wasn't brave enough to ask. Perhaps Lionel thought it was too late to make such a big change in his life. Perhaps your good opinion of him still mattered more than I did. But I suspect he just couldn't bear to break your poor mother's heart. I do know he compromised a bit by building that house for us and by spending more time with me. He used to tell your mother he was going fishing for the weekend and she seemed to believe him."

Luke nodded. "She would have. He's been going fishing all his life."

"Actually, no. Most times he said he was going fishing during the last twenty years, he was coming to see me. There used to be an old fishing cabin at Pretty Point where we'd meet. But it eventually got vandalised and was partially burned down."

Luke realised somewhat bitterly why his father had been so understanding about his no longer wanting to go fishing at Pretty Point. That had been when he'd turned twelve, exactly twenty years ago, the same year he'd met Ms Jessica Gilbert.

Luke looked at her and thought how breathtakingly beautiful she must have been back then. She was still very beautiful…

"I want to apologise for my father," he said, and meant it. "I don't think he treated you very well. Or fairly. And I think he knew it too. I'm sure his wanting to gift you the property at Pretty Point was his way of saying sorry, so of course you must have it. I've already told Celia that I will see to the deed being transferred to you."

Luke was moved by the emotion in her eyes. "You'd do that for me?"

"It's what my father wanted."

"Oh…oh, dear…" She dissolved into tears then and he could do nothing but take her into his arms and try to comfort her. A piece of cake, compared to taking her daughter into his arms.

"There, there," he soothed, stroking her hair and back. "Please don't cry."

"Lionel always hated me to cry," she sobbed.

No doubt, Luke thought ruefully. And I bet you cried often, you poor thing. It was wicked, what he did to you. Wicked. He should have walked away and let you find a decent life for yourself, with a man who could have given you a darned sight more than the occasional weekend. Whatever had possessed him?

Luke glanced over Jessica's shoulder to her even more beautiful daughter, and knew exactly what had possessed him.

A powerful force, physical passion. Especially in a man.

Luke vowed not to let his passion for Celia sway his good judgement. Come the end of this evening, he was out of here, never to return. But, while he had the chance, he was going to put this poor woman back on the path to some kind of future happiness, because the last thing he wanted on his conscience was Celia's mother topping herself.

"Why don't you take your mum upstairs to get dressed for dinner?" Luke directed at Celia. "You need to eat, Jessica," he added with a firm glance into her still teary eyes. "And to talk. We'll have a good chin-wag about Dad, shall we? You can tear strips off the old man, if you want to. And we'll down a couple of glasses of Helen's excellent wine. Shall we say ten minutes to dinner? You could manage that, Helen?"

Helen smiled at him. "No trouble."

"Good. Hop to it then, Celia. And for pity's sake, don't take as long as *you* did to get ready tonight. After ten minutes, I'll be coming up there to drag the pair of you downstairs personally."

Celia bristled, but then relented. Because he was right. This was exactly what her mother needed to do. To pull herself together and to talk about Lionel. To demythologise the man whom she'd falsely idolised. To have a proper wake for him, so to speak.

Then she might begin the healing process.

Celia hurried forward and led her somewhat dazed mother upstairs, plonking her down on the guest bed whilst she rustled up some clothes. She found a pair of stretchy blue jeans and a white cashmere sweater, neither of which needed ironing.

"Here, Mum. Put these on."

"He's remarkable, isn't he?" her mother said a bit dreamily as she did as her daughter ordered. "Just like Lionel."

Celia rolled her eyes. Her mother was such a romantic. It pained Celia to think she was more like her than she'd ever realised.

"He looks just like Lionel too," her mother added as she walked over to the dressing table and picked up her hair brush. "And he's just as forceful. There's something about a forceful man that's hard to resist, don't you think?"

Celia tried not to think of the way Luke had ordered her to undress this afternoon. Because thinking about such things made her want him to do the same again. And that just wasn't going to happen. Luke had been equally forceful on that score out at the front door.

"Have I time to put some lipstick and perfume on?" Jessica asked.

"If you're quick."

"What about my hair? I should really put it up. It's a mess."

"I don't think we've got the time for that."

"It won't take me long." And it didn't, her mother winding her hair around in her hands a couple of times and anchoring it in seconds with a few pins. "There. See? I was quick. Come on, let's get going. I want to talk to Luke some more. And *look* at him some more."

Don't we all, Celia thought ruefully as she followed in her mother's surprisingly brisk step.

The dinner was a great success, if her mother's

emerging good spirits were the basis for judgement. Luke was patience personified. And Aunt Helen looked very pleased with how things had turned out.

But Celia found the whole thing a trial. Just looking at Luke made her even more depressed inside, as did listening to her mother recount all the intimate little details she knew about Luke's life, things Lionel had told her over the years. Mostly his son's triumphs, both sportwise and academically.

Over the couple of hours she spent sitting at the dining table, Celia learned Luke had been captain of the basketball team, captain of the debating team, captain of his school of course. Luke, the youth, had been nothing short of an all round star! He'd won numerous awards during his university days as well, one being a rarely given scholarship to further his studies overseas, the architectural equivalent of being a Rhodians scholar.

At twenty-two, he'd jetted off for London, where he'd stayed on after finishing his studies, gaining invaluable experience by working for a highly prestigious international company that had offices in Paris, Rome and New York. All in all, Luke had stayed overseas for nearly eight years. When he'd returned two years ago he'd entered a competition to design a retirement village and had won. The prize had been a great wad of cash plus a lucrative contract to work for the architectural company that had sponsored the prize. He'd been working there ever since.

Aside from details of Luke's career, Celia also learned of several other personal crises in his growing-up years, in particular his breaking his leg during abseiling at a scout camp, thereby missing out on trying out for the Australian schoolboy basketball team— clearly considered a disaster at the time.

Luke now laughed about it, saying time put everything into perspective.

By the time coffee was served around nine-thirty, Celia realised Lionel hadn't exactly been demythologised during all this. He'd come across as a doting father who'd taken great pride in his quite remarkable son. Even worse was the realisation her own mother sounded just as proud of Luke, almost as though *she* were his mother.

Celia felt quite jealous.

"You know, Luke," her mother started up again as they all sipped their coffee, "your father was extremely relieved when you finally came back to live and work in Australia. He was worried you might meet some girl overseas and stay there for ever. He was over the moon when you became engaged to a Sydney girl."

Celia's coffee cup froze at her lips. *Engaged?* Had her mother just said *engaged*?

Her eyes went to his but he refused to meet them.

"If I recall rightly," Jessica said, sweeping on, oblivious to her daughter's stunned reaction, "your wedding is very soon. Unless you've decided to call it off after the accident, that is," she added a bit worriedly when she noted Luke's rather grim expression.

"No," he said. "No, the wedding's definitely going ahead, a fortnight tomorrow, as planned. I did think of postponing the ceremony for a while but, in the end, I decided nothing would be served by that. Isabel's parents had spent a lot of time and money organising everything, and I didn't think it would be fair on them. Or on Isabel, for that matter.''

Celia's knuckles whitened as her fingers tightened around her coffee cup.

''Your father wouldn't have wanted you to postpone anything,'' Jessica reassured him. ''He was very keen on your getting married, *and* on your Isabel. I hear she's very beautiful.''

''Yes,'' Luke agreed. ''Isabel's a lovely looking girl. And a lovely person as well.''

Now his eyes did go to Celia's. And she saw a wealth of apology in them. Yet no guilt. Amazing! No guilt!

She could barely believe it.

Luke was engaged! And the wedding was in a fortnight's time! Yet today, he'd been making love to *her*.

No, no, of course he hadn't been making love to her, Celia amended bitterly in her mind. He'd just been screwing her. That's all the Freeman men ever did to the Gilbert girls. Screw them.

Her coffee cup clattered back down into the saucer as a cold fury invaded her heart, and her eyes.

Luke put down his coffee cup as well, his own eyes closing briefly before opening again. When they did, they were quite unreadable.

''Speaking of the wedding has reminded me that I have a lot to do this weekend,'' he said in a flat but firm voice. ''So if you'll excuse me, ladies, I really do have to be going. Celia? Are you ready to go?''

''Any time you are,'' she replied through gritted teeth.

''You'll come back to visit some time, won't you?'' her mother asked him plaintively.

''Actually, no, Jessica. I won't. Not personally. My solicitor will be in touch, however. I'm very glad to have met you and talked with you, and I do wish you all the best for the future, but I think it wise to leave it at this one time.''

Her mother looked crestfallen, but resigned. She nodded. ''I can appreciate your feelings. It must have been a big shock for you, finding out about me. But you've been very decent about it all. And very kind. Let me just say how very sorry I am if what we did hurt you, but at least your mother never found out. And I did love your father very very much.''

When Luke stood up, walked round and bent to kiss her mother on the cheek, it took all of Celia's will-power not to jump up and scream all sorts of verbal abuse at him.

Only the thought of her mother's emotional health held her back. If Celia said anything at all about what Luke had done to her this afternoon, it might undo all the good he'd done here tonight.

He wasn't all bad, she conceded, just as Lionel hadn't been all bad. But both father and son had been unfaithful to the women they were supposedly committed to. And in doing so, they'd left a trail of emotional wreckage behind them.

Celia knew it would be a long, long time before she got over Luke Freeman. Maybe even longer than it would take her mother to get over Luke's father. Because Lionel was dead now, and Luke was very much alive. Celia had to live with the daily reality from now on that, somewhere in Sydney, Luke would be living with the lovely Isabel, married to her, making love to her, having children with her. Whilst she would be alone, alone with her regrets and her heartache.

CHAPTER TEN

"SAY something, for pity's sake," Luke ground out.

Celia glanced over at him, then turned and opened the passenger door. During the fifteen minutes it had taken for them to make their farewells and drive in total silence back to Pretty Point, her need for an angry confrontation with him had disintegrated. What would be the point? What would it achieve?

Without a word, she swung her feet out of his car and onto the gravel drive.

"I didn't tell you I was engaged to Isabel because I didn't want to hurt you any further," he threw after her in a pained voice. "You have to believe me, Celia."

Now she did turn to look at him. "Why must I believe you, Luke? Because it will make *you* feel better? You're a coward, just like your father."

"I'm no coward," he grated out. "And neither was my father. I've been thinking some more about what your mother said and I was wrong to condemn him. You were, too."

"Oh, come on. I had every right to condemn him!"

"No, be fair, Celia. Put yourself in my father's position. Whose happiness would you have chosen? He did what he thought he had to do. He put my happiness before his and, in the end, my mother's as well. He knew she couldn't have coped with his leaving her after all those years of marriage.''

''And what about *my* mother?'' Celia said, lashing out. ''Do you think she coped? You saw her. Your father nearly destroyed her.''

''He should have walked away right from the start, yes. But that would have been extremely difficult, under the circumstances. And your mother knew what she was getting into. She knew he was married after that first night and she kept on seeing him. She'll bounce back, your mum. She's tougher than you think.''

''And what about me?'' she threw at him. ''Do you think I'll bounce back after this?''

''You told me you were tougher than your mother,'' he reminded her.

Tears welled up in her eyes. ''Well, I'm not. I—I—Oh, just go! Go and marry your lovely Isabel. But I hope she knows what she's getting. A man who doesn't love her as she probably deserves to be loved. A man who just two weeks before his wedding forgot she even existed. Tell me, Luke, have you ever felt with Isabel what you felt with me this afternoon?''

He didn't say a single word, but his face told it all.

''No,'' she said, sneering. ''My betting is you'll be back too, just like your father. At least he had some excuse. What's yours, Luke? You're not even married yet. You should do the honorable thing and call your wedding off.''

His eyes looked haunted. ''You can't expect me to give up the substance for the shadow. I've only known you a few short hours. This thing between us—it—it won't last.''

''It lasted twenty years between our parents,'' she pointed out savagely.

''It lasted because they had an affair! They had all the excitement and the sex, and none of the mundane. They might not have been so happy if they'd married. It's hard to find happiness over the misery of others.''

''I hope you remember that.''

''You'll get over me.''

''I won't,'' she declared, and he stared at her in alarm.

''I've fallen in love with you, Luke Freeman. Oh, I know you think love can't happen as quickly as that. But it has, and nothing you say will change it. I love you. I love you. I love you!''

''Don't keep saying that.'' He groaned.

''Why? Because once again you don't want to hear it? You *are* a coward, Luke Freeman. A miserable coward. You don't deserve my love. You don't deserve any woman's love. I feel sorry for poor Isabel because she's going to be awfully short-changed in your marriage. I wonder how many nights you'll lie in bed with her, thinking of me, before you come crawling back up here, wanting another sample of the magic we shared today.''

''After I marry Isabel, I won't be back,'' he bit out. ''And that's a promise.''

''You'd better not because, let me warn you, if you do, I'll bring you down. With my love, and with my hate. Oh, yes, Luke. I'm not totally like my mother. I'm not nearly so sweet or forgiving. If you ever show up in my life again, I won't settle for just your body. I won't settle for anything less than your very soul. And once that's mine, you'll be the one who's destroyed. You have my promise on that!''

His face grew dark and his finger jabbed white hot fury at her. ''This is the very reason why I won't ever be back. Because I can't stand this sort of thing. I want peace in my life, not some crazy woman telling me she loves me one minute, then threatening me the next. You think you love me? Well, you don't. If you did, you'd have some compassion for me. Have you any idea what I've gone through these past two weeks? Sheer and utter hell! My parents killed and nobody to bury them but me. Can you imagine what it's like to choose coffins for both your parents? Choose the clothes they will wear for their funerals? Make all those awful decisions which have to be made? And then the funerals themselves, all the while trying not to break down, because men aren't expected to cry, are they?''

Celia stared at him in horror as his eyes actually glistened.

''But,'' he choked out, ''I've felt like crying. I still feel like crying when I think about it all. My parents...both gone. In a heartbeat. And then what happens? I discover that my beloved father, my hero, wasn't such a hero after all. Can you imagine how I felt when I found out he had feet of clay? How I felt when you answered the door today and I thought *you* were my father's mistress? A girl young enough to be his daughter. Yet you didn't tell me the truth, did you? Oh, no. You had your own private, vengeful agenda, Celia

Gilbert, and Luke Freeman's feelings didn't count. You deliberately let me think my father had been the worst kind of sexual predator.''

Remorse ripped through Celia as the reality of what she'd put Luke through hit home hard. ''Luke, I—I'm sorry. Truly. I was just trying to—''

''Protect your mother,'' he finished bitterly. ''Well, it's a pity you didn't think what results your charade might produce. Because no sooner had I started thinking of you as my father's mistress, than I started wanting you as my own. I was well on the slippery slide to hell long before you started crying and I took you in my arms. I'm in hell now, still wanting you so badly it's killing me. But it's not love driving me, sweetheart. It's lust. Pure, animal lust. At least *I* know the difference.

''So what am I to do, Celia? You tell me. Walk away like I've been trying to do? Or go with you back inside my father's decadent little love nest and take you to hell with me? You choose, darling. You choose.''

She stared at him, heart pounding, eyes widening. ''What do you mean? Take me to hell with you...''

''I mean just that. I still want you, in all the ways I've been thinking of having you from our first meeting. I don't love you and I won't pretend I do. You want my soul? It's yours, along with my body. Take it if you want it, because I'm tired of trying to do what's right. I'm tired of everything.''

Celia heard the torment in his voice and her heart filled with a sweet longing to comfort him, to take him in her arms and make him see that it wasn't just lust driving him. He *could* love her, if only he'd let himself.

He didn't love this Isabel. Luke wasn't the type of man to be unfaithful to a woman he truly loved. Surely he would see that, in time.

But she didn't have much time, did she?

"When do you have to be back in Sydney?" she asked abruptly.

"What's that got to do with anything?" he snapped.

"You said you didn't have a date with Isabel tonight. What about tomorrow night?"

"She's not expecting me back till the end of the weekend. She thinks I'm up here, revisiting my childhood past and getting in touch with my father's spirit. What a joke!"

"I don't think it's a joke at all," Celia murmured. "That's exactly what you've been doing."

He laughed. An awful sound. "I'm sure Dad's very proud of me for following in his footsteps to a T. Come on. Let's go inside and go to bed. That *is* what you want, isn't it?" He looked straight at her with a challenging gaze, his black eyes still glittering.

No, she thought despairingly. Not like this.

But if she sent him away...

She had one weekend, one weekend to make him see they were meant for each other.

"Yes," she agreed a bit shakily, knowing the risk she was taking but compelled just the same.

"And you don't want me to leave in the morning, do you? You want me to stay here with you all weekend."

"Yes," she said, more firmly this time.

"I thought so. Just don't go telling me how you love me all the time. I don't need any more romantic bulldust, or any more guilt trips. I don't need anything this weekend but you, naked and willing. Do you think you could manage that?''

Luke turned away from the hurt look on her face and climbed out of the car, slamming the door behind him. He knew he was being cruel. And he hated himself for it. But he also couldn't seem to stop.

In the space of one miserable day she'd turned his life upside down, and had made him do things he'd thought he'd never do. He was still doing them!

When he reached her side of the car, she was standing there, calmly waiting for him, no longer looking hurt, just breathtakingly beautiful in the moonlight. His flesh leapt at the sight of her and he abandoned all hope of resisting temptation.

''Why did I have to meet you now?'' He groaned frustratedly as he pulled her into his arms. ''And why did you have to be this beautiful?''

He didn't expect an answer, because he was already kissing her before she could do more than part her perfect lips.

His tongue met hers and they both moaned. His arms tightened around her and the urge to make love to her, then and there, was intense.

His need triggered an unwanted memory and his mouth burst up from hers. ''Damn and blast. I don't have any more condoms with me. Do you?''

She stared up at him with a desperation that must have reflected his own.

''No. But you—you—'' She broke off, her expression anguished.

"But I what?"

"You don't really need them. Not unless you think you do. I'm a regular blood donor. And I haven't been with anyone for months."

"Well, I'm no risk. You have my word on that. What about pregnancy?"

"No chance of that this weekend."

He looked at her and thought that a man would be crazy to trust a woman who claimed she loved him. But strangely, he *did* trust her.

Or did he just *want* to trust her? Had his normally careful character been corrupted by the thought of making love to her all weekend without having to worry about using protection, of staying inside her afterwards till he was ready to do it again. And again. And again.

The prospect of such pleasures was simply too much. "Fine," he bit out, grabbing her nearest hand and pulling her towards the house. "Come on before common sense returns and I change my mind."

He almost laughed at the hypocrisy of that last statement. Nothing was going to change his mind. Nothing was going to stop him, short of a bomb falling on top of them both.

He reached for where he'd seen her hide the key on a ledge and jammed it into the lock. "I trust you're not going to change *your* mind at the last moment?" he asked as he threw open the door.

"No," she said, her green eyes glittering wildly, her breasts rising and falling under her green top. She was as excited as he was, he realised. Too excited, perhaps, to think clearly.

Was this the kind of passion their parents had shared? If it was, then it explained a lot. His father's deceptions. Her mother's ongoing willingness to be used.

"You know you shouldn't always be so quick to take a man's word," he muttered. "Like you said earlier today, men lie to get sex, and they'd lie a lot to get what you're offering."

"You're not that kind of liar," she said with such confidence that he was momentarily rattled.

"You called me a coward a minute ago," he reminded her, pulling her inside and kicking the door shut behind them.

"I was angry with you."

"And you're not any more?" He pressed her up against the door, his erection almost at bursting point.

"I understand you better now."

He shook his head. "Well, I don't understand you, Celia Gilbert. And I don't want to. I just want to…"

"Take me to hell with you," she finished for him before he could say the crude word that had sprung to his lips.

"That's it, precisely."

"Impossible. Because I'm going to take you to heaven first." His breath caught when she snaked her arms up around his neck and reached up on tiptoe. "And I'm going to keep you there," she whispered huskily against his mouth, "all weekend long."

CHAPTER ELEVEN

CELIA woke to the sun streaming into the room and Luke still fast asleep next to her. Quietly she levered herself up on one elbow and stared down at him, her heart contracting as the memories flooded back, not just of the night before, but the whole of yesterday.

In a way, it all seemed unreal. Like a dream. Or a nightmare.

Luke's naked body sprawled on top of the bed beside her, however, was very real. As were the feelings just looking at it evoked within her.

She wanted to reach out and touch him again. Stroke him. Stir him. She wanted to make his flesh grow hard and huge once more so that she could straddle him and ride him one more amazing time.

Was that love? she now wondered. Wanting to do that?

Or was it just lust? as Luke had insisted.

The female psyche, Celia conceded, was geared to love, to seeing all relationships with romantic, rose-coloured glasses.

There'd been nothing remotely romantic in their first torrid encounter up against the door last night. Nor their second, on the rug, in front of the fireplace.

Basic was the word that came to mind.

But afterwards, Luke had been very tender with her,

apologising for his roughness as he'd carried her upstairs. Not that she'd really minded at the time. She'd been right there with him. As wildly excited as he'd been.

But she preferred the gentler lover he'd become once his first mad bursts of passion had been sated. She'd loved the way he'd washed her in the shower, kissing and caressing her all the while. And the way he'd dried her. So softly, yet sensually.

But nothing could compare with what he'd done to her when he'd carried her back to the bed. She'd vowed to take him to heaven, yet she'd been the one in heaven, with his mouth on her down there. She'd come so many times she lost count, till she'd begged him to stop.

He'd laughed, then had slid up her body and had eased himself back into her, bending her knees right back and hooking her ankles over his shoulders. She'd stared dazedly up at him as he'd rocked into her with a slow, voluptuous rhythm, his handsome face a study of intense concentration till eventually she'd begun moving with him, her hips lifting off the bed, her inner muscles squeezing him tight. He'd groaned then, and she'd known he'd been right on the edge. One more squeeze and he'd tipped right over.

She'd never watched a man come before. Not like that. She'd found it incredibly exciting, not minding at all that she hadn't come herself on that occasion.

"Witch," he'd called her afterwards, but smilingly. "Any more wine in that fridge downstairs?"

He'd brought a bottle of classic dry white back to bed and they'd drunk it together—straight from the bottle—and had talked and had laughed whilst she'd touched him and had kissed him, more and more intimately. She hadn't been able to help herself.

Of course, he hadn't minded. He hadn't minded at all. And before she'd known it she'd been on top of him and riding him, her nakedness on display for his eyes and hands, her earrings swinging back and forth with her rhythm. Once, he'd splashed some wine on her breasts and pulled her down so that he could lick it off. And when the wine had all gone, he'd rubbed the tip of the bottle against her till she'd splintered apart.

At the time, it had seemed so dizzyingly exciting.

Now, she didn't like to think about it.

Yet she had to think about it, didn't she? She had to think about the sort of woman she became when she was in bed with Luke: an uninhibited and wild creature who didn't seem to mind what he did to her, and whose ability to orgasm had increased a thousandfold.

Celia conceded it would be very easy to become addicted to having Luke as her lover, whether she was in love with him or not.

She believed her mother had fallen victim to a similar addiction with Luke's father, and that was why she'd never been able to break up with him. Lionel had been like a drug to her.

Celia couldn't bear the thought of ending up like her mother. And she might. She very well might, if Luke still married Isabel. And he'd given no indication as yet that he wouldn't.

Would she have the will-power to say no if he wanted her as *his* mistress? Would she send him away, or would she succumb, and keep stupidly hoping that he'd leave Isabel for her?

No. No. She couldn't do that to herself. She had to stop this right now!

Reefing her eyes away from Luke's magnificent male body she swung her legs over the side of the bed. The sound of her earrings tinkling had her reaching up and taking them off. Quietly, she slipped them into the top of the drawer of the bedside table. Best not wear *them* today. Luke had admitted during the night he found them an incredible turn-on and the last thing she wanted was to tempt Luke today. She just wanted to talk to him.

Celia sucked in a fortifying breath as she glanced at the bedside clock. It was just after ten.

Get up, she ordered herself. Get up. Get dressed, and go downstairs.

"And where do you think you're going?" Luke growled, snaking a long strong arm around her waist and pulling her back against him. His mouth nuzzled into her neck and his right hand homed in on a still sensitised breast.

Celia smothered a moan of pleasure. But, oh...he knew just what she liked. Or had learned to like during the night before. He'd been quite a teacher.

"I—I have to get up," she said, trying to ignore the exquisite sensation of his tugging on her nipple.

"Not yet," he said thickly, and angled his body to curl around hers.

When she felt his erection nudging between her legs, Celia stiffened.

No, don't think about how it feels when he's inside you, she told herself despairingly. Stop him, for pity's sake. Stop him!

She made some effort to struggle free and he grunted. "All right. Not so impatient."

She gasped when he slipped inside her.

"There. That better?"

He thought she'd been wriggling with frustration!

She wanted to cry. Instead, she moaned. It felt so good, so very, very good.

He started pulsing into her with short, rapid strokes and soon she was making whimpering little sounds, deep in her throat.

"You like that?" he muttered against her skin.

"Mmm," was all she could manage.

"And this?" His hand left her breast to reach down between her legs, touching her where a woman always likes to be touched.

"Yes," she choked out, squirming with pleasure. "No. Yes. No, don't. Stop it. I'll come."

"But I love it when you come. Come for me, Celia. Don't try to stop it. Let yourself go. A-h-h, yes. *Yes!*"

Once again, they climaxed together, and the pleasure was blinding. But, far too soon, it was over and reality came back to scorn her.

See? You're addicted to him already. You can't say no. He only has to touch you and you melt.

Self-disgust had her forcibly moving away from him whilst her recent release gave her some measure of will-power.

"Hey," he protested at his abrupt ejection from her

body, but she didn't answer him. She scrambled off the bed and bolted for the bathroom, locking the door behind her.

Luke sighed and fell back on the bed. He knew exactly what was bothering Celia. The same thing that had bothered him when he'd first woken up.

Guilt.

He'd tried to ignore his conscience, had tried to forget that he was still engaged to Isabel. And he'd managed, for the few minutes he'd been making love to Celia just now. Hard to think of anything much when he was inside that hot little body of hers.

But the reality of his fiancée had still been waiting there, at the back of his mind.

Now, it was well to the foreground, a problem he could no longer push aside.

Isabel deserved better than this kind of behaviour from him. Celia deserved better, too.

He wasn't being fair to either of them.

But what was he to do for the best?

Okay, so he didn't love Isabel. But he didn't believe he loved Celia, either. As he'd told her, love didn't happen that quickly. It wasn't love that had first driven him into Celia's bed yesterday. It had been a wicked combination of things: her beauty and sensuality; her tears and his own grief over his parents' deaths. His recent celibacy hadn't helped either.

But perhaps the most insidiously corrupting factor in all this had been his initial misconception over Celia's role in his father's life. His male mind had been set onto a seductively sexual path from the moment he'd clapped eyes on her, a dark decadent path that had somehow perversely appealed to his present frustrated state of mind and body.

His threat to take her to hell with him last night might have been borne out of that, but he hadn't taken her to hell, had he? She'd taken him to heaven, as she'd promised.

What a surprising lover she'd turned out to be!

So enchantingly sweet in the beginning. But in the end, so amazingly bold.

Luke heard the shower being snapped on and his mind shot back to last night, to the two occasions they'd showered together. How startled she'd been the first time when he'd taken the shower gel and had washed her with it. All over. Her eyes had grown wider by the second. Clearly, her sexual experience was very limited.

On their second visit, however, it had been her to take the vanilla-scented gel in her hands, pouring it into her palm and massaging him with it in all sorts of equally intimate places. One in particular. His gut twisted just thinking about how incredible *that* had felt.

Her newly discovered wantonness had excited him. Unbearably. He'd especially loved it when she'd gone down him later. Because he'd known she hadn't done that before, either. She hadn't done anything much before, from what he could gather.

Not like Isabel.

He grimaced. Isabel, again.

He'd honestly thought he was happy with Isabel in bed. And he was. Or he had been.

But it was never going to be the same again, was it? He'd never be able to go to bed with her in the future without thinking of Celia, without wanting her to *be* Celia.

Regardless of what his feelings were for Celia, and vice versa, she'd ruined the idea of his marrying Isabel. Because he knew he would not be able to stay away from her. Not for long. There was nothing for it but to call the wedding off. And the sooner the better. Today, in fact.

Luke threw back the sheet and swung his feet over the side of the bed, scowling as he glanced around the room. His clothes… Where were his clothes?

Downstairs, he remembered, all over the place.

Sighing, he rose and padded down the stairs where he collected his discarded clothes and dragged them all back on, minus the tie which he shoved into his jacket pocket. Then he picked up Celia's things, shaking his head over her ripped panties. He'd been like an animal!

But she'd seemed to like it. She seemed to like anything he did to her. She was going to be very pleased when he told her he was calling the wedding off.

Isabel wasn't, though. She was going to be upset. So were her parents. Nice people, both of them. Not wealthy, either. He hated the thought of doing this to all three of them.

At least he was rich enough now to make financial recompense for any expenses they couldn't recoup. He'd give Isabel a packet, too. She deserved it.

But no amount of money, he knew, would make up for the distress he was going to cause.

Celia opened the bathroom door just as Luke made it to the top of the stairs with her clothes. She had a towel wrapped around her head and was wearing a satiny cream robe. But not another darn thing, by the way the silky material clung to her skin as she walked into the room. It was going to be difficult doing the right thing and keeping his resolve to leave.

Only the thought of his imminent return—could he get back by tonight?—kept him focused.

Her eyes showed shock when she first noted his dressed state. But they swiftly grew cold and almost contemptuous. "You're leaving, I see," she bit out.

"Yes, I am," he began. "But I—"

"Please don't say another word," she snapped. "It's not necessary. I'm quite glad you're leaving. Now I don't have to ask you to, and there won't be a scene."

He frowned at her, wondering exactly what was behind this sudden change of attitude. After all, this was the girl who'd promised to keep him in heaven all weekend, who'd declared her undying love.

"Are you still angry with me about Isabel, is that it?" he asked, placing her clothes on the foot of the bed.

"No, that's not it." She reefed the towel off her head and her hair tumbled around her shoulders, a mass of damp dark red curls. She started rubbing it dry, and not quite looking at him. "The thing is, Luke, I realised this morning that you were right and I was wrong. I don't love you. It's just a sexual thing between us."

He frowned at her. How odd, he thought, that listening to her say what he'd actually said to her would make him see *he'd* been the one who was wrong. It wasn't just sex between them. It was something far stronger and far more special.

"Look, I won't be a hypocrite and say I didn't enjoy myself last night," she said, sweeping on. "I did. It was a real eye-opener. And an education all right. You've taught me how to come on cue and how to please a man, and for that I'm grateful. But given you *are* engaged, I'd rather leave things at a one-night stand. So thank you, but goodbye."

Luke could not believe what he was hearing. In fact, he *didn't* believe it. "You're lying to me," he stated firmly.

Her eyes finally met his. Such beautiful, expressive eyes when she wasn't acting. Clear windows to her soul, her frightened, hurt, sensitive soul.

"Why on earth would I do that?" she threw at him.

If she thought she could hide her vulnerability behind some falsely assertive façade, then she was way wrong. "Pride?" he suggested softly. "Conscience? Fear?"

"*Fear?*"

"Yes. You're worried that we'll end up like your mother and my father."

That rattled her. "And if I am, don't you think I have a right to be? I'd be a fool to think you're going to call off your marriage to Isabel because of me."

"But I am," he said.

She stared at him for a few startled moments, then laughed. "Oh, please. Don't insult my intelligence. Why would you do that? You've already said you don't love me, that you'd never give up the substance for the shadow. You're the one who's lying, and we both know why. You don't want to give up the great sex we had last night just yet.''

''No. I don't want to give *you* up, Celia. There's a difference.''

''No.'' She began shaking her head violently. ''No, I can't afford to believe that kind of thing.''

''Then, I guess it's up to me to *make* you believe me. I will be back, Celia. Today.''

''Well, I won't be here.'' Again, she flashed defiant eyes at him, and he almost smiled. A man who didn't know her as well as he did might have been fooled. But he *did* know her well, much better than he knew Isabel.

Strange, that.

''Yes, you will,'' he said. ''You'll wait for me.''

''And what makes you so sure of that?''

''Because you have to. Just as I have to come back. We were meant to be together, Celia. It was our destiny.''

''Our destiny?''

''Yes. You were the one who was right and I was wrong. We *have* fallen in love. I tried to argue against it in my mind but I can see that was very foolish of me. Because you can't argue with emotion. I've fallen in love with you, Celia. And you've fallen in love with me. End of story. Or should I say, the beginning of our story, if you want it to be. It's up to you.''

Celia stared at him. She wanted to believe him more than anything else in the world. But it was so hard to rise above everything she'd come to believe about men.

Yet, to be fair, Luke wasn't just an ordinary man. He

was an exceptional man. Sensitive. Kind. Deep. If she didn't trust *him*, then she'd never trust any man. Which meant she'd never have the things her mother never had, and which she'd always craved: a partner for life who loved her and wanted to have children with her.

She looked at Luke and wanted to have a family with him so very much. He'd be a wonderful father, she knew.

She had to believe in him. Because not to would make her such a coward. And she wasn't that.

"Yes. I...I'll be here," she admitted shakily, knowing that if he betrayed that trust, if he didn't return today, she would never recover.

"And I'll be back," he promised, coming forward to give her a polite peck on the cheek.

When his head lifted she gazed longingly up into his eyes. "Kiss me properly."

"I don't dare. You have great power in your lips, my love."

Her heart tightened. "Am I, Luke?" she whispered, her voice catching. "Am I really your love?"

He groaned, then swept her into his arms, his lips crushing down on hers.

She clung to him when his mouth finally lifted.

"Don't go," she said, sobbing.

"I don't want to. I *have* to. You yourself said you can't find happiness over the misery of others. I can't in all conscience leave it any longer to tell Isabel I'm not going to marry her. I promise I'll be back by dark. If I'm delayed for any reason, I'll ring. Come downstairs and write down your mobile number for me."

Celia knew he was right to go. But still, she didn't want him to.

"Hurry back," she called after him as he drove off. He waved, and was gone.

CHAPTER TWELVE

ISABEL'S parents lived in a neat federation-style home in the inner Sydney suburb of Burwood. An elderly couple, they'd given Luke the impression that they'd been very relieved when their youngest child had finally found a man she wanted to marry.

Isabel didn't look like a rebel, but Luke suspected she'd given her parents a few worries over the years. She'd had lots of jobs. Lots of lovers too, he'd gathered, though he was pretty sure her parents didn't know that.

Isabel was not a girl who confided often, or in great detail. They'd never had deep and meaningful discussions about their past relationships, just their future together. All Luke knew about Isabel's previous lovers were that they were losers, and she no longer trusted herself to fall in love with anyone fit for marriage and fatherhood. Which was why she'd decided to marry with her head, rather than her heart.

Luke wasn't quite sure what Isabel's reaction would be to his breaking off their engagement. No doubt she'd be upset and disappointed, but he doubted she'd be destroyed. No, definitely not destroyed.

Her parents would probably be *more* upset.

As Luke approached their house shortly before one, he was relieved to think that they would have already left for their regular Saturday afternoon's bowling down at their local club. Much better to tell Isabel by herself first.

Luke had rung her parents' number on the drive down, because that was where Isabel was staying till the wedding, but she hadn't been home. Apparently, she'd received a call that morning from the photographer she'd booked for the wedding with the news he'd broken a leg in a water-skiing accident and would not be able to do their wedding after all.

When he'd first heard this news, Luke had thought *good*. That was one thing they wouldn't have to cancel. But unfortunately, their accident-prone photographer had recommended a colleague and Isabel had already gone to meet this new chap.

''She just rang a little while back and she said she'd be home by one at the latest,'' her mother had trilled down the line.

Luke had thought about ringing Isabel on her mobile at the time but decided against it. He couldn't trust his voice not to betray something, and he wanted to deliver his news face to face.

Luke regretted that decision now as he slid his car into the kerb outside Isabel's front gate, because there was no sign of her stylish little navy car anywhere around.

It wasn't like Isabel at all to be late for anything and he wondered if fate was conspiring against him today. In desperation, he rang her mobile phone but she didn't answer. Another unusual occurrence, leaving him no option but to sit there and wait. Twenty agitating minutes passed before he spied her car in the side mirror coming round the corner from the main road.

His stomach was buzzing with butterflies by the time she parked behind him. How he hated having to do this.

They both climbed out from behind their wheels simultaneously, Isabel throwing him a startled look. ''Luke! What on earth are you doing here? I wasn't expecting you. Why didn't you call me?''

She looked beautiful as usual, but not quite her usual, serene self. Her hair was slightly mussed and she looked flushed in the cheeks as well. He supposed the photographer business had upset her.

His timing couldn't have been worse.

''I tried your mobile a little while back,'' he said. ''But you didn't answer.''

''What? Oh, I must have left the blasted thing behind at the studio. I took it out to ring Mum and tell her how long I'd be. Oh, too bad,'' she muttered, slamming the car door. ''It can stay there till tomorrow. I'm not going back now.''

She shook her head and threw Luke a pained look. ''You've no idea the dreadful day I've had. The photographer I booked for the wedding's had an accident and he made an appointment for me to meet with this other man who's not really suitable at all. Brilliant, but one of those avant-garde types who wants to do everything in black and white. I pointed out that I wouldn't have selected a wine-red gown for my maid of honour to wear if I'd wanted all the shots done in black and white. I was being sarcastic, of course, but would he listen to me? No! He even told me how he wanted me to wear my hair. As if I don't know what suits me best. I've never met such an insufferably opinionated man.''

Wow! Luke had never known Isabel to rave on like this. And she hadn't finished yet!

''Still, what can you expect from someone who fancies himself an artiste. You know the type. Struts around like he's God's gift to women. And he wears this earring in the shape of a phantom's head, of all things. What a show pony! Lord knows what our photographs are going to turn out like, but it's simply too late to get someone else decent,'' she muttered, before lifting a frustrated face.

''His name's Rafe, did I tell you? Rafe Saint Vincent. It wouldn't be his real name, of course. Just a career move. Nobody is born with a name like Rafe Saint Vincent. Talk about pretentious!''

Luke wished Isabel's tirade would come to a halt. He was feeling worse and worse by the moment. Carrying on like this was so unlike Isabel. This Rafe chap had really gotten under her skin. And now here he was, about to drop an even bigger bombshell.

Maybe she finally got the vibes, because she suddenly stopped ranting and stared at him. ''You know, Luke, you look like you've slept in your clothes. And you haven't even shaved. That's not like you at all. What are you doing here, anyway? I thought you were going to stay in your father's old fishing cabin up on Lake Macquarie for the whole weekend.''

"The cabin wasn't there any more. It had been torn down a few years before."

"Oh, what a shame. So where did you stay last night? In a motel? Or a tent?" she added drily, looking him up and down.

"No, Dad had built a brand new weekender on the same site. I stayed there."

"But—" she broke off and frowned "—how did you get in? You didn't break in, did you?"

"No, there was a girl staying there for the weekend and she let me in."

Isabel looked taken aback. "And she let you *sleep* the night?"

Luke sighed. "It's a long story, Isabel. I think we'd better go inside and sit down while I tell it to you."

She threw him an alarmed look. "Luke, you're worrying me…"

He took her arm and started propelling her over to the gate, but she pulled out of his grip and lanced him with panicky eyes. "You're not going ahead with the wedding, are you?"

He pressed his lips tightly together. No point in lying to her. "No," he confessed. "No, I'm not."

Luke was stunned when his oh, so pragmatic fiancée took this news very badly indeed.

"Oh, no," she cried. "No, Luke, don't do this to me!" And she buried her stricken face in her hands.

For the third time in the last twenty-four hours, Luke took a weeping woman into his arms and tried to comfort her.

"I'm so sorry, Isabel," he said.

"But why?" she cried quite angrily against his shirt, her hands gripping the lapels of his jacket and shaking them. *"Why?"*

"I've fallen in love."

Her eyes jerked up, shocked and sceptical. "Fallen in love! In less than a day?"

"No one is more surprised than me, I can tell you. But it's true. I came back straight away to tell you, and to call our wedding off."

"But love's no guarantee of happiness, Luke. I thought we agreed on that. It traps you and tricks you. It really is blind. This girl you've supposedly fallen in love with so quickly," she said, scornfully, "how do you know she'll be good for you? How do you know she won't make you miserable? You can't possibly know her real character, not this quickly. She could be playing a part for you, pretending to be something she's not. She might be a really bad person. A gold-digger, perhaps. A…a criminal, even!"

Luke was shocked by the extreme vehemence in Isabel's speculations. Clearly, someone at some time had hurt Isabel very badly. Some pretender. And whilst that thought made him understand her better, he was no longer able to embrace her once-bitten, forever careful cynicism.

True, he'd once thought he didn't want love and passion. But, since hearing his mother's history, Luke had worked out that strong emotions sometimes dredged up bad tapes from his early childhood, like when his mother had been unstable. Luke still didn't relish angry confrontations nor shouting matches, but he could no longer turn his back on the power and pleasure of true love. He felt confident that once his personal problems had been ironed out, his relationship with Celia would also bring the peace and contentment he was looking for. Because Celia, too, wanted that, he was sure.

"She's not any of those things," he told Isabel. "She's a good person. I just know it."

Isabel just shook her head. "I would never have believed you could be so naïve. A man like you!"

"I'm not naïve. Which is why I'm not rushing into anything. But I can't marry *you*, Isabel, feeling as I do about Celia. Surely you can see that."

Isabel let his lapels go with a disgruntled sigh. "Maybe I do and maybe I don't. *I'd* still marry *you*. I haven't much time for the highly overrated state of being *in love*."

"Maybe that's because you've never really been in love," Luke pointed out, and Isabel laughed.

"I'm an expert on the subject. But that's all right. You'll live and learn, Luke Freeman and, when you do, give me a call. Meanwhile, let's go inside as you said. I think I need a drink. Not tea or coffee. Something much stronger. Dad still has some of the whisky I gave him for his birthday. That should do the trick."

Luke frowned as he followed her into her parents' house. "But you don't drink Scotch?"

"Ah but I do," she threw over her shoulder at him as she strode into the lounge and over to the small drinks cabinet which held a small selection of decanters and glasses. "When the occasion calls for it," she added, and poured herself half a glassful. "Which is now. Today. This very second." And she quaffed back a darned good swallow. "Ah," she said with a lip-smacking sigh. "That hits the spot."

Luke couldn't help staring at her. This wasn't the Isabel he knew. This was someone else. She even *talked* differently.

"You want one?" she asked, and he shook his head.

Rolling the rest of the amber liquid in the glass, she walked over and curled herself up in one of the deep armchairs, her feet tucked under her. Scooping her blonde hair back from her face with one hand and lifting the glass to her lips with her other, she looked like some *femme fatale* from a *film noire*. If Luke hadn't been crazy about Celia he might have regretted breaking his engagement to this suddenly intriguing chameleon of a woman. If nothing else, life with her might have held more surprises than he'd been anticipating.

"I suppose she's beautiful, this Celia," Isabel said in dry tones.

"I think so." Luke settled himself in the chair opposite. No point in staying standing.

"What does she do?"

"She's a physiotherapist."

"And what was she doing, staying in your father's weekender? Did he rent it out, did he?"

"No. She was his mistress's daughter," he stated

rather baldly. But he was determined to tell Isabel the whole truth. She deserved nothing less.

"His *what*?" Isabel's feet shot out from under her as she snapped forward on the chair. Her glass, which was already approaching empty, remained frozen in mid-air.

"Dad's mistress's daughter," Luke repeated ruefully.

"No! I don't believe you. Not *your* Dad. With a *mistress*? That's impossible! He was one of the best husbands and fathers I've ever met. He was one of the reasons I wanted to marry *you*. Because I believed you'd be just as good a family man."

"As I said," Luke said drily, "it's a long story."

"And a fascinating one, I'm sure. It seems the Freeman men have a dark side I don't know about."

"Could be."

"I wish I'd known about it sooner," she muttered, and swigged back another mind-numbing mouthful of Scotch.

"What do you mean by that?"

"Oh, nothing. Just a private joke. I have this perverse sense of humour sometimes. Come on, tell me all the naughty details."

"I hope you won't be too shocked."

She chuckled. "Oh, dear, that's funny. Me, shocked? Trust me, darling. I can never be seriously shocked by anything sexual."

Luke looked at her with thoughtful eyes. "Did I ever really know you, Isabel?"

"Did I ever really know *you*?" she countered saucily.

Their eyes met and they both smiled together.

"You'll find someone else, Isabel," Luke said with total confidence.

"I dare say I will," she agreed. "But not quite like you, darling. You were one in a million. Your Celia is one lucky girl. I hope you'll be very happy together."

"Thanks, Isabel. That's very generous of you. But we won't be rushing to the altar. Which reminds me…I will, of course, be footing the bill for any expenses your parents have encountered with the wedding. I'll send them a cheque which should cover everything, and with some left over. And I'll be doing the right thing by you, too."

She shook her head as she slipped her solitaire-diamond engagement ring off her finger. "No, Luke. I wasn't marrying you for your money. I know you might have thought I was, but I wasn't. I was just pleased you were successful and stable. I wanted that security for my children. And for myself."

"I don't want that ring back, Isabel. It's yours. I gave it to you. You keep it, or sell it, if you want to."

She shrugged and slipped it onto a finger on her right hand. "If you insist. But I won't sell it. I'll wear it. It's a beautiful ring. Fortunate, though, that I didn't find any wedding rings I liked yesterday, so at least we won't have to return them. I'd better go get you your credit card while you're here."

"That can wait," he said before she could get up. "I want to finish discussing the rest of my financial obligations first."

She frowned. "What other financial obligations could you possibly have?"

"I owe you, Isabel. More than a ring's worth."

"No, you don't, Luke. I never lived with you. I have no claim on you, other than the expenses for the wedding."

"That's not the way I see it. You gave up your job to become my wife. You expected to be going on your honeymoon in a fortnight's time and possibly becoming a mother in the near future. Aside from that, married to me, you would never have had to worry about money for the rest of your life. I can't help you with the honeymoon or the becoming-a-mother bit now, but I can give you the financial security for life that you deserved."

"Luke, truly, you don't have to do this."

"Yes. I do. Now listen up. Firstly, I want you to have my town house in Turramurra. I'm temporarily moving back into the family home to live, so I don't need it. The furniture, too. It wouldn't fit any other place, anyway. You already have a key, don't you?"

"Yes, but…"

"No more buts, Isabel, please. The place is yours. I'll also have Harvey set up an investment portfolio for you as well which will give you a regular income for life. Only blue-chip stocks and shares. Nothing risky."

Isabel looked shocked. "But Luke, can you afford to do all that?"

"My father was a very rich man, and now so am I."

"I see. But still—"

"Call it conscience money, if you like, but please don't say no."

She thought about it for a few moments, then shrugged. "All right, Luke. I won't. I'd be a fool to, wouldn't I?"

"Absolutely."

She smiled a wry smile at him. "I always knew you were a winner. But I'd have preferred you as my husband, rather than my sugar daddy."

Luke sighed. "You've no idea how sorry I am about all this, Isabel. I wouldn't have hurt you for the world. You're a great girl. But the moment I saw Celia, I was a goner."

"She must be something, this Celia."

"She's very special."

"Okay, so tell me all. And don't leave out anything just because you think it might shock me. I told you. I can't be shocked in matters of the flesh. I'm not in love with you, so I won't be eaten up with jealousy."

Isabel was wrong. She *was* shocked. Goggle-eyed, to put it mildly, mostly by the length of his father's affair with Celia's mother.

"I still can't believe it of Lionel. He just didn't seem to be the type. Do you think he was really in love with Celia's mother all along, or was it just a sexual arrangement because of your mum's...er...personal problems?" she finished delicately.

"I honestly don't know. I'd like to think he loved her..."

"But you aren't sure that he did. And you'll never

know now, will you? And neither will that poor woman. I feel terribly sorry for her. She must feel like her whole life's been wasted."

Luke shook his head. "I have to confess I'm still very disappointed with Dad. Yet, who am I to judge, Isabel? This last twenty-four hours has taught me that we're all just human beings, with flaws and failings by the dozen."

"You can say that again. We also always think we'd do things differently if we had our lives over again," Isabel mused, "but we probably wouldn't. We'd probably make the same stupid mistakes all over again. And again. And again."

Luke cocked his head on one side and looked at her. "So what mistakes are you referring to? Would I be far out if I thought it had something to do with your falling in love with the wrong type of man in the past?"

She laughed. "I think it's too late for that kind of confidence, darling heart. Besides, I want to leave you thinking of me as the very sensible creature you liked and admired enough to consider marrying."

"And you're not so sensible?"

"I was with you."

"But not with other men?"

"Not with a couple of them. And one in particular."

"I see…"

She laughed again. "No, you don't. And you never will. Now, I'll go get you that credit card of yours…"

She was gone before he could say Jack Robinson, leaving him to speculate on the type of woman she'd been with other men. But she was back before his male mind went too far down that road.

"I presume you'll be returning to your Celia now?" she asked as she walked with him out to his car.

"I have to drop in at home first and pick up some clothes. But, yes, I'll be driving back up there as soon as I can."

"Drive carefully. And Luke..."

"Yes?"

"Thank you for the town house and the money. I do appreciate it. You really didn't have to, you know."

"I know. It was my pleasure. I'll get Harvey onto the paperwork first thing Monday morning."

"Whenever."

"No, the sooner the better. I'll also write a big fat cheque for your parents when I get back home, and pop it straight in a mailbox this very afternoon. What about the various cancellations for the wedding? Do you need any help with those?"

"No, I'll handle them. I'm the only one who knows everything, anyway. Mum left most of the arrangements up to me. She knows how stubborn I can be when I want something a certain way."

Luke blinked his surprise. Didn't sound like the very accommodating Isabel *he* knew.

But then, he didn't know her, did he? Not down deep.

"Thank heavens people haven't started sending gifts yet," she went on, bringing his mind back to practicalities.

"What about the honeymoon? You won't get anything back for that, even if you do ring and cancel. It's all prepaid and too late to expect any refund. Why don't we send your parents in our place?"

Isabel smiled. "You're just trying to suck up to them so that they don't kill you."

Luke grinned. "Absolutely."

"That's not such a bad idea. Mum was quite jealous when she found out where we were going. She said she'd always wanted to have a holiday on one of the Barrier Reef islands."

"Good. I'll pop the plane tickets and the details in the envelope with the cheque."

"You're being very generous, Luke."

"I feel very guilty."

"And so you should," she said, but with a smile.

"At least you won't need to hire that irritating photographer now," he pointed out.

Her left eyebrow arched in a sardonic fashion. "You're right," she said wryly. "That's certainly a bonus."

"But you still have to go back and get your phone," Luke reminded her.

"I suppose I shall," she said. "Now…"

"I must fly, Isabel. I promised Celia I'd be back by dark."

"Off you go, then. And do take care."

"I will."

Luke drove off with a much lighter heart than he'd arrived with. Isabel had given him a fright there for a moment, crying like that. But things had worked out reasonably well in the end.

Hopefully, she would fall in love one day. And not with some loser this time. Meanwhile, he'd make sure she didn't lack anything, financially.

Now, all Luke wanted to do was get back to Celia.

As soon as he arrived home, he went upstairs and showered and shaved, got dressed in casual clothes, packed a few more things in a bag, collected the honeymoon plane tickets from where he'd put them a few days before then hurried downstairs to his father's study.

It was a large room, large and masculine, with dark wooden furniture, book-lined walls and everything a successful man could wish for.

Luke sat down at the desk and ran his hands back and forth across the large leather top. It had never been this tidy when his father had been alive. It had always been littered with papers and plans and the monthly magazines his dad subscribed to. Ones about computers and fishing and wine. They had been his hobbies.

Aside from his mistress, of course, came the suddenly depressing thought.

Luke sighed then opened the drawers which he knew contained the things he wanted. Blank cheques. Stationery. Stamps. He'd gone through the desk the week before, a lousy job, worse even than going through his parents' wardrobes. There, he'd just given everything away to charity. His father's personal papers, however, had required more careful and personal attention and there were some things he simply hadn't been able to throw away. Not yet, anyway.

Ten minutes later the cheque for Isabel's parents was written and slipped into a business-sized envelope, along with a small letter of sincere apology and the plane tickets. Luke stuck on a stamp, addressed and sealed the envelope. All he had to do after that was pop it into a postbox somewhere.

Luke slid back the swivel chair from the desk and was about to stand up when his eyes dropped down under the desk and a memory struck from his childhood. He'd been playing in here one day without permission, pretending to be a cat burglar, if he recalled rightly. He'd been all of eight at the time and had just seen a movie about cat burglars on the television.

When he'd heard someone at the door, he'd dashed under the desk and had hidden there. A stupid place, if it had been his father coming in. But he'd been lucky. It had been his mother. She'd only stayed a minute or two and she hadn't seen him hiding under the desk. But, during that time, Luke had noticed a button built into the underrim of the desk. When his mother had left the room, he'd pressed it, and a secret drawer had shot out.

It had been disappointingly empty that time, and every subsequent time he'd snuck in to look in it. After a year or so, Luke had lost interest and had forgotten all about it.

But having thought of it now, he fished under the desk with his fingers and pressed the secret button. The drawer slid out, but it wasn't empty this time. It contained a couple of sheets of writing paper, folded over.

Luke picked them up and unfolded them, his heart racing with anticipation. The writing was definitely his father's and it was a letter, which began, "My Dearest Jess…"

Luke hesitated. It had been drummed into him from childhood never to read another person's mail. But this hadn't even been posted and he just had to read it, had to hopefully find out what kind of man his father had really been.

The letter was quite long. Two full pages.

Luke took ages reading, then rereading them.

By the time his head lifted, tears had filled his eyes.

He just sat there for ages, blinking, thinking.

"Yes," he muttered at last. "Dad's right. That's what he should have done and that's what I should do."

Rising, he popped the letter in his bag, picked up the other envelope and bag, and left the house, locking up after him. He threw his bag into the boot then climbed in behind the wheel, placing the envelope addressed to Isabel's parents on the passenger seat, intending to pop it into the first postbox he saw.

But as soon as he started heading north, Luke forgot all about that envelope, his head full of other things. Distracting things.

He'd been on the motorway for ages before he remembered.

He groaned, annoyed with himself.

Suddenly, he saw the sign saying the turn-off for

Gosford was coming up. There was sure to be a postbox there. Luke slowed then decided it would be silly to detour when the mail didn't even go at the weekends. He could easily post it on the Monday.

Having decided to keep on going, Luke sped up again. Unfortunately, the car travelling alongside him chose that same moment to accelerate and cut in ahead of him to take the exit.

Luke pulled his wheel to the left, breaking at the same time, but it was too late. They collided, metal crunching, brakes screeching, tyres smoking, both cars hurtling towards the side of the road.

Luke didn't even have time to swear before they hit the rock faces awaiting them and everything went black.

CHAPTER THIRTEEN

CELIA paced the deck, every now and then hurrying down the steps and going round the side of the house to stand and peer through the trees, hoping to see Luke's blue BMW coming along the road.

But it was never there. And now, it was nearly dark.

He'd promised to be back by dark.

Darkness fell and still, no sign of Luke. And no phone call, explaining why he'd been delayed. She wished she'd thought to ask him for *his* mobile number, but she hadn't. She did find Lionel's home number via directory enquiries. But there was no answer.

Eight o'clock came. Then nine. Then ten. Celia couldn't eat. Nor watch TV. She just paced the living room instead of the deck, every now and then going to the back door, opening it and peering into the night, looking for car lights.

By midnight Celia was forced to accept Luke wasn't going to come back. Not that night. Not ever.

It was at that moment she realised just how much she loved the man. Because the thought of never seeing him again was so overwhelming, she wasn't sure she could live with it. She couldn't breathe, couldn't think. All she knew was that she had to see him again, had to be with him again, no matter what.

"Marry Isabel, if that's what you want," she wailed to the empty room, "but don't leave me like this. Just let me see you every now and then. Let me…"

She broke off, appalled by what she'd just said, and what she was prepared to do to see Luke again. She *was* no better than her mother, whom she'd condemned all these years for being weak-willed and wishy-washy. If she couldn't learn from her mother's mistakes then what kind of fool was she?

A fool finally, deeply, insanely in love.

Celia began to cry then. She cried and cried and cried till she could cry no more. Finally, she fell asleep on the sofa, still clinging to the faint hope that Luke might turn up, that some circumstance of fate had prevented him from returning.

She awoke to daylight and someone gently shaking her shoulder, her heart leaping even in her half-asleep state.

"Luke?" she said before her brain registered it was her mother who'd roused her.

"*Luke?*" her mother repeated, frowning down at her daughter. "Why would you think I would be Luke?"

"What?" Celia pretended to be a bit fuzzy from sleep. "Sorry. I've just woken up. I'm still half asleep."

Her mother gave her a narrow-eyed look, her eyes taking in her daughter's appearance in one glance.

Celia knew she must look a mess after all the crying she'd done, plus sleeping in her clothes.

"So what are *you* doing here, Mum?" she countered swiftly as distraction.

It worked, her mother looking quite happily around the room now, rather than at her.

"I just couldn't wait to see the place again, now that this lovely house is going to be all mine. I didn't come yesterday because of what you said about needing some peace and quiet this weekend, but I thought you wouldn't mind my spending a few hours here today."

"You drove yourself, did you?"

"No. Helen wouldn't let me. She said I wasn't ready to drive yet, which is silly. I feel perfectly fine now. So much better after Luke's visit. But you know your aunt. Such a worrywart."

Celia thought that was a bit unfair. And just a tad ungrateful. Aunt Helen had been marvellous.

"Aunt Helen dropped you off, did she?" Celia asked as she swung her legs over the side of the sofa.

"Yes. She couldn't come in. She has to get ready to go to some luncheon with John at their club today. She saw your car was still here and asked if you could possibly drop me back at her place late this afternoon."

"Oh. Okay." The prospect of having her mother here all day was an awkward one. She hated the thought of having to hide her misery and act normal, when all she wanted to do was cry some more.

"I know it's out of your way," Jessica said, perhaps picking up on her daughter's reluctance.

"It's no trouble, Mum. Truly."

Jessica sighed. "Yes, it is. I've been nothing but trouble since Lionel died and I feel quite guilty about it. Trust me, come tomorrow I'm not going to be a burden any longer. I'm going to get my car back and I'm going to move back in here. I know it's not officially my place as yet, but I'm sure Luke wouldn't mind. Such a kind, generous man.''

The appalling thought crossed Celia's mind that maybe this house would never be her mother's now. Maybe Luke had changed his mind over lots of things, not just returning to her. Maybe he wanted nothing more to do with any of the Gilbert women and was going to marry Isabel in a fortnight's time, as planned.

Such thinking brought the deepest, darkest despair.

But, he couldn't marry her. *Could* he?

''What is it, Celia?'' her mother asked worriedly. ''What's wrong?''

''Nothing, I—I—''

''Please don't try to fob me off. I know there's something wrong. You think I haven't noticed you've been crying? On top of that, why did you sleep down here on the sofa when there's a perfectly good bed upstairs?''

Her mother sank down beside her on the sofa and placed a loving arm around her shoulders. Celia tensed, holding onto the last of her emotional control like some mountain climber gripping a cliff, knowing that to let go would be the end.

''There *is* something wrong, isn't there?'' her mother probed gently. ''Something to do with Luke Freeman, if I'm any guess. You didn't call out his name for nothing. And just then, when I brought his name up again, you looked very unhappy. You like him a lot, don't you? And you're upset because he's going to marry someone else.''

''Oh, Mum!'' Celia cried, and burst into tears.

''Oh, Celia…'' Her mother smoothed her hair gently back from her face as she used to when she'd been a child. ''I'm so sorry, darling. So sorry. I—'' She pulled back suddenly. ''What's this?'' And her fingers went to touch the love bite on her neck.

Celia's hand flew up to try and hide it, but her mother grabbed her hand and stared with uncompromising eyes into her own.

''If you think I don't know what that is, then you can think again, daughter of mine. Did Luke give that to you?''

Celia blushed.

''The bastard!'' Jessica spat. ''The miserable bastard. When? On Friday night after he left Helen's, when he was supposed to be driving home to his fiancée?''

Celia shook her head. ''No. Earlier.''

''*Earlier!* But you only met him that afternoon! Celia, how could you?''

''Oh, Mum, don't come that holier-than-thou stuff with me. You, of all people, should appreciate what happened. It was like it was with you and Lionel. The moment he took me in his arms, I couldn't even think straight.''

''And why, pray tell, did he take you in his arms in the first place?'' Jessica asked with barely held anger.

''Because I was crying.''

''Crying! Why were you crying?''

"What does that matter now? I was upset, about you and Lionel. And he was upset, about you and Lionel. We comforted each other and then we went to bed and it…it was fantastic! You must remember what that was like, don't you?" she threw at her mother in frustration and exasperation. "That's why *you* kept letting Lionel back into your bed, isn't it? Because you couldn't live without the way you felt when he was there. Well, I can't live without the way I feel when I'm with Luke. The trouble is I stupidly thought he couldn't live without the way he felt when he was with me. He said he'd break his engagement to Isabel and come back to me. But he hasn't," she cried, tears streaming down her face. "He's gone and changed his mind, that's what he's done. And I don't want to live any more," she wailed. "Do you know how that feels, Mum?"

Celia's words hung in the air. Charged and challenging.

"Yes," Jessica bit out. "I know exactly how that feels. And to think I thought Luke was so nice. A real gentleman. *Men!*" she sneered. "They're all the same. Especially the handsome ones. They think they can get away with anything. The trouble is," she added angrily, "usually, they can."

"I thought he loved me," Celia said, sobbing, and threw herself into her mother's arms again.

"I know, darling, I know. I thought Lionel loved me too. But he didn't. Not the way I loved him. If he had, he would have left his wife for me, just as your Luke would have left his Isabel. But he didn't, did he? He went back to her like they always do.''

The doorbell ringing had both women's heads snapping round to stare at the door, then at each other.

''Do you think…?'' Celia began, her heart pounding with instant hope.

''I don't know. Let's go and see.''

Celia raced to the door and wrenched it open. A policeman stood there, looking grave.

Celia's heart began plummeting down into a place it had never been before, a yawning black pit which went on and on and on.

Luke. Something had happened to Luke.

''Miss Gilbert?'' he said. ''Miss Jessica Gilbert?''

Celia almost fainted with relief. It wasn't her he wanted. He hadn't come to tell her Luke was dead.

''I'm Jessica Gilbert,'' her mother intervened, taking Celia firmly by the shoulders and holding her upright. ''This is my daughter, Celia. What's the problem, officer?''

''Gosford Hospital has been trying to contact you, ma'am, but didn't know your phone number or your address. They asked us for help and we were able to come up with this address from details on your driver's licence.'' The policeman pulled out a small notebook and consulted it before continuing. ''It seems a gentleman friend of your daughter, a Mr Luke Freeman, was in a car accident on the motorway late yesterday afternoon.''

Celia made some sort of whimpering sound and the policeman looked at her with kind eyes.

"He's alive, miss. But he is in intensive care and still unconscious."

Relief and worry mingled to overwhelm Celia. Oh, Luke, Luke, you *were* coming back to me, weren't you? I should never have doubted you.

She lifted teary eyes to her mother. "I have to go, Mum. Straight away."

"I'll drive you," Jessica offered. "You're not in a fit state."

"But…"

"Let your mother do the driving, miss," the policeman insisted.

Celia didn't like to enlighten him that, lately, it had been her mother who hadn't been fit to drive. That was why Aunt Helen had confiscated her car. But it seemed her mother was well on the way to recovery if the determined look on her face was anything to go by. Family crises did bring out the best in a person. Celia had been there for her mother a couple of weeks back, and now her mother was here for her.

"Thanks, Mum," she said with a sniffle or two. "I'll just run to the bathroom, then get my purse."

"I'll be going, then," said the policeman.

Both women thanked him, and soon they were on their way to Gosford Hospital, a good forty-minute drive away. Neither woman spoke, with Celia wringing her hands whilst Jessica concentrated on the road. The turn-off for Gosford Hospital could not come quickly enough for Celia. Eventually, there it was, but they were still quite a few miles away.

''Direct me from here,'' her mother asked once they were back on the Pacific Highway which only had two lanes on that section and was quite windy and narrow. ''You know these roads better than me. And Gosford Hospital, too.''

Celia did, having worked there briefly the previous year.

She knew exactly where to park and how to find intensive care. Not the easiest part of the hospital to locate with a lift ride first, then long, seemingly endless, corridors and turnings. By the time they arrived at the ward sister's desk, Celia's nervous tension had increased a thousandfold with her stomach feeling as if it had been on the Wild Mouse Ride at Sydney's Luna Park.

The nurse behind the desk was a stranger to Celia, a tight-lipped, pudding-faced biddy with all the tact and charm of a taxation-department auditor.

''No, Mr Freeman isn't dead or dying,'' they were brusquely informed at which point Celia struggled not to burst into tears again. For they would have been wasted on this tartar. ''He has a severe concussion, several broken ribs and extensive bruising down his right-hand side.''

''Has he gained consciousness at all?'' Celia asked anxiously.

''Mr Freeman came round briefly a while ago,'' the sister informed them. ''But he had a shot of pethidine for the pain and is back asleep now.''

"May we see him?"

The sister pursed her lips and frowned. "You're relatives, are you?"

"This is his girlfriend," Celia's mother piped up.

"*Another* girlfriend!"

"What do you mean, another girlfriend?"

"She means Isabel, Mum," Celia said with false calm. "Who else?"

"Yes, that's her name," the nurse confirmed. "Isabel."

Celia's heart sank once more. Maybe Luke hadn't been coming back to her at all. Maybe he'd just been coming to tell her he'd changed his mind and was going to marry Isabel.

"Celia?" a soft, female voice said from behind Celia's shoulder. "That *is* you, isn't it?"

Celia turned slowly, almost afraid of what she would see.

And she had every right to be.

Isabel *was* beautiful. Coolly, classically beautiful with thickly lashed blue eyes, an English-rose complexion and silky fair hair, which was sleekly up in a French roll with not a strand out of place. She was wearing a tailored cream linen trousers suit with a sky blue camisole underneath that matched the colour of her eyes.

Celia still had on the faded jeans and grey Sloppy Joe she'd dragged on late yesterday afternoon when the breeze off the lake had turned cool. She had not a scrap of make-up on and her hair was all over the place.

''I'm so glad the police were able to find you,'' Isabel said politely.

''I was at Mum's place,'' Celia replied, trying not to sound shaken by this woman's extraordinary beauty and composure. Impossible to call her a girl. She was a woman through and through. ''She drove me down straight away.''

''Naturally, Celia was too upset to drive,'' her mother pointed out a touch tartly.

''Naturally,'' Isabel agreed and, for the life of her, Celia could not detect any hint of sarcasm in the word.

So what was going on here?

There was only one way she was going to find out. Ask.

''Since you know about me,'' Celia said carefully, ''then I presume Luke must have told you what—what happened this weekend?''

''Oh, yes. He was totally truthful. Explained how he'd fallen in love with you and that he couldn't possibly marry me, under the circumstances. At the time, I thought he was crazy and told him so, but I've had some time to think about things since then, and I think he was right to call the wedding off. It would have been a disaster waiting to happen, on both sides.''

''You…you're not too upset about it, then?''

She smiled an odd little smile. ''Oh, I wouldn't go that far. But I'm a realist, Celia. It's you Luke loves, not me. Believe me, if he hadn't been unconscious when he was brought in here, it would have been you he'd have called to his bedside, not me. I was called by mistake. Apparently, there was this letter on the passenger seat of Luke's car which a policeman at the accident scene picked up. It had my parents' name and address on it. He found their number from directory enquiries and I answered. Once I got here, I gave the hospital administration section the job of finding you, which was impossible to begin with, since I only had your christian name to go by. I had to ring Luke's solicitor at home to come up with a surname, plus your mother's name. I presume you're Celia's mother? Jessica?''

Jessica nodded.

''I thought so. You're very alike. And before you ask, yes, Luke told me everything about you and his dad, too.''

''*Everything?*'' Jessica echoed disbelievingly.

''Pretty well everything,'' Isabel confirmed drily. ''To be honest, I didn't know Lionel had it in him. Luke, either, for that matter. It seems the Freeman men can be the very devil when it comes to stunningly beautiful redheads with gorgeous green eyes.''

Celia was astounded by such extravagantly generous compliments from this woman whom she considered far more beautiful than any woman she'd ever seen.

''I—I want you to know, Isabel, that I didn't set out to steal Luke away from you. It just…happened.''

Isabel reached out to pat Celia's arm in yet another generous gesture. ''I understand what happened more than you realise. Now, I think I'd best be going. Luke will come round again in due time. That's his bed down in the far corner of the ward. Oh, and don't be too alarmed by his bruises. The doctor said bruises always look worse than they really are.''

''I'm used to bruises,'' Celia remarked and Isabel nodded.

''That's right. You're a physiotherapist, aren't you?''

''Yes.'' Boy, Luke really did tell her everything, didn't he?

''That'll come in handy when he's recuperating. You'll be able to give him lots of lovely massages.''

Celia was taken aback by the wickedly sexy glitter that suddenly sparkled in those beautiful blue eyes. Not Miss Cool at all, she realised. Miss Naughty was more like it. Celia suspected that, despite the ladylike façade Luke's ex-fiancée wore so smoothly, she was probably hot stuff in bed.

Celia's first reaction was jealousy, but only for a split second. Any intimacy this woman had shared with Luke was in the past. He was hers now.

''You will stay with him today and see to his needs?'' Isabel asked.

No sexy innuendo this time. Just sincere caring.

''Of course,'' Celia promised. ''And Isabel...''

''Yes?''

''I'm really *very* sorry. You've been incredibly understanding about this. I know you must be still feeling terrible...inside.''

''As I said, not so terrible, now that I've adjusted to the idea. We weren't in love, you know. We were just...compatible. I thought it was enough. Obviously, it wasn't.''

"Being in love is what matters most," Jessica murmured rather wistfully, and Isabel's top lip curled over.

"I can't agree with that," she said. "But everyone's entitled to their opinion. Look, get Luke to ring me when he feels up to it, will you, Celia? He'll know where to find me. He gave me his town house in Sydney as a parting gift. And he's promised me loads of lovely money, so don't go feeling too sorry for me. I'll be fine."

"I'll just bet she will," Jessica muttered once Isabel was out of earshot. "Now, that's one tough cookie, despite her butter-wouldn't-melt-in-her-mouth appearance."

"I don't think she's all that tough," Celia mused. "I think she's just been hurt. Not by Luke. By someone else, in the past..."

"So what's got into you? You used to be the cynical one, not me. But enough of her, let's go and see Luke."

Celia had claimed she wouldn't be alarmed by Luke's bruises, but she *was* alarmed, both by them and the pallor of his skin. Her heart squeezed tight as she stared down at his sleeping form. She wanted to hold him so badly but, of course, that would have been stupid, and painful for a man with broken ribs.

Celia quietly drew the curtain around the bed and both she and Jessica pulled up chairs.

"He looks dreadful," Jessica said, echoing Celia's thoughts.

"I *feel* dreadful." Luke groaned, his eyes opening to slits first, then opening a little further.

Their eyes met and he smiled at her. "You found me," he said.

She picked up his nearest hand with both of hers and pressed it to her cheek. "You silly, silly man," she choked out. "I hope you weren't speeding."

Slowly, carefully, he shook his head.

"That's good." She kissed each of his fingers in turn, and her heart swelled up with such love for him.

"You must have been worried when I didn't turn up last night," he said hoarsely.

She looked into his eyes and smiled. "That's putting it mildly."

"Poor Celia..."

"She was in a dreadful state this morning," her mother piped up. "When the policeman knocked on the door, she collapsed."

"Mum, don't exaggerate. I didn't actually collapse, Luke."

"Close to," her mother muttered.

Luke brought her hand up to his mouth and kissed it. "You will marry me, won't you?" he murmured.

Celia stared at him.

"Now, look here," her mother piped up again. "You've only known each other for a day or so. That's not nearly enough time to make such a big decision as marriage."

Luke smiled at her. "How ironic that *you*, of all people, Jessica, would be the one to give us that advice."

"What do you mean?"

Luke propped himself up on his elbows before grunting painfully then dropping back onto the pillows.

"Look around the bed, Celia," he said, still grimacing. "Can you see my bag anywhere? It's black. A sports bag."

It was under the bed, in the special space made to put the patient's personal things when the bed was wheeled from room to room, which was often in a hospital.

"Here it is." She dragged it out.

"Open it. In it, on top, you should find a couple of sheets of paper folded over."

"Yes, here they are."

"I want you to give them to your mother to read."

Celia raised her eyebrows at her mother as she handed them over.

"I hope that will put your mind at rest, Jessica," Luke said, "in more ways than one."

CHAPTER FOURTEEN

"MY DEAREST Jess," it began.

Jessica looked up, her heart racing.

"Where—where did you find this?" she asked Luke shakily.

"It was in a secret drawer," he told her. "In my father's desk. I found it yesterday. Just read it, Jessica."

Her eyes dropped back to the paper but her hands were trembling. Fear of what she was about to find out gripped her heart like a vice. But nothing short of death could stop her from reading her lover's letter.

How strange it is that in all the years of our relationship, I have never written to you. No, not strange. Sad. Sad and unforgiveable. So much of what I have done to you has been unforgiveable, my darling. God, I regret so much. I should have left Kath as soon as I met you. I knew, that very first night, that you were the right woman for me.

But I was a coward. I couldn't bear the thought of my son hating me as I'd hated my own father. Still, that's no excuse. And now…now it is too late. It would kill Kath if I left her now, so we must continue as we have been.

But I had this dream a couple of nights back, in which

I died suddenly. And it's been bothering me ever since. So yesterday, I organised to give you the deed to our house. I should have done it earlier but, then, you never did like me giving you things. So independent, my lovely Jess. My brave, bold, beautiful Jess.

If only I could go back in time. But of course, you can't. But if I could, I would never let you go, right from that first night. I would be brave and bold too, if I had a second chance. I would not waste a minute of the precious gift of love God blessed us with.

Not many people love as we have loved over the years. With our whole bodies and hearts and minds. We were truly one, my darling, even when we were apart. I thought of you first thing in the morning every morning and last thing at night every night. I find myself writing this as though we're already in the past, I don't know why. That stupid dream, I suppose. But it has left me with an odd feeling of premonition. That is why I am putting my feelings down on paper just in case fate steps in and I don't ever have the chance to hold you in my arms again and tell you how much I love you. Have I told you that often enough, my darling? Have I given you at least some happiness as well as the pain?

I must close this as I have to go out shortly to some ghastly dinner party. I'd much rather be there with you, sitting on our deck, talking and sipping wine together.

Suddenly, I feel so sad. And I'm rambling. I told you about Luke getting married soon, didn't I? You know, I'm still not sure about him and that girl of his. They're too calm around each other. They never argue. Or hug, or kiss. Do you remember how we used to be during those first tempestuous months? Always arguing. Just so we could make up in bed. What passion we shared, my darling. What magic. That kind of magic only comes along once in a lifetime and, for some people, not at all. If only I'd realised that.

But we can't go back, can we? Still, at least I can tell you how much I treasured the times we spent together. Never forget me, Jess, because I'll never forget you, or stop loving you, no matter what. And please, please forgive me. I'm sure we will see each other again soon but, till then, I'll pop this in the mail to you first thing in the morning. Hopefully, the deed of your house shouldn't be long in following.

All my love, my darling,

Lionel.

Jessica touched his signature with her fingertips, silent tears dripping off her nose onto the paper.

Luke had a pretty good idea of what Celia's mother was feeling at that moment. He'd been more than moved when he'd read that letter. And so relieved that his dad had really loved his mistress, but had still cared enough for his wife not to destroy her faith in her husband, the one man whom she must have thought really loved her.

The letter had also galvinised Luke into action. Because no way were he and Celia going to end up like his father and her mother had!

Jessica looked up at him, her lovely eyes flooded. "You're right," she choked out. "Marry her. Soon."

Celia sucked in sharply.

"I will, don't worry," Luke said. "If she'll have me." And he looked at Celia. "Well, darling? Will you marry me?"

She looked a little bewildered but her answer was strong. "Of course I will."

"No hesitation? No doubts?"

"None."

"Incredible."

"There's a coffee shop down in the foyer," Jessica said, sniffling. "I'm going to take myself down there for a while. I'd like to read Lionel's letter again, in private, if you don't mind."

"We don't mind," Luke answered.

"You'll have to tell me what was in that letter," Celia whispered after her mother walked off, "or risk my dying of curiosity."

When Luke told her what was in it, Celia's heart turned over. "Oh, I'm so glad you found that letter," she said. "Poor Mum's been so desolate, thinking your dad didn't really love her."

"I know. I was worried he mightn't have as well. I feel much better knowing that he did."

"Sad, though, that they were never together as they should have been, as man and wife. I know Mum would have dearly loved to have had Lionel's child."

"Which is why we're not going to make the same

mistake, madam," Luke said firmly. "We're going to get married, pronto."

"How quick is pronto? I want a white wedding with all the trimmings. Mum will want that for me too, since she didn't have one herself."

Luke groaned. "What is it with women and weddings? That'll take weeks and weeks."

"Nothing's stopping us living together as soon as you're well enough to get out of here."

He smiled. "Now, why didn't I think of that? Where?"

"Where what?"

"Where shall we live together?"

"Well, I have this nice little flat behind the clinic where I work. It has all the essentials. A fridge. A television. A bed…"

"Sounds perfect."

"What about your job in Sydney?"

"My contract is up for renewal. I simply won't renew it."

"Just like that?"

"Just like that."

Celia grinned. "I love a decisive man."

"What about babies?"

Her eyebrows arched. "What *about* babies?"

"I want more than one."

"You know, you'll have to learn to ask, Mr Freeman," she said with a twinkle in her eye, "not just tell me."

"You're right. How many babies do you want?"

"I think four is a nice even number."

"Wow! That's two more than I had in mind."

"Shall we compromise with three?"

"Hell, no, let's be bold and go for four."

"But not during the first year," she replied. "I want you all to myself for a while."

"Tut-tut, you must *ask*, Ms Gilbert, not just tell me."

Celia bit her bottom lip and tried to look chastened. "Could I please have you all to myself for a year, darling?"

"Only on one condition."

"What's that?"

"You go on the pill. No more condoms for me."

"Done."

"How about a little kiss?" he asked softly.

"Luke Freeman, you're supposed to be too sore and sorry for such nonsense."

"Amazing what pethidine can do, isn't it?"

"Well...just a little kiss."

Their mouths touched lightly, sweetly.

"I love you," he murmured when their lips lifted slightly.

"I love you too."

"Put your head down here, beside mine," he said, patting the pillow next to him.

She did, closing her eyes when her nose touched his cheek. This will be what it'll be like, she thought, waking up with him in the mornings.

"I know other people will think we're rushing things," he whispered, "and so did I, till I read that letter my father wrote to your mother. He made me realise how important it was to seize the day because who knows what the future could bring? I decided then and there to come back and make you marry me.''

''*Make* me marry you?''

''*Ask* you to marry me,'' he rephrased.

She smiled. ''That's better, though actually, I rather like it when you're being forceful. Especially in bed.''

''Is that so?''

''Yes, that's so.''

''I'll remember that.''

''Luke…?''

''Yes, my darling?''

''I liked your Isabel.''

''I did too.''

''She wants you to give her a ring sometime.''

''I'll do that. Which reminds me, I gave her the town house I've been living in, and I'm going to organise for her to have an independent income. I hope you don't mind.''

''I don't mind at all. But money isn't everything, is it? I mean…I'd hate to think she's going to be miserable without you.''

''She didn't love me, Celia. She'll survive.''

''That's what she said.''

''And so will your mum.''

''Poor Mum…''

''No, don't think that. She experienced a great love in her life which is something a lot of people are never lucky enough to do.''

"We're even luckier then, aren't we?"

"Yep."

"I hope Isabel finds a great love one day."

"I hope so too."

"You are a very good man, Luke Freeman. You're going to make a very good father."

"I hope so. I had a good example set for me."

"Yes..." Celia nodded slowly. "Yes, as much as I hate to admit it, Lionel was a good father. You know, when I was a little girl I used to fantasise about Lionel being my *real* father."

"Really? That reminds me of something I've been meaning to ask you. Who *was* your real father? Or don't you know?"

"Oh, I know all right. He was just a boy. A classmate of Mum's. They got very merry at an end-of-year party and the result was me. Mum was just sixteen at the time. He was all of seventeen. When she told him she was pregnant, he wanted her to get an abortion. So did his parents. So did *her* parents. But Mum always did have a mind of her own. When her parents wouldn't support her decision to have the baby, she left home and supported herself.

"Gran and Pop came round later after I was born, but I never really knew them well. They died when I was a teenager. I never had anything to do with my real father. He seemed to want it that way. Which was perhaps why I was so vulnerable to your father's attentions. I thought he was wonderful."

"He *was* wonderful."

"If you say so, darling." Privately, Celia still wasn't

so sure about that. But she could afford to be generous, under the circumstances. "Do you know that when we have a baby, Lionel will be his or her grandfather, and my mother will be his or her grandmother. It's almost as if they *were* married, isn't it?"

"What a lovely way of putting it."

"It *was* destiny that we be together, wasn't it? Just like you said."

"Yes, darling, I think it was. Now, give me another little kiss, then why don't you pop downstairs and see how your mum is? Maybe she'll let you read that letter for yourself. I might have left some important things out."

Celia went downstairs to the coffee shop and found her mother sitting at a corner table, looking more serene than she'd seen her in years. Celia didn't have to ask to read the letter, her mum just handed it to her.

"Here," she said, smiling softly. "I want you to read this."

Celia still started reading Lionel's letter with a slightly cynical heart. But, by the time she finished, her eyes were full of tears.

"Oh, Mum," she cried, dabbing at them with a serviette. "Luke was right and I was wrong."

"About what, darling?"

"Lionel *was* wonderful."

"Oh, yes," her mother said, her own green eyes glistening. "Yes, he was."

Celia folded the letter over and handed it back. But not quite as wonderful as his son, she thought. No. Not quite *that* wonderful.

EPILOGUE

LUKE almost jack-knifed up from the massage table.

"Woman!" he complained as he slowly sank back down again. "What happened to the notion of healing hands? If your mother gave massages anything like you do, then my father would have run a mile."

"My mother gives a different type of massage," Celia said drily. "I'm not trying to relax you, I'm trying to make you mobile again."

"I was pretty mobile last night, wasn't I?"

"Oh, phooey. You just lay on your back while I did all the work."

"True." Luke sighed with pleasure at the memory. "Do you think we could try that again? After all, everyone else's gone home. It's just you, me and an empty clinic."

"Not just yet. Now, shut up and endure."

Luke shut up and endured. He'd only been out of the hospital for a week and he knew Celia was only doing what was best for him. But brother, when those amazingly strong fingers of hers had kneaded his right thigh muscle just now, he'd almost gone through the roof.

"Speaking of the clinic," Celia added as she worked on his calf, "Carol gets back from her maternity leave in a couple of weeks and I don't really want to stay on here. It's not my cup of tea. But the flat goes with the job, so we'll have to find somewhere else to live, I'm afraid. Sorry.''

''No need to apologise. What would you think about coming to live in Sydney with me? We could stay at the family home till I sell it.''

''You're still determined to sell it, Luke? From what you've said it's a lovely old place.''

''It is. But I think we should have a place of our own, something we designed and built together.''

''Oh, I'd love that.''

''Up this way.''

She beamed. ''You mean that?''

''I surely do. I can set up shop anywhere. It doesn't have to be in Sydney. So what say during the couple of months we have leading up to our wedding, we buy a parcel of land right on the Lake somewhere? I'll draw up the plans with your approval and submit them to council. Getting a builder will be easy. I know plenty of good builders. Then, they can build our dream home while we have an extended honeymoon overseas. You did say you wanted me all to yourself for a year, didn't you?''

''I certainly did.''

''Then, we'd be killing two birds with one stone, because it'll take a year for me to show you everything. You said you'd never been overseas before.''

''Never.''

''Then, I'll have to take you to London and Paris and Rome and New York. New York will blow your mind.

And then there's Tahiti. Now, *there's* a place for a honeymoon. Yes, we'll start in Tahiti, with nothing to do for a while except swim and lie back in hammocks and make love.''

"Sounds wonderful," Celia said dreamily. "Almost too good to be true."

Luke turned over and looked up into her eyes. "Nothing's too good for you, my darling."

She smiled down at him. "Such sweet talk will get you everywhere."

He cocked an eyebrow at her. "Will it get me a change in massage technique?"

"What did you have in mind?"

He picked up her hands and placed them right on where he had in mind.

"Gently now," he murmured when her hands began to move.

"Like this?"

"Mmm."

"And like this?"

He moaned softly.

She abandoned him for a second to turn and pick up a nearby bottle of fragrant oil. "I think we might need some of this, don't you?"

Luke was in heaven. There again, when Celia was making love to him, he was always in heaven.

"Do with me as you will," he said with a sigh of blissful surrender.

"Oh, I will," she said saucily. "I most certainly will."

Luke closed his eyes and wallowed while the woman he loved most certainly did.

* * * * *

SARAH'S SECRET

by

Catherine George

Catherine George was born in Wales, and early on developed a passion for reading which eventually fuelled her compulsion to write. Marriage to an engineer led to nine years in Brazil, but on his later travels the education of her son and daughter kept her in the UK. And instead of constant reading to pass her lonely evenings she began to write the first of her romantic novels. When not writing and reading she loves to cook, listen to opera and browse in antiques shops.

Don't miss Catherine George's exciting new novel, *The Rich Man's Bride,* out in April 2007 from Mills & Boon Modern Romance™

CHAPTER ONE

THE sky was ominous with the threat of approaching storm, but Sarah finally gave up trying to find a taxi during Friday rush hour and began hurrying at top speed through the dark, sultry afternoon. Hot and breathless, she was almost in sight of home when a curtain of rain poured from the heavens as though someone had thrown a switch. Lightning sizzled to earth almost at her feet, thunder cracked directly overhead, and with a scream she raced, panicking, through the alley that led to Campden Road. Drenched to the skin, she shot from the alley like a cork from a bottle and flew across the road through the downpour, straight into the path of a car. With a squeal of brakes the car slewed sharply to avoid her, but the front wing of the car caught her a light, glancing blow which sent her sprawling on hands and knees. Shaken and furious, she scrambled to her feet, shrugging off urgent hands which hauled her back on the pavement.

'Are you all right? Where the *hell* did you spring from?' yelled the stranger above another clap of thunder.

'Of course I'm not all right, you stupid idiot!' She glared up at a wet male face haggard with shock. 'Can't you look where you're going?'

'I *was* looking,' he flung at her. 'For which you can thank your lucky stars, lady. If my reactions had been slower things could have been a sight worse. You came out of nowhere!'

'I did *not*. I was just crossing the road.'

'You mean you shot across without looking.'

'Look here, *I'm* the injured party,' she retorted furiously, then bit back a scream, her teeth chattering as lightning forked down again close by, followed by another crack of thunder.

The man seized her arm. 'You're in shock. And soaked to the skin. Get in the car. I'll drive you to the hospital—'

'The way *you* drive? Not a chance!' Sarah pulled free so viciously her head swam as she bent to retrieve her scattered belongings, and the man caught her by the shoulders to hold her steady for a moment before bending to help her. Their heads banged together, she recoiled with a yelp, and with a muttered apology he handed over a bunch of keys, frowning when she winced as she took them.

'You *are* hurt.' He seized one of her hands, where the rain was sluicing grit and blood from a scrape, but Sarah snatched it away, horribly conscious, now, of hair dripping round her face in rats' tails, and blouse soaked to a transparency the man had obviously noticed. Colour flooded her face.

'It's only a scratch. I'll live,' she snapped. 'Which is no thanks to you.'

'If you won't go to a hospital at least let me drive you home.'

'*No.* I am home. I live over there,' she shouted as thunder boomed around them.

'Then I'll get you there in one piece.' Ignoring her protests, he took her briefcase, grasped her by the elbow and hurried her across the road through the sheeting rain.

'I should take you to a hospital,' he insisted, but Sarah shook her head, refusing to meet his eyes as he handed over the briefcase.

'Unnecessary.'

'Is there someone inside to take care of you?'

'Yes, there is. You can go now.' Sarah unlocked the front door of one of the tall Victorian houses lining the road, muttered a word of ungracious thanks, went inside, and slammed the door. She dumped her bags down in the gloomy hall, knees trembling as reaction hit her, but unmoved now when thunder cracked overhead. She was safe.

'Good heavens, just look at you,' said her grandmother, hurrying downstairs. 'You're soaked to the skin.' She frowned as she saw Sarah's knees. 'What happened? Did you fall?'

Sarah made light of her wounds and went to the bathroom to get her sodden clothes off. She mopped at her grazes, then returned to the kitchen, wrapped in a towelling dressing gown. She sat down at the table, surprised but grateful to find tea waiting for her, and rubbed at her wet hair with a sleeve while she gave an account of her adventure.

'You should go to the police!' said Margaret Parker severely. 'You could have been badly injured. I suppose it was the usual boy racer taking a shortcut to the town centre?'

'Not this time. It was a *very* angry adult of the species, who insisted I was to blame.'

'And were you?'

'Certainly not!' Sarah met her grandmother's eyes, then shrugged. 'Well, yes, I suppose I was, really. I was in my usual panic, so I didn't look properly before crossing the road.'

'You really must try to control your irrational fear of storms, you know.'

'Not entirely irrational,' said Sarah quietly.

Margaret Parker backed down at once. 'Was the man objectionable?'

'Not exactly. But he was steamingly angry. Once he knew I was in one piece he obviously wanted to shake the living daylights out of me.'

'Typical male! What sort of age was he?'

'No idea. We were both soaked to the skin, and I didn't have my contacts in, so one way and another my powers of observation were on the blink.' Sarah eyed the rain streaming down the window. 'Good thing I don't have to drive through this to collect Davy today.'

'But you're going to the theatre tonight,' Margaret reminded her.

'Heavens, so I am.' Sarah groaned, then shook her head wearily. 'I just can't face it tonight, peeved though Brian will be. If I ring him now I'll catch him before he leaves the office.'

'Surely you'll feel better by this evening?' said her grandmother disapprovingly. 'Brian won't be happy if you let him down at the last minute.'

'I'm sure he'll understand if I explain.' Sarah heaved herself up from the table to peer through the window. 'The storm's moving away a bit, so I think I'll soak my wounds in a hot bath. I feel a bit shivery.'

'Reaction. It will soon wear off. Was the man hurt, by the way?'

'No idea. But serve him right if he was!'

Margaret raised an eyebrow. 'I thought you were to blame?'

'I was.' Sarah smiled wryly. 'Which is so *aggravating*. I want someone else to blame. Preferably him.'

When Sarah rang Brian Collins his reaction was just as predicted.

'Sarah, you do realise that I had the devil of a job to

get tickets?' he demanded irritably, then climbed down a little. 'Though I'm sorry you're feeling unwell, of course.'

'And I'm sorry to cancel at the last minute. But there must be someone else you can take, Brian?'

He was silent for a moment. 'Since Davina's not there for once I could just return the tickets and spend the evening at home with you.'

Sarah blenched. '*No*—no, don't do that, Brian. I'd hate you to miss the play on my account. I know you were looking forward to it.'

'Very well, then,' he said, resigned. 'I'll ring you next week.'

Sarah rang off, her eyes thoughtful. Her association with Brian Collins, undemanding in most ways though it was, had definitely run its course. He was a nice, conventional man, pleasant enough company for an occasional evening out, but there were two major drawbacks to their relationship. One was an ongoing argument due to Sarah's refusal to become physically involved. The other was that in theory Brian felt he should get on with children, but in practice found it so difficult Davy couldn't stand him.

Not, thought Sarah, as she lay in a blissfully hot bath later, that Brian sees very much of her. Nor can I let Davy rule my life for ever. One day she'll be up and away and I'll be free to do as I like. Chilled by the idea of Davy grown up and independent, Sarah pulled the bathplug and concentrated on the episode in the storm instead. But, hard as she tried to bring her rescuer's face into focus, it remained a dark, rainwashed blur. He'd been a lot taller than her, and strong, by the way he'd manhandled her. But otherwise she had only a general impression of broad shoulders outlined by a soaked white shirt, dark hair and eyes, and a face so haggard with shock that if she met him again in the street she probably wouldn't recognise him. Which, all things considered, was probably just as well.

By the time Sarah was dressed the sky was clear, and she began to relax at last. And, though it was strange to be without Davy on a Friday evening, she wasn't sorry to have this particular one to herself after her scary little adventure.

On her way out for her bridge evening Margaret Parker came down from her apartment upstairs to hand over a supermarket bag. 'I forgot this in all the excitement—the shopping I did for you this morning.'

Sarah thanked her, handed over the money, then groaned as the buzzer sounded on the outer door. 'I hope that's not Brian on a flying visit before the theatre.'

'Sarah, really!' remonstrated her grandmother.

But when Sarah spoke into her receiver she found it was a florist's delivery. 'Are you sure it's for Tracy?' she asked, surprised.

'No name, just the number of the house,' said the disembodied voice.

Sarah hurried to open the front door, taken aback when she was handed an enormous bouquet of fragrant lilies.

'How thoughtful,' said her grandmother in approval. 'Brian, of course?'

'Actually no,' said Sarah, not without satisfaction, and handed over a card which read, *'With sincere apologies, J. Hogan.'*

'A courteous gesture,' conceded Margaret reluctantly.

Sarah shrugged. 'Just salving his conscience.' She thought for a moment. 'Hogan. The name's familiar. I wonder if he's on our firm's database?'

'Did he look familiar?'

'Couldn't tell. I doubt if I'd even know him again.'

Later, taking pleasure in having the entire house to herself, Sarah made herself some supper and settled down to enjoy it on the sofa in her sitting room, with the glass doors open to the garden at the back of the house.

'Nice move,' she told the striking arrangement of lilies.

During the evening a very excited Davina rang up to ask if they were doing anything special the next day.

'No, darling. Why?' asked Sarah.

'Because Polly's mummy says can I go bowling with them tomorrow and stay the night again? Can I? *Please?* Here's Mrs Rogers,' she added, before Sarah, astonished, could say another word.

Alison Rogers gave assurances that they would be delighted to keep Davy for another day. Sarah expressed grateful, rather bemused thanks, and, after a few instructions on behaviour to an ecstatic Davy, arranged to collect her on Sunday instead of the next day.

Sarah's feelings were mixed when she returned to her book. It was the first time Davy had spent a night away from her, apart from school, and the child was obviously having such a good time with Polly she was even happy to skip part of her weekend at home. Suppressing a wry little pang at the thought, Sarah felt pleased that Davy was beginning to spread her wings at last. At nearly nine years old Davina Tracy was tall for her age, but an endearing mixture of maturity and little-girl dependence. To want to spend her precious weekend away from Sarah was a first in Davy Tracy's young life.

Next morning Sarah felt no ill effects after her adventure in the storm, other than the discovery that Mr J.

Hogan's car had left a spectacular bruise on her thigh. Hoping she'd left a corresponding dent somewhere on its chassis, she went off to load the washing machine, then took her breakfast out to the table in the sunlit courtyard outside the sitting room windows. Sarah went through the Saturday morning paper while she ate, and had read it from cover to cover by the time her grandmother came outside in her gardening clothes.

'You look fully recovered this morning, Sarah,' Margaret commented.

'I'm fine now. It seems funny without Davy on a Saturday morning, but I did enjoy the extra hour in bed. And I've read all my favourite bits of the paper in one go for once. By the way,' Sarah added, pulling up the leg of her shorts, 'take a look. My souvenir of yesterday's adventure.'

'Does it hurt?'

'Only if I bump into something.' Sarah stretched luxuriously. 'It's a lovely day. Once I've hung out my laundry I'm off into town for some shopping. Can I fetch you anything?'

Sarah's Saturdays were always given over to Davy. And, much as she looked forward to spending them with her child, it was a pleasant change to be on her own for once, free to browse as long as she liked in the numerous bookshops in the town. After treating herself to a cut-price bestseller she made a preliminary foray through the summer sale in the town's largest department store, then went up to the coffee shop on the top floor. While she enjoyed a peaceful sandwich Sarah couldn't help comparing it with the pizza Davy invariably clamoured for, and hoped her child was enjoying something similar with the Rogers family.

Sarah lingered over coffee afterwards, looking down

on a view of the Parade through the trees, and afterwards went down a couple of floors to find a dress in the sale. With regret she dismissed a rail of low-cut strappy little numbers. As usual, her aim was a dress for all seasons: office, prize day at school, even the odd evening out.

Eventually, after checking the price tags of every possibility in her size, Sarah found a dress in clinging almond-pink jersey. It draped slightly, sported a minor designer label, and displayed exactly the right length of long, suntanned leg she was rather vain about. She examined herself critically, checked on her back view, and decided she could do no better with the money she could afford.

When she got home Sarah went up to her grandmother's flat to hand over the vitamin pills Margaret had asked her to buy, showed her the dress, then reported that she was off to read in the garden for a while before getting on with her homework.

Sarah went out with her new book to lie on an old steamer chair under an umbrella for a while, a brief interlude which did nothing at all, later, for her enthusiasm for the work she always brought home with her. Her job entailed a nine-to-three working day for a specialist recruitment firm, where she dealt with client liaison, database management, and the most urgent of the daily correspondence. The bulk of the latter she took home with her, to finish on a computer supplied by the firm for the purpose. It was an arrangement that suited both Sarah and her employers, and she was well aware that the job was as ideal as she was ever likely to find in her circumstances. The salary was generous for part-time work, and the hours were convenient for someone with a child. Her grandmother shared some of the responsibility for Davy, but Margaret Parker was an active member of her church, played bridge regularly, and served on the committees of several high-profile charities. She led such a busy social life Sarah asked her to look after Davy only in emergencies.

Later that evening, when Margaret Parker had gone off to the theatre with a friend, to see the play her granddaughter had missed out on, the doorbell rang just as Sarah was switching off the computer.

'Ms Tracy?' said a man's voice through the intercom. 'My name's Hogan. Could you spare a moment to talk to me, please?'

Her eyebrows rose. What on earth did *he* want? But, eager to find out, Sarah asked him to wait a moment, exchanged her glasses for contact lenses, did some lightning work with a lipstick and hairbrush, then opened the front door to confront a tall man dressed in jeans and a plain white shirt. Now it was dry his hair wasn't black but dark blond, tipped with gold at the ends. And the eyes she'd thought dark were the ultramarine blue of one of Davina's crayons. Sarah liked the look of him now she could see him clearly. And suddenly wished she were wearing something more appealing.

'I apologise for intruding on a Saturday night,' he said, after a silence spent in gazing at her with an intensity she found rather unnerving, 'but I wanted to make sure you came to no harm yesterday.'

Sarah hesitated, then opened the door wider. 'Please come in.' She led the way along the hall to the sitting room, opened the glass doors and took her visitor outside. She motioned him to one of the chairs at the garden table, and sat down.

'Thank you for seeing me,' he said at once, the blue eyes very direct. 'I was worried last night after you refused to let me take you to a hospital.'

'The fault was more mine than yours, Mr Hogan,' she admitted reluctantly. 'And thank you for the flowers. They're beautiful.'

'My olive branch.' He smiled a little. 'Actually, this is my second visit of the day. I came round to see you this morning, but you were out.'

Sarah smiled back, then on impulse offered him a drink.

A flash of surprise lit the striking, dark-lashed eyes. 'Are you sure I'm not keeping you from something?'

'Not a thing,' she admitted reluctantly, wishing she could say that some handsome escort was about to sweep her off to dine and dance the night away.

'Then thank you. I'd like that very much. It's thirsty weather.'

'I'm afraid it's just beer or a glass of wine.'

'A beer sounds wonderful.'

Sarah hurried off to fetch one of the cans kept for the man who helped in the garden, filled a stein which had once belonged to her father, then half-filled a glass for herself and topped it up with Davy's lemonade.

'Time I introduced myself properly,' said her visitor, rising to his feet when she got back. 'Jacob Hogan.'

'Sarah Tracy,' she responded with a smile, and sat down, waving him back to his chair.

'I kept thinking I should have insisted on taking you to the hospital yesterday,' he said ruefully. 'You were on my mind all evening.'

Sarah shrugged. 'You needn't have worried. My main problem was fright. Not just from the encounter with your car, either. I suffer from chronic cowardice in thunderstorms. Which is why I wasn't paying attention to the traffic.'

'Understandable.' He leaned back in the chair as he

sipped his beer, looking relaxed, as though he meant to stay for a while. Something Sarah, rather to her surprise, found she didn't object to in the slightest.

She looked at him questioningly. 'Your name's familiar. The Hogan part.'

'Tiles,' he said, resigned.

Sarah smiled. 'Oh, of course! Pentiles. We used them in the new bathroom. Imported, and *very* expensive.'

He shook his head. 'Not all our lines. We provide for all tastes and pockets.'

'I know. I read about your company in the local paper. Quite a success story.'

'Then you probably know my father started it off with just one hardware shop?'

She nodded. 'He obviously expanded big-time at some stage. Is it true that you now have retail outlets all over the country?'

'Pretty much. The whole thing took off at amazing speed when I finally persuaded Dad that ceramic tiles were the way forward.' He shrugged. 'These days people expect more than one bathroom—power showers, bigger kitchens, conservatories—all good for our line of business.'

'Is it entirely family-run?'

'The only Hogans in Pentiles are my father and myself. My brother's CV is more glamorous. Liam's an investment banker, and lives in London.' He smiled. 'I distribute tiles and live here in Pennington. I was making a detour through Campden Road to my place yesterday, trying to dodge rush hour traffic in the town centre.' His eyes gleamed. 'At which point you gave me the worst fright of my entire life.'

'I gave *you* a fright?' Sarah said indignantly. 'For a

moment my life flashed past before my eyes. I've got the scars to prove it, too.' She held out her grazed palms.

He leaned forward to inspect them, and for a wild moment Sarah thought he was going to kiss them better, but he sat back, giving her the straight blue look again.

'I apologise. Again. So, Miss Tracy. You know about my tiles. May I ask what you do with your life?'

Wishing it was more interesting, Sarah described her job briefly, then offered him another drink. And wished she hadn't when he took this as a signal to leave.

'I didn't mean to take up so much of your time,' he said, getting to his feet, then smiled warmly, his eyes crinkling at the corners. 'Thank you for seeing me. And for the beer.'

When Sarah led the way inside he paused, his attention caught by a photograph on a side table. On their one and only excursion as a threesome Brian, who prided himself on his skill with a camera, had snapped Sarah and Davy laughing together from their perch on a five-barred gate. The result was so happy Sarah had framed it. Bright sunshine gleamed on two heads of glossy nut-brown hair, and picked out gold flecks in identical brown eyes.

'She's yours, of course,' commented her visitor. 'The likeness is remarkable. How old is she?'

'Davina will be nine soon.'

'*Nine?*' His eyes were incredulous as he turned to look at her. 'You must have been very young when she was born!'

Sarah nodded. 'Eighteen.' She went ahead of him along the hall to open the front door, and held out her hand to her unexpected guest. 'It was very kind of you to come round, Mr Hogan. And I assure you that my dignity was the worst casualty during our encounter. Not counting my temper,' she added ruefully. 'I'm sorry I screamed at you like a fishwife.'

'Hardly surprising—you'd had a hell of a shock. I was shattered myself.' He took her hand very carefully for a moment, mindful of the grazes, and gave her a look she couldn't interpret. 'I hope your wounds heal soon, Mrs Tracy.'

'Actually, it's *Miss* Tracy,' she corrected casually, and smiled. 'Thank you for coming, Mr Hogan.'

His sudden answering smile held a warmth Sarah responded to involuntarily. 'It was my pleasure—a great pleasure,' he assured her. 'And I answer to Jake.'

CHAPTER TWO

SARAH was reading when her grandmother called in to report on the play. Margaret Parker's eyebrows rose when she heard about the unexpected visitor.

'Hogan? I'm sure I've heard that name somewhere quite recently.'

'You probably read his success story in the local paper. He's the brains behind Pentiles.'

'The tiles we used in your bathroom? How impressive.'

'He called this morning, too, while I was out. You were probably in the garden and didn't hear the bell.' Sarah gave her grandmother a challenging little smile. 'Actually, I'm glad I was out. It meant I enjoyed a pleasant interlude in the garden with a very attractive stranger. Spiced up my Saturday evening no end.'

'You've changed your tune since last night,' said Margaret tartly. 'Although you should be grateful to this Mr Hogan for making you miss the play.' She looked down her nose. 'The ex-soap star may have drawn the crowds in, but Oscar Wilde was probably spinning in his Paris grave at her interpretation of Lady Windermere.'

'Oh, dear. You think Brian disapproved?'

'Her costumes displayed so much cleavage I'm sure the male half of the audience were *very* happy.'

Sarah chuckled. 'Brian's not that sort.'

Margaret's mouth tightened. 'All men are that sort. As you very well know.'

Sarah took a while to get to sleep that night, trying to

remember exactly what she'd read about Pentiles. She knew that Jacob Hogan had taken over the family business when quite young, and eventually turned it into its present success story. But to her annoyance she couldn't remember if a wife had been mentioned in the article.

She sighed despondently. Not that it mattered. Men tended to lose interest in her once they found she came as a package with Davy. One look at her child's photograph had probably killed all personal interest on Jake Hogan's part. Brian, to his credit, had insisted that Sarah's responsibilities as a single parent made no difference to their relationship. And in principle, she conceded, they probably hadn't. Not that this had ever worried Sarah much because she had known from the beginning that, no matter how much her grandmother stressed Brian's eligibility, there was no future in the relationship. Quite apart from the problem with Davy, he just didn't appeal to Sarah in the normal male-female way.

Jake Hogan, on the other hand, appealed to her a lot. In every way. A fright and a graze or two were a small price to pay for meeting the most attractive man to enter her life to date, even if it was just a one-off experience.

Next morning Sarah drove out of town for a couple of miles to make for the Rogers home, where screams of laughter could be heard coming from the depths of its vast, wild garden when she arrived. Alison Rogers welcomed her into the house and took her straight to a big, comfortably untidy kitchen, where it was pleasant to sit for a while and chat over coffee while Don Rogers went to collect Polly and Davina.

'Thank you so much for having Davy,' Sarah said gratefully. 'This was quite a big step for her. She's never wanted a sleepover before, let alone a whole extra day away from home.'

'She told me that,' said Alison, pleased. 'We're flattered. And as far as we're concerned Davy can make a return visit any time. It was far less trouble for us than keeping Polly entertained on her own. Now she's a weekly boarder our daughter demands our undivided attention every minute of the day at weekends. I expect it's the same with Davy.'

'Absolutely!'

'But you have to cope on your own, which must be hard.' Alison bit her lip. 'I'm sorry, Sarah. I didn't mean to get personal. But Davy told us she's never had a daddy.'

'That's right,' said Sarah cheerfully. 'Men don't feature in Davy's life, so I hope your husband didn't find her too much of a nuisance.'

'Don took to her on sight—as you can see.' Alison got up to point through the window, where her large husband was tearing towards the house in mock terror, with two little girls chasing after him, screaming in delight.

Sarah laughed as she watched Don Rogers capture a little girl under each arm and run with them into the house.

'Right,' he panted as he set them down. 'Which one would you like, Sarah?'

'Mummy!' Davy launched herself at Sarah to hug her, looking flushed and grubby and thoroughly pleased with herself. 'We went bowling and had pizzas and we talked *all* night.'

'Most of it, anyway,' said Alison indulgently.

'You've obviously had a marvellous time,' said Sarah, ruffling Davy's hair.

'Mummy says Davy can come *every* weekend,' said Polly hopefully.

Her father chuckled. 'We might like that, but I think Sarah would miss her.'

'How about coming to stay with Davy and me some time, instead, Polly?' suggested Sarah. 'Our garden's not as big as yours, but we could go swimming, and to the cinema, maybe.'

Polly clamoured at once for permission, a date was set for two weeks later, and Alison suggested Sarah drove Polly back afterwards. 'Join us for Sunday lunch that day. Davy too, of course. We'll invite some of the neighbours in, make it a party.'

Sarah made no attempt to hide her pleasure. This was the kind of invitation which never came her way. 'That's so kind of you, I'd love to.'

On the way home Davy chattered incessantly, giving Sarah every detail of her stay with Polly. 'Mr Rogers is lovely,' she said with enthusiasm. 'Mrs Rogers, too,' she added hastily, 'but she couldn't play with us all the time, because she had to do cooking and stuff.'

'A woman's lot,' said Sarah with a dramatic sigh, and Davy giggled.

'You don't cook *all* the time.'

'True. Grandma's making Sunday lunch at this very moment.'

'What are we having?' said Davy, eyes sparkling.

'I know about lots of vegetables, because I did them for her before I came out. And I'm sure Grandma's rustling up something yummy to go with them.'

When they hurried upstairs in Campden Road, delicious scents of roast chicken came wafting from Margaret's kitchen. She came down to meet them, smiling with a warmth she never showed Sarah as she opened her arms for Davy to fling herself into them and give a second account of her activities over the weekend.

'Goodness, what an exciting time you've had,' said Margaret fondly. 'Now, go and wash in my bathroom, Davina Tracy. Lunch is nearly ready.' She exchanged a look with Sarah as the little girl raced off. 'She obviously enjoyed herself.'

'She certainly did. But brace yourself, because we've got Polly on a return visit in a fortnight.' Sarah's lips twitched. 'You could always take off on holiday a few days sooner than scheduled.'

'Certainly not,' said Margaret briskly. 'I shall be here as usual. But the Rogers child will be your responsibility, Sarah, not mine.'

The rest of the day went by in a flash, with only time for the cake Margaret always made for Davy's tea before Sarah drove the child back to school. This was a task she never looked forward to, though it was easier these days, now Davy had made friends. During her first term Davy had hated going back to school on Sunday evenings, and had been so tearful the journey had been purgatory for Sarah.

Given her own choice of education Sarah would have kept Davy at home and sent her to a local day school. But Margaret Parker had contributed to the money Sarah's parents had put in trust for school fees at Davy's birth, and had made sure that when the time came the child was sent to Roedale. And if Sarah suspected that Margaret had chosen the school for its social cachet, rather than its excellent academic record, she kept her thoughts to herself.

So, although Anne and David Tracy had died on holiday when Davina was only five, Sarah had kept her promise and eventually sent the child as a weekly boarder to the girls' school Margaret Parker had persuaded them to choose. But Sarah had never imagined beforehand how painful it would be to part with Davy every term-time Sunday evening.

When Brian rang after the weekend, with a belated enquiry after Sarah's health, she agreed readily when he suggested they had dinner together the following evening, glad of the opportunity to tell him it was over between them.

Over dinner at Brian's favourite restaurant Sarah listened patiently while he gave her a detailed account of the play she'd missed.

'The actress who played Lady Windermere was particularly good,' he informed her. 'Beautiful creature.'

'So I've heard,' murmured Sarah absently, her mind on the kindest way to tell him it was over between them. In the end Brian gave up on her, openly relieved when she refused pudding and coffee. He walked her back to the car at such a pace she assumed he was in a hurry to get home, then sat silent for a moment, making no move to switch on the ignition.

'Sarah, there's something I need to tell you,' he informed her heavily.

Because he'd taken the exact words out of her mouth she eyed him in surprise. 'Talk away, then, Brian.'

'I'm sorry I was poor company tonight,' he began, staring through the windscreen. 'Because, well—oh, dammit, there's no easy way to say this.'

'Are you by any chance giving me the push, Brian?' asked Sarah unsteadily, desperate to laugh.

'I wouldn't have put it quite like that,' he protested, and shot a hunted look at her. 'Look, my dear, I hate to do this to you in your particular situation.'

She stiffened. 'My situation?'

'Don't be offended,' he implored her. 'I think you do a wonderful job as a single parent. But—well—the truth is, Sarah, I'm just not cut out to be a stepfather,' he added in a rush.

Since Sarah, in her wildest dreams, had never cast him in the role, she agreed readily. 'No, Brian, I don't think you are.'

'But I must be honest. That's not the only reason,' he went on doggedly, and took a deep breath. 'It's been obvious to me for some time that a physical relationship between us is never going to happen, Sarah. And, contrary to the impression I may give, I'm a pretty normal kind of man, with the usual male needs, you know.'

'Oh, Brian, of course you are,' said Sarah in remorse. 'I'm sorry I couldn't fulfil them for you. I never meant to hurt you.'

'I know that, my dear.' He patted her hand. 'So I'll be straight with you, Sarah. I've met someone else. Amanda's just joined the firm. I took her to the theatre when you cancelled, and we found we were—well— instantly compatible in that way. Highly compatible. In fact I spent most of the weekend with her. Something which was never possible with you, because of Davina. Amanda knows I'm with you tonight, of course,' he added. 'But she was very sporting about it.'

'Good for her,' managed Sarah, trying to get her head round the idea of Brian involved in a hot, passionate relationship.

'I hope this isn't too upsetting for you,' he said, tugging at his tie. 'I wouldn't hurt you for the world.'

Sarah took a deep, steadying breath. 'Brian, I'm not upset and I'm not hurt. Truly. In fact I'm very happy for you. Now, drive me home.'

When she got in Sarah went straight upstairs to break the news she knew very well would annoy Margaret Parker. 'Sorry to interrupt, Grandma, but I thought you should know right away that Brian doesn't want to see me any more.'

Margaret stared in horror. 'Why ever not?' Her eyes narrowed suspiciously. 'What did you do to offend him, you silly girl? Brian Collins is such a good catch. His father owns half of Pennington—'

'It's more a case of what I didn't do,' interrupted Sarah.

'I don't understand.'

Sarah met her grandmother's eyes squarely. 'Oh, I think you do. I know you dislike the word, but sex was to blame.'

Margaret stiffened. 'Then you have only yourself to blame. You, of all people, know what happens when a woman drops into a man's arms like a ripe plum!'

Sarah's eyes flashed coldly. 'You've got it all wrong, Grandma. *Lack* of sex was the problem. I never cared for Brian in that way. So he's found someone who does. And good luck to him.'

Margaret Parker's face was a study. 'I—I see. I apologise,' she added with difficulty.

'Apology accepted.' Sarah turned at the door for her parting shot. 'And to top it all Brian came clean and admitted he couldn't see himself as Davy's stepfather.'

Feeling liberated after the departure of Brian from her life, Sarah rushed home from work the next afternoon to sit out in the garden and make the most of the heat wave. Not bothering to cook, she ate salad, and left the firm's daily quota of mail until the evening, when it was cooler. Margaret Parker, in conciliatory mood after the misunderstanding over Brian, had added extra salad vegetables to the shopping she'd offered to undertake for Sarah, and never mentioned the subject again, adhering to the rule of non-interference kept to on both sides from the day Sarah had taken Davy to live in the house in Campden Road.

To achieve privacy and independence for both Sarah and herself, Margaret Parker had divided her home into two separate, self-contained apartments before they'd set up house together. Though she would have infinitely preferred a place of her own for herself and Davy, Sarah knew this wasn't practical, and never forgot that she was a lot better off than many in her situation as a single parent. She had the huge advantage of a low-rent home, a steady, if not lavish, income from her job, and the knowledge that Davy's education was financially secure at a reputable school. Even if it wasn't the school of Sarah's choice. And now Davy had started boarding Sarah enjoyed evenings out with friends made through her job—if she were honest, she enjoyed herself more with Esther and Maggie from the agency than dining out with Brian.

Although Sarah was happy enough with her life she was human enough to yearn sometimes for an extra dimension to it, a feeling which intensified the next morning, when she received a long-expected wedding invitation from Nick Morrell, her closest friend from college days. He enclosed a note, urging her to bring her current man with her and stay for the dance afterwards, and emphasised that the old crowd were all looking forward to seeing her again.

Sarah's own standing within their group had been unique from the first. She had been afraid beforehand that her fatherless baby would be a handicap where friendships were concerned. But to her surprise and gratitude Davy's existence had been accepted as part of life

by the kindred spirits met at university, both male and female. Nick Morrell had been one of the friends close enough
to invite home, to meet her parents and play with Davy,
and they had kept in close touch ever since. But now Nick
was acquiring a wife things would be a lot different.

Sarah mulled over the invitation as she walked to
work, very much aware that if she went to the wedding
she would be the only one of her group without a partner. Though even if they'd still been on that kind of
footing Brian wouldn't have served the purpose. Unless
they'd undergone a sea change lately, her crowd were a
flippant, wise-cracking bunch. Sober Brian, anything
but, just wouldn't have fitted in. But she had a new dress,
she reminded herself. And the wedding was mid-week,
so no problem with Davy. She was due some time off.
All she needed were some shoes and a place to stay
overnight. A wedding present was an essential expense
whether she went or not. She decided to book a room
right away at the hotel Nick had recommended. It could
always be cancelled if she changed her mind.

After an even busier day than usual Sarah was glad
to escape at last, and, hoisting her bulging briefcase, set
off through the crowds thronging the pavements in the
afternoon sunshine. Sarah rarely took the car into work
in summer, relying on her walk to and from the town
centre for her daily quota of exercise. She was hurrying
for home, her thoughts on tea in the garden, when a car
stopped a little way ahead and a familiar male figure
leaned out, formal in a dark suit.

'Hello, there. Can I give you a lift?' Jake Hogan
asked, smiling.

Oh, yes, please, thought Sarah, and returned the smile
warmly as he reached over to open the passenger door
for her. 'How nice of you. Though I shouldn't, really.'

'You don't accept lifts from strange men?'

'Never!' Her eyes danced. 'Though I really meant that the walk is my daily gesture at keeping fit.'

He cast a comprehensive glance at her as they left the busiest part of town behind. 'It won't affect you much to skip it for once. You were hurrying,' he added. 'Do you need to get home urgently?'

'Only for tea in the garden.'

'Pleasant prospect,' he sighed. 'I'm on my way to a meeting.'

'In this neighbourhood?' she said, surprised.

'No, not really.' When he pulled up in Campden Road he switched off the ignition and turned to give her the smile she'd been thinking of rather a lot since the previous Saturday. 'Actually, my meeting's in town. But I spotted you hurrying down the street, so I did a quick U-turn to drive you home.'

Sarah felt a rush of secret pleasure. 'I might not have been going home,' she pointed out.

'In which case I would have driven you wherever you wanted to go.' His eyes crinkled. 'Or you could have refused politely and waved me on before I got nicked for kerb-crawling.'

Sarah laughed. 'I was very grateful for the ride. And now I'll let you get to your meeting,' she added, undoing the seatbelt.

'Don't go for a moment, Sarah,' he said quickly, and fixed her with the familiar straight blue look. 'I'm glad we met again, because this is the type of question I couldn't ask over the phone. You're not obliged to answer, of course, but there's something I'd like to know.'

Sarah eyed him warily. 'What is it?'

'It's personal,' he warned.

'Go on.'

'Does your little girl's father share your life?'

She shook her head. 'No. He never has.'

His eyes lit with gratifying relief. 'In that case, Sarah Tracy, will you have dinner with me?'

Oh, yes, please, she thought, for the second time in minutes, then gave him an equally straight look. 'If you'll answer a personal question yourself.'

'As many as you like.'

'Just one. Are you married?'

He shook his head, laughing. 'No, Sarah, I'm not. So say yes.'

'Yes, then,' she said, and smiled. 'When did you have in mind?'

'Tonight?'

Sarah stared at him, surprised, and for a moment considered saying she had other plans, just to sound less eager. But only for a split second. 'Yes. Tonight would be fine.'

'Good. I'll call for you at eight.'

Sarah waved as he drove off, then went indoors to find her grandmother coming downstairs, frowning.

'I saw you getting out of a strange car, Sarah. Who brought you home?'

'Jake Hogan.' Sarah looked her grandmother in the eye. 'He asked me out to dinner tonight.'

Margaret's face hardened. 'Are you going? You hardly know the man.'

'I'm going out for a meal, Grandma, not a dirty weekend.'

'Don't be coarse!' Margaret turned to go back upstairs, but Sarah called after her.

'By the way, I had an invitation to Nick Morrell's wedding this morning.'

'Really? If it's when I'm away in Italy I won't be able to look after Davy for you,' was the instant response.

'Actually it's mid-week, when she's in school,' said Sarah, swallowing the angry retort she longed to make. 'I must go. I've got homework to do before I'm free to enjoy myself,' she added deliberately, and gained the hollow victory of knowing her arrow had found its target, by the look on Margaret Parker's face.

But Sarah refused to let the incident affect her buoyant mood as she hurried off to deal with the contents of her briefcase. She could sit in the garden tomorrow. Tonight she was dining out with Jake Hogan.

Work done in record time, Sarah went off to shower in the small bathroom lined with Jake Hogan's Pentiles. After a prolonged session with a hotbrush and all the cosmetic aids at her disposal, she dressed, and, as a gesture of conciliation, went up to her grandmother's sitting room to say she was about to leave. 'Will I do?'

Margaret eyed the linen trousers and amber sleeveless top with surprise. 'You wear that to work.'

'I'm keeping the new dress for Nick's wedding.'

'So you're definitely going, then?'

'Of course I am. You know I'm fond of Nick. I booked a room this morning. Anyway, I haven't a clue where I'm being taken tonight so I thought this rig would do for most places.' She looked her grandmother in the eye. 'And in case you're worried about the expanse of bare flesh I shall wear my jacket all evening even if I fry.'

Although Margaret Parker had been too offended by Sarah's parting shot to wish her a good time, from the moment Sarah opened the door to Jake Hogan she knew the evening would be a success. His fawn linen jacket was creased just enough to look good, and his smile filled her with an anticipation she had never felt before sharing a meal with Brian.

'You look wonderful, Sarah,' Jake informed her.

So did he, but she kept that to herself in case he took it as a come-on. 'Thank you.'

'In this heat I thought you might like a meal in a pub garden tonight,' he said, handing her into his car. 'But if not we could eat at that place near the Pump Rooms in town.'

'I've been there just recently,' she said quickly. For the farewell meal with Brian. 'Eating al fresco sounds wonderful.'

And it was. Jake drove her deep into the Gloucestershire countryside to the Trout Inn, a pretty, unpretentious pub with a stream actually flowing through the garden.

'This is so lovely,' said Sarah, looking round her with pleasure as he led her to the table he'd reserved. 'You knew how I'd choose, then.'

He gave her an outrageously smug smile. 'I booked at the other restaurant, too. I'm a belt and braces kind of guy.'

She laughed. 'What happens when you don't turn up there?'

'I told them to free the table if we hadn't made it by eight-thirty.' He shrugged. 'They were happy. I'm a good customer.'

'You dine there a lot?' she asked, picturing a succession of glamorous companions.

'Lunch mainly, with clients.'

Sarah sat back in her chair while Jake went off to get drinks, putting on mental brakes. She'd only just met the man. Who Jake Hogan entertained to lunch, dinner or breakfast—especially breakfast—was none of her business. Nevertheless, she liked the idea of business clients better than other women. She grinned at her own absurdity, the smile still in her eyes when Jake came back with drinks and a menu.

'You look happy. I'm glad you like it here.'

'It's the kind of place Davy would love, too,' she said, deliberately bringing her child into the conversation.

Jake gave her a questioning look over his glass of beer. 'Did you have to pay someone to stay with her this evening?'

Well done, thought Sarah. Some men changed the subject the moment she mentioned Davy. 'No. She's a weekly boarder at Roedale.'

'Your old school?'

She shook her head. 'At her age I went to the school in the village where I was born. How about you?'

'Liam and I are also products of state education.' He smiled wryly. 'But with differing results. Liam's were uniformly spectacular, mine less so. I joined the family business straight after fairly respectable A-levels. But Liam can boast an Oxford degree, plus an MBA from that high-powered place in France.'

'Impressive,' said Sarah, not sure she liked the sound of Liam Hogan and his credentials.

'Would you mind if I took my jacket off?' Jake asked.

'Not in the least. I'm too warm in mine, too,' she said, ignoring her promise to Margaret.

Jake helped her out of her jacket, eyeing her bare brown shoulders with appreciation. 'You've obviously been on holiday recently.'

She shook her head, smiling. 'Part of it is natural skin tone, the rest fresh air. We've had a heatwave, and I finish work at three. A short session in the garden after work every day is a lot cheaper than a foreign holiday.'

'You obviously never burn.'

'I keep under an umbrella and use sunscreen. After my day in the office I yearn for fresh air.' She leaned back in her chair, relaxed. 'Where do you get *your* tan? Golf?'

'No, genetics. My mother's Italian. We get *our* skin tone from her.'

'Unusual with fair hair.' And very, very appealing to Sarah.

Jake waved a menu at her. 'What do you fancy? Obviously the trout's good.'

'I'll pass on that,' she said hastily. 'My father used to fish for trout when I was young. With far too much success for my liking.'

He laughed. 'Does he still do it?'

'No.' She hesitated. 'Both my parents are dead.'

'I'm sorry.' Jake reached across to touch her hand fleetingly. 'That must be doubly tough on you with a little girl to look after.'

Not a man to shirk sensitive issues, approved Sarah. 'It was at first. Davy was so inconsolable I had to bottle up my own grief to try and help her through it. But don't let's talk of sad things,' she said briskly. 'I don't want to spoil your evening.'

'There's no way you could do that,' he assured her, and tapped the menu. 'So what would you like to start?'

Sarah cast an eye down the list. 'These all sound so tempting. I adore this kind of thing, but if I order one I never get through a main course.'

'Then don't have a main course. I vote we choose two or three starters each, then share the lot.'

'Can we do that?' she said, smiling in delight.

'You can do anything you like,' he assured her softly, with no smile at all.

CHAPTER THREE

PREPARED from the first to enjoy the evening, Sarah found her pleasure increased by the minute as they worked their way through baby asparagus wrapped in parma ham, crab cakes, a *millefeuille* of goat's cheese with roasted red peppers, spicy chorizo sausage, fettucine with smoked salmon, and a platter of home-baked bread. And she was well aware that not all her enjoyment came from the food. The intimate process of dipping into each other's plates was an ice-breaker which rapidly created a rapport between them new to Sarah since her student days.

'Have some bread to fill up the corners,' said Jake, buttering a slice for her.

'This was a brilliant idea,' she assured him indistinctly. 'Are you sure you won't have more corners to fill? This is a pretty light meal by average male standards.'

'I object to the label of average male,' he retorted, grinning. 'Anyway, I ate a large lunch. How about you?'

'I eat a sandwich at my desk every day.' She shrugged. 'As I said, I finish work at three, so I never take a lunch break.'

He frowned as he speared a slice of chorizo. 'Don't you get tired without a proper break?'

'I've been doing it for years. I'm used to it.'

'So, besides work, what else do you do?'

'Cinema, theatre, and so on. Usually with women-

35

friends.' She hesitated. 'And until recently I went out with a man on a more or less regular basis.'

'What happened?'

'He jilted me last Tuesday.'

'Good God, why?' demanded Jake blankly.

Sarah's eyes danced. 'He found someone else. Besides, he felt he wasn't cut out to be a stepfather.'

Jake eyed her searchingly. 'Was there any likelihood of that?'

'Not the remotest chance! It wasn't that kind of relationship. Besides, Davy didn't like him. Though my grandmother did.'

'Is your grandmother's approval vital to you?'

'Fortunately, no, because it's hard to come by where I'm concerned. Her soft spot is reserved for Davy.'

He pushed the asparagus towards her. 'You have that; I'm not keen on it.'

'Really? I love it. I'll swap for the chorizo.' Sarah eyed the plates with respect. 'These are all very generous for starters.' She looked up in sudden suspicion. 'Wait a minute. Did you—?'

'I told them to be generous,' he said, unrepentant. 'At lunch today I was given allegedly king prawns the size of my thumbnail for a first course, so it seemed best to be on the safe side tonight.'

Sarah shook her head, laughing, and applied herself with relish to the asparagus.

'Do you see much of your grandmother?'

'We live with her.' Sarah explained the arrangement in Campden Road.

His lips twitched. 'Did you tell her how we met?'

Sarah laughed. 'I could hardly avoid it. She was there when I arrived looking like a drowned rat.'

His eyes locked on hers. 'I'm sorry I knocked you

over. But on the plus side, if I hadn't I wouldn't have met you. And, as must be perfectly obvious to you, Sarah Tracy, I'm very glad I have.'

'So am I.'

Their eyes held for a couple of heartbeats, then Jake said abruptly, 'How about some pudding? They do a great one here with pecans and honey ice-cream. But you must eat a whole one yourself, or you don't get coffee.'

'I don't want coffee, but I will eat the pudding,' she assured him, because ordering it and waiting for it, and eating it, meant more time spent alone with Jake Hogan in the pretty garden which was empty now, as the evening grew cool. And she had other plans for coffee.

'We could go inside if you're cold,' he offered, as their plates were cleared away.

'I'd much rather stay here.'

'Good. So would I.' He gave the order for their puddings, then moved his chair closer. 'Sarah, maybe it's too soon to ask this, but when you know me better—as I fully intend you shall—you'll find I tend to go straight for what I want.'

Sarah raised an eyebrow. 'That sounds ominous.'

He smiled, his teeth showing white in the dusk. 'Not really. I just want to repeat this kind of evening as soon as possible. Are you by any miracle free this Saturday?'

She shook her head regretfully. 'I'm afraid not.'

Jake leaned closer, his eyes probing. 'You mean you really are tied up, or am I rushing things, taking too much for granted?'

'No,' she said candidly. 'You're not. But this is where problems always arise with my social life. I'm never free at weekends because of Davy.'

'Where was she last Saturday?'

'Enjoying her very first sleepover with a school-friend.'

Jake eyed her thoughtfully. 'But if you live with your grandmother wouldn't she look after Davy for one night?'

'I never leave Davy on the only two nights she spends at home.' Sarah touched her hand to his to emphasise her regret. 'Otherwise, Jake, I'd be only too happy.'

His hand captured hers and held it. 'That's some comfort. But I'm disappointed. Now I shan't know what to do with myself on Saturday.'

'What do you normally do?' she asked, looking at their clasped hands.

'Like you, I also had someone in my life until recently.'

'Just the one?'

'Absolutely. Though there were others in the past before her.' He gave her one of his straight blue looks. 'But just for the record, Sarah, I'm strictly a one woman at a time type.'

She returned the look steadily. 'So what happened with your lady?'

'Like your friend, she preferred someone else—ah, here comes pudding.' Jake released her hand without hurry, but remained close as they ate, chuckling at Sarah's unashamed sounds of appreciation.

'That was wonderful,' she sighed, scraping up the last smear of sauce. 'All of it. In fact I enjoyed this meal more than any I've had in the most expensive hotel in town.'

And not just because of the food.

'So have I.' He leaned closer. 'Did the idiot who jilted you take you to the Chesterton a lot, then?'

'No,' she said, and gave him a demure little smile. 'Brian liked the one near the Pump Rooms.'

'Ah! So that's why you turned it down tonight.'

'Partly. Though when you mentioned eating in a garden it was no contest.'

At last, with a reluctance Sarah shared, Jake got up. 'It's getting cool. Would you like to go inside?'

'Not really. It looks very hot and crowded in there.' She turned to look up at him as he helped her on with her jacket. 'Would you like some coffee at my place instead?'

His smile was answer enough. 'Just give me a minute to settle the bill.'

Sarah's mind worked at top speed while she chatted on the short journey home with Jake. The leap of heat in his eyes at her suggestion warned her to make it clear, without offending him, that coffee meant just coffee. It was not a habit of hers to invite anyone back to share it. Sarah had always met Brian in town, and rarely asked him back to Campden Road to avoid encounters with the all too obviously approving Margaret. Oliver Bryce, the man she'd known before that, had always been in a hurry to get home to the babysitter after their evenings out, so the coffee situation had never arisen with him, either. Not counting visits from college friends, Jake Hogan, if he only knew it, was being granted a rare privilege.

When they arrived Sarah led the way to the sitting room, for the first time that evening ill at ease. 'Do sit down. I shan't be long—'

'Sarah, don't bother with coffee.' Jake caught her by the hand, his eyes very serious. 'Which doesn't mean I'm about to leap on you. I meant I'd sooner have a glass of water.'

She flushed, feeling ridiculous. 'Right. Water it is.'

When she got back with it Jake turned away from the photograph, looked at her closely for a moment, then turned back to study Davy again. 'Exactly the same tortoiseshell eyes and shiny brown hair. Something in the expression, too. The resemblance is remarkable,' he added.

'Would you like to take off your jacket?' she asked, to attract his attention away from Davina.

Jake put his glass on the table near the lilies he'd sent her, and removed his jacket, his eyes teasing as he grinned at Sarah. 'Relax,' he ordered. 'I never ravish a lady on a first date, I swear.'

Sarah laughed awkwardly, feeling her colour rise. 'I'm glad to hear it. Won't you sit down?'

'Yes,' he said promptly. 'If you will, too.' He took her hand and drew her down beside him on her sofa. 'Now, tell me why you're on edge, Sarah. Bad experiences in this situation before?'

'No, not at all.' She braced herself. 'I've never asked anyone back here before.'

He gave her an incredulous look. 'Never? How long have you lived here?'

'Nearly four years.'

'Is this because your grandmother shares the house?'

'Not really. She converted the house into separate flats for the express purpose of privacy for both of us.'

Jake took her hand. 'I'm hoping against hope I know the answer, Sarah, but why me?'

Sarah shrugged. 'I was enjoying the evening, and it's not very late, so it just seemed the natural thing to do.'

His grasp tightened. 'Actually, you pre-empted me. I was just about to suggest coffee at my place. Would you have come?'

She smiled a little. 'You didn't ask so we'll never know.'

'I'll ask next time,' he warned.

'Is there going to be a next time?'

'Damn right there is,' he said, and kissed her. Then stared in astonishment as she immediately scrambled out of reach, her face flaming at the blank surprise on his face as he promptly removed himself to the other end of the sofa.

'I meant what I said,' Jake assured her. 'No ravishing on the first date, Sarah. Just a kiss, I swear.' He drew in a deep, unsteady breath. 'Though from my point of view it was a rash move to share our meal in that particular way.'

Afraid to trust her voice for a moment, Sarah raised a questioning eyebrow, and Jake smiled wryly.

'I meant, Miss Tracy, that for me the entire meal was a subtle form of foreplay. Couldn't you tell?'

'No. I thought we were just getting on well together.' She hesitated. 'So if you had asked me back to your place, and I'd agreed, you would have taken it for granted I was saying yes to a whole lot more than coffee?'

'No, Sarah, absolutely not.' Jake stood up, holding out a hand to help her to her feet. 'Like you, I simply wanted to prolong our time together.'

She looked up into his eyes. And believed him.

'So when can I see you again?' he went on, as though the awkward little incident had never happened. 'You said Saturday's out, but how about Sunday evening?'

Sarah felt an overwhelming rush of relief. She had been so sure Jake would give up on her after her embarrassing little rejection. She couldn't tell him that if she'd followed her instincts she would have let him kiss her as much as he wanted. Because with him she wanted it too. But that way danger lay. As she knew better than most, instincts had to be reined in, not followed blindly. Yet even on such short acquaintance she was sure that Jake would never force her to anything. And she wanted to see him again. She always felt a bit down after taking Davy back to school. Time spent with Jake Hogan would be the perfect antidote to her usual Sunday evening blues.

'Yes. I'd like that,' she said at last.

'That took a long time,' he said dryly. 'What shall we do?'

She smiled at him. 'If it's fine I'd like a drive to somewhere pleasant with a view, then a long, leisurely walk.'

'That's a first,' said Jake, laughing. 'No lady in my past ever asked to go hiking before.'

'No hiking—just a Sunday evening stroll, please!'

'Whatever you want. What time do you get back from Davy's school?'

'About six.'

'I'll be here soon after, then.' He looked down at her for a moment, then bent and kissed her forehead. 'Goodnight, Sarah Tracy.'

'Goodnight, Jake Hogan.' She stepped back, her eyes suddenly serious. 'Thank you for this evening. I enjoyed it very much.'

'So did I.' Jake followed her to the front door. 'Next time you can introduce me to your grandmother,' he said with a grin, and crossed the pavement to his car.

Sarah watched him get in, raised her hand in response to his wave as he drove off, then went back in the house and closed the door, her eyes wistful. The man was a charmer. Unlike comfortable, friendly Oliver, or staid, unimpassioned Brian, it would be all too easy to fall in love with Jake Hogan.

CHAPTER FOUR

SARAH was about to leave the office on Friday afternoon to collect Davy, when Alison Rogers rang her cellphone number.

'Sarah, I'm in a fix. My car won't start, and Don's in London until tonight—'

'No problem, I'll pick Polly up,' said Sarah promptly. 'You just caught me; I'm on my way right now.'

'You're an angel! I'll ring the school and let them know. See you soon—I'll have tea and buns waiting.'

When Sarah collected them later Polly and Davina were in tearing spirits to be going home together, and full of their practice for sports day. They piled into the car, straw boaters askew, gingham dresses rumpled, both of them excited because Davy had beaten everyone in her class in the sprint.

'But Polly came second at skipping,' added Davy.

'Well done, both of you!'

Polly smiled at Sarah expectantly. 'Are you staying to tea? Mummy always bakes stuff on Friday, ready for when I come home.'

'Please can we?' urged Davy, hovering as Sarah stowed their belongings away.

'Yes, but we won't stay long. I'm sure Polly's mummy saw quite enough of you last weekend. Now, tell me what else you two have been up to this week, besides races. How about boring stuff like sums, and so on?'

When they arrived at the Rogers house, Alison came

running out to greet them. 'You saved my life,' she said gratefully, after embracing her daughter. 'Take Davy off to wash hands, Polly. Sit down, Sarah,' she added, 'you look tired. Hard day?'

'No more than usual. It's just a rush on Fridays to get off on time to drive to Roedale.'

'Davy told me you work at home in the evenings as well.'

'Part of the deal with my employers. It only takes up an hour or so.' Sarah shrugged, smiling. 'In my circumstances the arrangement's very convenient. When Davy's home I work after she's gone to bed.'

'Hard graft just the same.' Alison put plates of cupcakes and cookies on the table, went to call the girls, then sat down to pour tea.

'Thank you,' said Sarah, accepting her cup. 'I rang my grandmother before I left to tell her we'd be later today.'

'I've heard a lot about Grandma. Though I thought she was your mother.'

'No, she dotes on Davy, but she's actually *my* grandmother.'

Davina came running in with Polly, very much at home in her friend's house. The girls polished off several cakes and cookies, swallowed down large glasses of the milk Davy always objected to at home, then rushed out to play in the garden.

'Peace at last,' said Alison with satisfaction, and refilled Sarah's cup. 'Have another cookie to assuage my guilt.'

'Why guilt?' said Sarah, amused.

'It suddenly struck me that you'll be picking Polly up *next* week as well.'

'I don't mind in the least. But I'll have that cookie. They're delicious.'

'With the life you lead I don't suppose you get much time for baking,' said Alison with sympathy.

Sarah shook her head, laughing. 'Actually, I do. Since Davy started boarding I have a lot more time to myself, socially and otherwise. But no baking. I'm hopeless at it. Lucky for us, my grandmother's an expert. She also makes Sunday lunch for the three of us.' Sarah smiled. 'But during the week I fend for myself, or go out. Something I do a lot more than I used to now Davy's in school. Beforehand I hated the thought of parting with her, even on a weekly basis, but now she's settled in I confess I'm rather enjoying my new freedom.'

When she was finally able to tear Davy away Sarah drove home to find a message on her machine, but she sent Davy off to find Margaret before she allowed herself to listen to it.

'Jake, Sarah,' said familiar tones. 'Just reminding you about Sunday.'

As if she needed reminding! But she played the message again twice, just to listen to his voice. Like a schoolgirl with a first crush, she thought sheepishly.

Margaret came down with Davy to announce that she was going out shortly, and had taken the liberty of making the sauce for their pasta supper.

Davy's eyes lit up. 'With lots of tomato in it? Goody.'

'Thank you, Grandma,' said Sarah shortly. 'But I could have managed.'

'Out of a jar, no doubt,' said Margaret, after Davy rushed off to change. 'By the way,' she added coldly, 'more flowers came for you today. I put them in water in the kitchen.'

'Who are they from?' said Sarah, surprised.

'I've no idea. The card was addressed to you.'

Sarah hurried to the kitchen to take a card from the envelope propped beside an enormous bunch of brilliantly coloured zinnias. 'They're from Jake Hogan,' she told her grandmother, who had followed behind to find out.

'Again,' commented Margaret. 'He obviously enjoyed the evening with you.'

'We both did. I asked him in when he drove me home.'

'You've never done that before,' said Margaret accusingly.

'Don't worry. He didn't stay long.'

'I know. I heard him leave.'

'Then you know exactly how long he stayed,' said Sarah evenly.

Margaret's mouth tightened. 'I don't mean to be hard on you, Sarah, but you're obviously attracted to this man, so do please be careful. Try to look at things from my point of view.'

'Oh, I do. All the time.' Their eyes clashed for a moment. 'But sometimes, Grandma, try to remember that I have a point of view too.'

Davy talked non-stop through supper in the kitchen with Sarah, giving her a blow by blow account of every minute at school during the week. 'It's nice to be home, though,' she said, with a heartfelt sigh.

Sarah gave her a searching look. 'I thought you were liking school better these days.'

Davy nodded vigorously. 'I am. But I still like being home with you best.'

Sarah gave her a hug. 'You do your stuff in front of

the TV while I clear up, then we'll watch a video. *Father Goose*, if you like.'

The film was one of Davy's favourites. And, because there was no such thing as too much Cary Grant for Sarah, they both enjoyed their evening together, as usual. But Davy sighed mutinously when Sarah rewound the video tape.

'I suppose you've got work to do now.'

'Afraid so. But it's time you were asleep anyway. It's way past school bedtime.'

'Which is why I prefer it at home!'

Next day Davy was up early, eager to make the most of every minute as usual, and after breakfast Sarah took her into town for the usual programme of a swim at the leisure centre pool, followed by shopping for new jeans before Davy's invariable choice of a pizza lunch.

'What would you like to do now?' asked Sarah, as they left the restaurant. 'It seems a shame to sit in a cinema on an afternoon like this. There's a craft fair on in the park.'

'Hot dogs and doughnuts?' said Davy hopefully.

'Probably. Though how you can even think about them straight after lunch beats me,' said Sarah, laughing.

'I've had a week of school dinners! Let's go.'

As they strolled together through the town centre Sarah caught sight of their reflections in a shop window, and with regret realised that her child was growing up very fast. Davy, as usual, chattered nineteen to the dozen as they walked, her face animated in the frame of bright brown hair still damp round the edges from her swim.

'Next year there's a school trip to France,' Davy said eventually, and gave Sarah a hopeful glance. 'Will I be able to go?'

'Of course,' said Sarah without hesitation, though extras of this kind meant a lot of creative juggling with her finances. 'But thank you for giving me due warning.'

'I don't have to go,' said Davy bravely.

'Of course you do. I can have some peace and quiet without you.'

Davy giggled, then tugged Sarah's arm. 'There's a man waving at you over there, Mummy.'

Sarah's heart gave a thump when she saw Jake crossing the road towards them.

'Who's that?' whispered Davy.

'A friend,' Sarah whispered before he reached them. 'Be nice.'

'Hello, Sarah.' Jake smiled at her, then turned his attention to Davy. 'Hi, there. I'm Jake Hogan.'

Sarah, prepared to give a surreptitious dig to prompt a polite response, was surprised to see Davy return Jake's smile far more pleasantly than she'd ever managed with Brian.

'Hello, I'm Davy Tracy,' she told him. 'Well, Davina, really. But Mummy only says that when she's cross.'

'I know all about that,' he assured her. 'When my mother calls me Jacob I shake in my shoes.'

Davy's eyes widened. 'Even though you're grown up?'

'Especially now I'm grown up!' He turned to Sarah. 'Are you out for a walk, or can I give you both a lift somewhere?'

'That's very kind of you,' she said, smiling, 'but we're not going home yet. We went for a swim, had lunch, and now we're making for the show in the park.'

Sarah was tempted to ask him to join them. But from past experience with Brian she knew that Davy would probably object to having a stranger muscle in on her precious Saturday.

'Sounds like fun,' said Jake. 'Enjoy yourselves. Nice to meet you, Davy.' He smiled at Sarah, hesitated a moment, then with one of his straight blue looks said goodbye and went off in the opposite direction before she could thank him for the flowers.

'Is that a new friend?' asked Davy, as they made for the park.

'Yes. I met him quite recently. Why?'

'He's cool. Not a bit like Boring Brian,' said Davy, then made a face. 'Sorry!'

'I should think so,' said Sarah, trying not to laugh. 'And for your information, miss, I don't go out with Brian any more.'

'Really?' Davy's face lit up. 'Is that because of Mr Hogan?'

'Certainly not. Brian and I decided to call it a day, that's all.'

Davy danced a little jig of jubilation. 'Great! I was really, really afraid you were going to marry Brian and I'd have to call him Daddy.'

Sarah couldn't help laughing. 'There was never any question of that, muggins.'

'Thank goodness. Not that I'd mind if you did get married one day,' added Davy magnanimously. 'Someone like Polly's dad would be fab.'

'I'll keep it in mind!'

Davy loved everything about the afternoon, delighted when she found that a dog show was part of the entertainment. She went into raptures over the irresistible Labradors, and clapped the elegant, obedient German Shepherds, then went wild with excitement when teams of mongrels raced against each other through obstacle courses. In between events she downed a hot dog, and several doughnuts, and after a few determined attempts knocked down enough skittles to win a small white rabbit with blue eyes.

'Do you think Grandma would like this?' she asked, as they eventually began trudging home.

'That's a nice thought. I'm sure she'll love it.'

'That's for me?' said Margaret with delight when Davy handed it over. 'And you won it? Thank you so much, darling. What's his name?'

Davy gave Sarah a wide, wicked grin. 'How about Jake?'

Sarah gave her a kindling look and despatched her off for a bath. 'You reek of doughnuts, young lady.'

'So does this rabbit,' observed Margaret, when Davy was out of earshot. 'Why Jake?'

Sarah explained their chance encounter with Jake Hogan. 'She told me she likes him more than Boring Brian.'

Margaret gave a reluctant laugh. 'Oh, dear. ''Out of the mouth of babes'', and all that.'

Sarah gave her a narrowed look. 'Are you telling me you agree with her? Yet you wanted me to marry Brian.'

Her grandmother passed a hand over her immaculate hair, looking defensive. 'I just want security for you, Sarah.'

'*If* I ever marry, which is unlikely in my particular circumstances, I'm fool enough to want a whole lot more than mere security.' Sarah yawned suddenly. 'Sorry. I need to scrub the reek of fast food from my person.'

When Davy was safely delivered back to Roedale next day the entire process was a lot happier than usual for Sarah, with the prospect of Jake's company to look forward to. Right from Davy's first day at Roedale Sarah had made a habit of taking herself to bed early on Sundays to get the evening over with.

But tonight, she thought jubilantly, I'll be with Jake—and slammed on the mental brakes again when the thought triggered off alarm bells. Careful, she warned herself.

But when Sarah turned into Campden Road she saw Jake leaning against the bonnet of his car, waiting for her, and knew that the alarm bells had rung too late. It would be all too easy to fall madly in love with Jake Hogan. She was halfway there already, if she were honest with herself. And because this particular form of madness had never troubled her before the early-warning signs had gone unnoticed.

Almost before she'd stopped the car Jake opened her door to help her out. 'At last. I made the mistake of turning up early. I was getting impatient.'

'Hi,' she said, smiling. 'Come in for a minute.'

Jake followed her through the front door, closed it behind him, then glanced at the stairs. 'Is your grandmother in?'

'No. Why?'

He took her in his arms very carefully and, when she didn't resist, let out a deep breath and held her close. 'Because I've been wanting this since I left you on Friday night,' he whispered. 'But don't worry, I won't kiss you unless you ask me nicely. Even though I wanted to kiss you when we met yesterday, too. Could you tell?'

She flushed. 'No, of course not.'

'Were you pleased to see me?'

'Yes. So pleased I forgot to thank you for the flowers,' she said breathlessly.

He grinned down at her. 'Or were you too chicken to mention them because Davy was with you?'

'Not at all.' She smiled. 'But you don't have to keep sending me flowers, Jake.'

'Why not?' he said casually, and released her, his eyes alight with something which made Sarah back away.

'If we're going walking we'd better get moving,' she said hurriedly. 'So read the Sunday papers for a minute, Jake, while I park the car.'

'Where?'

'There's a garage at the bottom of the garden.'

'Give me your keys and I'll do it.'

Sarah gave instructions about the lane running behind Campden Road, told Jake to come back through the garden, and while he was gone rushed to add a few touches to the face which glowed at her from the mirror. She changed her school-visit linen skirt and leather sling-backs for pink cotton jeans and powder-blue suede loafers, then hurried to the back door just as Jake appeared outside.

'Thank you,' she said, taking her keys. 'The car stays there now until I fetch Davy next Friday.'

'So what happens if you get caught in a thunderstorm on the way home from work again?' he demanded.

'I shall study weather forecasts with more attention in future.'

'Do you have a cellphone?'

'Yes.'

'Good. If you're in any doubt ring me and I'll drive you home.'

Sarah's eyes danced. 'What happens if your secretary tells me Mr Hogan's too busy to talk to me?'

'I'll give strict instructions to the contrary. And before I bring you back tonight we'll exchange numbers.' He gave her the familiar look. 'Ring mine any time you want, night or day, Sarah. Now, let's go for that walk.'

Jake drove her to the outskirts of town to park outside a restaurant which had once been a railway station. 'We'll leave the car here while we stroll along the walkway they've made along the track. It used to be a local branch line once. They do rather good home-made food during the day. Have you never been here before?'

Sarah shook her head. 'Not since the makeover. But I will in future. Davy could even ride her bike along here.'

'I bring the kids here sometimes, with theirs,' he told her, and laughed at the look on her face. 'I own to a couple of sisters, too, both of them married with a brace of children each.'

'Ah! So that's why you were so relaxed with Davy.'

'It wasn't hard. She's a cute little girl.'

'Don't say little in front of her, please! Davy thinks she's pretty grown up.' Sarah pulled a face. 'We had quite an argument over clothes yesterday. She tried to con me into buying her some utterly gruesome shoes, as worn by her favourite pop star.'

'Did you give in?'

'No. I compromised. An art I'm learning with Davy now she's growing up so fast. I let her have the embroidered jeans she wanted, but not the shoes. She must respect the line I draw.' Sarah smiled up at him. 'Which she does, most of the time.'

'Maddy's girls go running to their father if she says no—' Jake halted, his eyes dark with remorse. 'Hell, Sarah—I'm *sorry*.'

'Don't be. I'm not the least sensitive on the subject,' she assured him, with a smile designed to convince him she meant it. 'So, tell me how your sister's husband copes with feminine wiles.'

'Sam learned early on to turn a deaf ear to his daughters in preference to getting a black eye from his wife. My sister inherited my mother's temper. Paula's boys are older, and more interested in electronic gear than clothes.'

'It must be fun, being part of a big family,' she said enviously.

Jake shrugged. 'Fun sometimes, mayhem at others. Those of us who live locally are expected to turn up regularly for Sunday lunch with my parents. Liam, too, now and then. My mother doesn't regard living in London as an impediment to visiting the family.'

'Is your brother married?'

'No. But attached. Temporarily.'

Sarah raised an eyebrow at his tone. 'You don't like the lady?'

'Liam does, which is more to the point.' Jake glanced at his watch. 'Come on, let's go back to my place and have some supper.'

'I had a big lunch,' she warned him. 'My grandmother cooks for us on Sunday, and demands clean plates.'

'I'm sure you can find room for some of my mother's cannelloni. She sends me home with something from her freezer every time I visit, convinced I don't eat properly.'

'And do you?'

'I did the other night,' he said quietly. He cast a glance along the leafy, deserted walkway, then took her hands and brought her round to face him. 'I keep thinking of the way we shared the meal, Sarah Tracy.'

She looked up at him steadily. 'So do I.'

He looked at her mouth, shook his head with regret, and began to walk with her again. 'This was a very good idea of yours. I spend far too much time cooped up in places with recycled air. Next time,' he went on, 'we could bring Davy.'

Sarah shook her head firmly. 'I'd rather not involve Davy in my social life.'

Jake frowned. 'Why? Because your recent friend jilted you?'

'Not at all. Davy was delighted about that.' Sarah gave a sudden chuckle. 'Apparently she'd been horribly afraid I'd marry Boring Brian and she'd have to call him Daddy.'

Jake gave a shout of laughter that attracted amused glances from a couple passing by with a dog. 'And is he boring?'

'I suppose so, a little. Which is why I was about to let him down gently and call it a day. But before I could he took the wind out of my sails by dumping me instead.' Sarah laughed ruefully. 'Which cut me down to size pretty effectively!'

'The man's an idiot,' said Jake dismissively, then shot her a glance. 'Is Davy opposed to marriage altogether, then, where you're concerned?'

'Not at all. She informed me on Saturday that she fancies a daddy like Polly's, for preference.'

'How does Polly's daddy feel about that?'

Sarah chuckled. 'It's her mummy who would raise objections, I imagine, so because I like Alison Rogers very much I'll pass on that one.'

Jake halted. 'You don't mean Don Rogers's wife?'

'Yes. Do you know her?'

'I certainly do. Her husband's firm deals with my legal affairs. Good man, Don.'

'Small world!'

'In this town it's unavoidable. In fact,' added Jake as

they resumed their stroll, 'it's strange I haven't run into you before.'

Sarah laughed. 'Unfortunate turn of phrase! But it's not surprising we haven't met. I didn't go out much socially until last autumn.'

'What happened then?'

'Davy started at Roedale. Before that all the time left over from my job was spent in chauffeuring her to various after-school things, like ballet and swimming lessons, overseeing homework, and just being there for her.'

When they got to the car Jake handed her in, looking thoughtful. 'And was that enough for you, Sarah?'

'I've had a pretty normal social life during the last few months,' she told him as he slid in beside her. 'There was someone else before Brian.'

'If you tell me that guy broke up with you as well I just won't believe it.'

'No. I managed to get in first with Oliver.'

'It wasn't working with him, either?'

'No.'

'Why not?'

'He was a widower, for a start—'

'And Davy didn't like him?'

'She never met him.' Sarah shrugged. 'Oliver has a small son. And because I refused to involve Davy in outings as a foursome it died a natural death. Besides, the poor man still hankered after his dead wife.'

Jake drove in silence for a moment, then gave her a swift, sidelong look. 'Just for the record, Sarah, I don't hanker after anyone.'

She was very glad to hear it. 'Not even the lady you mentioned?'

'No. I own to siblings and parents who sometimes

interfere in my life, but generally speaking I'm not bringing much excess baggage to our relationship, Sarah.'

Relationship?

'I've obviously stricken you dumb,' he said after a while. 'Is the idea so unattractive to you, then? The moment I saw you—'

'I was soaking wet and screaming at you in fury,' she reminded him.

He shrugged. 'I knew, just the same.'

'Knew what?'

'That I wanted you in my life. So I sent flowers and came hammering on your door. And when you finally opened it, I stood transfixed.'

'Because I looked so much better dry?'

'You clean up well,' he agreed with a grin, then turned a wry blue look in her direction. 'But then I saw Davy's photograph and assumed you were married. Surely you noted my relief when you said you were *Miss* Tracy?'

She gave him a thoughtful glance. 'How old are you, Jake?'

'Thirty. Why?'

'You're successful, and no turn-off in the looks department. So why aren't *you* married? Or at least spoken for.'

'I've never even come near to it. No sinister reason, I swear,' he added. 'I'm straight, by the way, in case you had doubts.'

'None at all,' she assured him, smiling.

Jake parked the car outside his apartment block and took her hands, his eyes very serious as they held hers. 'Right. So when it comes to a relationship I meant you could choose any kind you want, Sarah, as long as it includes me.'

CHAPTER FIVE

JAKE'S home was a large modern apartment with a balcony overlooking the River Penn. Big windows and gleaming wood floors, walls painted uniformly cream and almost bare of ornament, were all a far cry from the gloomy, crowded old house Sarah shared with her grandmother.

'Have you been here long?' asked Sarah, entranced by the light and space.

'You mean it looks bare?'

She shook her head. 'I like it a lot.'

He looked pleased. 'When I first got a place of my own I lived in a furnished flat in a house very much like yours. A move which mystified my mother, who couldn't see why I had to leave the comforts of home. Eventually I heard along the grapevine that this was coming on the market, and I was lucky enough to snap it up straight away. But I'm proceeding gradually with furniture, buying things when I find them. And at the same time trying not to offend my mother, who desperately wants to help.'

'Why not let her?'

Jake smiled ruefully. 'Her taste runs to pictures and mirrors and cushions, and every inch of floor space covered by carpet. Which is fine in my parents' house. But definitely not here.'

Sarah nodded, deeply envious as she looked at the fringed Art Nouveau rug in subtle shades of chestnut and rose, chairs and sofa upholstered in suede the colour of honey to echo the leather metal-studded screen in a corner. Niches had been fitted with downlighters and glass shelves, but the latter were empty except for a solitary bronze nude.

'Liam gave me that as a moving-in present,' Jake told her. He leaned against a wall, arms folded, watching Sarah's face as she took time to look at everything before moving across the room to admire the view.

'No curtains,' she commented, noting the blind furled away at windows that slid open on to a balcony.

'That came with the flat. It looked good to me, so I left it.'

'You were right.' She turned to smile at him. 'It's a shame to hide the view.'

'There's a good one in here, too, only smaller,' he informed her, showing her into a kitchen fitted out with beechwood and stainless steel, and a window with a different angle on the river.

'This room doesn't look used much!' she commented.

Jake smiled. 'I did some hectic tidying up this morning to impress you.'

Sarah *was* impressed. By everything in Jake's home. 'Don't you have someone in to clean?'

'Never on Sundays.' He gave her the straight look which usually presaged some equally straight talking. 'You don't have to inspect the bedroom, by the way. It's not an obligatory part of the tour.'

'Of course I do,' she said briskly. 'I've heard a lot about this place, but I've never been in one of the apartments. I want to see everything—especially the bathroom. I assume it's done out in the very best Pentiles can provide?'

Jake took her to inspect it. 'I had it altered before I moved in. The former tenant put in a sort of Roman sunken bath with a mosaic backdrop up to the ceiling. To me it looked like the communal bath we all jumped in after rugby matches at school. I couldn't live with it.' He smiled. 'I was pleased the man used Pentiles for the purpose when he had it done originally, of course, but I swapped it all for conventional fittings, and a minimum of Pentiles' finest round the bath.'

'No power shower?' said Sarah in mock disapproval.

'That's in my own bathroom. Come through the bedroom and take a look.'

Sarah was unsurprised to find walls and even the linen on the wide bed all in the same uniform cream. A fitted carpet in tawny wool added a note of warmth, but, not counting the built-in cupboards which housed Jake's clothes, the only piece of furniture was a solitary bedside table with a bronze lamp. The effect should have been spartan in such a large room. But when she thought of her own room at Campden Road, with her desk and computer crammed in with the bedroom furniture brought from her family home, she envied Jake the space and tranquillity. Envied him the entire flat, she thought with a sigh, as he opened a door on the far side of the room so she could take a quick look at the shower housed in bronze glass.

'So. What's the verdict?' he asked as they went back to the kitchen.

'I'm green with envy,' she said frankly.

Jake looked pleased as he hooked a leather-topped kitchen stool over to the window. 'Gaze at sunset on the river for a while—I shan't be long.'

'Can't I help?'

'No. Just sit there looking decorative while I work.' Jake took the cork from a bottle of wine. 'Shall I throw a salad together?'

Sarah shook her head, smiling. 'Not for me. I eat so much of it lately I'll pass on that for once, Jake, thanks. But some bread would be good.'

'My mother gave me a loaf baked with her own fair hand. So in a minute we'll take all this into the other room and picnic. Because, as you may have noticed, I don't possess a dining room.'

'Would you use one much if you did?' she asked.

'Probably not. There was a dining room originally, but the Roman bath tenant did away with it to make one big living space. Right,' he added, as the timer went off, 'if you'll take the wine and the glasses, I'll bring the tray. Then I'll come back for our cannelloni.'

When Jake handed her a steaming, savoury plateful Sarah received it doubtfully. 'Shouldn't we eat this out on the balcony? I'd hate to mark this upholstery.'

'It won't matter if you do. The suede is man-made and guaranteed, I was assured, to repel stains. So far it's keeping its word.'

They sat together on the sofa, which Jake pulled nearer the window to watch the sunset. And though the cannelloni was delicious, and Sarah possessed more appetite for it than she'd expected, she knew perfectly well that, just like the evening at the Trout Inn, it was Jake's company that made the meal special.

'That was wonderful,' she said at last, as she mopped up sauce with her bread. 'Your mother's a great cook.'

'I thought of trying to impress you by pretending I'd made the cannelloni myself,' Jake confessed, grinning. 'But I stuck with the truth.' He refilled her glass, then got up to take their plates. When he came back he settled beside her with a sigh of content. 'So what do you usually do after you've taken Davy back on Sunday evenings?'

'Mope a lot and go to bed early with a book.' Sarah smiled at him. 'This is a *great* improvement.'

'Thank you.' Jake moved nearer and slid an arm round her shoulders. 'It's a big improvement on my Sunday evenings, too.'

'What do you normally do?' she asked, resisting an urge to lay her head on his shoulder.

'Nothing much. After family lunch I talk shop with my father, then I come back here and get stuck into some paperwork.'

Sarah turned her head to look up at him. 'Every Sunday?'

The thick lashes descended like shutters. 'Lately, yes. Before that I spent my weekends in London for a while. Not that many, as it turned out.'

'Why not?'

'As I told you, she met someone else,' he said shortly.

Something in his tone made Sarah uneasy. 'I really must be going,' she said, getting to her feet. 'Thank you for supper.'

He leapt up, frowning in surprise. 'Don't go yet. I didn't mean to snap.' He put a hand on hers. 'Look. I said I wasn't bringing any baggage to our relationship, Sarah, and I meant it.'

She gave him a look as straight as his. 'We don't have a relationship—'

'Of course we do. Admit it.'

'All right. But we won't if you still hanker after the lady.'

'There's no question of that.' Jake touched a hand to her cheek. 'Come and sit down again so I can explain. Then, if you still want me to, I'll drive you home.'

Jake switched on a couple of lamps and resumed his place beside her. But this time he kept his distance.

'I met the lady in question in London,' he began, staring out into the darkening sky.

Sarah gave him a hostile look. Couldn't he even bring himself to mention her name?

'We were both after the same taxi, so we shared it, and things went on from there pretty rapidly,' Jake continued. 'She works in advertising, earns a lot of money, and loathes the country. I could never persuade her to come down here. So I went up to her place at weekends instead. Then before you could even call the arrangement a habit she met someone else. End of story.'

'But you still care?' asked Sarah quietly.

Jake's head swivelled, his eyes bright with surprise. 'Good God, no. I was bloody angry at the time, but if you mean was my heart broken, definitely not. It was never that kind of thing.'

'Then what kind of thing was it?'

His eyes remained steady. 'A fling, pure and simple.'

'So why do you mind so much?'

'Because she lied to me. Kept me on a string even though she fancied someone else. It was the other man who insisted she tell me.'

'So why hadn't she told you before?'

'She said,' replied Jake sardonically, 'that she couldn't bring herself to hurt me, which was a bit dramatic when all we'd had together were a couple of weekends of wining and dining. And bed, of course. Not earth-shattering stuff, by any stretch of the imagination. Any of it. When I pointed this out she lost it and slapped my face, at which point I lost *my* temper, stormed out of her flat and drove home.' He was silent for a moment, his eyes absent, then smiled at Sarah in apology. 'Sorry! I didn't mean to bore you with my past.' He slid closer and kissed her before she could dodge away. 'I had a very different plan in mind for you for this evening,' he whispered.

She sprang up, eyeing him in suspicion. 'Plan?'

'Turn of phrase, nothing more,' he said, taken aback. 'I just wanted to spend time getting to know you better.'

With a session in bed at the end of it? Sarah's chin lifted. 'I think I will go home now, please.'

Jake rose to his feet, frowning. 'Why so soon? If I swear not to lay a finger on you, Sarah, will you stay for a while?'

She shook her head, refusing to meet his eyes. 'It's getting late; we both have work tomorrow—'

'And suddenly you just can't wait to get away.' He looked at her in silence for a moment, giving her time to change her mind. When it was obvious this wasn't going to happen he shrugged negligently, his eyes suddenly cold. 'Let's go, then.'

Sarah sat silent on the way home, cursing her ingrained tendency to take flight at the first hint of sexual danger. This time it had spoiled an evening which up to then had been idyllic. The walk, the meal had been perfect. Then the mere mention of bed had ruined everything.

When they arrived in Campden Road Jake pointedly left the engine running. He got out of the car, and with punctilious courtesy helped her out, then saw her to her door, brushed aside her thanks for the meal, and drove off.

Sarah spent a very restless night afterwards. Had she really expected Jake to beg her to stay? Fond hope! The easy charm was a very effective disguise for the steel underneath. Not that it mattered any more, because she'd blown any chance of getting to know him better. All because Jake Hogan had uttered the buzz words 'plan' and 'bed'. And to cap it all they hadn't exchanged telephone numbers after all.

No more a lover of Mondays than anyone else, Sarah found her prevailing mood of deep depression made the next day so much harder to bear than usual that her colleagues even asked if she were coming down with something. To demonstrate that she wasn't she drove herself so hard that in addition to her usual work she finished most of the day's correspondence during office hours, then stayed on late to finish the rest.

When Sarah emerged into rain pouring down from a sky as dark as her mood, she trudged along under an umbrella, wondering why on earth she'd polished off the mail in the office when there was a whole evening yawning ahead of her with nothing to do. She was sunk so deep in gloom she jumped yards at a touch on her arm, and whirled round to come face to face with Jake Hogan. He looked tall and unfamiliar in a belted raincoat, a dripping hat pulled down over eyes that held none of their usual smiling warmth.

'You worked late today,' he said, without greeting.

'Hello, Jake,' Sarah retorted pointedly, to disguise how utterly delighted she was to see him. 'What are you doing here?'

'Waiting for you, and getting drenched for my pains. I'll drive you home.' Without waiting for consent he took her arm to hurry her to the car waiting at the kerb, but said nothing about his reason for waiting for her. They were halfway to Campden Road before Sarah could bring herself to break the silence between them.

'I'm sorry about last night,' she said at last, staring at the rain sluicing down the windscreen.

'So am I.' He slanted a baffled look at her. 'What the hell did I *do*?'

'You said you like the truth,' she said after a while.

'Normally, yes,' agreed Jake heavily. 'This time, probably not.'

Spit it out, Sarah told herself. Get it over with. 'You said you wanted to be part of my life in whatever way I chose.'

He nodded, his face sombre. 'I did. And I meant it.' He parked the car outside the house, took off the hat, tossed it into the back seat, then turned to look at her. 'I still mean it.'

Sarah returned the look steadily. 'Jake, how long did your association with the advertising lady last?'

His eyes narrowed. 'Not very long at all. Three—no, four—weekends. Probably no more than ten days or so, all told.'

'But right from the start you were sleeping together?'

Jake's eyes lit with sudden comprehension. 'Yes. I went to stay in her flat, and she took it for granted I'd share her bed.' He shrugged. 'It's common enough practice, Sarah.'

'So common that bed was the plan you had for me last night, too?'

Jake stared at her in brooding silence for so long Sarah was on the point of getting out of the car when he finally spoke.

'You mean you can't bear the thought of that, Sarah? With me?'

'No,' she admitted, flushing. 'I don't mean that at all. But it's not going to happen just the same, Jake. No bed. Just friendship.'

He took her hand. 'You might change your mind as you get to know me better.'

'I wouldn't count on it.' Sarah looked away. 'I enjoy your company, but that's as far as it goes, Jake.'

He put a finger under her chin and brought her round to look at him, the hard planes of his face softened a little. 'Is it a case of once bitten, twice shy, Sarah?'

She nodded mutely, taking refuge in an explanation he could accept.

Jake took her hand in a firm, warm clasp. 'I still want to spend time with you, Sarah.'

'I want that, too,' she assured him.

He relaxed visibly. 'So what are you doing tonight?'

'Nothing much.'

The brooding look disappeared, replaced by the sudden familiar smile which breached every defence she possessed. 'There's a Clint Eastwood film on at the Regal. If I promise—Scouts' honour—just to hold your hand, will you come?'

Sarah's smile matched Jake's, her dark mood suddenly vanished. 'An offer I can't resist. Will you throw in popcorn?'

'Ice-cream, too, if you're good.'

'Done!'

They went to the cinema together that night, and held hands, just as Jake had promised. And when he drove Sarah home he gave her a brief goodnight kiss in the car, then saw her to her door. He took her to dinner at the Chesterton the following evening, and to the theatre later in the week to see the local repertory company tackling Ibsen. But when Jake brought her home after the play the brooding look reappeared when they arrived in Campden Road.

'I suppose that's it until next week, then?'

'Afraid so.' Sarah chuckled. 'If I live that long! Tomorrow Davy's bringing Polly home with her for the weekend. After which we take Polly back and join the

Rogers family for Sunday lunch.' She smiled at him. 'I'm really looking forward to that.'

'Will you be up to seeing me on Sunday evening afterwards?'

'Probably not,' she said with regret. 'I may just want to crawl into bed.'

Jake frowned. 'Which means Wednesday before I see you again. I'm away on Monday, and I'll be tied up until late on Tuesday evening.'

Sarah eyed him in dismay. 'And Wednesday's out for me. I forgot to tell you. I'm going away for a couple of days next week.'

'You *forgot*?' he repeated wrathfully. 'Where are you going?'

She hesitated. 'Jake. It's early. Want some coffee?'

His eyes gleamed. 'You're asking me in?'

'Yes. Are you coming?'

'What do you think?' Jake slid out of the car at top speed, sprinted round it to let her out, then hustled her across the pavement to her door.

'Why the rush?' demanded Sarah, laughing as she put her key in the lock.

'In case you change your mind on the way!'

Margaret Parker emerged from the kitchen as Jake hurried Sarah into the hall.

'Hello, Grandma,' said Sarah blithely. 'This is Jake Hogan. Jake, meet my grandmother, Margaret Parker.'

'Good evening, Mr Hogan,' said Margaret formally.

Jake smiled and held out his hand. 'How do you do, Mrs Parker?'

Margaret took the hand briefly, and even managed a smile. 'How was *A Doll's House*?'

'The understudy had to go on as Nora, and she just

wasn't up to it,' said Sarah, making a face. 'Good thing you decided to give it a miss this week.'

'I'm no Ibsen fan. By the way, I'm afraid you caught me raiding your kitchen, Sarah. I was out of coffee.'

'Come and have some with us,' offered Sarah, but Margaret declined politely, told Jake she'd been pleased to meet him, then took herself back up to her own quarters.

'I see where you get the tortoiseshell eyes,' commented Jake, watching Sarah as she put out cups.

'My mother had them, too. The distaff genes dominate the looks in my family.' Thank God, thought Sarah, as they went into the sitting room.

'Not a night for sitting outside,' she said with regret. 'Last week it was too hot to breathe; this week it's cold enough for autumn.'

'Never mind our famous climate,' said Jake, putting the tray down. 'Tell me where you're going next week.'

'To a wedding.'

'Whose?'

'Old college friend.' She shrugged. 'I must make the effort to go, because Nick's a good friend. And some of my old college crowd will be there—'

'Do I hear a but?' asked Jake.

Sarah nodded. 'The wedding's midweek, which means no problem with Davy, and I had time owing to me at work—I even bought a suitable dress the other day.'

Jake eyed her face as she poured coffee. 'So what's the snag?'

'Pretty feeble, really.' She pulled a face. 'I'll be the only one on my own. The others come in pairs.'

'And you mind that?'

'I do, rather. At this kind of wedding in the past I

always had Nick for company. But this time he's the bridegroom, so I'll be a spare wheel.'

'Does your invitation include a partner?'

'Yes.' She smiled wryly. 'Nick put a note with the invitation, telling me to bring my current man with me.'

Jake gave her one of the direct looks she was coming to know. 'Then why don't you?'

Sarah's eyes widened. 'Are you saying *you* would come with me?'

'Remember I told you I'm strictly a one at a time kind of guy?' said Jake elliptically.

'Yes. Why?'

'I assume you function on the same principle?'

'Of course I do.'

'Then as far as I'm concerned we're a couple.' He gave her a mocking little bow. 'If you want a partner for the occasion, I'm yours. I even own a morning coat.'

Sarah gazed at him, her mind working overtime. The offer was tempting. Very tempting. 'I'm staying overnight,' she warned.

'I'll book a room at the same hotel, then.'

'But can you just take off like that—from Pentiles, I mean?'

'The firm won't grind to a halt if I'm away for a day or two,' he said, then gave her a smile tinged with arrogance. 'I *am* Pentiles, remember. I take time off when I want.'

Sarah frowned. 'If you do come with me,' she began, choosing her words with care, 'my friends will probably read more into it than you'd like.'

'Than *you'd* like,' he corrected. 'I don't see a problem. Just introduce me as a friend.'

'The female section of the group will take one look at you and flatly refuse to believe that!'

Jake frowned. 'Why?'

'You know perfectly well why,' she retorted irritably. One look at those dark-rimmed blue eyes and gold-streaked hair, plus the physique that went with them, and she'd probably be beating girlfriends off with a stick.

'But it's true. I am your friend,' he pointed out. 'Not entirely by choice, on my part, I admit. I'd like a closer relationship. Much closer. But I know damn well I must toe the line or you'll send me packing.' His eyes glittered with sudden heat. 'Sometimes I can't believe I've been tamed so easily.'

Sarah gave him a fulminating look. Jake Hogan might be lounging at ease on her sofa, but with that particular light in his eye he looked about as tame as the average free-range lion.

'If you do come to the wedding—' she began, but he held up a hand.

'I *am* coming. I like weddings.'

'You must be the only man I know who does!'

'As I keep telling you, I'm not the average male,' he reminded her affably. 'And on the subject of weddings I speak from experience, having survived the nuptials of two sisters and several cousins, featured as best man at two of them, and still lived to tell the tale.'

Against her will Sarah began to laugh. 'Oh, all right. Then thank you, Jake. You win.'

'I always do.' He grinned at her. 'So where's the wedding?'

Sarah wasn't in the least surprised to learn that Jake knew the area she mentioned. She listened, amused, while he spoke at persuasive length, first to the receptionist at the Greenacres Hotel in Norfolk, then to the manager, turning on the charm to an outrageous degree before giving his credit card details to secure a room.

'Only one in the place, due to the wedding. The manager was reluctant at first to let me have it, because it's a brand-new renovation and isn't quite finished. But I persuaded her to have it ready by the time I need it,' he said afterwards, and gave Sarah a smile of such blatant triumph she laughed in his face.

'You were shameless. I suppose a technique like that wins for you every time,' she said severely, but he shook his head, sighing.

'Not quite. If I thought it did I'd try it with you, Sarah.' He looked at his watch. 'Time I was off.'

'Look, Jake, if you change your mind,' she said awkwardly. 'About the wedding, I mean, please feel free to do so.'

Jake got up, pulled her to her feet and took her by the shoulders, his eyes utterly serious. 'I won't change my mind. If it makes life easier for you to have a partner at this wedding I'll be there for you, Sarah. We're friends, remember. That's what friends are for.'

Impulsively she reached up to kiss his cheek. 'Thank you, Jake.'

He stepped back, a pulse throbbing visibly at the corner of his mouth. 'Don't mention it,' he said huskily. 'Goodnight, Sarah.'

She walked with him to the door and held up her face for their customary friendly kiss, but he pulled her into his arms and kissed her with such heat and hunger she was speechless when he let her go.

'I'll ring you.' He smiled crookedly into her dazed eyes, then went out to the car and to her intense disappointment drove off, with no mention of meeting again before their trip to Norfolk.

CHAPTER SIX

SARAH was too busy to miss Jake over the weekend. At least, not as much as she'd expected. From the moment she collected Davy and Polly from school life was so hectic her only respite was in bed. There was a picnic tea in the garden when they got home on the Friday afternoon, and a trip to McDonald's later. Once the children were in bed in Davy's room Sarah finished off the work she'd brought home, then fell into bed herself to get some rest in preparation for next day.

The two little girls were up early, Davy eager to introduce the excited Polly to their Saturday programme of swimming, lunch, and cinema. After the film Sarah drove them home to play in the garden before supper, then finished off the day with a round of board games. Margaret surprised Sarah no end by joining in to make up a four.

'Thank you,' said Sarah gratefully, after she'd packed the lively pair off to bed. 'I thought you were going out tonight.'

'I had lunch with Barbara today, instead of our usual supper. We went over arrangements for the Tuscany trip.' Margaret eyed her granddaughter searchingly. 'Sarah, purely as a matter of interest, how does Jake Hogan feel about your no-weekend rule?'

'If he objects he's not saying so. Besides, I laid my cards on the table about Davy from the first. Most of them, anyway,' she added with a sigh, then eyed her

73

grandmother warily. 'By the way, Jake's going to Nick's wedding with me.'

'*Really?*' Dark eyebrows shot to meet the hair that was still as brown as Sarah's under its frosting of silver. 'In what capacity, exactly?'

'As my friend.'

Margaret said nothing for a moment, then gave Sarah a searching look. 'Is that all he is?'

'Of course.' Sarah met the look head-on. 'That's all he can be.'

Sunday morning was fine, with a forecast promising sunshine which augured well for the Rogers' barbecue. After packing Davy's bag for the school week, Sarah wandered round the garden in her dressing gown for a while to gauge the temperature, then went into her room to change into a raspberry linen skirt. She added a plain white shirt, rolled the sleeves to just below her elbows, then went to collect the girls.

'Ready for the off?' said Margaret, on her way downstairs to say goodbye to Davy.

'Yes. Though I'm not sure about the skirt. I'm not exactly up on what the well-dressed barbecue guest is wearing this season.' Sarah made a face. 'I'll feel very silly if everyone else is in jeans.'

But when she delivered Polly to her parents Sarah was relieved to find that only Don was in jeans. Alison was wearing a strappy cotton dress.

'Have you been good?' Alison asked, hugging her daughter, who at top speed proceeded to itemise all the fab things she'd done in Pennington, then rushed Davy into the garden to play.

'I hope you're not worn out, Sarah,' said Don. 'Sit down, have a drink, and relax.'

Sarah took the reclining chair he offered, and assured her hosts that Polly had been no trouble at all over the weekend. 'As you said, it's easier with two. Though I'm afraid they didn't get to sleep very early.'

'They will tonight, back in school,' said Alison comfortably. 'In the meantime thank heavens we're lucky with the weather. Let's just sit for a minute and enjoy the sun. The others aren't due for a while.'

Sarah found it very pleasant to relax for a while in the Rogers' friendly company. When the guests arrived she was introduced to Ned and Helen Fenwick from next door, followed by three more couples from the neighbourhood, and found she was quickly absorbed into the friendly, animated group. When some of the men gave Don a hand with the chicken and steaks he was cooking, or topped up drinks, Alison enlisted Sarah's help in transferring the rest of the food from the house to the trestle table laid under the shade of the sheltering fruit trees.

Glad to be of use, and well aware that Alison's plea for help was to make her feel part of the scene, Sarah hurried to and fro with salads and relishes and baskets of bread. When everything was ready she ducked into the cloakroom to tidy up, then heard the doorbell ring and went out into the hall to let in a belated guest. And stared, speechless, at the sight of Jake Hogan, grinning at her in outrageous triumph, dressed in faded jeans and a shirt which matched his eyes.

'Jake!' called Alison, coming into the hall. 'Long time no see. Hurry up, you're late. Have you met Sarah Tracy?'

'I certainly have,' he said, thrusting a bag of bottles into Alison's arms before kissing her on both cheeks. 'How are you, Ally?'

'A lot older than when I saw you last,' she said, laughing. 'Thank you for these, you extravagant man. Come and have something to drink, then we can eat. Don's been hovering over that barbecue so long he must be medium rare himself by now.'

When Alison hurried back to her guests Jake took Sarah's arm to delay her. 'Are you glad to see me?'

She eyed him accusingly. 'You didn't tell me you were coming.'

'Don didn't invite me until Friday.'

'Rather a coincidence!'

'Not exactly. I just made it my business to contact Don over the phone on Friday. I mentioned I hadn't seen Alison for ages, and that was it.'

Sarah gave him what was meant to be a severe look. 'You didn't think to give me a ring and tell me?'

'I wanted to surprise you.' Jake took her hand. 'Tell me you're pleased, Sarah.'

'I am,' she said, relenting. 'Very pleased.'

'Good.' He gave her the eye-crinkling smile which turned her bones to jelly. 'Where's Davy?'

'Out in the garden with Polly.'

'Will she object to my presence?'

'She's having too good a time to object to anything, so come on; we'd better join the others.'

Sarah had been enjoying herself well enough up to that point, but now Jake Hogan was one of the guests her party spirit soared to the point of euphoria. He accepted a beer and did the round of introductions, then perched himself on the footrest of Sarah's recliner.

When Helen Fenwick asked if anyone had been to the Playhouse that week Jake surprised Alison by saying that he'd taken Sarah there.

'I didn't know you two knew each other so well,' she said, surprised.

'Didn't you?' said Jake blandly. 'How's Polly?'

'Getting filthy in the garden with Sarah's little girl—oh, heavens, what now?' Alison jumped up in alarm as her daughter came tearing across the lawn in distress.

'Davy's stuck up a tree, Sarah, and can't get down,' Polly wailed.

In one fluent move Jake leapt up, pulled Sarah to her feet, and ran with her after Polly.

'You see to the meat, darling.' Don tossed his utensils to Alison, and took off after the others at top speed. 'Is she in one of the oak trees, Polly?' he panted, catching up with his daughter.

'Yes, Daddy. And she's *bleeding*!'

Sarah blenched when they found Davy high above the ground, clinging to a branch of one of the trees edging the Rogers' property.

'Hi, Davy,' said Jake breathlessly as they reached her. 'How did you get up there?'

Davy peered down at him in surprise. 'Hello, Mr Hogan,' she shouted, then her voice quavered. 'It was easy-peasy getting up, but now I'm stuck. I can't get down.'

'Did you hurt yourself?' called Sarah, determinedly calm.

'Only a bit. I scraped my knee.'

Don Rogers, who was a lot heavier than Jake, opted to station himself at the foot of the tree as catcher, leaving Jake to work his way up steadily from branch to branch. When Jake reached a fork in the tree below the frightened child he smiled at her in reassurance and stretched up an arm. 'Right then, Davy. Give me your hand.'

'I can't let go,' she gasped.

'Yes, you can, sweetheart. Just one hand. You can still hang on with the other.'

Sarah watched, heart in her throat, while Davy, apparently reassured by something in the smiling blue eyes trained on hers, fearfully detached one hand and put it into Jake's.

'Good girl!' Don called.

'Now, lean down a little bit and put the other one round my neck,' instructed Jake.

Polly clutched Sarah's hand as with agonising slowness Davy detached her hand and slid her arm round Jake's neck to let him take her weight.

'Well done,' he said, holding her securely. 'Now we're going to climb down a bit.'

'And then Jake is going to hand you down to me,' called Don, smiling up at Davy. 'Just like pass the parcel.'

'OK,' she said bravely, and clung to Jake like a limpet while he made it down to a secure foothold before lowering her into the waiting arms below.

'Here's Mummy to inspect your wounds,' said Don, and gave Davy a kiss. 'And now I must get back to my labours or our lunch will be cinders.'

Polly rushed to inspect the wound, but Davy assured her airily that it was just a scratch, then to Sarah's pride turned to Jake with a beaming smile of gratitude. 'Thank you very much for getting me down, Mr Hogan.'

He grinned as he ruffled her hair. 'Any time, Davy. Glad to be of service.'

'Now, let's go and tell Alison you're in one piece and apologise for holding up lunch,' said Sarah.

Later she took the freshly scrubbed girls to join the

others at the long trestle table, and found Don taking sly pleasure in lauding Jake as the hero of the hour.

'Maidens in distress a specialty,' Jake said flippantly.

'All ages?' called Alison from the foot of the table, to general laughter.

'Absolutely,' he said with a grin, holding Sarah's chair for her.

With Davy safe and sound Sarah settled down to enjoy the party. The food was delicious, and tasted even better for being eaten in the open air in convivial company, and to add to her pleasure Davy, seated the other side of Jake, spent most of the meal chattering happily to him.

The company gathered round the table enjoyed themselves so much that when people finally began to leave it was almost time for Davy and Polly to go back to school.

'I'll take Polly with us,' offered Sarah, as Alison went inside with her to collect her child's belongings together. 'I'm sure you two could do with a breather after working so hard over lunch.'

'Are you sure?' said Alison, obviously tempted.

'It seems pretty pointless for both of us to make the same journey.'

'Or we could take Davy with us?'

'I'd rather do that myself, and explain to her house mother that she had a bit of a fright up the tree.' Sarah smiled sheepishly. 'I'm fussing, I know—'

'Of course you're not fussing,' said Alison, and gave Sarah a knowing little smile. 'By the way, I didn't know Jake Hogan was a friend of yours.'

'Small world,' said Sarah casually. 'Now, we'd better get those two out of the bath.'

When the two girls ran downstairs, transformed from

grubby hoydens into neat little schoolgirls, Jake was still chatting in the garden with Don.

'Hey, look at you two,' he said, jumping up. 'Who waved a magic wand?'

Alison laughed, and looked at her watch. 'There's time, yet, Sarah. Have some tea before you go. And you two sit quietly and don't get dirty, please.'

Sarah was only too pleased to stay on a while, but deep down couldn't help feeling wistful. To the onlooker the four of them looked so much like two conventional couples with a child apiece she was pierced with a stab of longing for the impossible.

After Alison took Don into the house with her, apparently in need of his help to make a pot of tea, Jake moved his chair closer to Sarah's.

'Have you recovered from the drama with Davy?' he asked quietly.

'I'm used to it. She has a real thing about trees, but she never learns. At one time or another she's been stuck up every one of ours in the garden at Campden Road,' Sarah told him, her eyes on the girls as they sat on a rug on the grass, playing some absorbing private game.

'But other than that you've had a good time today?'

Sarah turned to look at him, her eyes luminous. 'Better than good. I've never been to anything like this before.'

Jake frowned in surprise. 'Why not?'

'It doesn't take rocket science to work that one out, Jake.' She shrugged. 'All the people here today were couples.'

'You don't get invited to parties?'

'Some. Colleagues' birthdays, Christmas drinks with the families of the men I work for, the odd charity bash. Which is how I met Brian. But no family affairs like this.' Sarah straightened in her chair. 'I'm whingeing. Sorry.'

'Don asked if we were seeing each other,' said Jake casually.

Sarah frowned. 'What did you say?'

'The truth. Because we are seeing each other. Literally.' He heaved a dramatic sigh. 'My ego wasn't up to admitting that ours was a no-kisses type of romance.'

She flushed. 'I wouldn't say no kisses at all.'

'Next best thing,' he whispered, as Don came back hefting a tray.

Much as Sarah would have liked the day to go for ever, shortly afterwards it was time to see her young passengers into the car and say her goodbyes. 'We've had such a good time,' she told her hosts.

'Come again soon,' said Don genially, and cocked an eyebrow at Jake. 'Both of you.'

'Dinner next time,' said Alison, nodding. 'Then we'll have more time to talk.'

'I'll ring you, Sarah,' said Jake, and she gave him a quick, embarrassed smile, conscious of the interest from the other two. Jake popped his head inside the open window at the back of the car. 'Mind you keep out of trees, Davy. You too, Polly.'

The giggling children promised, waved at Alison and Don, and Sarah drove off to a chorus of goodbyes. When she got to Roedale Sarah had a quick word with the house mother to give the reason for Davy's grazed knee, gave both girls a hug and drove back to Pennington, anticlimax creeping up on her, stronger with every mile. Her Sunday evening blues were back in force. But not for the usual reason.

When she'd parked the car in the garage at the bottom

of the garden, Sarah wandered aimlessly up the path, rounded the shrubbery and felt a leap of unadulterated joy at the sight of Jake sitting at the patio table, reading the Sunday papers.

He jumped up as she approached, smiling rather warily. 'Mrs Parker let me in. Do you mind?'

'Of course I don't,' said Sarah, so obviously meaning it his eyes lit up in response as she sat down in one of the chairs at the table. 'Second surprise of the day.'

'I wanted to see you alone,' he said matter-of-factly, and drew a chair up close beside her.

'Why didn't you say so earlier?'

'Originally you said you'd be too tired. So I thought you'd say no. And we need to make arrangements for the wedding.'

'You could have rung me.'

'I could,' he agreed. 'But I like this much better.' He looked at her steadily. 'So I rang your grandmother's bell. She was on her way out to church, so I offered to wait in the car until you got back from Roedale, but she suggested I wait in the garden instead.'

'I'm glad she did. It's a very *nice* surprise,' she said after a while, her eyes falling.

'For once I could tell,' he said dryly. 'Normally you don't give much away, Sarah Tracy.'

'I'm not the effusive type. Want a drink?' she asked.

'Not really. I just want to sit here with you in the cool of the evening and talk, or not talk, as the case may be. I enjoyed the day so much I wanted it to last longer.'

'So did I,' she confessed.

'Good.' Jake stretched out his long legs with a sigh. 'Have you remembered that I'm in London tomorrow? I'll be back at the grind on Tuesday afternoon, but I'll work late so I can take off for Norfolk with a clear conscience.'

'Look,' said Sarah quickly, 'if the trip is causing problems for you—'

'It isn't.' He turned to smile at her. 'As I keep telling you, I like weddings.'

'As long as you're not the bridegroom, I suppose!'

'Not a bit of it. Come the day, I'll enjoy my own wedding most of all,' he assured her, and held her eyes with the intensity which always braced her for what was coming next. 'Did you never consider getting married, Sarah?'

'No,' she said, after a taut little silence. 'Never.'

'Not even to Davy's father?'

'Him least of all.'

'And you obviously don't want to talk about it,' he said after a moment, and turned his attention back to the sunset. 'Right. So what time shall I come for you on Wednesday?'

'Early, I'm afraid. The wedding's not until three, but it's a fair trip, and I'll need time when we arrive to tidy up and change into my finery. Which reminds me,' she added. 'Do you possess a golf umbrella?'

He grinned. 'No. But I can borrow one. Why?'

'So we can arrive in church in reasonable nick if it rains, of course.'

'I'll see to it,' he promised.

While the shadows lengthened, and the sun disappeared over the trees at the end of the garden, they went on talking with the easy familiarity of friends of a lot longer standing than they actually were, at peace with the world and each other.

'I've enjoyed today,' said Jake at one stage, and shot

a look at Sarah. 'I didn't spoil things for you by gate-crashing the party?'

'Not in the least.' Finding it easier to admit in the fading light, Sarah told him the truth. 'I was delighted to see you, Jake.'

'Thank God for that. But you realise that Don and Alison now have us pigeonholed as a couple?' he added.

'Next time I see them I'll tell them we're not,' she said, unconcerned.

'Why?' Jake demanded. 'Maybe we're not exactly the sort of couple they think we are. But we're definitely a pair of some kind, Sarah.'

'If the subject comes up I'll say we're just good friends.'

'Which will convince them beyond all doubt that we're lovers.' Jake heaved a sigh. 'Which we're not, alas.'

Sarah shivered suddenly, and rubbed her arms. 'It's getting chilly. Let's go inside. I'll make some supper.'

Switching lights on as she went, Sarah led the way to the kitchen. 'How do you feel about omelettes?'

'Enthusiastic,' he assured her. 'Though I didn't come here tonight expecting to be fed.'

'What exactly did you expect?'

Jake's smile was wry. 'Very little, Miss Tracy. A habit I'm learning fast where you're concerned, to avoid disappointment. Can I do something?'

'No.' She flashed a gleaming dark look at him. 'Just sit there and look decorative while I work.'

He threw back his head and laughed.

The kitchen, which had originally served the entire household, was now Sarah's private domain. But years before it had been renovated to Margaret Parker's requirements, with modern appliances and cupboards, and plenty of space for pots of herbs on the broad ledge of a window Sarah's master builder grandfather had enlarged to give his wife a better view of the garden. These days Margaret's state-of-the art kitchen was upstairs in her self-contained flat, converted from a small spare bedroom with the same view.

When they sat down to eat puffy omelettes flavoured with parsley and chives, Jake attacked his with gusto.

'Though after the lunch we ate I hadn't expected to be hungry again today,' he commented.

Sarah glanced up at the clock on the wall. 'It's after nine. Hours since lunch. Have some more bread.'

'This is a big kitchen for just you, Sarah,' he said, eyeing his surroundings.

'Especially as my main activity in here is throwing a salad together! But in its heyday it would have served a big household, probably as much as a dozen or so originally.' She smiled. 'Three attic bedrooms and four double bedrooms, one with dressing room. But originally only one bathroom—with a solitary lavatory inside it— to serve all the occupants. At one time there was another, in an outhouse at the back, but that was kept for the servants' use, in the days when people had such things.'

Jake smiled. 'Sounds like the setting for a television costume drama.'

Sarah got up to take their plates, then made coffee. 'It's a huge contrast to the home I grew up in. My father was a civil engineer who worked in hotel construction all over the world. He had a house built for my mother, complete with every gadget and convenience possible to make life easy for her.'

'Was your mother delicate, then?'

'She wasn't the most robust of people, it's true, but that wasn't the reason. It was just the way Dad was with her. Always.' Sarah leaned against the counter, waiting for the coffee to perk. 'I only realised how special their marriage was when I was old enough to notice other people's. My parents idolised each other.'

Jake looked at her questioningly. 'Did that mean you felt excluded?'

'Good heavens, no. I felt part of the equation, always.' She brought the coffee pot over and sat down to pour.

He leaned over to touch her hand. 'So there was no problem with them when Davy was born?'

Sarah kept her eyes on her task. 'Not in that way.'

Jake leaned back again. 'But it must have been pretty tough for a teenager, just the same.'

'Not nearly as tough as for some. Because Davy was born in my gap year I was able to take up my college place, as planned. And I led a normal, rackety student life during term, but switched back to the role of Mummy when I went home—' Sarah stopped abruptly. 'This isn't something I normally discuss, Jake.'

'I'm very much aware of that. Thank you, Sarah. And now,' he added briskly, 'what time shall I call for you on Wednesday morning?'

'I'd like to get there by twelve if possible,' she said, grateful to him for changing the subject.

'Right. I'll be here at six.'

'Sorry to get you up at that hour.'

'Not a bit of it. I wake early most mornings,' he assured her. 'And I'd rather start when the roads are relatively quiet. We can stop for coffee somewhere, to break the journey, and grab something to eat at the hotel when we get there.'

Sarah smiled at him gratefully. 'This is very good of you, Jake.'

'As I keep saying, Miss Tracy, it's what friends are

for.' He got up reluctantly. 'Thank you for supper. Shall I help wash up?'

She shook her head, laughing. 'You're just too good to be true, Jake Hogan. I'll let you off the dishes in case your halo gets too tight.'

He grinned. 'I only offered so I could stay longer!'

'You can do that anyway. Come back to the sitting room for a while.'

He followed her into the other room and sat down with her on the sofa. 'Good. Now we can practise behaving like the old friends we're supposed to be. Though that isn't difficult. Not for me, anyway.'

'Nor for me.' Sarah turned her head on the sofa-back to look at him. 'I'm very glad you came to the lunch today, Jake.'

'So am I.' He smiled into her eyes. 'I'll send flowers to Alison tomorrow. Though she won't know I'm really thanking her for an entire Sunday spent with you. Not something that's likely to occur often, alas.'

'True,' Sarah agreed with regret.

'Would Davy really object if the three of us spent time together?'

'Probably not. But that isn't going to happen just the same, Jake.'

He was silent for a moment. 'Why not?'

She sighed. 'Because you and I may not remain— friends, Jake. So I can't risk any attachment to you on Davy's part. Her world fell apart when my parents died. It's taken from that time almost until now to give her any real sense of security. This wavered badly when she went to board at Roedale, but she's getting back on course again now and I want her to stay that way.'

Jake looked across at the photograph of the two smiling faces, then turned back to Sarah. 'So are you saying you've never had a relationship since Davy was born?'

'No, I'm not. I had boyfriends in college, like everyone else, but nothing significant. And Davy was never involved.' Sarah looked away. 'I led a perfectly normal life—or what I thought of as a normal life—until my parents died. After that everything changed. We had to move in here with my grandmother, and you know the rest.'

'So you won't let a man into your life in case the relationship harms Davy,' said Jake slowly.

'Which has been no problem up to now,' she admitted.

Jake reached out a hand to turn her face to his. 'Up to now,' he repeated inexorably. 'Does that mean you'd consider a closer relationship with me if it weren't for Davy?'

Sarah nodded wordlessly, then closed her eyes, suddenly defenceless when he drew her into his arms. 'Please, Jake!'

'Please what?' he whispered, and kissed her very gently.

It wasn't fair, she thought wildly. The merest touch of Jake's lips roused all kinds of hot, unbidden responses never experienced with the most passionate overtures from anyone else.

'Don't push me away, Sarah. You need a little tender loving care,' he whispered, raising his head a fraction.

'Is that what this is?' she said unevenly, and closed her eyes against the heat in his.

'Yes,' he said tightly. 'And it's killing me, because I want a hell of a lot more.'

He kissed her again, and this time the kiss was hot and hard, and for the first time she answered it in kind, shivers running down her spine as his tongue met hers and his hands slid upwards beneath her shirt to caress her bare back. Her breasts tautened in anticipation of the caresses she was sure would happen any second as the kiss deepened. The growing hunger of it set her body alight, and she gasped as his fingers sought the nipples straining against the thin cotton of her shirt. Heat streaked through her from his fingertips, the shock of it causing such turbulence her inevitable defence mechanism sprang to life, and she jerked away violently, hands outstretched to ward him off.

Jake gave a smothered groan and leapt to his feet to stand at the windows, his chest heaving as he stared out blindly into the dark, while Sarah slumped into a corner of the sofa, feeling as though she'd been dropped from a great height. It was a long time before she could trust her voice, but at last she cleared her throat, her dark eyes heavy with remorse. 'I'm sorry, Jake.'

He stayed where he was, his back turned to her. 'So am I,' he said tersely. 'Because you're a puzzle I just can't solve. I want you, Sarah. And it hurts like hell to know you don't want me.'

'Ah, but I do,' she said miserably.

Jake turned sharply, his eyes blazing into hers. 'So why—?' Colour leached suddenly from his face. 'Sarah, for God's sake, tell me! Were you raped?'

Sarah jumped up to take his hands. '*No*, Jake. It was nothing like that.'

Jake held her close, his cheek rubbing against her hair as he let out a deep breath of relief. 'Thank goodness for that, at least.' He pulled away a little and smiled down at her. 'Maybe one day you'll be able to tell me about it. When you know me better. Which I'm determined you will. Better than anyone else in the world, in fact. But for now I'm going to let you get some rest and take myself off home.'

'Thank you, Jake,' she said huskily.

'What for, exactly?'

Sarah's eyes were luminous in her flushed face. 'Everything.'

CHAPTER SEVEN

MARGARET PARKER left for Pisa with a group of friends next day. And without her formidable presence the atmosphere in the house seemed lighter. Far from feeling lonely or nervous, Sarah was happy to have the place to herself, her spirits rising even further when Jake rang.

'Just thought I'd report in, check that all was well with you, Sarah.'

'How nice of you.'

'I *am* nice.' He chuckled. 'My day has been incredibly boring, so tell me about yours.'

'Much the same as usual, except for a shopping spree after work. And I've been chatting to Nick, the amazingly jittery bridegroom. He rang earlier to make sure I was coming.'

'Did you mention me?'

'I certainly did. He told me to say he's looking forward to meeting you, then went on at enormous length about the virtues of his Delphine. The man's head over heels in love at last!'

'You don't mind that?'

'Of course not. Nick and I have always been the best of friends. But there was never anything else between us.'

'So I've no reason to feel jealous?'

'None at all.' Sarah paused. '*Are* you the jealous type, Jake?'

'Only when you're concerned, it seems,' he said lightly. 'So tell me about your shopping spree.'

91

'I hired a hat for the occasion.'

'One of those big cartwheel affairs?'

'No. Small and frivolous.'

'Can't wait to see you in it. What else did you buy?'

'The wedding gift—'

'I'm glad you mentioned that. As well as the pleasure of talking to you, Miss Tracy, I rang to pick your brains. What shall *I* buy the happy pair?'

'Since you've never met them, you don't need to buy them anything.'

'What did you choose?'

Sarah described the hand-carved wooden fruit bowl she'd chosen, but glossed over the fact that its price tag had put paid to new shoes. 'We can both sign the card,' she suggested.

'Then I insist on paying half—I won't ruffle your feathers by offering to foot the entire bill!'

'Wise man,' she said, laughing. 'Half will do nicely.' So nicely she might search through the sales for shoes next day after all.

'I'll be home latish tomorrow evening, Sarah, but I'll be with you bright and early on Wednesday.'

'I'll be ready. Goodnight, Jake. Thanks for ringing.'

'My pleasure.'

Her pleasure too, Sarah acknowledged as she got ready for bed. Added to the sexual attraction which grew stronger every time they met, she liked every last thing about Jake Hogan. His smile, his voice, his looks. His touch. The mere thought of his hands on her skin and his mouth on hers, and— Her mind veered away sharply. She knew she was a frustrating puzzle to Jake, but there were some vital missing pieces to put in place before she could even begin to consider the kind of relationship he wanted. And which she was beginning to want just as much.

Sarah was in the middle of packing the following evening when Jake rang her doorbell, demanding entry.

She let him in, her delight undisguised at the sight of him. Then her eyes widened in dismay. Something had happened. He couldn't take her to the wedding after all. 'Something wrong, Jake?'

'I just needed to see you,' he said simply, and kissed her briefly.

Sarah was so pleased to hear it she kissed him back. 'I thought you'd come to say you couldn't make it tomorrow,' she said, as they went into the sitting room.

'Not a bit of it,' he assured her, and sank down on the sofa, stifling a yawn. 'I've spent the last two days working my socks off to make sure I can leave Pentiles to its own devices for a while.'

'Have you eaten?'

'Yes. I took pity on my staff and had something sent in between meetings. So right now I just want to sit and hold hands with you for a few minutes.' Jake held up his hand and Sarah took it, letting him draw her down beside him.

'You look tired,' she commented.

'I am. But I shall get myself to bed early tonight. And then tomorrow I'm yours,' he assured her. 'All through the meetings and presentations I missed you yesterday, Sarah. I missed you today, too. Which is why I'm here, even though I'll be seeing you in the morning.' His grasp tightened. 'And not just for the kiss—which I couldn't help when I saw the worried look in those beautiful eyes.'

'Worried I didn't have a driver for tomorrow,' she agreed with feeling.

He moved closer. 'Would you have been disappointed?'

'Yes.' Sarah looked down at their clasped hands. 'And
not just because I didn't want to go alone, either.'

Jake put a finger under her chin to turn her face up to
his. 'Can it be the lady's warming towards me?'

'You know I am!' She met his eyes steadily. 'But the
situation still stands, Jake.'

He nodded, resigned. 'But the odd friendly kiss can't
do any harm. In fact,' he added, melting her with the
eye-crinkling smile, 'it would do me a whole lot of
good.'

For answer she tilted her chin in invitation.

Jake kissed her gently, then took her by surprise by
lifting her onto his lap. When she leaned into him instead
of struggling to get away he gave a relishing sigh and
held her close. But after a moment or two his arms tightened, and heat flared in his eyes, the pupils extending to
cover the blue iris. Sarah gazed into them, spellbound,
and with a smothered sound he bent his head and kissed
her, his tongue caressing hers. She melted against him,
responding with such fervour their hearts were thudding
in unison when the need for air forced them to separate.
Breathing hard, Jake straightened with reluctance and
gazed down into her dazed face.

'I was wrong. That did me no good at all.'

'I know what you mean,' she said unevenly. 'If those
are your friendly kisses what are the passionate ones
like? Don't demonstrate!' she added hastily, then
frowned. 'That's an unsettling look in your eye. What's
wrong?'

Jake was silent for a moment, then gave her an oddly
bleak smile. 'I keep wondering about your old pal Nick

Morrell.' He gave her a hard, devouring kiss by way of illustration. 'Were you on these kind of terms with him?'

Sarah shook her head vehemently. 'No. Not like this. Never like this. With anyone.'

'No one at all?' Jake smoothed the hair away from her forehead, his eyes holding hers.

'I know what you're asking, Jake.' She would have slid from his lap, but he held her fast. 'All right. I'll tell you just one thing, Jake, on condition we don't talk about it any more.' She sat rigid for a moment, then sagged against him, burying her face against his shoulder. 'Other than my grandmother, no one knows that Davy owes her existence to a single moment of misguided sympathy.'

Jake stroked her hair in silence for a moment, then stood up with her and set her on her feet. 'Thank you, darling. It can't have been easy for you to tell me that. And now I must go. See you in the morning.'

'You were right, Jake. You are definitely not the average male.' Sarah smiled crookedly. 'Any other man would be hammering at me with more questions.'

He kissed her again. 'I admit I want to know every last thing about you, Sarah, but I promise I'll be patient until you can trust me with the entire story. So get some sleep, darling. It's going to be a long day tomorrow.'

Jake arrived next morning on the stroke of six, as promised, in jeans and a navy jersey over a thin shirt, which was so similar to Sarah's choice of clothes she laughed as he gave her a swift kiss.

'We look like twins,' she told him.

'Not quite,' he said with a grin, giving her a head-to-toe survey.

Jake refused coffee in favour of leaving immediately

to avoid the morning rush hour, stowed Sarah's belongings in the car, then waited while she made sure the house was secure.

'My grandmother's on holiday,' she explained, sliding into the passenger seat. 'But I've plugged in the gadgets that make the lights come on, and cancelled the milk and newspapers, and double-checked all the windows and doors.'

'Then you were alone in the house last night?' asked Jake as he drove off.

'Yes.'

He slanted a look at her. 'But you didn't tell me that in case I carried you up to your bed and demanded my evil way, I suppose?'

'I sleep downstairs, so it doesn't apply,' she said, unmoved. 'And, believe it or not, I just forgot to mention it.'

'I believe everything you tell me, Sarah.'

'Good. Anyway, it was Grandma's trip to Italy which originally gave me doubts about going to the wedding. But the school has my mobile number, and the details of the hotel in Norfolk, and Alison offered to stand in as back-up for Davy if the need arises.' Sarah shivered. 'Which I devoutly hope it won't.'

Jake touched her hand for an instant. 'Of course it won't. But even if it does I'll get you back here at the speed of light.'

'I hope that's not your normal approach to motorway driving?' she asked, laughing.

'Don't worry, you'll arrive in one piece, but I may need a bit of guidance to find the actual spot once we leave the A11.'

'No problem, I'm a brilliant navigator,' she assured

him. 'But we've got a lot of motorway to get through yet before I start grappling with a map.'

Jake drove not only with speed, but with such skill Sarah relaxed when she found he was capable of paying attention to the road at the same time as giving details of his trip to London, which had included a meal eaten with his brother.

'Did you tell him about me, Jake?'

'Yes.'

Sarah gave him a wry glance. 'Was he surprised? Or didn't you tell him about Davy?'

'Of course I did. We're pretty close, Liam and I. We like to know the other is enjoying life.'

'And is Liam enjoying his?'

'The work part, yes, as usual. But his romance has come unstuck.'

'Poor Liam.' Sarah changed the subject to talk about the wedding, which had put a strain on the accommodation available in the area. 'Nick says the bride's family lives in a vast old rectory, which will be crammed to the rafters with as many relations as possible to leave room in the area for the other guests.'

'Talking of which, how, exactly, do I introduce myself to your chums?' asked Jake.

'As Sarah's friend, of course.'

'A bit lukewarm for my taste. You won't allow lover, I know, and I draw the line at boyfriend. How about partner?'

She shook her head. 'That implies that we live together.'

'As we would, if I had my way,' he said, startling her.

'But how can you want that when we've never even—?' she began, then stopped, colour flooding her face.

'Made love?' He sent her a smouldering look, then returned his attention to the three lanes of motorway crowded as far as the eye could see by this time with London-bound traffic. 'The fact had not escaped my attention, Sarah. Though the foretaste I've been granted makes it obvious we'd be good together. More than good. Sensational.' He drew in a deep breath. 'Now for pity's sake let's change the subject—it's bad for me when I'm driving.'

They stopped later at a motorway service restaurant for coffee and toast and a breather for Jake, who declined Sarah's offer to help with the driving.

'Not,' he assured her, 'because I refuse to let a woman drive me. But I don't want you to arrive at the hotel too tired to enjoy the wedding.'

'Thank you,' she said, her smile so warm Jake reached a hand across the table to take hers.

'Are you aware of the effect of that smile of yours?'

'No,' she said, surprised.

'I thought so. Be sparing with it today. With other men,' he added.

Sarah's eyes flashed. 'Orders, Jake?'

'Advice, not orders.' He wagged an admonishing finger. 'I'm your escort, Miss Tracy, so save that particular smile for me.'

It had been cool with early-morning mist when they started out, but by this time the sun was so hot they discarded their sweaters before resuming their journey.

'"Happy the bride the sun shines on,"' said Sarah.

'It's going to be a scorcher,' agreed Jake, and donned dark glasses for the rest of the journey.

Due to Jake's powerful car, and his skill as a driver, plus the added bonus of Sarah's navigating skills, they arrived at the Greenacres Hotel shortly after eleven.

Sarah spotted the bridegroom in the bar with a trio of friends, and all four of them came rushing to greet her the moment she appeared in the doorway. Grinning broadly, Nick Morrell got there first, and gave her a crushing hug before passing her on to Frances and Grania, then to Paul, completing the circle of friends who had once shared a house with Sarah in student days.

Once the hugging and kissing had abated, Sarah took Jake by the hand and drew him forward. 'This is Jake Hogan, everyone.'

Jake was immediately pounced on by both women, but Nick interrupted, laughing, so he could introduce Paul Bailey, his best man.

'Present company came to provide moral support, to make sure I don't get too nervous to remember my lines. Order more coffee, Paul, would you? The others will be back shortly,' said Nick, putting an arm round Sarah. 'Ben—Grania's husband,' he told Jake, 'is out searching the neighbourhood for a bed for the night.'

'With my Tom as guide, which is worrying, because he's never been to this neck of the woods before,' put in Frances. 'We tried wheedling at the little place we're in, but no luck. Everything's booked solid locally for the wedding.'

'It's all my fault,' said Grania penitently. 'I meant to book the minute I got the invitation, then it went clean out of my mind. By the time I got round to it there was no room at any inn at all.' She pulled a face. 'Ben is not pleased with me. I've grovelled to the receptionist here for first refusal if a cancellation comes in, but that's a pretty fond hope. Never mind. We can always sleep in the car.'

'The men can do that,' said Frances instantly. 'You can bunk in with me.'

Grania shook her head. 'That's sweet of you, Fran, but I wouldn't dream of putting Tom out just because I was an idiot. Anyway, Sarah, let's get on to more important subjects. We want to hear all about your gorgeous Davy—' She halted, casting an uncertain glance at Jake.

'Apart from getting stuck up a tree on Sunday,' he said quickly, 'Davy's doing fine.'

There were instant demands to see photographs, and exclamations over the child's extraordinary likeness to Sarah now she was growing up.

'We all feel a bit proprietary about Davy, Jake,' Nick explained. 'We've known her since she was in her buggy.'

'I envy you that,' said Jake quietly.

'She's a poppet,' said Grania, and smiled proudly. 'Talking of which, guess what, folks?' She paused dramatically. 'We're hoping to achieve something similar ourselves by Christmas!'

The stop-press news brought a flood of congratulations and kisses all round, then Nick looked at his watch and blenched, instantly transformed into panicking bridegroom mode.

'Sorry, must dash. Promised to collect my brother from the station. Coming, Paul? See you all in church.' Looking harassed, he thrust a hand through his dark curly hair, thanked everyone for the gifts, then hurried off with Paul.

'Poor dear,' said Frances, shaking her head. 'I thought women suffered bridal nerves, not laid-back people like Nick.'

'Ben was just the same,' said Grania, and sighed deeply. 'Oh, dear. I hope he comes back with good news.'

'So do I,' said Sarah, then turned to Jake. 'Perhaps we'd better check in.'

'Right. I'll bring the luggage in.' He smiled warmly at Frances and Grania. 'Good to meet you. I'll see you later.'

After he'd gone out to the car Sarah's one-time housemates pounced on her.

'Does this mean you're going to give Davy a daddy at last?' asked Grania eagerly.

Sarah shook her head, flushing. 'We're just friends.'

'Pull the other one, ducky,' said Frances, laughing. 'The man's obviously nuts about you—and not at all happy to see Nick cuddling you, either.'

'Stop it, Fran,' said Grania, who had always been the one to look out for Sarah most in the past. 'You're making her blush. But Jake's definitely a charmer. Have you known him long?'

'Not very long,' said Sarah, smiling as she saw Jake beckon from the foyer. 'I must dash.'

'I'm famished, as always by this time of day,' said Grania, patting her middle. 'So when you're settled in come back down and have a snack lunch with us, Sarah. Ben and Tom should surely be back by then.'

'Love to. See you later.'

Sarah hurried from the bar to take her hatbox from Jake. 'Could we talk somewhere before checking in?' she muttered in his ear.

'Yes, of course. There's a sofa over there.' He gave her a searching look. 'Sit down. Tell me what's wrong, and what I can do to help.'

She smiled gratefully. 'Jake, what sort of room did you book?'

To her astonishment he looked embarrassed. 'You'll laugh.'

'Of course I won't. Did they put you in the broom closet, or something?'

'Quite the reverse. They let me have the spanking new bridal suite. Not required by your friend and his bride, obviously.' He shrugged. 'It was that or nothing.'

'You're joking! What on earth does it cost?' she said, giggling.

'Don't ask.' He took her hand. 'So tell me, what's your problem, Sarah, and how can I solve it for you?'

She sighed. 'It's just that Grania's pregnant.'

Jake nodded. 'And you're worried at the idea of her sleeping in the car.'

'Exactly. I feel guilty because I booked a double room, and heaven knows what size yours is. It seems so awful not to hand one of them over, but—'

'There's obviously more, so spit it out.'

Sarah looked at him in appeal. 'This sounds stupid, but even if you agree to let me share with you I don't want the world to know we originally booked separate rooms.'

Jake's eyes gleamed. 'Run that past me again. You actually want to share with me?'

'So Grania can have my room, yes,' she said impatiently. 'There must be a sofa I can sleep on?'

'You'd better hope so,' he said, after a pause, 'because any bridal suite worth the name is certain to have a double bed.'

'I realise that. Would you mind sharing with me?'

Jake let out a deep breath, a wry twist to his lips. 'No, Sarah. I wouldn't mind at all. But are you sure about this?'

'Of course I'm sure. So what do we do?'

'Tell the receptionist we double-booked by mistake, and to pass your room on to your friend without mentioning you,' said Jake promptly. 'What's Grania's surname again?'

'Forrester.'

'Right. Wait here.'

Jake crossed the hall to the reception desk, and Sarah looked on, impressed, while the Hogan charm went into overdrive as he explained the apparent mistake. The young woman behind the desk listened with rapt attention, then nodded with enthusiasm, smiling warmly at Jake. She sent an envious, dewy-eyed look in Sarah's direction, and went off towards the bar.

'What on earth did you say?' whispered Sarah, when Jake rejoined her.

'That I'd booked the bridal suite as a special surprise for you, unaware that you'd already made a reservation. And don't worry, I emphasised that you were not only anxious that Mrs Forrester should have yours, but wanted the arrangement kept secret to avoid any embarrassment.'

'What embarrassment?'

'I gave her a mysterious smile and didn't specify. It seemed to go down well.'

'It must have. I think she's already gone to find Grania. Better make ourselves scarce.'

Crammed into the small lift with their luggage, Sarah suddenly broke up with laughter, and Jake sagged against the wall, joining in.

'I would have been hopeless as a spy!' he said, when he could get his breath. 'It was hard to keep a straight face when I was doing my bit with the receptionist.'

'But doing it so *well*,' mocked Sarah, as the doors opened on the top floor.

'Just for you,' he reminded her.

'What's the room number?' she asked, as they went out into a corridor.

'We haven't arrived yet,' said Jake, leading the way past closed doors. 'We foot it the rest of the way, up those stairs at the end.'

Intrigued, Sarah followed him up to a landing, where it was immediately obvious which room was theirs because there was only one door.

'Former attic bedrooms now converted into bridal suite,' said Jake. He put down the bags and unlocked the door.

Sarah went ahead of him into a long, light-filled room, her eyes drawn instantly to a tester bed with filmy white drapes. She looked away quickly, concentrating on the décor instead. 'Well, well,' she said, as Jake closed the door behind him. 'You should feel right at home here.'

'Why?'

'It's like your flat. Pale colours, white bed. Almost minimalist. Not everyone's idea of a bridal suite.'

'Which it isn't tonight,' Jake said with regret.

'True.' Sarah laid her hatbox and garment bag on a narrow settle grouped with a pair of chairs and a table under one of the windows. 'Where do I hang my things?'

Jake went over to a series of brass handles let into one wall and pulled on one to discover a wardrobe. 'And over there,' he added, pointing to a door in the other wall, 'must be the bathroom.'

Because she was the one who'd asked to share Sarah did her best to hide any awkwardness. 'Right,' she said briskly. 'Grania asked us to join them for a snack lunch when we're ready.'

'Good, I'm hungry,' said Jake, unzipping the cover from his morning coat. 'I'll just hang this up, then I'll leave you to sort out your gear. I'll wait for you in the bar.'

Sarah smiled at him with gratitude. 'Thank you, Jake. This is very good of you.'

'A beautiful woman asks to share my room and it's good of me to agree?' Jake shook his head, his eyes gleaming. 'If I *were* good I'd offer to give the room up to you and sleep in the car, Sarah. But I can't see that happening, somehow. Don't be long, and don't forget to bring the key with you,' he added, and left her alone.

Afraid that her solution to Grania's problem was likely to cause quite a few for herself, one way and another, Sarah hung her dress away, pleased to see that it had survived without creasing. She unpacked her bag, then opened the door into the bathroom. And laughed out loud. Mirror-tiled walls reflected opulence the exact opposite of the bedroom's restraint. The interior designer had gone overboard with gold dolphins. They were inlaid in the glass housing the shower, frolicked on the filmy curtains at the window, and accessed water to the sunken circular tub. Several more held up shelves laden with every bathtime luxury a guest could possibly need, and they even bordered fluffy white towels piled on a gilt chair. Everything your average sybarite could possibly want, thought Sarah, amused.

She washed her face, touched it up again, then went back into the bedroom. But no sofa had materialised by magic in the meantime. Not counting the small, decorative settle under the window, and the sunken tub in the bathroom, the only place to sleep was the ineluctably bridal bed.

CHAPTER EIGHT

THERE was an air of celebration in the bar when Sarah joined the others. Tom Hill and Ben Forrester made a great fuss of her, while Grania, euphoric with relief, gave the news that there had been a cancellation after all.

'So Grania won't have to sleep in the car,' Jake said, smiling at Sarah as he seated her beside him.

'Thank God,' said Ben fervently. 'I'm pretty damn relieved myself, I can tell you. We went right through the list we were given, plus a few more places we found on the way, but no luck.' He gave a rueful look at his wife. 'I don't mind telling you, I dreaded breaking the news when I got back.'

'But he didn't have to because miracles do happen sometimes after all,' said Grania, elated. 'I can hardly believe our luck.'

'Is the room comfortable?' said Sarah, avoiding Jake's eye.

'Small and basic, but compared with the alternative it's utter luxury!'

'By the way, Tom, I told Grania you could sleep in the car, and she could share with me if the worst came to the worst,' Frances told her husband, then laughed with everyone else at the comical dismay on his face.

'Of course I'd have done that,' he said loftily, then grinned. 'But I'm bloody glad I don't have to.'

Sarah was happy to be among the friends she rarely saw these days. And it was a double bonus to find that Jake not only blended effortlessly into the group, but had gained much approval for his forethought in ordering pots of coffee and an enormous platter of assorted sandwiches for the lunch everyone needed to eat quickly before going off to change for the wedding.

'Good man,' said Ben fervently, munching. 'I'm famished after knocking on all those doors. Emotionally drained, too,' he added with drama. 'Good thing we're having coffee. A beer would knock me flat.'

'Not that you're allowed one, anyway, with champagne to come later,' said Grania, and smiled warmly at Jake. 'This was such a good idea of yours. Thank you.'

'How long have you known Sarah, Jake?' asked Frances curiously.

'Not long enough,' he assured her.

'How did you meet?'

'He ran me over in his car,' explained Sarah, and grinned at the startled faces turned in her direction. 'You did ask!'

'She gave me the worst fright of my entire life,' said Jake, shuddering.

'Good heavens,' said Grania, awestruck. 'Were you hurt, Sarah?'

'Just a graze or two and a bruised thigh. It was my fault, really. Jake did his utmost to avoid me. I literally shot out into the road in front of him. In the middle of a thunderstorm,' Sarah added, laughing at the instant comprehension on the assembled faces.

'Ah! All is revealed,' Frances told Jake. 'Sarah goes bananas in a storm. In our student days the faintest rumble of thunder sent her diving into the broom cupboard.'

Lunch over, it was decided to make a move and meet in the foyer at two-fifteen for the short drive to the church.

'Tom and I can direct you, needless to say,' said Ben,

grinning. 'After this morning we know every nook and cranny in the entire neighbourhood!'

After Frances and Tom were waved off the others made for the lift.

'Bit of a tight fit,' commented Ben. 'Push up, Sarah. What floor are you on?'

'Right at the top,' said Jake.

'So are we,' said Grania, pleased.

'We're a floor above that again,' Sarah explained, glad they were crowded so closely together she couldn't see Jake's face.

They left the others at their door, then went on up the stairs, Sarah amused by the look on Grania's face as she watched them go.

'She likes you, Jake.'

'Good. I like her, too. And the others.' He smiled at her. 'One way and another I'm going to enjoy this wedding very much.'

Sarah gave him a narrowed look as he closed the door behind him. 'Why?'

'Because your friends are good company and I'll be spending the day with you.' He waved a hand at the bed. 'Or did you imagine I meant the pleasure of sharing that?'

'No. Though you'll have to,' she said, unruffled. 'There's nowhere else to sleep.'

'So I've noticed. Do you snore?'

Sarah laughed. 'I've no idea. Do you?'

'I've never had complaints,' he said blandly, then gave her the familiar laser-beam look. 'Sarah, I know perfectly well you didn't ask to share because you lust after my body. I'll sleep on the floor. It wouldn't be the first time. So don't let worries about tonight spoil your day.'

Sarah went over to Jake and touched a hand to his cheek. 'You're a lovely man, Jake Hogan.'

To her surprise colour rose in his face as he captured the hand and kissed it. 'Thank you kindly, Miss Tracy. No one's ever said that to me before.'

'You amaze me,' she teased. 'Right, while you hang your things up I'll use the bathroom. Though do take a look inside first.'

Jake crossed the room and stood still on the threshold. 'Good*night*!' He went inside to inspect it, then came out looking smug. 'A bit over-dolphined, but the mirror tiles are Pentiles' best, I'm happy to say. Now put a move on, room-mate, I need a shave.'

Sarah had a very quick shower, then emerged in one of the dressing gowns provided by the management. 'Right. Your turn.'

While Jake was in the bathroom Sarah dressed rapidly, then sat down at the dressing table to do her face, and the hair she'd been up before dawn to wash. She brushed the long, in-curving bob into place, threaded her mother's amethyst and pearl drops through her earlobes, checked the toenails painted the night before in the same clover-pink as her dress, then slid her feet into two strips of kid the colour of her suntanned skin. She got up and did a twirl as Jake came out of the bathroom swathed in the other dressing gown.

'Will I do?'

'Oh, yes, Sarah, you'll do,' he said in a tone which brought swift colour to her face.

'Thank you.' She smiled awkwardly. 'I'll read one of the magazines over there while you get dressed.'

Sarah kept her eyes glued to the pages, well aware that it was idiotic to feel so—so what? Shy? Ridiculous. She'd shared a house for years with Nick and Paul, and with other male students staying from time to time. But none of them had ever been more than friends. Whereas Jake Hogan was something else entirely.

'You can look up,' he said in amusement. 'I'm decent now.'

Sarah cast her magazine aside with relief and watched while Jake fastened a waistcoat in charcoal-grey silk, then knotted a matching tie under his gleaming white collar.

'Will *I* do?' he asked, slotting gold cufflinks into place.

She looked him over in approval, from thick, gold-tipped fair hair, to the gleaming toes of his shoes. Jake appealed to her strongly enough in ordinary clothes, but in formal wedding gear he was spectacular. 'Perfect,' she said. And meant it.

Jake gave her a wry glance. 'If only I were, Sarah.' He checked his watch. 'Time you were putting on your hat.'

Sarah removed the lid from the box, and took out a saucer of white straw decorated with loops of stiff white ribbon and a spray of pink rosebuds in a nest of tulle. 'They added the roses after I took my dress to the shop—good match, aren't they?'

'Perfect. It's a very sexy little hat, but how the devil are you going to anchor it on?' said Jake.

'One of the rosebuds is a hatpin in disguise.' Sarah removed it, planted the hat off centre to let a couple of rosebuds trail over one temple, then speared the confection into place. She turned from the mirror, smiling. 'What do you think?'

He looked at her in silence for a moment. 'I'd better not tell you,' he said at last, and trailed a finger down her cheek, leaving a ribbon of fire on her skin. 'On your mark, get set, then.'

Sarah gathered up a small clutch purse, gave Jake a mocking little curtsy, then made for the door. 'Let's go.'

The wedding ceremony was an informal, riotous affair, with a troupe of small bridesmaids and pageboys who required quelling from time to time while Delphine Bartlett was joined in holy matrimony to Nicholas Morrell. But because the bride turned a beaming smile on the miscreants and obviously didn't mind a bit, no one else did, either. Jake, well versed in the ways of small children, was even able to field a small pageboy making a run for it at one stage, and handed him over with a grin to the perspiring father in pursuit.

'Well done,' whispered Sarah, impressed.

'I'm good with children,' he murmured, and took her hand in his again, to Grania's deep approval.

After the general photo-session later, Tom and Ben took a few shots of their own little group, then Jake took the camera to record the group of friends with the bride and groom and the best man.

'Though why the devil did you have to wear such a gigantic hat, Fran?' grumbled Tom, as he tried to stand close on Jake's instructions.

'It's my sister's Ascot hat,' she retorted. 'It was very good of her to lend it to me.'

'Pity she didn't have a cheeky little number like Sarah's!'

By this time the smaller fry in the wedding party were getting out of hand, and Nick and Delphine made a run for the lych gate, laughing and dodging showers of confetti as they dived into the car for the drive to the bride's home for the wedding breakfast.

'Though why it's breakfast in the afternoon, I'll never know,' said Grania as Ben helped her into the car as if she had *Fragile* marked across her forehead. 'Relax, darling. I'm pregnant, not incapable.'

A marquee, which had served two of the bride's sisters in the past, stood waiting in the sunlit garden of the old rectory, which, according to Nick, the Bartletts had been restoring and renovating ever since their marriage, thirty years before.

'Shall I carry you?' Jake asked as he helped Sarah out into the paddock serving as car park. 'Those shoes aren't made for walking, Miss Tracy.'

'The grass is bone-dry, so I'll manage, thanks.' She smiled at him. 'Come on. This is where you get to kiss the bride.'

'It's not the bride I want to kiss,' he muttered, then grinned as the others joined them, demanding the reason for Sarah's hectic colour.

'It's the heat,' she said, avoiding the gleam in Jake's eye.

After a session of kisses and congratulations the bride and groom circulated amongst the guests, so obviously happy and comfortable together Sarah watched them wistfully until she found Jake's hostile eyes trained on her face.

'Wishing you were the bride?' he asked in an undertone.

'Of course I'm not!' she returned tartly. 'Weddings make women sentimental, that's all.'

He leaned so close his breath was hot on her cheek. 'To me it looked as though you were indulging in a little of the hankering you objected to on my part.'

'What are you two murmuring about?' demanded

Frances. 'Can't have you canoodling at this hour. Have some more champagne.'

'Jake thinks I'm feeling miserable because Nick's married at last,' said Sarah, amused to see she'd startled Jake by her bluntness.

'Why on earth should you be miserable?' asked Grania, surprised.

Ben patted her hand indulgently. 'She means Jake's a bit jealous of Sarah's relationship with Nick, darling.'

'Are you, Jake?' demanded Frances, eyes sparkling.

'Yes,' he said candidly.

'No need,' Grania assured him. 'They were always thick as thieves, of course, but both of them went out with other people all the time. Nick used to moan to Sarah about his love life—though I don't think it was a two-way thing. She was never very communicative about herself.' She smiled. 'She's certainly kept you a dark secret.'

'Would you kindly stop talking about me as though I wasn't here?' complained Sarah, and eyed Jake militantly. 'Happy now?'

'If he's not,' said Tom with a suggestive wink, 'you can always make it up to him later.'

To Sarah's relief the bride and groom chose that moment to join them.

'You look pretty gorgeous, Sal,' said Nick. 'Doesn't she, Jake?'

'Absolutely,' agreed Jake, deadpan, then turned to the bride. 'So do you, Mrs Morrell. I wish you every happiness.'

'Thank you so much.' Delphine exchanged a luminous look with Nick. 'Every time someone calls me Mrs Morrell I get this funny feeling here.' She touched the pearl-embroidered silk at his midriff.

'Me too,' her new husband assured her dotingly.

'You're a very lucky man, Nick,' said Sarah, and gave Delphine a kiss. 'You won't mind if I say I think you're lucky too?'

Later, in the marquee, Tom and Ben switched the place cards so that Sarah sat between them at their table, leaving Jake opposite between their wives.

'Don't be cross; they don't see her very often these days,' said Grania, correctly interpreting the look on Jake's face.

'How could I object with you and Frances for company?' he said, smiling.

When the speeches were over and the cake cut, the top table was cleared away to make room for dancing to records played by a local disc jockey. The bride and groom took to the floor to much affectionate applause, and waltzed slowly and inexpertly round the floor. This time Sarah made sure she displayed no sign of the wistfulness Jake had misunderstood earlier.

When the bridal pair came to a halt the waltz gave way to an old Fred Astaire number, and some of the older guests promptly took to the floor to dance to something familiar while they had the chance.

Jake got up and came round the table to Sarah. 'Dance with me?'

Because her hat had been taken for safe-keeping to the car before the meal, they could have danced cheek to cheek, in tune with the song. But constraint still lingered between them, until at last Sarah raised her head to meet the brooding blue eyes.

'I'm not, you know,' she said, very distinctly.

'Hankering?' He almost tripped her up as he missed a step.

'Yes. At least, not after Nick.' She met his eyes very

deliberately and felt her pulse leap as his lashes dropped to hide his blaze of reaction.

'You mean that?' he muttered into her hair.

Sarah nodded mutely, and moved closer into arms which tightened in response.

From then on the evening was pure bliss for Sarah. She danced once each with Tom and Ben, and even boogied wildly with Nick at one stage, when the music hotted up later in the evening. But for the rest of the time Jake kept her close, either on the dance floor, or sitting with an openly possessive arm round her at the table, to the great satisfaction of Frances and Grania. At last a fanfare blared over the amplifiers and Nick and Delphine reappeared, dressed in travelling clothes.

'Tell us where you're going?' yelled someone.

'Unspecified destination,' said Nick, laughing, then took his bride by the hand and hurried her out to the car, where two sets of parents were waiting to make sure that nothing objectionable was added to the usual assortment of balloons and old boots.

Grania heaved a sentimental sigh as they waved the happy pair off. 'I know the honeymoon's in Mauritius, but I wonder where they're going tonight?'

'Nick said he'd booked the most romantic hotel he could find,' said Sarah.

'He's always told Sarah everything,' said Frances, and patted Jake's hand. 'But don't worry. That's bound to change from now on.'

Jake smiled at her appreciatively, and took Sarah's hand. 'Want to dance some more?'

She glanced at the others—at Grania, drooping against Ben, and Frances, yawning widely. 'Whatever happened to the gang who could party all night?' she teased.

'It's late, it's hellish hot, and we got married!' said Ben. 'Come on, mother of my child. Past your bedtime.'

'Mine too,' yawned Tom.

They said their farewells to the bride's parents, then, due to Grania's current dislike of breakfast, the group arranged to meet in the Greenacres bar at eleven the following morning for coffee before going their separate ways.

'That all went very well,' said Sarah, as she got in the car. 'I can't thank you enough for coming with me, Jake. It made all the difference.'

'No thanks necessary,' he assured her. 'It was a great wedding. Even the speeches were short.'

'Though Nick's was surprisingly sentimental. He's more the flip one-liner type normally.'

'Ah, but he's never been a bridegroom before.'

Back at the hotel they went up in the lift with Ben and Grania, who by this time was speechless with fatigue and heat. When the doors opened on the top floor Ben scooped his wife up in his arms and, with a grinning goodnight to Sarah and Jake, bore his tired, waving little burden off to their room.

'Are you as tired as Grania?' asked Jake, following Sarah up the stairs.

'No. Just terribly hot. But then, I'm not pregnant. At her stage expectant mothers need all the sleep they can get. Even more after the baby arrives,' she added ruefully.

'As you know from experience,' he said, unlocking the door.

In their room lamps were lit and the covers turned down on the bed. Averting her eyes from it, Sarah packed her hat away in its box, then sank down on the settle and with a sigh of relief kicked off the new sandals. 'I may not be as exhausted as Grania, but I'm so hot I couldn't have danced any more tonight.'

'I'm not surprised,' he said, eyeing the tall slender heels. 'How can you even walk in those beats me, let alone dance.'

'It's a girl thing,' she said, laughing.

Jake smiled as she waggled pink-tipped toes. 'You have very pretty feet, Sarah.'

'Really? I'd never thought of feet as pretty, mine or anyone else's.' She looked at them in surprise, then up at Jake. 'It's hot in here. The new bridal suite obviously doesn't run to air-conditioning. Don't you want to get out of that coat?'

'Urgently. But it seemed over-familiar, somehow, to start stripping the moment we came through the door.'

'Go ahead,' she said, curling up as he began to hang his finery away. 'Jake?' she added, once he was down to shirtsleeves.

'Yes, ma'am.' He smiled at her encouragingly.

'We need to talk finances.'

'Why?'

She waved a hand at the room. 'This must be hugely expensive.'

His eyes glittered menacingly. 'Don't even think of offering to share costs.'

'Why not? I would have paid for the other room.'

'But you're not paying for this one.'

Sarah glowered at him. 'Then you can forget about going halves with the wedding present.'

Jake closed the wardrobe door and leaned against it, arms folded, belligerence in every line of him. 'I fail to see why.'

'It's only fair.'

He stared at her in frustration for a moment, then shrugged. 'All right. But I win over the room.'

'OK.' Sarah smiled at him cajolingly. 'Though it makes the next bit awkward, Jake.'

'Go on,' he said, eyes narrowed.

'I'm desperately thirsty. So if I ask to have something sent up will you at least let me pay for drinks?'

'You don't have to.' With a triumphant smile Jake opened the end cupboard door to reveal a small refrigerator and a shelf full of glasses. 'I investigated while you were in the bath earlier on. How about some champagne?'

'I was thinking more of mineral water!'

'There's some of that, too. You can have it later. The champagne's only a half-bottle, so your share won't knock you out. I'll even let you ruin it with fruit juice if you like.'

'How kind!'

Jake half filled a champagne flute and topped it up with orange juice, poured a glass of wine for himself, then opened the windows to the sultry night before he sat down on the chair drawn up to Sarah's settle. 'I think we've toasted the bride and groom well and truly already, so this one's for us,' he said, touching his glass to hers.

'To us,' repeated Sarah, and sipped her drink. 'Mmm, lovely. In fact the entire day was lovely, Jake. Except for one particular incident,' she added tartly.

He shrugged. 'Sorry about that. You were looking at Nick with such yearning in your eyes I was jealous as hell.'

'It was envy, not yearning, Jake.' She drained her glass and put it down on the table. 'Nick's the last of my crowd to get married, which leaves me as the only single one left. For a moment I couldn't help envying the security the others take for granted in their relationships.'

Jake nodded slowly. 'Whereas you bring Davy up alone.'

Sarah reached out to touch his hand. 'Which is no hardship, Jake, I assure you. Blame my split-second of envy on wedding-day emotion. I was back on course right away, I promise.'

'Good. By the way, talking of Davy, she told me that Polly's dad is running in the fathers' race on sports day,' said Jake, the sudden change of subject startling Sarah considerably.

'She didn't tell me there was a fathers' race—oh, *no*!' She eyed him in alarm. 'I suppose that means there's a mothers' race, too.'

'Oh, yes. And Davy's entered you for it.' Jake's lips twitched. 'That's not all. At the Rogers' lunch she suggested I run in the fathers' race with Don, but I had to explain that, not being a father, I wasn't eligible.'

'Good heavens!' said Sarah, astounded. 'She never said a word to me, the monkey. Sorry she put you on the spot like that.'

'*I'm* not sorry. I took it as a good sign.'

'Of what?'

'That she approves of me, possibly even likes me. Which,' added Jake, putting his glass down, 'brings me to a subject I've been waiting for the right time to discuss.'

'What is it?' she said warily.

His eyes locked on Sarah's. 'When I booked this room I didn't foresee that you'd be sharing it with me. But now you're a captive audience I have something to say. So listen, Sarah.'

'For heaven's sake, Jake,' she said impatiently, 'you're making me nervous. Just say it, whatever it is.'

He stood up abruptly, something in his attitude sending Sarah's heart racing with apprehension by the time he spoke.

'You must know that I'm in love with you,' he said at last, taking her breath away. 'And I believe you're not indifferent to me, either. Is that true?'

Sarah nodded mutely, her eyes fixed on his.

'I've thought about this a lot,' he went on. 'And it's obvious you won't allow yourself anything warmer than friendship with me, or even let yourself respond to me normally, because of what happened first time round.'

'But—'

He held up a hand. 'Let me finish. With you I want—need—so much more than friendship.' Jake breathed in deeply, a pulse throbbing beside his mouth. 'I know I said brave things about being satisfied with whatever relationship you wanted. But the kind *I* want, darling, is marriage.'

CHAPTER NINE

BECAUSE her heart was pounding and the room was very warm, Sarah sat perfectly still, needing all her energy just to breathe. 'You say you've given this thought,' she said at last.

Jake sat down again, long legs outstretched, the animation draining from his face. 'Do I take that as a no?'

She gave him a long, troubled look. 'Have you taken Davy into consideration?'

'Of course I have.'

'But you're only thirty years old, Jake. Which is pretty young to take on a nine-year-old child.'

'Older than you,' he pointed out.

'That's different.'

'I know. You're her mother. But, unlike your defecting friend, I'm sure I could make a good stepfather. I like Davy. And maybe I don't shape up to Don Rogers in her eyes, but I think she likes me. Or could do, given the chance to get to know me.' He turned to look at her. 'You won't expose Davy to any temporary arrangement with a man in case she gets hurt. I understand that. But in this case temporary doesn't come into it. I want you for keeps, Sarah. Both of you.'

Sarah blinked, then blinked again more rapidly, but tears poured down her cheeks, and, lacking something to mop them up, she knuckled them from her eyes and gave a loud, unromantic sniff.

Jake got up to fetch a container of tissues from the

bathroom. 'Compliments of the management,' he said, handing it to her.

Sarah mopped her eyes, blew her nose, then gave him a damp smile of apology. 'Sorry about that. I don't do tears much.'

Jake swung her feet to the floor and sat down, putting his arm round her shoulders. 'I didn't mean to make you cry. And if the thought of marrying me affects you like that perhaps we'd better forget all about it.'

Easier said than done, thought Sarah despairingly. Until he'd brought the subject up she'd had no idea she wanted to marry Jake. Or hadn't allowed herself to consider the possibility.

'If we did marry,' she began, tensing as she felt his arm tighten, 'wouldn't your family find it strange you'd chosen a woman with a child, rather than a more conventional bride?'

'I've no idea,' he said, shrugging. 'If you were past the age of having more children it would be different. But you're what? Twenty-seven?'

She nodded.

He raised her face to his, giving the smile that did such damage to her defences. 'I'm sure we could provide Davy with a couple of siblings with no trouble at all, my darling.'

It wasn't fair, she thought in anguish. The endearment, reinforced by a clamouring voice in her head which urged her to say yes, was hard to fight. Suddenly her resistance vanished, and she yielded to the arms which closed round her. Why should she fight? It would be so good to have a man in her life. And not just any man, but one she could trust, and who was happy to include Davy in his proposal.

'Jake,' she said at last, raising her head. 'I know this

isn't the answer you deserve, but would you give me a little time to think it over?'

He gave her a searching look, then shook his head. 'I'd like to be noble and say take as much time as you want. But if you're going to turn me down I'd rather you did it now—made it a clean break.'

Sarah felt a rush of pure dismay. 'So if I say no that's it? Over and out?'

'I want you for my wife, Sarah, with everything the word implies. I won't settle for anything less.' His eyes darkened. 'Do you feel anything for me at all?'

'You know very well that I do,' she said with heat, and detached herself from his hold. 'In fact, I can't think straight when I'm so close to you.'

'Which is encouraging,' he said wryly as she stood up.

'Jake,' said Sarah with sudden decision. 'If you'll wait until morning I'll give you my answer then.'

'A recipe for a sleepless night, if ever I heard one! Not,' added Jake, heaving a sigh, 'that it was going to be restful anyway.' He got up and gave her a swift, hard kiss. 'Go on. You take the bathroom first. In the meantime I shall pitch my tent.'

Sarah gave him a grateful smile. 'Thank you, Jake.'

'What for this time?'

'For the proposal. It's my first.'

He narrowed his eyes at her. 'And last, too, if I have anything to do with it.'

When Sarah came out of the bathroom, feeling desperately hot in the hotel dressing gown over her cotton nightshirt, Jake had set up a makeshift bed on the floor, with blankets and a pillow.

'That looks horribly uncomfortable,' she said, eyeing

it guiltily. 'This is all my fault. I shouldn't have asked to share.'

'I could hardly make the suggestion myself,' he pointed out. 'But the moment I heard Grania was expecting a baby I began trying to work out some way of giving her my room without embarrassing you.'

She grinned. 'It would have been pretty hard for Grania and Frances to swallow that we weren't sleeping together.'

'Why?'

'Because they think you're a charmer, and sexy with it!'

'I only wish you shared their enthusiasm,' he said dryly.

Sarah gave him a wry little smile. 'Actually, I do.'

With a growl Jake started towards her, stopped dead, then turned on his heel and strode off to the bathroom, slamming the door shut behind him.

Sarah took off the dressing gown and slid under the covers, then turned off the lamp at her side of the bed. This, she thought despondently, was going to be a long, long night. She felt hot and restless, but forced herself to keep very still when Jake crossed the room to turn off the other lamp. She waited, perspiration beading her upper lip. And knew she had no earthly right to feel disappointed when he let himself down on the floor instead of sliding into bed with her.

Convinced that heat and tension would keep her awake all night, Sarah lay so still that eventually she dozed, only to wake with a violent start as the room lit up and thunder rolled. The curtains blew out into the room on a gush of hot wind as rain sheeted down outside, and she lay rigid, heart hammering, determined not to make a sound. But when the storm moved ominously closer she burrowed under the pillows to shut out the lightning which lit up the room. They were insulation neither against the noise, nor against her gasp of fright. Jake got up to close the windows against the rain blowing in, then switched on the lamp. He sat on the edge of the bed, removed the pillows and pulled Sarah into his arms.

'Are you all right?' he asked, smoothing her hair as she hid her face against his bare chest.

'No, I'm not!' she wailed as another crack of thunder shook the room.

'Don't worry. There's a lightning conductor on the roof,' he said into her ear. 'You're shivering. Are you cold?'

She shook her head vehemently. 'Anything but. Sorry about this, Jake. I'd better shut myself in the bathroom until it's over.'

'There's a window in there, too,' he pointed out. 'Festooned with dolphins, but not lightning-proof.'

Sarah gave a smothered scream as lightning forked through the room a split-second before thunder cracked overhead. She clung on to Jake for dear life, and he went rigid for a moment, then laid her back down on the bed.

Sarah gazed up at him beseechingly. 'Don't leave me!'

Jake looked down at her, jaw clenched, then he slid in beside her, drew her into his arms, tucked her head against his shoulder and pulled the sheet over them both. 'Is that better?'

'Better' didn't begin to describe it, thought Sarah as another crack of thunder propelled her against him. 'Much better,' she whispered against his throat.

Jake lay motionless as an effigy, but Sarah felt heat baking from his body into hers, and her heart thumped when she registered that his only covering was a pair of thin cotton boxers. Which were no disguise for his arousal.

When another crack of thunder sent her burrowing closer Jake groaned and tried to thrust her away, but Sarah clung to him with such desperation his control abruptly snapped. His arms closed round her like steel bands, making it impossible for her to flinch away. He kissed her hungrily, savagely, his mouth ravaging hers as though the elements had stripped away the charm to leave the basic man in command. His lips and tongue demanded a response she gave with such abandon the breath tore through his chest as his pillaging mouth left hers to move down her throat. His hands slid up her thighs to caress the outline of her hips and waist, then he stripped the nightshirt over her head and tossed it on the floor. Lying propped on an elbow, Jake hung over her, his fingers tracing a path from her parted mouth to her thighs, the silence broken only by their rapid breathing now the storm had begun to move away. Sarah knew that he was giving her the opportunity to change her mind, to draw back as she always had long before this stage was reached. But for the first time it was different. She wanted this. She wanted Jake. When she held up her arms in fierce entreaty his eyes lit with such heat her breath caught as his hands slid upwards to cup her breasts and lift them to his hungry mouth.

'Jake, I must—' she gasped, but he swung his body over hers and stifled her words with a kiss so explicit it sent everything out of her head.

'Don't stop me now, darling,' he breathed against her lips. 'I want you so much it hurts. But I want you to need this as much as I do.'

He went on kissing her, and she gave a stifled moan

as his mouth moved down to join the fingers caressing her breasts. Sarah shivered at the almost unbearable feelings he was plucking from deep inside her as he pulled on each sensitised nipple, igniting all the need he could ever want. Jake slid a hand between her thighs to find the hot, liquid proof of it, and drew in a deep, unsteady breath of pure satisfaction, his eyes holding hers as his long, expert fingers caused waves of sensation which flooded her with such hot, throbbing pleasure she choked back a scream, then lay with astonished eyes still locked with his as the aftershocks faded. He smiled triumphantly and kissed her parted mouth, then slid over her to lie between her thighs.

'Jake—' she tried again, but he laid a finger on her lips.

'Do you want me?' he demanded.

'*Yes*. Desperately—but I've never done this before!' she blurted.

Jake stared at her in utter disbelief. He would have pulled away, but Sarah revolved her hips against his in fierce demand. 'This is how much I want you,' she said through her teeth. 'So, having got this far, you'd better make love to me now or I'll go mad. *Please!*'

Jake needed no second bidding. He entered her with a smooth thrust she responded to with a sharp intake of breath at the small, tearing pain of it. His head flew up, but Sarah smiled up into his questioning eyes and locked her hands behind his neck. 'Don't stop!'

'I can't,' he groaned, and moved inside her. Sarah made a relishing little sound of appreciation, discovering that pain had been replaced by pleasure which grew fiercer and hotter as Jake made love to her with all the skill at his command. Her emotions heightened by the storm, Sarah responded with such fervour to the unfamiliar bliss of possession that his careful expertise quickly deserted him, and he crushed her close as they surged together towards fulfilment which overtook him long before he'd intended, and he lay gasping in her arms in the throes of a climax he knew she hadn't shared.

'Darling, I'm *sorry*,' he groaned, and rubbed his cheek against hers in contrition.

Sarah gave him a lazy, exultant smile. 'Don't be. One each. Only fair.'

Jake laughed deep in his throat, and smoothed the damp hair away from her forehead. 'Next time,' he promised, 'we'll make it together.'

He rolled over onto his back and drew her against him, one hand smoothing her hair as their heartbeats slowed. Sarah felt such a wave of love for him she heaved in a deep, tremulous sigh and reached up to kiss him.

'Thank you,' he whispered. 'Was that for anything in particular?'

'Your extraordinary forbearance.'

Jake turned his head to look at her, making no attempt to misunderstand. 'I love you, Sarah. And I admit I'm poleaxed. Neither of which entitles me to ask questions you're not ready to answer.'

'Yes, it does,' she said at once, and smiled at him. 'If we are going to marry—'

'No doubt about it,' he assured her with arrogance.

'Then you deserve an explanation.'

Jake looked at her in silence for a moment. His eyes, reverted now to their normal colour, were thoughtful. 'I won't deny that part of me is burning with curiosity, my darling. But before any explanations let's have a drink and just relax for a while.'

Sarah agreed gratefully. Her emotions were running so high it seemed a good idea to calm down for a while before she told him the truth about Davy. 'Only I'll have that mineral water this time.'

Jake pulled the sheet over her, then went to the drinks cupboard and filled two glasses with a mixture of mineral water and fruit juice.

'Nothing stronger for you?' Sarah said, surprised.

Jake sat beside her and leaned against the pillows, smiling into her eyes. 'No. I'm intoxicated enough already.'

She gave him a speaking look of thanks, drained the glass quickly, set it down on the bedside table, then wriggled close to him. 'It's been a very eventful day.'

Jake finished his own drink, then put his arms round her. 'And night,' he added, rubbing his cheek over her hair. 'And just in case you have any doubts I'm spending the rest of it right here in this bed. With you.'

'Of course you are.' She smiled up at him. 'Because you don't snore, Jake. At least you haven't done so far.'

He grinned. 'Probably because I haven't been to sleep.'

'No wonder. It must have been horribly uncomfortable on the floor,' she said with sympathy.

'That was only a contributory factor. The real reason for my insomnia was right here, in this bed but out of reach.' Jake kissed her. 'How did you expect me to sleep in those circumstances?'

'I'm not out of reach now,' she pointed out.

'No,' he agreed huskily, and pulled her closer. 'Are you tired, darling?'

'Not in the least,' she said, surprised to find she was right. 'I thought people went straight to sleep after making love.'

'We obviously haven't made love enough yet,' he said promptly, and Sarah laughed.

'If you're going to make love to me again, Jake—'

'No if about it!'

'Then I'd like a shower first.'

'Brilliant idea.' He slid out of bed and held out his hand.

In spite of sharing the ultimate intimacy with Jake only minutes before, Sarah felt irrationally shy as she slid naked from the bed. Colour flooded her face when her nipples hardened in response to his caressing gaze. His breathing suddenly rapid, Jake picked her up and carried her into the bathroom to set her on her feet in the shower stall. He turned on the spray and held her close against him, kissing her as he smoothed scented gel over her hot, wet body, and Sarah did the same for him in return, no longer shy at all. He groaned like a man in pain as her seeking hands brought him to full arousal, and he switched off the spray and parted her thighs with an invading knee. They clung together in hot, wet contact as they kissed with increasing wildness, until at last Jake tore his mouth away, snatched up a towel to dry her with unsteady, urgent hands, then carried her back to bed.

They surged together at once, all preliminaries swept aside. Mouth to mouth, hands entwined, their bodies fused together in a union Jake fought to keep slow and gradual. But soon Sarah was overwhelmed by the pulsing reality of her first climax, and, feeling her innermost muscles clenched round him, Jake released his control and collapsed on her, gasping endearments against her parted mouth.

It was a long time before either of them had the breath

or inclination to speak. At last Jake turned over on his back and pulled Sarah close.

'This,' he said gruffly, 'is where one asks how was it for you?'

She smiled up at him, her gold-flecked eyes glittering in the lamplight. 'Does one?'

'I thought you might be unfamiliar with the protocol. In the circumstances,' he added, pulling her higher so he could kiss her.

'Because I'm new at it, you mean.'

'Precisely. An extraordinary, glorious fact I'm still trying to take in.' He let out a deep, unsteady breath. 'I'm very grateful to the storm for making you seduce me.'

Sarah reared up in indignation. 'Is that what I did?'

'In a way.' Jake smoothed her tumbled hair, his eyes suddenly sober. 'I wouldn't have initiated this myself, darling. Not tonight, anyway.'

'Why not?'

'Because I was damned if I'd take advantage of the situation.'

'Halo problems again,' she chuckled, and rubbed her cheek against his bare shoulder. 'You're one of a kind, Jake Hogan.'

He glowered at her. 'I'm not, you know.'

'All right, all right. I won't talk about halos again.'

'Good. Because human failings are beginning to get the better of me right now.'

'Curiosity?'

'Absolutely.' Jake sat up, rearranged the pillows and held out his arms.

Sarah slid into them with a sigh of pleasure as he drew the sheet over them. 'At least you can now understand why I wouldn't—couldn't let myself respond to you,

Jake.' She looked up at him with sombre eyes. 'In college it was no problem to duck out of all the bed-hopping the others were involved in. Nor with anyone since. But with you, for the first time, I wanted this almost from the start. Even though it meant letting you into the secret I've never shared with anyone.'

'I still can't take it in,' Jake said, equally grave, and kissed her gently. 'Davy's so like you I just can't believe she's not your child.'

Sarah's eyes filled with unshed tears. 'She is mine in every way that matters, Jake, just not my actual daughter. Davina Anne Tracy is my sister.'

CHAPTER TEN

'YOUR *sister*?' Jake stared at Sarah incredulously, then slid out of bed, shrugged on the robe and fetched the tissues, holding her in his arms while he blotted her eyes with such tender care the tears overflowed.

'Sorry, sorry.' She rubbed her wet face against his chest. 'Tears twice in one night. Personal best for S. Tracy.'

Jake waited until she was calmer, then fetched a shot glass from the minibar. 'Medicinal cognac. Down with it, darling.'

Sarah drank the mouthful of fiery spirit, and felt better as the warmth spread through her. She coughed a little as she handed Jake the glass. 'Thank you. Though I hate the stuff—I hate to think of your hotel bill in the morning, too.'

He said something rude about the bill, then got back into bed beside her. 'Sarah,' he said firmly, as she curled up against him, 'if it makes you unhappy, don't tell me any more.'

She touched a hand to his cheek in gratitude, but shook her head. 'I want you to know everything, Jake. And I won't cry again. Promise.'

The story began one bleak January day with a funeral. David Tracy had just gone back from leave to the work he was doing on a hotel construction in Malaysia, and because Sarah had been back in school after the Christmas holidays, and working hard for exams, Anne had left her in Campden Road with her grandmother and made the long journey to Cumbria alone.

'When she was doing her teacher training,' Sarah told Jake, 'my mother had a friend called Tony Barrett. They were very close, rather like Nick and me. Best of friends. They went to each other's weddings, and the two couples got on well together. For years Tony brought his wife Lisa to visit us, and we went up to Cumbria to visit them.'

Anne Tracy had gone to see Lisa Barrett twice during her long, protracted illness, and the moment Tony rang to say his wife had finally died Anne had set off for Cumbria again. After the funeral, when all the guests and relatives had gone, Tony had begged Anne to stay on for a day or so to help him sort through his wife's belongings. The first night alone in the house together, when he'd gone to her room in desperate distress, her only thought had been to comfort him.

'My mother was small, and Tony Barrett was a big man,' said Sarah without inflection. 'And due to his wife's illness he'd been celibate for a very long time.'

'So the inevitable happened,' said Jake quietly.

Tony Barrett had been wild with remorse afterwards, and Anne Tracy, sick with misery and guilt over the entire episode, had driven home at first light, determined to block it out and never think of it again.

'I was shaping up for A-levels, and too taken up with my own concerns for a while to notice that my mother was quieter than usual after she came back,' Sarah said remorsefully.

But eventually Sarah had noticed, and grown worried. Anne had looked haggard from loss of sleep, and tried so hard to be bright and animated Sarah had known that underneath something was terribly wrong.

'So I demanded to know if she had cancer, like Lisa Barrett.' Sarah heaved a sigh. 'It shocked her into telling me she was pregnant. At first I was so relieved to know she wasn't terminally ill I couldn't understand why she was in such a state about being pregnant. She was only thirty-nine. Finally she broke down, and told me that not only was Tony Barrett to blame, but that she'd had such a bad time when I was born that my father insisted on a vasectomy. It was the thought of telling him which was killing her.'

'God,' said Jake, wincing. 'What a situation.'

Margaret Parker had been appalled when Anne finally confessed the truth, and in her frantic desire to avoid scandal had instantly advised abortion. But Anne, who'd had strong beliefs on the subject, hadn't been able to bear the thought of that. But she hadn't been able to bear the thought of causing her husband so much hurt, either, and had become so distraught that the entire subject had had to be dropped for a while.

'Grandma insisted on moving in with us during that awful time,' said Sarah. 'She told me she was afraid to leave Mother alone while I was in school, but, looking back, I'm sure she used the time to keep hammering at her to get rid of the baby.'

'Your father wasn't told?' asked Jake.

'No. In spite of my grandmother's attitude, Mother was looking and feeling much better by the time he came home on leave. Grandma went back to Campden Road, and my parents were so happy just to be together again Mother couldn't bear to spoil things for Dad. Before he went back to Malaysia he told her he intended to see the job out before he came home again, which meant autumn at the earliest. Normally Mother would have been in despair at the long parting, but for once she was relieved.'

'Did she see a doctor?' asked Jake.

Sarah shook her head. 'We lived in a small village where everyone knew everyone else. My father was born and brought up there, and the doctor was his personal friend.'

Jake was silent for a moment, frowning. 'All this was a heavy load for a teenager to cope with, Sarah.'

'Even heavier for my mother, Jake.'

The unwanted baby had been due to arrive some time in early autumn, and the moment Sarah finished her exams that June Margaret Parker had insisted the three of them went off to Cornwall for the rest of the summer.

'We did that every year anyway,' said Sarah. 'Polruan Cottage stood on its own, a fair way out of the nearest village, and although even by that stage Mother didn't look pregnant, she refused to go a step farther than the garden. I'm convinced she'd persuaded herself that because she didn't want the baby she'd miscarry and Dad would never have to know.'

'But surely she was in need of medical attention?'

Sarah nodded. 'That was part of Grandma's reason for moving us down there once abortion was no longer a possibility. It was her home turf, and her oldest friend had once been a midwife. Mrs Treharne was let in on the secret, sworn to silence, and checked on Mother regularly. Life got easier after that.'

The advent of Jenna Treharne had been very necessary one evening in July, when, right in the middle of a violent thunderstorm, it had seemed that Anne's wish was about to be granted and she'd gone into premature labour. Deaf to her patient's protests, Jenna had called am ambulance and accompanied Anne and Margaret in it to the hospital in Truro, leaving Sarah, who had not long passed her driving test, to follow them alone in her grandmother's car, not only rigid with terror when lightning forked around her as she drove through the rain, but desperately afraid her mother would be dead before she got to the hospital. But it had been hours later when Anne Tracy, exhausted and in need of a blood transfusion, gave birth to her daughter. And though baby Davina had been a couple of pounds lighter than she would have weighed full-term, she'd been in remarkably good shape otherwise.

'Mother was kept in hospital while Davy had a stay in an incubator before they were discharged,' said Sarah. 'And after they got back to Polruan Cottage the baby was fine. Mother was the problem.'

Because her closest friends knew about the vasectomy Anne had been in despair about returning to her own home with a baby. She'd been in a poor state physically after the birth, and mentally at such a low ebb that Jenna had given dire warnings of clinical depression, and worse. So Margaret had taken complete charge of Anne while Sarah looked after the baby right from the first, taking the hard work involved in her stride. Because she'd been young and fit Sarah had soon got used to broken nights, and nappy changes, and the endless round of sterilising and making up bottle feeds. It had been the arguments with her grandmother which were hardest to bear, because Margaret Parker had kept urging Anne to have the baby adopted.

'By that time,' said Sarah, 'I felt that Davina belonged to me. My baby. I couldn't bear the idea of adoption. Nor could my mother. Then my grandmother said something that made it all so simple.'

'What was that, sweetheart?' asked Jake, holding her closer.

'In one of her outbursts she said it would have been far better if the baby had been mine. There would have been tongue-wagging, but because I was so young it would have been accepted more easily—by my father as well as everyone else.' Sarah breathed in deeply. 'Afterwards, when my mother was asleep, Grandma persuaded me to claim Davy as mine. Somehow she'd got it into her head that I was to blame for everything. That if I had gone to Cumbria with Mother, instead of insisting on staying home to study, none of it would have happened.'

'How on earth did she work that one out?' said Jake, incensed.

'She wasn't very rational at the time. But once I'd thought it over I decided for myself that it was the best thing to do. Not,' added Sarah fiercely, 'for my grandmother's sake, but for my mother and father and their marriage. So next day I went to register Davy's birth, and the registrar took it for granted I was the mother anyway. Which means the birth certificate reads: ''Mother—Sarah Anne Tracy. Father—blank.'''

'What a crazily brave thing to do.' Jake looked down at her in wonder. 'You do know that giving false information like that is illegal?'

'My mother's name was Sarah Anne, like me. She called herself Anne. So it seemed almost right…'

Jake shook his head. 'And no one ever questioned it?'

'My mother went up like a rocket. For a while I was terrified I'd sent her over the edge. But after endless arguments I hit below the belt and pointed out the grief it would save my father. And because of my grandmother's desperate urging Mother, who was in no fit state to put up a fight, finally capitulated. Though not without a long list of conditions, mainly about my education. As for my reception back home—' Sarah shrugged. 'I'd had a struggle with my weight as a teenager. So when I returned from Cornwall with a baby, weighing a stone less due to stress and sheer hard work, it caused the expected stir, but no one ever doubted that Davy was mine.'

Jake rubbed his cheek over her hair. 'But you'd been born and brought up in your village, too, darling. Didn't you mind?'

'Of course I did. But I didn't have a boyfriend, so I knew no blame could be attached to anyone. And I'd already left school. But I admit it hurt badly when my so-called best friend took off in a huff because I refused to tell her about Davy's father.' Sarah shrugged. 'But none of that was important against saving my parents' marriage. I cancelled my gap year *au pair* job in France, and because my mother was still so fragile I looked after Davy myself. So from the day she was born she was all mine.'

The worst part for Sarah, once Davy had safely arrived, had been writing to her father to give him news which, however well-intentioned, was nevertheless a lie. But David Tracy had rung the moment he had her letter, accepted Sarah's refusal to name the father, and assured his daughter of his love and support, and his willingness to help Anne with the baby as long as Sarah agreed to take up her college place, as planned. By the time he'd eventually come home for good Anne had fully recovered physically, and was so happy to be reunited with her husband that, all too aware of the alternative, she'd finally achieved total acceptance of Sarah's quixotic gesture.

'And, seeing them so happy together, I never regretted it for a minute,' said Sarah. 'For that first year I insisted on looking after Davy full-time, but Mother took over when I went to university, and with Dad's help looked after her baby herself—as she'd wanted to all along. It was a terrible wrench for me to leave Davy, but I was normal teenager enough to enjoy the usual student scene once I was part of it. Though I went home a lot more often than the friends I made because I couldn't bear to be parted long from Davy.' She smiled up at Jake. 'She adored my parents, but *I* was Mummy.'

Sarah had eventually achieved her English degree, and returned to live at home while she followed it up with a computer course. Eventually she'd got a job in a software firm, and shared Davy with her parents.

'Then when she was five they went on holiday and never came back. They were killed when the coach transferring them from hotel to airport crashed. And my life changed completely. Left with full responsibility for Davy, I had to sell the family home, which had been mortgaged to put me through college and pay Davy's school fees, so it didn't fetch as much as expected. It just gave me a bit of a cushion in the bank, so I could take a part-time job, but we had to move in with my grandmother. Which wasn't an ideal situation for either of us, but it won her no end of brownie points with her friends. The rest you know.' Sarah gave a sudden, inelegant yawn. 'Sorry, Jake! Confession may be good for the soul, but it's jolly tiring.'

'It's been a long, eventful day,' said Jake, settling her close against him. 'It's an amazing story, Sarah. But just one more thing. Was this Tony Barrett ever told about Davy?'

Sarah shook her head. 'No. It was one of the conditions Mother made when I wouldn't let her tell Dad the truth. But because she refused to have anything to do with him afterwards I always felt sorry for him, so maybe one day, when Davy's old enough to cope with the truth herself, I'll leave it to her to decide whether she wants to get in touch with Tony.' She smiled ruefully. 'He doesn't have any children, so there's no gothic-novel possibility of Davy falling in love with her brother one day.'

When Sarah woke the sky was just getting light, and she was still held fast in Jake's arms. She moved a little, his lashes flew up and his eyes, vividly blue in the morning light, lit up as they met hers.

'Good morning,' she whispered.

'A fantastic morning,' he agreed, kissing her nose. 'Did you sleep well?'

'I must have done. I've only just surfaced. So you obviously don't snore.'

'Of course I don't. You don't, either.'

'That's a relief.' She stretched luxuriously, and felt him tense against her.

'If you do that,' he warned in a constricted tone, 'there could be consequences.'

Sarah looked up into the darkening blue eyes, and smiled into them as she deliberately stretched again.

Jake gave a stifled laugh and held her closer. 'Tell me, Miss Tracy, what are your views on making love by dawn's early light?'

'I don't have any, Mr Hogan—yet,' she said provocatively.

'Something I'd better put right, then. Another first,' he added with blatantly male satisfaction, and began to pay slow, subtle attention to every inch of her until Sarah made it passionately clear she could endure the delicious agony no longer, and Jake surged inside her to take her on a fiery, gasping quest for the rapture they achieved almost in unison.

It was a long time before either of them spoke afterwards, but at last Jake raised his head. 'Well?' he demanded.

Sarah let out a deep, unsteady breath. 'I now realise why the others were so keen on this.'

'The others?'

'The other students I knew. Those you've met, and a lot more besides. I was the only one who kept my bed strictly to myself.'

Jake propped himself up on an elbow to look down into her face. 'You must have had a few problems with that?'

'Quite a lot, at first. But eventually it was taken for granted that my experience with Davy was the problem.' Sarah smiled up at him. 'You're the only one who knows the truth.'

Jake trailed a caressing finger down her cheek. 'I still can't believe I was your first lover. I thought I was dreaming when—'

'When I ordered you to make love to me?'

'Orders I was deliriously happy to obey!' Jake kissed her at length, then rubbed his cheek against hers. 'Tell me you love me.'

Her dark eyes narrowed ominously. 'If I didn't, Jake Hogan, none of this would have happened in the first place. Storm or no storm.'

'Tell me just the same,' he commanded.

To Sarah's embarrassment shyness overtook her again. 'I love you,' she muttered, eyes falling.

'Again.'

She stared up at him resentfully. 'If you keep on making me say it I might change my mind.'

'In which case,' said Jake very softly, 'I'd have to resort to measures to change it back.'

The mere thought of the measures he had in mind hurried Sarah's breathing. Then her stomach gave a loud, embarrassing grumble, and he threw back his head and laughed.

'You're hungry!' Jake bent his tousled head to kiss the place which protested. His lips lingered, moved downward, then stopped abruptly.

'What's the matter?' she demanded.

He raised his head to give her a smile which made her toes curl. 'Making love to you, Sarah Tracy, is addictive.'

Sarah flushed and looked away. 'If you'll hand me the dressing gown I'll have a bath. What time's breakfast?'

'Eight o'clock, right here. I ordered it last night. Though we can eat downstairs if you prefer.'

'I don't. I'd much rather have it here, in private. But I hope you ordered a lot of food!' She smiled at him as she scrambled into her robe. 'Shan't be long. I'm off to play with the dolphins.'

He sighed. 'Alone, I suppose.'

'If breakfast is arriving at eight,' she retorted, 'very definitely alone!'

After the emotional and physical demands of the night Sarah felt tired, but utterly happy as she shared breakfast with Jake.

'I wasn't sure what you'd like,' he told her, 'so I took a chance. Coffee, fresh fruit compote, scrambled eggs with grilled bacon, plus the usual toast and butter and so on.'

'Perfect.' Sarah tucked in with gusto. 'I never eat much breakfast normally, but I'm hungry this morning.'

'So am I.' He leaned close to kiss her cheek. 'Our recent activities tend to do that.'

'Do they?' Sarah gave him a sparkling, gold-flecked glance. 'You'd know more about that than me.'

'True.' Jake was abruptly serious. 'But this is a first for me, too, Sarah. I don't deny that there have been women in my life before. Women whose company I enjoyed. But with you it's different.'

'Why?'

'Because I've never loved anyone before,' he said simply.

She gave him a luminous, rather shaky smile. 'Thank you, darling.'

'Say that again.'

'Thank you?'

He leaned nearer. 'No. The darling bit.'

She brandished her fork at him. 'I want to get on with my breakfast, my darling Mr Hogan, so let's leave the endearments until later.'

Later, packed and ready to join the others for coffee, Sarah sighed regretfully as she took a last look around the room.

'Are you glad I persuaded them to let me have the bridal suite?' said Jake.

Sarah nodded fervently. 'Because we were the first to sleep here it seems like ours. I hate to leave it.'

'We can come back any time you like.' Jake looked down at her with the familiar straight look. 'Which brings me to the next important subject. How soon can we get married?'

'If it were just up to me I'd say as soon as possible,'

she assured him. 'But there's Davy to consider. I'd like
to give her time to get used to the idea.'

'Do *you* need time?'

She gave him a wicked little smile. 'None at all.
You've sold me on the idea already.'

When they went downstairs to the bar the others were
waiting for them.

'Good morning, you two,' said Frances, smiling. 'We
thought of you last night, Sarah. I hope you cuddled her
during the storm, Jake.'

He grinned. 'I rather enjoyed the storm myself.'

'I bet you did,' said Ben with relish, as the others
laughed.

'We're embarrassing Sarah,' said Grania quickly.

'Not in the least,' said Sarah, and exchanged a long
look with Jake. 'In fact we've got something to tell you.'

Jake kissed her swiftly, then turned to the others with
a triumphant smile. 'Last night I asked Sarah to marry
me. And she said yes.'

After their announcement, it was a long time before
Sarah and Jake managed to make their farewells, and
head for home.

'It occurred to me, too late, that maybe you might not
want our intentions made quite so public yet—if at all,'
said Sarah, when they were finally on their way.

'Are you serious? I want the whole world to know—
a.s.a.p. But Davy first, obviously. So how do we approach that?'

Sarah gave it some thought. 'Perhaps you'd like to
take us both to the Trout on Saturday evening, to eat in
the garden there if it's fine. Davy would love going out
for a grown-up dinner.'

'Done,' he said promptly. 'Will you tell her straight away?'

'No. I'll wait until Sunday morning, after she's spent time with you.' She smiled at him. 'So you'd better put on the charm for Saturday night.'

To her surprise Jake was unamused.

'I never deliberately set out to charm, Sarah,' he said shortly. 'And even if I did I would never try it with Davy.'

Sarah touched his hand in penitence. 'I'm sorry. You obviously didn't like that. But I witnessed your masterly performance with the receptionist, remember?'

He nodded, keeping his eyes on the road. 'I admit that I pull out the stops when absolutely necessary. But never with you, Sarah. You get the plain, unvarnished Jake Hogan, always.'

'Which is all I want, ever,' she assured him.

They stopped for a snack after they left the motorway, then drove back in the afternoon to Campden Road.

'Gosh, I'm tired,' said Sarah, as they went inside the quiet house. She smiled at him. 'You must be, too.'

'We had very little sleep last night,' he reminded her, taking her into his arms. 'I suggest you go to bed for a while, darling. On your own, unfortunately. I'm just going to check on things at Pentiles, then I'll take my gear on to the flat. What time shall I come back?'

'Whenever you like. I'll make supper.'

'Perfect.' He kissed her swiftly. 'Then after that let's have an early night. Together.'

'Even more perfect,' she assured him, and kissed him back at such length Jake lost all enthusiasm for anything to do with work.

'Go,' said Sarah, pushing him away. 'I'll be waiting when you come back. About eight?'

Jake shook his head as he went to the door. 'Seven.'

Instead of taking a nap Sarah rang the school to report that she was back home in Campden Road. Then, feeling that the occasion called for something special by way of a meal, she got the car out to go shopping for food. She rushed home with her spoils afterwards, had a bath instead of a rest, then set to with a will in the kitchen. A few minutes short of seven she was dressed and ready in a sleeveless white T-shirt dress, her hair shining and her face alight with a glow which owed nothing to cosmetics. The courgette flowers she'd splurged on were stuffed with a savoury cheese mixture, ready to deep fry, a salad lacked only its dressing, and two steaks waited in a marinade, ready to grill. She'd laid the kitchen table with a yellow cloth, and as a finishing touch put out blue saucers to hold the fat yellow candles she'd bought.

When the phone rang Sarah went cold. Jake wasn't coming! He'd had an accident. Then she flushed with guilt because she hadn't thought of Davy first. And found it was neither Jake nor the school with bad news, but Margaret Parker making a brief duty call from Florence.

When Jake arrived, right on the stroke of seven, Sarah threw open the door with a smile of such passionate welcome he took her in his arms, careless of the bag of bottles he was carrying.

'I just had a phone call,' she said breathlessly, once he'd stopped kissing her.

'Something wrong with Davy,' said Jake sharply.

'No. It was my grandmother, reporting in from Florence.' Sarah smiled sheepishly as she went ahead of him to the kitchen. 'But I was certain it was you, saying you couldn't come.'

'Why on earth should you think that?' he said, mystified, and put the bottles on the table. 'The champagne should be chilled, by the way.'

Sarah put it in the fridge, then turned to face him. 'Because I felt so happy. I was sure something had happened to spoil it.'

Jake took her hands, his eyes spearing hers. 'Sarah Tracy, I swear I will never consciously do anything to make you unhappy. Believe it.'

Sarah did believe it, and made it plain in a way Jake liked so much it was a long time before she came back to earth sufficiently to think of food. 'This won't do,' she said severely. 'Time I started dinner.'

Because Jake insisted on helping her the meal took rather longer to arrive at the table than Sarah had intended. But despite too many cooks everything turned out well. Jake was lavish with his praise, and the occasion was made even more festive by the champagne which Sarah enjoyed much more than the wine at the wedding.

'Why is that, do you think?' she said dreamily.

'Simple, my darling. We're drinking it to celebrate our engagement.' Jake grinned. 'In which case I could probably have got away with something a lot less pricey than this.'

'Cheapskate!' Sarah made a face at him. 'Though you're absolutely right.'

'But for tonight I wanted only the best.' Jake assured her.

'I did, too.' Sarah chuckled. 'Surprising though it may be, Mr Hogan, courgette flowers and fillet steaks are not part of my normal diet.'

Later they made for the sofa in the sitting room and left the curtains open so they could watch the sun set over the garden, Sarah curled up against Jake in utter contentment.

'We must make the most of this, Jake,' she said with a sigh.

He nodded. 'Tomorrow night you want free for Davy, of course, but I'll see you both on Saturday evening. How do I play that? Do I just drop you back here afterwards?'

'If she's happy you can come in for coffee.'

Jake snapped his fingers suddenly. 'Don't move. I'll be back in a second.' He went out into the hall for his jacket and came back with a square leather box. 'Go on, open it,' he said, handing it to Sarah.

She looked at him questioningly, then opened the box, her eyes like saucers when she found four rings inside.

'I knew you wouldn't want to make it official until Davy's in on it, but I was determined to put a ring on your finger tonight, Sarah,' said Jake. 'My name is good with the jeweller in the Parade. He let me bring these to see which one you preferred. Don't worry about the size. That can be adjusted.'

Sarah closed the box with a snap and climbed into his lap to kiss him. 'I love you so much, Jake Hogan.'

He shook her slightly. 'Hell, you scared me, Sarah. I thought you were going to throw the box back at me.'

For answer she kissed him with such fervour both of them forgot the rings and everything else for a while.

When Jake released her at last Sarah sat up to open the box again.

'Which one do you like best?' she asked breathlessly.

'Which, roughly translated, means which one costs least, I suppose! All four rings carry much the same price tag, which the jeweller was kind enough to remove before handing them over.' Jake grinned. 'You see? I'm getting to know you so well!'

Sarah was dazzled by all the rings. But the one she loved at first sight was a cluster of tiny diamonds set in a cushion round a raised central ruby.

'The others are modern, but that one's circa 1905—Edwardian,' said Jake, and took it from its slot to slide on Sarah's finger.

'That's the one,' she said immediately.

'Try the others on.'

'No point. I want this one.'

'Then, just like me, Sarah Tracy,' said Jake huskily, 'it's yours.'

CHAPTER ELEVEN

To SARAH'S relief the evening with Davy was a great success. Full of excitement about going out to grown-up dinner, Davy was impatient for Jake to arrive, and when he did greeted him with an enthusiasm which delighted him. She was impressed by his car, loved eating in the Trout's garden, and chattered away to Jake during the meal as though she'd known him all her life.

When Davy was in bed later, Jake followed Sarah into the sitting room and took her in his arms, rubbing his cheek against hers.

'I'd say that that went pretty well!'

She hugged him tightly. 'Wonderfully well. Tomorrow I'll give her the news.' She drew back to look up at him. 'Unless you'd rather I waited until you tell your family.'

'I was coming to that. How soon do you think you could bear the ordeal of family Sunday lunch *chez* Hogan? I warn you now, Mother will round up all the usual suspects for the occasion, so if you can't face that just yet I can leave it a while.'

'Only until my grandmother comes back. I'd better break the news to her first, but after that any time you like. I'm looking forward to meeting them.'

'We'll take Davy along too, of course.' Jake chuckled. 'By the way, when you were making coffee just now she repeated her invitation to sports day.'

Sarah laughed. 'Something tells me it won't take her

long to get used to the idea of *you* as a stepfather.' She sobered. 'Though you'll really be her brother-in-law.'

'No one else on the planet needs to know that,' said Jake emphatically.

'True.' Sarah breathed in deeply. 'But I'm so glad *you* do. I never thought I'd find anyone I could share my secret with, Jake. Ever.'

He kissed her very gently. 'I'm grateful for the privilege. And now,' he added with regret, 'I must go. But I'll be waiting on tenterhooks tomorrow, to hear Davy's reaction to the news.'

'I'll come straight to your place from Roedale,' promised Sarah. 'Though somehow I don't think there's much to worry about.'

Sarah was right. When she broached the subject next day, straight after breakfast, Davy positively fizzed with excitement.

'Yippee! I *like* Jake. Does he like me, Mummy? Can I tell Polly? When are you going to get married? Will you wear a long white dress? Can I be bridesmaid?'

'Jake likes you very much,' said Sarah, limp with relief. 'And of course you can be bridesmaid. But we have to wait until Grandma gets back before we tell anyone.'

'OK,' said Davy, obviously happy to agree with anything. Her suntanned face glowed with satisfaction. 'I like Jake a lot,' she added, in case there was any doubt.

'More than Brian, obviously,' said Sarah dryly.

Davy gave her a scornful look. 'Jake's cool. He talks to me as if I've got a brain. I asked him to come to sports day. I hope he does.'

Sarah laughed. 'I'll tell him.'

'Ring him now!'

'Thank God,' was Jake's response when Sarah informed him of Davy's approval. 'Now I can enjoy

Sunday lunch. Though it's going to be hard to keep the news to myself.'

'Just another few days and the entire world can know,' Sarah promised him.

With Davy back in school, and Margaret Parker still away, Jake took it for granted that Sarah would spend every possible moment with him, and she rushed home every day to do her homework in record time before he arrived. He refused to let her cook, and took her out to eat or ordered something in, but, whether they spent time in Campden Road or at his flat, by mutual consent the evening always ended early, in bed.

'It won't always be like this,' said Jake one night, as they lay in each other's arms, quiet at last. 'But right now I need to make the most of every minute.'

'You mean before my grandmother gets home and Davy finishes school?' Sarah moved back a little to look into his eyes. 'Look, Jake, are you really sure about this?'

He grasped her by the shoulders. 'Loving you?' he demanded.

'No. I know you love me—'

'I should bloody well hope so by now,' he said fiercely, and kissed her hard. 'So no more doubts, woman. At the moment I tend to rush you to bed the moment I see you, which means we haven't discussed certain aspects of our future. So, as soon as my ring is officially on your finger instead of round your neck, I suggest we start thinking about somewhere to live. A house that's big enough for you, me, Davy, plus any future additions. So don't even think of backing out now, Sarah.' He smiled suddenly. 'You can't now, anyway. I've paid for the ring.'

'Then of course I won't. I love that ring.' Sarah buried her face against his shoulder. 'I love you, too, Jacob Hogan.'

'In that case,' he whispered, 'let me remove any last, lingering doubts from your mind, my darling. You belong to me. And I'm going to have you.'

'Now?'

'Now!'

When Sarah picked her grandmother up from the airport Margaret Parker received the news with deep misgiving as they drove home.

'This comes as a shock, Sarah. I've always hoped that one day you'd find someone to trust with the truth, of course, but you've only just met this man.'

'But I knew from the first that I could trust Jake,' Sarah assured her. 'And quite apart from that I like him so much, as well as being madly in love with him.' She turned steady eyes on her grandmother's set face for a moment. 'I think I deserve this. So try to be happy for me. Please.'

Margaret Parker let out a deep sigh. 'Very well, Sarah. I'll do my best. When will I have the opportunity for congratulations?'

'This evening. Jake's coming to dinner. He wanted to take us out, but I wasn't sure how you'd feel after the flight so he's having a meal sent in.'

'How kind of him,' said Margaret, thawing somewhat. 'Have you met any of the Hogan family yet?'

'Not yet. We were waiting for you to get back. Jake's just waiting for me to give the go-ahead before telling his parents. At which point,' Sarah warned, 'he says his mother will immediately gather the Hogan clan together for a celebration meal to meet the three of us.'

Margaret eyed Sarah searchingly. 'How did Davy take to the idea of Jake as a stepfather?'

'With tremendous enthusiasm. She's even invited him to sports day. Now, tell me all about Florence.'

With Jake on terrific form, and Sarah, ring prominently displayed, so obviously floating on a pink cloud, Margaret Parker unbent enough to drink a congratulatory toast in the champagne Jake had brought, but she retired to bed straight after the meal.

'Jet lag,' she explained, as she said goodnight.

'Jet lag after a two-hour flight?' said Jake, once she'd gone upstairs. 'Or does she disapprove of me?'

'Not of you, personally.' Sarah shrugged. 'She's just in a state because you know the truth. You'll have to give her time to come round. I didn't expect her to be happy about it straight away.'

He took her in his arms, rubbing his cheek against her hair. 'The important thing to me is that *you* are happy.'

'I am. Blissfully,' sighed Sarah. 'Though I hope your family shows more enthusiasm than Grandma did.'

'Of course they will. I'll tell them this weekend, to give my mother enough notice to kill the fatted calf.'

'I'm a bit nervous,' confessed Sarah.

Jake turned her face up to his, his eyes utterly serious. 'You have nothing to worry about where my family is concerned. But even in the unlikely event that they do disapprove, it won't make a shred of difference, Sarah. As long as you love me, nothing else matters.'

When Jake arrived on the Friday evening Davy rushed to open the door to him, and told him in no uncertain terms that she was thrilled about the forthcoming wedding. Over supper Davy chattered incessantly, and was

almost as downcast as Sarah when she heard Jake was
away next day.

'But it's Saturday. I hoped you'd go swimming with
us, Jake,' she said, disappointed.

'I'd much rather do that than talk boring old business
in Birmingham,' he assured her. 'The people I need to
see are only available tomorrow, unfortunately.' He
slanted a glance at Sarah. 'Let me take you out to
Sunday lunch instead.'

'Grandma always cooks that,' said Davy.

'We'll ask her to come out with us, to give her a rest.
Then the following weekend you can all have Sunday
lunch with *my* family,' said Jake.

It was a prospect which occupied Sarah constantly
during the time away from Jake, but when he arrived to
take them out for Sunday lunch, as arranged, he made a
thumbs-up sign when Sarah opened the door to him, and
told her that his entire family were delighted with his
news.

'Liam, too,' he added.

'I'm looking forward to meeting him,' said Sarah.
Which wasn't exactly true. She had qualms about meeting all the Hogans. 'Grandma thanks you for your invitation, by the way, but she's not feeling too good.
Migraine.'

'I'm sorry about that. Tell her I hope she'll join us
next time.'

Much to Davy's delight Jake drove her back to
Roedale later, where her day was crowned by the triumph of telling Polly about the wedding.

'No problem about going back to school tonight,' said
Jake, laughing as the child made a bee-line for her
friends.

'She's settled in very well now—even wants to stay

on a week for summer school. They make dens in the school grounds, put on plays, go on picnics, and so on,' said Sarah on the journey back to Jake's flat. 'I'm glad Davy's spreading her wings at last.'

'Does it mean extra expense?' asked Jake. 'If so, let me pay, darling.'

She smiled at him gratefully. 'Thanks for the offer, but it's sorted already, from my nest-egg fund.'

He gave her one of his straight looks. 'When I'm her stepfather I'll consider it my prerogative to foot her bills, Sarah.'

'And so you shall. But not until we're married.' She shrugged. 'Silly, I know, but it would seem too much like tempting fate beforehand.'

'Sarah.' Jake took her in his arms as they went up in the lift. 'I know life's dealt you a tough hand to play in the past, but from now on things will be different, I promise. You have my personal guarantee.'

Sarah was happy to believe him. Other than her grandmother's lukewarm attitude to her engagement, the only cloud left on her horizon was the prospect of meeting Jake's family. Despite Jake's assurances to the contrary, she was still convinced that the Hogans would have preferred their son's bride to produce a daughter after the marriage rather than nine years beforehand.

Glad of the pink dress for the occasion, Sarah decided that new shoes would be good for her morale. The frivolous sandals worn to the wedding wouldn't do to meet her future in-laws. A little frisson of excitement ran down her spine at the mere thought of in-laws, just the same, simply because it brought home the reality of marrying Jake.

As soon as Sarah finished work next day she hit the shops. An hour later, in possession of classic fawn

pumps, she was on her way back to the office to collect
her usual homework when her heart gave a leap of recognition as she caught sight of Jake in the familiar car
he'd parked under the trees in the Parade. She hurried
down the pavement, waving to attract his attention, then
dropped her hand, colour draining from her face when a
woman slid into the passenger seat and brought Jake's
face down to hers. Rooted to the spot, Sarah stared in
sick disbelief while she watched him kiss his companion
with a casual familiarity which turned her stomach. Yet
for the life of her she couldn't look away. When he
raised his head at last he looked straight at Sarah, raised
a quizzical eyebrow, gave her an outrageous wink,
smiled his famous, eye-crinkling smile and drove off.

Sarah walked back to the office in a daze. She collected the mail, said her goodbyes, and started for home
through a world disintegrating in jagged pieces all
around her. But Sarah's numbness gave way to anguish
as she thought of Davy. What possible explanation could
she give Davy for changing her mind about marrying
Jake? The truth was too unpalatable for herself, let alone
a nine-year-old child. What a fool she'd been. And she
had only herself to blame for letting it get so far. It had
been her own fault, right from asking to share the bridal
suite to the point where she'd literally begged Jake to
make love to her.

'You look terrible. What's wrong?' demanded
Margaret Parker, who was paying off a taxi when Sarah
arrived home.

'The engagement's off,' said Sarah, and closed the
door behind them as they went inside.

Her grandmother stared in astonishment. 'Good heavens, Sarah. Why?'

'I've just seen Jake with another woman.'

To her credit, Margaret Parker patted Sarah's shoulder in an attempt at comfort. 'Could it have been a sister, perhaps?'

'I certainly hope not, the way they were kissing.' Sarah's eyes flashed gold fire.

'Where on earth was all this going on?'

'In a car parked in full view in the Parade.'

Margaret's eyes widened incredulously. 'There must be some mistake, surely.'

'If someone else had told me I might have swallowed that. But seeing is believing. He looked straight at me after—after kissing the woman.' Sarah's teeth began to chatter. 'He—even *smiled*—at me.'

Margaret marched her granddaughter into the kitchen. 'Sit there. I'll be back in a minute.'

Too dazed with misery to wonder where her grandmother was going, Sarah sat slumped at the kitchen table until Margaret came back with a glass.

'Brandy. Drink it up.'

Sarah, rather astonished by her grandmother's concern, obeyed, spluttered as her teeth knocked at the glass, then as the taste registered tears ran down her cheeks. 'He gave me brandy when I told him my story at the hotel,' she sobbed. 'I *trusted* Jake. What a fool I was!'

Margaret handed her a tissue. 'I can't deny I disapproved when you said you'd confided in him, but after getting to know him a little I would have sworn myself that Jake Hogan could be trusted.'

Sarah blew her nose, then took a deep breath. 'It's not just for myself. I can get over it. It's Davy I'm concerned about. She likes Jake so much.' She shuddered. 'But I just can't bear the fact that he knows such personal things about me.'

'How did you come to tell him?'

'We—we made love after the wedding.' Sarah blushed to the roots of her hair. 'Because of Davy it was the first time for me, of course. So I had to explain.'

Margaret nodded bleakly. 'It had to happen one day, because you take after Anne in so many ways.'

Sarah bristled. 'What do you mean?'

'Anne was just like you, head over heels in love the moment she met your father. Because you were on the way soon afterwards they got married right away. But you arrived late, unlike Davy, so no one ever knew.'

'That must have been a relief for you,' said Sarah acidly.

'It was.' Margaret shrugged. 'I know you think it's ridiculous, but respectability has always been of prime importance to me. I care about public opinion.' She hesitated. 'But Anne couldn't help the nature she'd inherited.'

Sarah stared at her grandmother, forgetting her anger and grief for a moment. 'Are you saying that Mother took after *you*, Grandma?'

Margaret smiled wryly. 'Impossible to believe, obviously. And you're right. It was your grandfather, not me.' She braced herself. 'He was unfaithful to me almost from the first, you see. Anne never knew because he was discreet, and I took great care to keep it from her. But living a lie takes a toll. And it made me very hard on Anne when she was growing up. And you too, Sarah.'

'Heavens, Grandma,' said Sarah, frowning. 'I had no idea.'

'Perhaps you can understand, now, how desperate I felt when she told me what had happened with Anthony Barrett. I was demented at the thought of your father's grief, the reaction of my friends—' Margaret breathed in deeply, looking every year of her age for once, and more. 'None of which is any excuse for the sacrifice I demanded of you.'

Two pairs of gold-flecked eyes met each other in silence for a moment.

'It's been hard at times, but I don't regret it,' said Sarah at last.

Margaret cleared her throat rather noisily. 'So. What will you do when Jake comes for you tonight?'

'That's not going to happen!' Sarah's jaw clenched. 'He *saw* me looking at him and he didn't care a bit.'

Sarah was so sure Jake wouldn't turn up she settled down in front of her computer to tackle the pile of mail she'd brought home. Wearing glasses because her eyes were too sore for contact lenses after crying so much, she did her best to concentrate, but it was hard to compose lucid syntax when her mind was going round in circles like a demented bee, trying to find some logical explanation for what she'd seen.

Sarah was still so sure Jake wouldn't come she picked up the receiver from force of habit when the doorbell rang, then stiffened in fury when she heard his voice over the intercom.

'Hi, darling, let me in. It's eighteen long hours since I kissed you—'

'Get away from my door, Hogan!' she spat. 'Or I'll call the police.' She slammed down the receiver.

The bell rang again at once. 'Did you hear me?' she shouted through the intercom.

'For God's sake, Sarah, what the hell's *wrong*?'

Only everything, she thought bitterly, and left the receiver off the hook, steeling herself to ignore the frantic demands crackling through it. After a while it went quiet, and she put it back. With relief, she assured herself. Glad she'd persuaded her grandmother to go out as planned, Sarah tried again to concentrate, then jumped out of her skin when a hard hand dropped on her shoulder.

'What the hell was all that about?' demanded Jake, his eyes blazing as he hauled her to her feet.

'Take your hands off me,' she flung at him, and backed away as far as she could in the crowded bedroom. 'How did you get in here?'

'Through the back garden. I picked the lock on your kitchen door. I advise you to change it.' He was breathing hard, a white line round his mouth. 'And don't start on about the police again. Before I move an inch I demand to know what's wrong.'

Sarah pushed her glasses up her shiny nose, glaring at him through them. 'Oh, *please*,' she said scornfully. 'Don't come the innocent with me. You know exactly what's wrong.'

Jake stood with arms folded and legs apart, looming large in the confined space. 'Actually, I don't,' he said with menace. 'Elucidate.'

She thrust a hand through her hair, glaring at him. 'Did you actually think you could come here and take up where we left off after—after what I saw today?'

Jake stared blankly. 'What the devil are you talking about?'

Sarah clenched her hands to keep from hitting him. 'You. In a car. Snogging with some female in full view of passers-by. Including me. You *saw* me. You knew I'd seen you. But you laughed in my face.'

'It wasn't me,' he said flatly.

'I had my lenses in,' she snapped. 'I *know* it was you.' She moved to the door. 'Get out, Jake. Now. Or I will call the police.'

'Sarah, there's a simple explanation. If you'll just listen—'

'Get out of my sight!' She marched out into the hall and opened the front door.

Jake followed her, gave her a look which could have cut glass, then brushed past her and went out to his car. Sarah banged the door shut, deflated, and collapsed on her bed in angry tears. Hey, she reminded herself after a while, you don't do tears. She went into the bathroom, scowled at the Pentiles lining it, washed her face and brushed her hair, polished her glasses, then went back to work.

Due to severe lack of concentration it took longer than usual for Sarah to finish. She was in the kitchen, thinking about what, if anything, to eat for her supper, when the doorbell rang again. Breathing fire, she answered the intercom and heard Jake's voice.

'A word, please, Sarah.'

Her instinct was to tell him to get lost, but she'd calmed down enough by this time for curiosity to get the better of her. She went along the hall to open the door, then stood, wide-eyed, when she found two men on her doorstep. Both tall, both fair, dressed in jeans and white shirts, they regarded her with eyes of identical ultramarine-blue, one pair gleaming with amusement, the other steel-hard with determination.

'We'd like to come in,' said Jake at last.

Heart pounding, Sarah inclined her head regally, and stood aside for her visitors to go past. 'Come to the sitting room.'

'This is my brother, Liam,' announced Jake.

Sarah could see that for herself.

'Hello, Miss Tracy,' Liam said, in a voice so like

Jake's it made her shiver. 'I didn't realise who you were this afternoon.'

The penny dropped so abruptly Sarah threw a wild look at Jake, who nodded in grim confirmation.

'You refused to listen to explanations earlier, so I brought Liam along in the flesh to clarify things.'

'I was the one you saw today,' explained Liam. 'If you want further proof, Serena's outside in the car.'

'The girl you saw *Liam* kissing,' said Jake with emphasis.

'Oh,' said Sarah faintly, beset by several violent emotions all fighting at once for the upper hand.

'It's a common mistake,' said Liam ruefully. 'We're often mistaken for each other.'

'But now you're both together the difference is obvious.' To Sarah, anyway. Ignoring Jake, she managed an icy little smile for his brother. 'Sorry to bring you out of your way like this. If I'd known the truth beforehand it wouldn't have been necessary. Jake mentioned a brother, but forgot to say you were twins.'

CHAPTER TWELVE

'CUE to make myself scarce,' said Liam. 'Mustn't keep Serena waiting.'

'Won't you bring her in for a drink?' said Sarah politely.

Liam shook his head. 'Some other time, perhaps.' He held out his hand. 'Sarah, I'm very sorry for the mix up.'

'Not *your* fault,' she assured him, and shook his hand briefly.

'You take the car, Liam,' said Jake. 'I'll get a cab.'

'By all means go with your brother,' said Sarah, with hauteur.

'I'm staying!'

'And I'm going,' said Liam hastily. 'I'll see myself out.'

After he'd gone the silence in the room was deafening. In the end Jake was first to break it. He thrust a hand through his hair and turned away to stare into the twilight beyond the window.

'I should have told you Liam was my twin.'

'Why on earth didn't you?' she demanded.

Jake turned to look at her. 'It's caused problems before.' His mouth twisted. 'I was going to tell you before Sunday, obviously.'

'Sunday?'

'When I introduced you to my parents and my family, including Liam.'

Past tense, noted Sarah in alarm.

'Have you changed your mind about that?' she asked with care.

He met her eyes. 'No. Have you?'

She looked away. 'I bought some new shoes.'

Jake moved a little closer. 'A pity not to wear them, then.'

'And Davy would be desperately disappointed.'

'So would I,' he said huskily, and closed the space between them to take her in his arms. 'Is this allowed, or will you call the police?'

'No.' She let out a deep, shaky breath, her knees suddenly giving way as she sagged against him, and Jake picked her up and sat down with her in his lap.

'That,' he said roughly, as his arms endangered her ribs, 'was the worst couple of hours of my entire life.'

'It's been a lot longer than that since I saw Liam,' she said, shuddering. 'When I saw you—him—with another woman I was *heartbroken*!'

Jake swore with colourful violence and tipped her face up to his. 'I've had a word with my little brother about making an exhibition of himself in public places.'

'Little brother?' she said, diverted.

'Half an hour younger.' For the first time that evening Jake's smiled appeared. 'I gave him hell for fooling about with Serena in full view of passers-by.'

'Not your style at all,' agreed Sarah. 'But you can see my mistake. It was your car, Jake.'

He nodded grimly. 'Liam still brings his car down here to be serviced—won't trust London garages. After he'd dropped it off he borrowed mine for the day. Liam's also used to city anonymity. He tends to forget that we share a face well known in these parts. But I prefer to keep my love life private.' Jake bent his head and kissed her, and with a sigh of thanksgiving Sarah responded with fervour fuelled by relief.

She sat up suddenly, biting her lip as she pushed her hands through her hair.

'What now?' he demanded.

She groaned. 'It just struck me that your brother must wonder what on earth you see in me. I look such a fright!'

'Is that all?' Jake let out a snort of relief and pulled her back against him. 'Actually, my darling, I like the dishevelled look so much I could eat you.' He kissed her by way of illustration, and went on kissing her, until they were hot and breathless and in need of a great deal more than kisses. 'I suppose your grandmother's due home any time now,' said Jake, breathing hard. 'I want you like hell, darling, but in the circumstances I'd better go home while I can.'

Sarah licked the tip of her tongue round her lips, her eyes glittering with invitation. 'Take me with you?'

'Oh, God, yes,' he said fervently, and in minutes they were in Sarah's car, a few things thrown in her overnight bag and a note left for Margaret. With Jake at the wheel they arrived at his apartment building with a speed which should have had them stopped by the police. He parked the car, took Sarah by the hand and rushed her through the foyer into the lift, his hands under her shirt and his mouth on hers before the doors closed.

When they reached the flat Jake kicked the door shut behind him, dropped Sarah's bag and yanked her up on her toes against him. She gasped against his mouth as he cupped his hands around her bottom, the proof of his need hot and hard against her through two layers of denim. Their kisses grew wilder, her thighs parted involuntarily, and he lifted her against him so she could lock her legs about his hips. He held her cruelly tight against his erection and strode to the bedroom with Sarah clasped close in his arms, her head buried against his shoulder.

They collapsed together on the bed, Jake hard and heavy on top of her, and Sarah lay under him, returning his kisses feverishly, revelling in the weight and feel and aroused male scent of him. When the urge to mate grew overpowering he got to his knees on the bed and pulled her up with him, to undress her, both of them on fire with such desperate need they tore at each other's clothes with rough, impatient hands until they were naked together. And then he was over her and inside her and he gave a hoarse, visceral groan of satisfaction as Sarah's hands dug into his lean hips to draw him deep into her innermost core.

Their impassioned loving was too wild to last long, but so overwhelmingly sweet in its intensity Sarah's cheeks were wet when it was over.

'Tears?' whispered Jake, kissing them away.

'Only because I'm happy.' She gave a deep, unsteady sigh. 'It's almost worth quarrelling to make up like that.'

'Almost,' he agreed. 'But not quite. In future I vote we pass on the fight and cut straight to the good part.'

The rest of the week went by on wings. Margaret Parker, rather to Sarah's surprise, made it plain she was relieved to see her grandchild so happy again, and astonished Sarah by indicating, as delicately as she could, that she quite understood if Sarah wished to spend every night with Jake until Davy came home for the weekend.

'Actually, I don't,' said Sarah. 'But last night it was late by the time everything was sorted. We just needed more time together to recover.'

'Does Jake find my presence in the house inhibiting, by any chance?' said Margaret dryly.

Sarah grinned. 'Probably. Though going back to his place last night was my idea, not his.'

'In my day, of course, officially one had to wait until legally shackled before sharing a bed.'

'Officially?'

Margaret gave her a wry smile. 'This may come as a surprise, Sarah, but sex isn't a modern invention. It was all too popular with some in my day too.'

The following Saturday Davy had her wish and Jake joined them for a swim and lunch and a trip to the cinema. Then, because it was a beautiful evening, Sarah suggested a stroll in the park before going home.

'Just like a real family,' said Davy with satisfaction as the three of them walked through the sunlit park. 'Can I have an ice-cream?'

Sarah gave Jake an apologetic smile. 'She's a bottomless pit.'

'Which will please my mother enormously,' he said, handing over the money. 'She's been cooking for days.'

Davy thanked him, then spotted one of her schoolfriends with a dog on a lead, and asked permission to run off to talk to her.

'I'm nervous about tomorrow,' said Sarah, watching Davy with the other little girl and her family.

Jake halted and took her hand. 'Don't be, darling. Liam heartily approved, by the way.'

'Even though I had glasses on and looked a mess?'

'Right. So imagine what effect you'll have when you're all dressed up to impress.'

Sarah shook her head. 'I don't want to *impress*, Jake. Just to reassure your parents that their firstborn isn't making a great big mistake by marrying me.'

'Which I'm going to do as soon as humanly possible, whatever their verdict,' he informed her.

To round off the evening they went back to supper at Jake's flat, which Davy liked so much it was an effort to get her home afterwards.

'Are we going to live here with you, Jake?' she asked.

'Not big enough, sweetheart. Mummy and I are going to find a house with a special room in it just for you,' he said, ruffling her hair.

When they got back to Campden Road it was uphill work getting Davy to bed.

'It's a big day tomorrow,' said Sarah firmly. 'Lunch with Jake's family, then back to school. So sleep now, please.'

Jake held up his arms when she got back to the sitting room. 'Come and tell me you love me.'

'I love you,' she said promptly, and curled up against him on the sofa. 'So you haven't changed your mind about being a stepfather?'

'No.' Jake kissed her. 'I like Davy. And she obviously likes me. And I know very well that life isn't all swimming and fun, like today, and later, when she's a teenager bristling with hormones and attitude, things may get rocky now and then. But because she's a little duplicate of you in every way it's easy to think of her as mine already, Sarah.'

'Thank you, Jake.' She breathed in deeply. 'This is all so perfect I keep thinking something will go wrong.'

He tapped her cheek gently. 'That part's already happened, due to Liam. From now on it's plain sailing.'

'Is he bringing Serena tomorrow?'

'No fear. She's just an old flame. Serena was in school with us. Since then she's been married and divorced twice. Liam sees her now and then, when he's down, but he wouldn't dream of bringing her to a family get-together. That's strictly for serious relationships, like yours and mine, darling.' He smiled. 'At time of going to press Liam is firmly unattached.'

Sarah kissed him, then with regret stood up. 'I'm sorry to see you go, darling, but I need an early night so I can scintillate tomorrow.'

Jake returned the kiss, then reluctantly let her go. 'I'll come for you at twelve tomorrow. If you bring Davy's school gear I can drive you straight back to Roedale.'

'I think we'd better come home first, so she can have a bath before going back to school.'

'Probably a good idea,' Jake said, chuckling. 'You may have had enough of the Hogans by that time.'

The fateful Sunday dawned so bright and sunny Sarah gave up the idea of a formal dress and high heels. When Jake arrived he grinned when he found Sarah and Davy in identical white T-shirts Margaret had brought as presents from Florence, Davy's worn with embroidered jeans and Sarah's with the raspberry linen skirt.

'You both look gorgeous,' he said, and eyed Sarah's flat white sandals. 'What happened to the new shoes?'

Sarah smiled sheepishly. 'The heels were a bit much for a hot day like this.'

'You look nice, too, Jake,' said Davy, eyeing his pale linen trousers and blue shirt.

'Thank you, sweetheart,' he said, touched. 'I'll just say hello to your grandma, then we'll be off.'

The Hogans lived the other side of Pennington, in a house set in two acres of beautifully kept garden. When Jake turned into the drive it was already full of cars. Children could be heard shouting in the distance, and Davy looked suddenly anxious.

'Are they bigger than me?' she asked Jake as he helped her out.

'Not much. Don't worry. They won't bite.'

A man with greying fair hair came hurrying towards them, familiar blue eyes bright with welcome. 'Hello, son. Introduce me to your beautiful ladies.'

Jake put an arm round them both. 'Dad, this is Sarah Tracy and her daughter Davina. Only she prefers Davy.'

'Welcome to the family, Sarah,' said John Hogan, and to her surprise kissed her on both cheeks. 'My wife's Italian,' he explained, eyes twinkling. 'I've acquired the habit.' He turned to Davy, who was watching him expectantly. 'Am I allowed to kiss you too, pet?'

She smiled and held up her face, and after planting a kiss on her cheeks he took her hand and led the way into the house, where his wife came rushing through the hall, smoothing back her greying black hair.

'Jacob!' She clapped her hands together as she saw Davy. '*Bellissima*, how lovely to meet you.' She swept Davy into a hug, then whispered in her ear. 'Now introduce me to your *mamma*.'

'Her name is Sarah Tracy,' said Davy, reassured by the warmth of her reception.

'How do you do, Mrs Hogan?' said Sarah. 'It's very kind of you to invite us.'

She was immediately folded into a scented embrace. 'You shall call me Teresa,' said Jake's mother, kissing her warmly. 'And the little one is Davy, Jake tells me.'

'After my father, David.'

'Ah!' Teresa patted her cheek. 'I know about your parents—so sad.'

'Mamma,' said Jake hurriedly, 'are the others in the garden?'

'Can't you hear?' said his father, smiling. 'Your

mother shut them out there so she could meet Sarah first. And Davy, too,' he added, taking her hand. 'Come on, pet, let's go and find someone for you to play with.'

Sarah tensed, but Jake put a comforting arm round her as the little girl went off with his father.

'You must be so proud of her. She is so sweet,' said Teresa fondly, and turned smiling black eyes on Sarah. 'And so like her *mamma*.'

'Is Liam here yet?' asked Jake.

'No,' said his mother, with an ominous flash of eye. 'He is late.'

'He'll be here, don't worry.'

'Come,' said Teresa, taking Sarah's hand. 'I must introduce you to the rest of my family. They want so much to meet you.'

Jake's sisters, Maddalena and Paula, a handsome vivacious pair, took after their mother, both in colouring and the exuberance of their welcome as they introduced their husbands and children.

'You boys,' Paula told her sons, 'must look after Davy. She's a guest.'

'And you two, no squabbling for once,' Maddy told her daughters. 'This is a special day. Your uncle is going to marry this lovely lady, and Davy will be your new cousin.'

Sarah watched the children take charge of Davy, who, far from being dismayed by the prospect, was soon absorbed into the gang as they planned how to pass the time before the meal.

'She'll be fine,' Jake assured her, then looked round with a smile as a familiar figure came strolling from the house. 'At last, the prodigal. Now we can break out the fatted calf.'

Liam embraced his parents, then with a grin at Jake

kissed Sarah on both cheeks. 'Welcome to the family, Sarah. He's a good guy,' he whispered in her ear. 'Only don't tell him I said so.'

The meal was an exuberant affair, with everyone helping themselves from a table groaning with good food. The adults took their plates outside, where chairs of every description were set close together on the paved area outside the dining room window. The five children sat on a groundsheet on the lawn to eat theirs, Davy so obviously enjoying herself Sarah relaxed enough to eat everything Jake put on her plate as she answered questions from his sisters about her grandmother and Davy, where they were going to live, and what she was going to wear for the wedding.

'Forgive my wife's enthusiasm,' said Sam, Maddy's husband. He grinned at Sarah. 'She's been trying to get her brothers married for years.'

'I don't mind,' Sarah assured a rather heated-looking Maddy. 'I'm afraid we still need some fine tuning on the details.'

'House-hunting first,' said Jake, and took Sarah's hand. 'And as far as I'm concerned a wedding date as soon as possible.'

She smiled at him with a look of such glowing agreement Teresa Hogan clapped her hands in appreciation and urged everyone to eat more food and drink more wine.

Jake got up, taking Sarah's plate with his. 'I'll bring you some of my mother's famed ice-cream,' he promised, and went over to Davy to ask her preference.

'My parents are very pleased with Jake's fiancée,' said Liam, taking the chair next to Sarah.

'I'm glad. They're very kind.' She smiled at him, but the familiar blue eyes were very serious.

'I'm sorry for what happened the other day, Sarah.'

'You weren't to know I'd see you.'

'But anyone else passing by could have seen me and made the mistake you did.' His mouth twisted. 'In London I'm anonymous, of course. But here in Pennington the Hogan twins are well known.'

'Not to me they weren't,' she said tartly. 'If I'd known about the twin part it would have saved me a lot of grief that day.'

'And it was grief,' he said penitently. 'I could see that when Jake marched me to your door that evening. I could have kicked myself for causing him any more problems.'

Sarah would have liked to ask what he meant, but at that moment Jake came out from the house with handfuls of ice-cream cones, and the younger members of the party rushed to meet him, Davy included. He was laughing and licking his fingers as he came back to Sarah.

'Sorry. I saw to the small fry first. I'll bring some for you right away.'

'Sit down,' said Liam, jumping up. 'I'll do it.'

'You two getting on well together?' asked Jake, watching his brother walk away.

Sarah nodded. 'Liam's very fond of you.'

'Of course he is. We're twins.'

'Now he tells me,' she said dryly, and handed him some tissues. 'Mop yourself up.'

'I was rather hoping,' he whispered, 'that you'd offer to lick me clean.'

'What on earth are you saying to make Sarah blush like that?' demanded Maddy. She looked round suspiciously. 'It's very quiet. Where are the children?'

'Gone to play hide and seek in the shrubbery,' said Paula, and lay back, relaxed. 'Sheer bliss. Don't have any boys, Sarah. Little girls like Davy must be so much easier.'

'Don't you believe it,' said her sister with feeling.

'Are you two trying to frighten Sarah off?' demanded Jake wrathfully.

'Now then, girls,' said Liam, handing Sarah a crystal dish full of different kinds of ice-cream. 'I brought two spoons. You can share with her, Jake.'

Sarah had such a happy time with the Hogan family she was sorry she hadn't brought Davy's school things, as Jake had suggested, so they could stay longer.

'You will stay longer next time,' said Teresa firmly, 'when you bring your grandmother. We would so much like to meet her.'

'I like your family, Jake,' said Davy on the way back to Campden Road. 'Josh and Michael said I can go and play computer games with them some time, and Nina and Chloe asked if I can go to their house for a sleepover in the holidays, Mummy.'

'How very nice of them,' said Sarah, from the depths of the pink cloud she was occupying. 'It's been such a lovely day.'

'So you enjoyed it after all, darling,' said Jake, touching her hand fleetingly.

'I feel silly now, because I was so nervous beforehand.'

'Whereas the Hogans, *en masse*, took to you on sight,' he said simply, 'just as I said they would.'

When they got to Campden Road Margaret was sitting in the garden. She got up, smiling affectionately, when Davy shot out through the French windows to report on the wonderful time she'd had.

'My family were very sorry you didn't join us, Margaret,' said Jake, 'so no getting out of it next time.'

'I shall look forward to it,' she told him, and held out her hand. 'I've put your things ready, Davy, but you need a bath before you're fit to go back to school. No,' she added as Sarah started forward. 'You sit out here with Jake for a bit, and I'll see to Davy.'

'I think your grandmother's thawing towards me,' said Jake.

Sarah nodded. 'She's different with me these days, too. She found it hard at first, knowing that you were in on the family skeleton, but she's basically a sensible woman. She knew it had to happen some time.'

'Thank God it happened with me,' said Jake, and perched on the foot of Sarah's old steamer chair. 'Come and sit here with me.'

She slid into the chair with a sigh, smiling at him as he took her hand. 'You know, Jake, normally I never even think about it, but when I was watching Davy romping with your sister's children today, it was hard to believe I'm not really her mother.'

'But you are, in every way but biological fact,' he said quietly. 'And no one could be a better mother than you are, Sarah. Davy's a great kid. Which is all down to you.' The straight blue look gave due warning that something serious was coming next. 'Which, talking of children, brings me to an overdue apology.'

Sarah gave him a slow, comprehending smile. 'No apologies, Jake. I don't mind. In fact, I'm glad.'

Jake let out a deep breath, and kissed the hand he was holding. 'That hellish misunderstanding was the culprit. The other times I was prepared—'

'I've been meaning to ask about that,' she said, delighted when his face reddened. 'Were you that sure you'd get lucky after Nick's wedding, then?'

'Not at all,' he retorted, then grinned ruefully. 'But when you asked to share my room I didn't dare trust in my increasingly shaky will-power. Fortunately the men's room at the hotel was fully equipped. Which was just as well when the storm brought things to a head.' His eyes met hers with a look which brought matching colour to her own face. 'But by the time we got to my place after the quarrel I was so desperate to make love to you my brain stopped functioning.'

Sarah kissed him. 'So did mine.'

'You're not sorry we could be having a child, then?' he said, with such deep satisfaction she kissed him again.

'No, Jake Hogan. Not in the slightest.'

They sat together in dreamy silence for a few minutes, until Margaret coughed tactfully and came out to join them.

'Davy's ready, but not exactly fired with enthusiasm for the return to school. Which is only natural after such an exciting weekend.'

'Right,' said Jake, pulling Sarah to her feet. 'Let's go.'

Davy was waiting in the hall by her bag. 'I don't feel well,' she said mutinously.

'Too much pasta and ice-cream, maybe,' said Sarah. 'Tell you what, if your tummy's protesting you can sit by Jake in the front, and I'll take a back seat.'

Davy waved goodbye to Margaret, then brightened a little when Jake put a selection of the latest hits on the CD player. Sarah slid into the back seat with a yawn.

'Gosh, I'm sleepy,' she said, and leaned back gratefully against the leather. 'Wake me if I snore.'

Which totally failed in its aim to win a smile from

Davy, who sat hunched in her seat, apparently absorbed in the music.

Jake drove Sarah home afterwards, stayed to share a snack supper, then left early. 'You look in need of a good night's sleep, Sarah,' he said firmly. 'On our own, alas. Never mind. I shall warm my lonely bed with the thought that soon you'll be sharing it with me every night. So get some rest while you can.'

The following evening Sarah got home from work feeling rather flat, because Jake was in London for the day, and might not make it home in time to see her. She ate a quick supper, then settled down to finish off the work she'd brought home. When Jake rang during the evening, as promised, he told her he wouldn't be home until after ten.

'In that case,' said Sarah, disappointed, 'I'll have another early night and come round to your place tomorrow evening.'

'Early,' he ordered.

She smiled as she put the phone down, then put her feet up on the sofa, suddenly so tired she hadn't the energy to get ready for bed. When her phone rang again every hair rose on her spine when a crisp voice said, 'Irene Kendall here, Miss Tracy.'

'Is Davy ill, Mrs Kendall?' demanded Sarah in alarm.

'It's not that, Miss Tracy. Do you have someone with you?'

'Yes. But just tell me what's wrong—*please*!'

'I regret to tell you that Davina is missing.'

Sarah gasped. '*Missing?* How could she be? Have you searched for her?'

'Of course. She went to bed as usual, but when her house mother made the rounds just now Davina's bed was empty. Everything possible has been done to find her before I rang you, both in the school itself and the grounds, but without success. I hoped so much that she would be with you.'

'I would have rung you at once if she had been. But she's *not*,' said Sarah, her voice cracking. 'Have you called the police?'

'I wanted to make sure Davina wasn't with you. But I'll contact them at once.'

'I'll get in the car—'

'No, Miss Tracy. Please. You must stay home in case Davina contacts you. The moment I hear anything I'll ring you. Please do the same for me if—when you have any news yourself.'

'Yes, of course,' said Sarah unsteadily. Phone clasped in her clammy hand, she raced upstairs to tell her grandmother.

'Dear God,' said Margaret, white as a sheet. 'Right,' she said, pulling herself together. 'Let's not panic. We'll go downstairs and make tea.'

'I don't want any tea,' snapped Sarah, then closed her eyes in remorse. 'Sorry, sorry.'

'Brandy, then—no, maybe not, in case you need to drive.'

'Where to?' said Sarah blankly.

'To fetch Davy when they find her.'

They exchanged a long, silent look, full of dread knowledge of all the things that might happen to a lost child, then went downstairs to wait together.

'I'm afraid to ring Jake,' said Sarah, pacing up and down the sitting room. 'He's on his way back from London. If I tell him about Davy he'll probably break the sound barrier up the motorway.'

'What time is he due home?'

'About ten.'

'Ring him after that.' Margaret got up. 'I'll make that tea.'

When the phone rang at nine-thirty Sarah almost dropped it. 'Hello?' she said, her voice hoarse with hope.

'Sarah?' said Jake. 'Something's wrong. What's up?'

She told him tersely. 'But I have to hang up now, Jake, in case—'

'Right. I'll be with you as soon as I can.'

He rang off before Sarah could implore him to drive safely. Silently Margaret handed her a mug of tea.

'I feel so helpless!' Sarah began to pace, then dropped the mug with a crash when the phone rang again.

'Irene Kendall, Miss Tracy. No news, I'm afraid. The police have been here, so I'm just letting you know you'll receive a visit from them shortly. They're searching the grounds as we speak, obviously of the opinion that our search wasn't carried out efficiently.'

At any other time Sarah would have smiled at the indignation the efficient Mrs Kendall couldn't keep out of her voice. 'I'm sure it was.'

'My only consolation is that it's still light at this time of the year.'

'True,' said Sarah desolately.

'I'll ring off now, to keep your line open. Try not to worry too much, Miss Tracy.'

'Is she serious?' exploded Sarah. 'Try not to *worry*!'

'It's the kind of meaningless thing people say when there's nothing else *to* say,' said Margaret, then tensed as the doorbell rang.

'Jake did break the sound barrier,' said Sarah, and ran to open the door to him, then let out a sobbing cry of joy when she found Davy looking up at her with heart-rending doubt on her tearstained face.

'I had to come home,' she said. 'Don't be cross.'

Sarah hugged her cruelly close, then looked up to find Davy hadn't arrived alone. Alison Rogers stood a little way apart, watching them, her car waiting at the kerb.

'Alison!' cried Sarah.

'Mrs Rogers brought me home,' said Davy, knuckling tears out of her eyes.

Alison gave Sarah a sympathetic look.

'I saw Davy walking along the road into town, so I offered her a lift.' She smiled. 'I didn't have a phone with me so I brought her straight here. She's fine, Sarah, just upset.'

'Oh Alison, I can't thank you enough…'

'I'm just glad I saw her,' said Alison. 'Look, you obviously need to talk. I'll leave you in peace. See you later, Sarah. Bye-bye, Davy.'

Sarah watched with pride when Davy held out her hand to her rescuer.

'Thank you very much for bringing me home.'

'A pleasure, Davy.' Alison's eyes twinkled as she shook the small, grubby hand. 'But let's not meet again like that, please. Your poor mother must have been frantic.'

Davy gave Sarah a forlorn look. 'Were you?'

'You'll never know how much!' Sarah turned to Alison with a grateful smile. 'Thank you again.'

'My pleasure. Goodnight.'

Davina saw Margaret hovering in the hall and flew into her arms. 'I just *had* to come home, Grandma,' she sobbed. 'Before I went back on Sunday I heard Mummy saying she wasn't my mother. I've been thinking and thinking about it all the time, and I just couldn't bear it in school a minute longer. So I sneaked out after lights out, and waited for a bus. Only it didn't come, and I started walking, then a car stopped and Polly's mummy brought me home.'

Sarah felt physically sick. She closed the door, gazing at the child clasped in Margaret's arms, her mind frantically trying for an explanation Davy could cope with.

'First of all, young lady,' said Margaret firmly, meeting Sarah's eyes over Davy's untidy head. 'I think you should have a bath, and by that time we'll all be feeling a lot calmer. You gave us a dreadful fright, Davina Tracy.'

'I'd better ring Mrs Kendall,' said Sarah, pulling herself together.

Davy turned round in alarm. 'She *will* be cross with me!'

'Not when I explain,' said Sarah firmly. 'You go off and have a scrub in Grandma's bathroom while I ring her.'

Shortly afterwards Jake arrived, his face so haggard Sarah held out her arms, smiling jubilantly to reassure him.

'Davy's home! Grandma's taken her upstairs for a bath.'

'Thank God.' His hug endangered her ribs. 'What on earth happened?'

Sarah explained, then looked up at him in anguish. 'It's all my fault. She overheard when I was talking to you about not being her mother. And now I've got to find some way to explain.'

Jake led her into the kitchen. 'Make me some coffee, darling, while we think of the best way to tell her.'

Comforted by the 'we', Sarah put the kettle on, then leaned against Jake when he put his arm round her.

'You would have had to tell her one day, Sarah.'

'I know.' She looked up at him in appeal. 'Will you stay while I talk to her?'

'I'll do whatever you want,' he assured her. 'But will Davy want me around in this situation?'

'I don't know. But *I* want you.'

He kissed her swiftly. 'Then I'll stay.'

When Davy came in with Margaret her eyes lit up at the sight of Jake, obviously pleased to see him, and he swept her up in his arms.

'Next time you want to go walkabout you ring me and I'll fetch you myself, Davy Tracy,' he said with mock menace, and sat down with her on his lap.

Davy settled herself comfortably in Jake's hold, her questioning eyes on Sarah. 'Grandma said you'd explain once I was clean.'

'Right, then,' said Sarah, bracing herself.

Margaret met her eyes. 'I said you'd tell Davy who her mother was.'

The slight emphasis on the word 'mother' clarified things for Sarah. 'I was going to tell you this when you were older, Davy—'

'I'm nine,' Davy interrupted hotly. 'Not a baby.'

Sarah's eyes filled. 'No,' she said thickly, 'you're not. Thank you,' she added, when Margaret handed her some kitchen paper.

'Am I adopted, then?' blurted Davy.

'Good heavens, no, darling.'

'But if you're not my mummy who is?'

Sarah took a deep breath. 'It was your lovely granny, Davy. But she was so ill after you were born she just couldn't look after you. So she gave you to me. You were my very own baby right from the first, though I had to share you with Granny and Gramps later on, when she was better—Grandma, too.' Sarah smiled lovingly.

'You were lucky, really, because when you were little you had four people to spoil you.'

'I asked Sarah to be your mummy,' said Margaret huskily. 'Anne—your granny—was so ill, you see, and I was much too old. I thought Sarah would be the perfect mummy for you. And I was right, wasn't I?' Unaccustomed, painful tears welled in her eyes as all three of them waited with bated breath for Davy's re-action.

It seemed a very long time before Davy let out a deep sigh and slid off Jake's lap to go to Sarah. 'I didn't think I could be adopted, really, because everyone says I look just like you.'

And thank God for it, thought Sarah, weak with relief.

'Are you hungry, darling?' asked Margaret, blowing her nose. 'I could cook something.'

'I've got a better idea,' said Jake, and grinned at Margaret. 'Let's ring up for a giant pizza. Do you like pizza, Grandma?'

'I've never tasted it,' she confessed, smiling. 'But I'm sure it's delicious.'

The weeks before summer term ended at Roedale were a halcyon time for Sarah. Jake went with her to sports day and watched Davy win the sprint, and displayed his pride as openly as any father there when the winner's ribbon was pinned on her shirt. This momentous event was eclipsed only by the wedding, which took place soon afterwards, with Davy as chief bridesmaid, fol-lowed by Nina and Chloe, when Sarah walked down the aisle in the long white dress Jake had insisted on for his bride. There were so many contenders for Davy's com-pany while her mother was away on honeymoon that in

the end she spent part of it with the Rogers family and
part of it with Nina and Chloe, and in between was
chauffeured on regular visits to Margaret, to reassure her
that Grandma wasn't lonely.

The housing situation had been solved with remarkable simplicity, and to Margaret Parker's deep approval.
Her bosom friend Barbara lived alone in a large house
not far from the Rogers home, and the lady was only
too happy to move into the ground-floor flat in Campden
Road and sell her house to Jake and Sarah.

'But we'll live in my flat while the renovations are
being done,' said Jake, on the first night of their honeymoon.

Sarah looked out at the moonlight silvering the garden
of the Greenacres Hotel and pinched herself hard.

'What's the matter?' he demanded as she winced.

'Just making sure I'm not dreaming.' She gave him a
wry, wondering smile over her shoulder. 'You must admit it's a touch unreal. Not so long ago I was a hard-
working single parent, then *wham* I fell in love with the
unique and wonderful Mr Jacob Hogan.'

Jake laughed and turned her in his arms to look down
into her face. 'Not unique, exactly. I'm one of a pair,
remember.'

'Not to me,' said Sarah firmly. 'You, my darling husband, are one of a kind.'

Jake kissed her by way of appreciation, then kissed
her again at length. 'It's getting cold,' he whispered.
'Let's go to bed.'

'It's not cold at all,' she said, laughing. 'Though I like
the idea of bed. But first,' she added, 'there's something
I've been meaning to ask you.'

'Ask away.'

'When you took us home to your parents the first time

Liam apologised for the infamous car incident, and said he'd caused you enough trouble already. What did he mean?'

Jake gave her a wry smile. 'You remember I told you that my London lady met someone else she preferred?'

'Vividly.' Sarah reached up and kissed him. 'Though I don't understand how she could!'

'Thank you, my darling.' He kissed her back. 'But I introduced her to Liam one weekend.'

'What happened?'

'She forsook me for my identical twin.'

'*What?* The woman has no taste. Besides, you and Liam aren't really identical.' Sarah smiled up at him. 'To me, darling, you're unique.'

'Definitely time for bed,' said Jake, and picked her up.

'Will making love be different now we're married?' asked Sarah, when he laid her on the wide white bed that had filled her with such misgiving the first time she'd seen it.

'Probably,' said Jake, his eyes gleaming with anticipation. 'I've never made love to a married woman before.'

'Same here with a married man.'

'Or any other man at all,' said her husband, with deep satisfaction.

'True.' Sarah gave him a glowing smile and held up her arms. 'Only you, Jake Hogan. Only you.'

MORGAN'S
SECRET SON

by

Sara Wood

Childhood in Portsmouth meant grubby knees, flying pigtails and happiness for **Sara Wood**. Poverty drove her from typist and seaside landlady to teacher, till writing finally gave her the freedom her Romany blood craved. Happily married, she has two handsome sons: Richard is married, calm, dependable, drives tankers; Simon is a roamer – silversmith, roofer, welder, always with beautiful girls. Sara lives in the Cornish countryside. Her glamorous writing life alternates with her passion for gardening which allows her to be carefree and grubby again!

CHAPTER ONE

JODIE looked around the immaculate apartment, gave a satisfied twitch to her hip-hugging skirt and went to unbolt the door.

'Hi, Chas! Come in,' she invited amiably.

A flurry of New York's winter snow hurled itself past Chas's muffled figure and settled on the newly polished wood floor.

'You'll have to clear that up before it stains,' he directed, frowning at the innocent flakes. 'Hurry up! Fetch the—'

'No, Chas,' she purred, very cat-got-the-cream. 'I *won't*!'

She had no intention of slaving away for him. She was waiting for his reaction to her outfit, and when it came it was highly satisfying. Startled by her refusal, he looked her up and down and then did the tour again, all the way from her high-heeled red thigh boots to her new and classy hairstyle.

'Wowee, babe! You're a real knockout!' he declared in surprise.

She smiled to herself, thinking of the blow she was about to deal him. 'In more ways than one, Chas. Would you help me on with this?' she asked sweetly.

'Sure... Uh...are we going somewhere?'

He was more than puzzled by her assertive attitude, and his fingers hesitated on the warm amber-red jacket she'd handed to him.

'Just *me*!' she trilled.

Wonderfully in control, Jodie slipped her arms into the jacket then flung a heavy honey-gold cape around her shoulders, her once-nervy hands as steady as a rock. Then she dropped her bombshell.

'I'm leaving. Permanently. Here are my keys. The apartment's all yours. *You* go wipe the floor!'

He gaped. Jodie noticed for the first time that his teeth were rather uneven and his lips were thick and wet. She shuddered. Love really had been blind!

'But...but you're crazy about me!' he protested. 'And...I love you!'

'No,' she corrected, feeling contemptuous because he'd deliberately turned on his low, sexy voice. It was so gravelly it could have gritted Manhattan. But it did nothing for her. He was out of her system! She jammed her fabulous felt hat over her shiny chestnut bob and set the brim at a wicked angle. 'You love yourself and you love the person you tried to create,' she said, exulting in her coolness. 'Ever since I came into your office as a junior you've done your best to make me into what you wanted: a cross between a domestic servant, a hard-nosed career woman and an insatiable tigress in bed. I'm fed up with being on antidepressants because I don't measure up, and I'm sick of trying to work out some PR promotion for you whilst scrubbing saucepans in a *thong*!'

'You're exaggerating!' he gasped.

'Perhaps, but you can't deny that would have been your wildest dream come true!' Her eyes flashed, green and sparkling, as she warmed to her theme. 'No wonder I was a bag of nerves! No wonder this kitchen's seen more charred remains than a fire fighter on overtime! Well, if you want Superwoman, go train someone else. I want out.'

'You can't!' Chas said in desperation, as she picked up her new suede gloves purposefully.

'*Watch.*'

'But...we could have babies!'

She froze at his last-ditch, sneaky attempt to keep her, then swivelled around, her jade eyes glittering with such ferocity that Chas quailed. For the past six years she'd longed for marriage and children. Chas had refused.

'Good*bye*!' she said coldly. 'You can pick my car up from JFK airport!'

'You're not serious! Where's your luggage?' he scorned.

'In the car already.' Feeling free as a bird, she opened the door.

'Wait a minute! Where—where are you going?' he wailed.

'England,' she replied more softly, happiness lighting her face. 'To be with my father.'

'*Whaaat?* You're mad! I know he wrote to you, but that was six months ago and you haven't heard anything since! If he's the sort of guy to abandon you and your mother when you were barely a year old, he's hardly going to cheer when an emotional cripple lands on his doorstep!' Chas bellowed nastily.

'I'll ignore that vicious remark,' she said, utterly calm and collected. 'I fully understand why he might have changed his mind about seeing me. Anyone can get cold feet over a situation like this. But I've realised that I *have* to meet up with him. He's my only living relative and I have to *try*.'

Taking charge of her life was such fun! Why hadn't she done it long ago? Seven years she'd worked for Chas! For six of those she'd been living with him! She gave the stunned Chas an amused glance.

'You'll find the thongs and the push-up bras in my top drawer,' she murmured. 'Enjoy.'

Elated, she swept out into the snow. She felt gorgeous, dressed in new and sensual—rather than uncomfortable and tacky—underwear. Over it she wore an outrageously expensive tangerine silk T-shirt, the slim-fitting amber suit with its shockingly brief skirt, a theatrical cape, hat and boots. She had become a new woman in every way—and she was setting out on an adventure.

Seemingly all legs and slim suede boots, she wriggled into the driving seat, gave a little wave to the open-mouthed Chas and giggled. Then she drove away, her thoughts returning to that moment when she'd opened the letter for the first time.

The sincerity of her father's affection had burst upon her like a ray of sunshine and hope. *Your loving father, Sam,* he'd signed it, and the breath had caught in her throat when she'd read those words. Someone cared. Someone really loved and wanted her. The tears came to her eyes as she remembered and she had to hastily dash them away or end up flattened by a bus.

Her mother had died when she was small. Foster-parents had brought her up, and now she recognised that they had begun the curbing of her naturally happy, outgoing nature with their rigid rules and punishments. Love had never figured. Not true, unselfish, accepting love. But now things would be different.

Jodie beamed cheerfully at a cab driver who was trying to cut her up and she let him through with a friendly wave. She laughed out loud when the man hesitated, unable to believe what he was seeing. But she was on top of the world and in love with everyone—Chas excepted!—even cab drivers.

Soon, she thought dreamily, she'd be arriving at her father's house in the south of England. He would have her letter announcing her arrival by now, and he could hardly refuse to see her when she'd come so far.

Just in case he did, there was Plan B. She'd booked into

a nearby hotel, from where she planned to work on his heartstrings until he agreed to a meeting.

She felt sure he wouldn't reject her. Something, someone, had dissuaded him from answering her many letters, she was sure. She understood only too well how other people could cloud one's judgement.

It had taken her this long to realise that Chas's advice—to forget her father—had been totally selfish. For years she'd relied on Chas, becoming increasingly dependent and subservient. But now she saw him for what he was: a bully and a control freak.

Her present confidence came from the fact that her father had been so eager for her to visit, and had even asked for her mother's address. A pang went through her. The weeks of loneliness and bewilderment after her mother's death had been so awful that she could recall them with crystal-clearness even now.

That was all over, though. Her eyes sparkled. This was the happiest she'd ever been in the whole of her life. No clouds on the horizon, no thongs, and a case stuffed to the brim with sizzling citrus and scarlet clothes!

'Brace yourself, England,' she cried with a laugh, seeing the sign for the airport. 'Here I come!'

With Jack hooked expertly over his shoulder and his hands slippery with suds, Morgan finally succeeded in opening the door.

Why did people always call when he'd just got the baby in the bath? It was one of life's irritating mysteries—and it was getting beyond a joke.

He grunted when the postman's cheery, gossip-ready face hove into view. Village life in rural Sussex had its drawbacks. People expected to chat, to share information.

And there were too many busybodies around trying to find out what the devil he was doing in Sam Frazer's house.

The postman had taken a step back. Morgan realised he'd been scowling and modified the severity of his expression.

'Morning,' he muttered. It still sounded like a veiled threat, even to his ears. Must do better!

'Recorded delivery,' the postman said, warily handing over the package.

'Thanks,' he said, mustering a little more grace.

He signed for the letter with his free hand and gave it a cursory glance. For Sam. He dropped it onto the pile of unopened mail on the hall table which was waiting till Sam's health improved, and made to shut the door. He had a million things to do.

'Er...baby all right?' enquired the postman meekly.

With a concealed sigh, Morgan mused that curiosity must be stronger than fear.

'Fine.'

'Must be five weeks old now. I love kids. Can I have a peep?'

It would have been churlish in the extreme to refuse, tempting though it was. Resigned to having Jack poked about by any number of strangers in the next few months, he pushed back the folds of the hooded towel which he'd wrapped around Jack's wet body and his face softened as two tiny boot-black eyes stared back at him.

'Like his father,' observed the postman, making funny faces for Jack's benefit.

'Is he?'

How a snub-nosed scrap of humanity could look anything like an adult, he couldn't imagine! Ironically everyone declared that Jack resembled Sam.

Guilt and resentment sucked relentlessly at his stomach. It was terrible being torn in two like this... He stared bleakly at the baby, despising himself for what he'd done, almost sick with anger and worry.

'We were all sorry to hear Mr Frazer had been rushed into hospital again. How *is* he?' persisted the postman with genuine sympathy.

'Critical,' Morgan jerked, all hell breaking loose in his heart.

'That's bad! He's had some rotten luck since he moved in last summer.' The postman patted his hand comfortingly. 'It was a nice funeral you gave his missus,' he said soothingly. 'Lovely oration.'

Morgan winced and didn't correct him. Teresa hadn't been married to Sam—a fact which had virtually caused her death.

He supposed that the postman was trying to be kind, but Morgan did not want to be reminded too vividly of that terrible day when he'd stood in the driving rain watching Teresa's coffin being lowered into the ground.

And then there'd been the expressions of sympathy to deal with. Teresa's London friends knew his secret: that he'd had an affair with her, before she'd switched to Sam.

They had stared with open curiosity at his hollow eyes and shocked appearance, whispering salaciously behind their hands.

He had known what they were saying. He'd overheard a comment: 'Did he never stop loving her? Is that why he's so distraught?'

The knife twisted even more sharply in his guts. What a hypocrite he was, a sham, a fraud! God! reliving it all was unbearable. He had to get away.

'Thanks,' he croaked, and had to stop to clear his throat of the clogging emotion.

The postman took advantage. 'Good on you for looking

after their baby—not many men would do that. Close relative, are you?'

'Not exactly. Excuse me,' he said stiffly, before the relationship could be investigated—and endlessly dissected during some idle coffee morning. 'His bath water's getting cold.'

He shut the door with a sigh of relief and instinctively hugged Jack closer, as if that could protect him from anything bad anyone might say or do.

But danger had literally threatened. Perhaps it was just as well that Sam had been rejected by his daughter. She would have jeopardised Jack's future. And that, Morgan thought darkly, was something he couldn't bear.

The baby felt soft and warm against his chest and a lump came back into Morgan's throat as emotion spilled in a flood of liquid heat through his body.

Teresa's death had stunned him. It had been the last thing he'd expected. And now...

What had he got himself into? The deception was getting harder to maintain. Every time he visited Sam the secret of Jack's birth burned inside him like a red-hot poker, souring his relationship with the man he admired and respected and loved more than any other.

Morgan groaned. Blurting out the truth would make him feel a hell of a lot better—but it would crucify Sam. Probably catapult him into a fatal decline.

'I can't do it!' he rasped in despair.

But...he loathed deceit and despised people who were so feeble they had to tell lies.

His eyes darkened with pain as he tried to face the inevitable and make the ultimate sacrifice. The truth would have to be locked up inside him and never revealed while Sam lived, however much that went against his own wishes.

and desires. There were two people weaker than himself
involved, and they had needs greater than his.

'Jack… How small and defenceless you are… And yet
you don't know the trouble you've caused, little one,' he
said quietly to the baby, who gave him that black glass
stare and rooted around with his mouth, blind instinct
prompting him to search for his non-existent mother's
breast.

'Poor little scrap,' Morgan whispered, offering a knuckle
in compensation. The small mouth clamped around it, digging in hard, and the black lashes fluttered in bliss. 'No
wonder Sam adores you,' Morgan murmured, enchanted as
always. 'You'd make anyone's heart soften. Let's get to
that bath and make you all clean for your…'

He couldn't say it. Some things were impossible to deal
with, and assigning fatherhood was one insurmountable
hurdle he hadn't yet come to terms with.

Morgan took the baby up to the nursery feeling like a
heel. He was caught in a web of lies. Here he was, fooling
Jack with a knuckle to suck instead of the real thing. And
in the future he'd be deceiving the child every single day
of his life.

But he didn't want to! Stricken, he stopped in mid-stride,
fighting the souring anger, desperately trying to suppress
his own needs. All his paternal instincts—previously hidden even to himself—were clamouring for the truth to be
known. His head told him that was impossible. Head versus
heart. A soul-destroying battle. Which would prevail?

Anguish distorted his features. Emotion flooded unchecked within him, his customary tight self-control eroded
by exhaustion and shock.

For a terrifying moment he felt an overwhelming need
to throw back his head and let rip a primal yell of anger
and frustration. Only the presence of the child stopped him.

Slowly his heart rate became regular again as the anger became ruthlessly suppressed.

For Jack's sake he gritted his teeth and continued the interrupted bath rituals, blocking out everything but the immediate needs of the tiny, dependent baby.

When he'd finished they settled in front of the log fire in the drawing room, and as Jack sucked enthusiastically on the bottle Morgan watched, his harrowed features relaxing into a deep awe. This was his compensation, the joy amid the grieving.

To him, the child was a miracle of perfection. Dark-haired, flawless skin, thick black lashes. Smiling, he touched the little hand with its long, slender fingers and minute fingernails. Jack's hand curled around his finger in an impressive grip of possession. Morgan's heart ached.

This was his son, and he wanted everyone to know it.

CHAPTER TWO

BLEAKLY he acknowledged the impossibility of that dream. 'Sam will be proud of you,' he promised with an effort.

The urgent hungry expression on Jack's face was slowly vanishing and a soft, blissful look of repose had begun to replace it. The small features smoothed out, the impossibly arched mouth slackened with sleep.

Desperate for sleep himself, Morgan adjusted his arm so that the two of them could rest in comfort. Just a few minutes for a catnap, he promised himself vaguely. Unfortunately his teeming thoughts wouldn't allow him to rest.

He hadn't found a daily help yet, and the kitchen needed clearing up. After that, he had to sterilise a load of bottles, make up a new batch of feed, put the washing on and do some ironing. Some time today he had to ring the office to see if it still existed. Then he and Jack would wrap up and go to see Sam.

He groaned at the catalogue of things which needed doing. It was eleven-thirty and he hadn't even shaved—let alone found time to grab a morning coffee! But when he wasn't by Sam's bed, doing essential chores or looking after the baby, he was pacing the floor night after night, and his energy levels were at rock bottom.

More to the point, his mind was consumed with guilt. He'd never done anything wrong in his life before and this secret was testing his self-respect and control to the limit.

He knew he was on a short fuse. Was it any wonder? Morgan's black brows screwed together in a fierce frown.

His big capable hands curled around the tiny baby who slept, oblivious to everything around him. Jack made Morgan feel both protective and envious.

His eyes grew hazy as he contemplated the future. For years he'd done whatever he'd wanted, gone where he'd pleased, lived as free as a bird. Now circumstances had clipped his wings and it was hard to adjust.

Once he had been free to fly to exotic sites and absorb their meaning, to discover that feverish excitement of seeing one of his designs take shape on his drawing board—and then grow in reality on the site, at one with its environment.

But in one brief moment with Teresa Frazer he had created and designed something which had turned his world upside down. For the rest of his life he'd never forget the moment when he'd turned up at the hospital and she had confessed that Jack was his son, not Sam's. Jack had been conceived while they were still together—before Sam even knew of Teresa's existence.

He winced, seeing again that once-beautiful face, hideously mangled by the car crash which had brought him hurrying to Sussex from his London flat. He hadn't doubted her word for a second. She had been so desperate to tell the truth, and too aware that she was close to death to waste her time with lies.

Morgan thought of Sam's breakdown when news of the crash had come through, how it had been he, Morgan who'd been with Teresa for her last conscious moments before the emergency Caesarean.

It had been *he* who'd first held his baby, *he* who'd wept with unrestrained joy and amazement. He hadn't shed tears since he was eleven, but the suddenness of fatherhood had overwhelmed him.

Emotion had filled his heart to bursting. He'd wanted this

child. *His* child! And yet he had known even then that he'd have to surrender him for the sake of a slowly dying man. Jack must be registered as Sam's son.

Such joy and sorrow mingling together as he had never known...

Morgan passed a shaky hand over his face. He owed *everything* to Sam. But this was the cruellest price to pay!

Racked with despair, he bent his weary head and gently kissed the downy forehead. The warmth of the fire and the accumulation of several sleepless nights began to blur his mind. His thoughts became less focused and finally he slept, briefly free from his troubles and the destructive, shameful deceit.

The closer Jodie came to the village where her father lived, the more breathless and excited she became. Discovering his existence had been the most wonderful thing that had happened to her. Her heartbeat quickened. She dearly wanted this to work. It *must*! All her hopes were resting on it.

Her eager eyes took in the scenery with its voluptuously smooth hills—incongruously called Downs, according to the map. Sheep grazed on the emerald grass of the tiny fields and swans were lazily decorating a meandering river.

And then she saw it: an old-fashioned signpost pointing the way down a country lane. She turned off the main road, her heart singing with unrestrained delight.

It was getting dark, even though it was only about four o'clock in the afternoon. In her headlights she could pick out quaint flintstone cottages strung out sporadically along the lane. Occasionally there would be a small Tudor cottage, with black and white timbers, a thatched roof and pretty garden.

As she passed each house she slowed the car to a crawl,

so she could read the names, her mouth increasingly dry
with nerves. At last, in the rapidly fading light, she spotted
the one she was looking for: Great Luscombe Hall.

'Be there!' she begged in a heartfelt plea.

Nervously she headed down a long drive, her hands gripping the steering wheel in a mixture of panic and anticipation. Her forest dark eyes widened. There was a moat!
Awed, she steered the car over the wooden bridge that
spanned it. It had never occurred to her for a minute that
her father might be wealthy!

Adjusting to this fact, Jodie brought the car to a halt in
front of the house. Her heart was beating hard in her chest
with anticipation. Great Luscombe Hall was a rambling,
timbered manor house with a roof made from huge slabs
of stone, and its façade had been constructed with enough
oak beams to make a fleet of ships.

'I can't believe this!' she whispered.

With trembling fingers she switched off the lights and
the engine and leapt out, her body tensed in expectancy.

And then she heard a furious barking. She shrank back,
terrified to see a Collie hurtling towards her.

'Help!' she croaked, freezing to the spot. Her terror-
stricken gaze was pinned to the dog's white fangs. 'G-g-
good, dog!' she squeaked unconvincingly.

'He's friendly,' snapped a hard male voice. 'His tail's
wagging, can't you see?'

Her father! Forgetting the animal, she looked hopefully
towards the house, a warm, happy smile bursting forth and
illuminating her eyes. It faded almost immediately. This
couldn't be him. He was too young. This was…who?

She swallowed nervously. The dishevelled, raven-haired
man was glaring at her suspiciously from the shadowy
doorway. Darkness surrounded him, a mere chink of light

coming from the door he'd pulled to, as if he were defending his castle from intruders.

Extreme tiredness made her head swim with odd, fanciful images—the black-watered moat, the medieval manor and with its looming, jettied upper storey, and the sinister stranger.

She noted that his hair was wild and wind-tousled, his black brows thick and fierce and the angular jaw covered in five o'clock shadow. Wide-eyed with apprehension, she took in his hostile stare, crumpled crew-neck sweater and jeans and wondered if she'd come to the wrong house.

'Great…Luscombe Hall?' she queried shakily.

'Yes!' he clipped.

No mistake, then. And he was just a man, she reminded herself. Bad-tempered, unfriendly and unwittingly threatening, but nothing more. It was time her adrenaline climbed down to normal.

'Then, hi!' she called, rallying her spirits. When she took a step forward she felt the dog's nose against her thigh and her courage faltered. 'You're *sure* I can move without losing a leg or two?' she asked, worried.

Searingly dark eyes brooded on her poppy-coated lips and she felt the hairs rise on the back of her neck. He'd just stared, that was all. But a flash of something almost sexual had slid briefly through her body.

'He's eaten already,' he dismissed. His mouth remained hard, as if hacked from granite by a sculptor who didn't know how to do curves. 'You want something?' he shot.

It wasn't the most gracious welcome she'd ever had! Jodie thought he sounded as if he'd got out of the wrong side of bed—and not long ago, judging by his rumpled state. Who could he be—the gardener? No—he'd been indoors. And the house might look grand enough for a butler, but not one who looked so untidy and…dangerous.

Handyman perhaps. He could have been under the floor-boards fixing something, hence his mussed-up hair.

Mystified, Jodie risked walking to the house. The dog bounded about her, circling as if she were a wayward sheep to be brought into line, and she smiled at its antics—though her city upbringing stopped her from trusting it enough to offer it a friendly pat.

'Here, Satan!' ordered the man sharply.

She hid a grin. Satan! That said volumes about his owner! She watched thoughtfully as the dog whirled around and flew over to its master, sitting to heel and gazing up anxiously. How severely had the dog been chastised till that level of obedience had been achieved? Fresh from living with a bully of her own, she felt her dislike of the man rack up a notch.

Close up, he seemed to tower over her slender frame, and she felt almost smothered by the tense atmosphere which surrounded him. It was clear from his manner that he was harassed and impatient, suggesting he had better things to do. Boilers to repair, pipes to lag, she thought with a sublime ignorance about maintenance. So she got to the point.

'I've come to see my father,' she told him briskly, though her joy suddenly shone through as she thought of their imminent meeting. Her fears vanished completely and she beamed, suddenly awash with happiness. This was a moment to cherish.

The man drew in his breath sharply and his eyebrows collided fiercely over his nose, as if she'd just confirmed his worst suspicions.

'Your...*father*?' he repeated ominously.

'Sam Frazer,' she confirmed, before the frown screwed up the man's entire face.

'*Sam!*'

He looked devastated. He'd gone quite pale beneath his olive complexion. Jodie took pity on him. Thinking only that she was seconds away from seeing her father for the first time, she gave an ecstatic grin and said, 'Yes! It's going to surprise a lot of people, I imagine. I'm pretty knocked out too—this house isn't what I'd expected at all. I'd imagined my father in a little cottage with roses over the door, and wearing tweedy things with leather patches on the elbows. This is really grand!'

'Is it?'

Jodie's voice faltered a little at the contempt in the man's eyes. But she wasn't to be put off. 'Sure it is. Now, if you're wondering, I'm his long-lost daughter from New York,' she explained. 'You'll want credentials, I suppose. Understandable. You can't let anyone in, can you? Somewhere...I have his letter...' Eagerly she scrabbled in her bag and produced it. 'It's a bit blurred in places because I cried over it,' she pointed out hurriedly. 'And it's coming apart at the folds because—'

'I get the picture,' he said tightly.

He shot her an unreadable look from under his brows then switched on the porch light and bent his tousled head to study the first few lines. Jodie restrained her urge to leap about from one foot to the other and yell, Let me in—now! and contented herself with idly observing him as an exercise in self-discipline.

It surprised her to see that his hair was gorgeous: thick and silky, gleaming with the brilliance of a raven's wing in the light. Her thick brown lashes fluttered with unwilling feminine admiration as her gaze took in his killer looks and the sheer masculinity of his angled jaw and powerful shoulders. Then her eyes widened in wonder. There were some creamy stains on his black sweater.

She was just pondering on this odd fact when the hairs

began to rise on the back of her neck and she sensed that he must be studying her again, with that bone-slicing stare. She looked up and gasped. His expression was one of utter repugnance.

'He wrote this six months ago,' he said icily.

'I *know* that! I replied immediately—'

'Really?'

'Yes!' Her face went hot at his disbelief. 'I did!' Her brow furrowed when she realised what his doubt must mean. 'Are you telling me that my father didn't get my letters?' she asked in dismay.

'Correct.'

Exasperated by the monosyllabic responses, she drew her brows into an even deeper frown.

'That's impossible. I wrote several times in quick succession—and I telephoned twice—' she said with dignity.

'If that were true—*if*,' he interrupted coldly, 'why did you come?'

Her eyes widened. 'Because I want to see him, of course! Something doesn't add up here. I sent those letters. They can't all have been lost.'

'I agree. He had no letters from you. So you must be lying. I think you'd better leave.'

She glared and clenched her fists in angry distress, her mouth beginning to tremble. Hot tears pricked the backs of her eyes. It would be tragic if this was as far as she got! So near, so far...

'I'm not going till I see my father! I *did* write!' she insisted in desperation. 'Something's happened to the mail. A wrong zip code, maybe. I spoke to a woman on the phone. I'm not imagining that. I asked for Sam Frazer, said who I was, and she told me he didn't want to see me—'

'Well, that final comment is true, at least,' he drawled. 'I suggest you turn around and go home.'

He'd turned and was about to shut the door when she lunged forward and jammed herself in the gap. The dog barked excitedly, its teeth snapping close to her thigh.

'Ouch!' she gasped. 'Get this door and this dog off me!'

The pressure of the door was removed from her protesting flesh.

'Leave!' ordered the man.

Glowering, she stayed put; the dog backed away obediently. She rubbed her arm and thigh, conscious that she was deliberately being intimidated by the man's looming bulk.

'What did you do that for?' he asked impatiently. And then, with a small thread of concern in his voice, 'Are you hurt?'

'It's nothing,' she dismissed. 'But I couldn't let you slam the door in my face. I've flown across the Atlantic to see my father. Surely he can spare a few moments of his time?'

'No. He can't.'

Her imploring face lifted to his. 'Just a few moments... I won't bother him for long, but... You must let me in,' she said, her voice trembling with emotion. '*Please!* You've no idea what it's like not to know your father! I need to see him so badly—even if it's just the *once* and never again! It's not much to ask, surely? To see what he looks like, to hear his voice...' Her own voice cracked up annoyingly. 'I—I don't even have a *photograph*! Let me have memories of him to take away with me, if nothing else,' she added in a croaky husk. 'Imagine how you'd feel in my position!'

'Hell.' His growl was followed by a long pause, as if he was struggling against his better judgement. Jodie waited with bated breath, willing him to relent. 'You'd better come in,' he muttered grudgingly, to her great relief.

Then, before she could gather her wits, he'd turned on

his heel and was walking into the beamed hall beyond, the dog at his side. She stared at his daunting back with irritation. This guy wasn't a servant to anyone. He oozed authority with every flicker of his ink-dark eyes. He wasn't pleasant, either.

But everything pointed to the fact that he knew her father well. And the hostile welcome must be because he knew that her father had been disappointed and upset when her expected letters didn't arrive.

No. Correction. There was another reason. This guy *might* be the person who'd dissuaded her father from going ahead with the reunion. If so, she had to persuade the guy that he had nothing to fear from her.

Jodie gave a feeble smile. Fear! He wouldn't be afraid of the devil himself if he came calling!

Suddenly she started, remembering the recorded delivery. That must have arrived—proof enough! She would call his bluff.

In seconds she crossed the dark oak floor and caught hold of the man's arm. It felt hard and muscled as it tensed beneath her fingers. His whole body became stiff and taut, as if she'd invaded his space. Crushed by his cold dislike, she let her hand slide away.

'I'm sorry,' she said hastily. 'But I had to stop you before you reported back to my father. I want you to know I'm not lying. I can prove that I had the right address and that he must have had my letters.'

The hard, uncompromising gaze pierced into her brain and she felt giddy.

'How?'

With an effort, Jodie pulled herself together. She might be tired and woozy, but this was important.

'I sent a letter by recorded delivery to say I was coming. It must have been safely delivered into the right hands; it's guaranteed! And if that arrived, then so did all the other letters!' she said in triumph.

'Ah.'

She followed his gaze to a circular table which groaned under a pile of unopened mail. Her letter lay on the top. Her mouth opened in amazement that anyone could be so cavalier.

'How can you claim the rest of my mail's gone astray?' she exclaimed in horror. 'It's probably all lurking beneath that heap!'

'No. That's just ten days' worth,' he said curtly.

'Ten…! But you can't leave mail unopened! And where are my previous letters, then? In a landfill site?' she spluttered, aghast.

'Don't be ridiculous! All his earlier mail has been dealt with. So will this when… You look hot,' he said, changing the subject abruptly. 'Let me take your cape.'

He came up behind her and his hands were on her shoulders before she could move. But his touch seemed tentative, as if he would have preferred to avoid contact. The pure wool cape slid away, slithering across her firm breasts in a shimmer of gold.

'Your hat,' he ordered, appearing in front of her and holding out his hand.

He looked her up and down, and then again—perhaps startled by the vibrancy of her colour scheme, she thought with a flash of amusement. She let a smile sneak out, her hopes rising—she'd got this far at least. What did she care what had gone wrong in the past? This was now and she was here, and somewhere in this house was her own dear father.

Jodie removed her hat with a flourish, giving her head a little shake as she did so.

'Let's not get twitchy over what happened. There's obviously been a muddle. The important thing is that I see him now,' she said happily, silky brown hair still swinging around her delighted face.

His lips tightened into an uncompromisingly grim line. 'Come into the study,' he ordered.

She was left with her mouth open in astonishment as he strode away. This, she decided angrily, was another control freak. He told women to jump; they asked How high? Chauvinist!

She followed, the dog prowling alongside her, but she paused on the threshold of the lamp-lit room he'd entered. Her father wasn't there. Her hands curled into angry fists as she checked the room again.

The stranger stood with his feet planted firmly apart in an attitude of domination. He leant, squire-like, against a carved beam which spanned an enormous recess…an inglenook, she decided, raking around in her mind for her limited knowledge of medieval houses.

Logs the size of small tree trunks crackled and blazed in a massive iron basket, filling the timbered room with the sweet aroma of pine. Books lined the walls and a desk, chaotically littered with papers, sat squarely in a mullioned bay window, its deep window seat backed by a dozen or so scarlet cyclamen in oriental pots.

'You're busy, I'm in a hurry, so I won't hold you up any longer,' she said, her chin high. 'You know why I'm here. Tell me where my father is!'

Her face went hot. He was examining her in intense detail and warmth was creeping through her as he did so.

'Sit!' he ordered.

'Good grief! What do you think I am—a dog?' she declared indignantly.

'I was talking to Satan. He's just behind you in the doorway. Perhaps you'd like to sit down as well, though?' he suggested, a faintly dry humour briefly appearing in his eyes.

She grinned. At last he was beginning to unbend a little. 'Sorry!' she said blithely. 'I'm not used to orders being barked at dogs.'

His eyebrow rose at her implied criticism. 'Collies are intelligent and powerful. He knows he's not allowed in the reception rooms, though he tries it on every now and then. You rule them, or they rule you. All dogs need a pack leader.'

'And you're it?' she said with a smile, wondering if his philosophy extended to women.

'For the moment. Please, make yourself comfortable.'

The cream leather armchair he'd indicated looked as welcoming as a warm bed and she sank into it in relief. 'That's better! It's been a long journey,' she confided, stretching her long limbs luxuriantly and giving a little wriggle to ease her stiffness. 'I've been driving on the left side of the road for the past four hours and my brain has been protesting every inch of the way. I suppose I could have stopped overnight somewhere, but I kept going because I longed to be here.'

Misty-eyed again, she ventured a smile, but received nothing in return.

'I'll get you some tea,' he drawled. 'Stay!' he ordered.

Jodie wasn't too sure if this had been directed to her or the dog. 'I'd rather see my father straight away,' she said hurriedly. But not quickly enough. His long jean-clad legs had swallowed up space so quickly that he was almost out of the room. Balked again, she called, 'And if it's no trouble, I'd prefer coffee... Oh, for heaven's sake!' she fumed in exasperation.

Morgan strode to the kitchen, and once he was there and

out of sight he stopped dead, knowing he had to gather his composure before he faced Jodie again.

He needed space. Time. A brain that wasn't fuzzy with exhaustion and which could deal with the problem her arrival had created.

Focus. He must concentrate... Cursing softly to himself, he ruthlessly shut out everything but the alarming situation.

He had a choice. To refuse Jodie any access to Sam, or—when Sam's health improved—he could coax Sam to see his daughter. He closed his eyes, fighting for objectivity.

If he could persuade her to go then life could continue as before. And one day Jack would return to him.

He felt dark emotions swirling inexorably in his mind, denying him clarity of thought. Because he knew with a gut-wrenching pain that if Jodie was ever reunited with Sam then he could lose his son for ever.

Jodie was Sam's next of kin. When Sam died, which the doctors said would be within a year or two, she would automatically be responsible for Jack's future welfare.

And he, Morgan, would be out on his ear.

A devil was driving him, whispering in his ear wickedly that he could eliminate all danger by stating the cold, unvarnished truth: that her father had rejected her utterly. It would be so simple—and he wanted his son so badly that he tortured himself by listening to the voice in his head even though he knew he should, in all honour, endeavour to bring father and daughter together.

But Sam had been adamant. 'She's like her mother!' he'd declared with wild conjecture, when he'd given up all hope of hearing from Jodie. 'Selfish, flighty and heartless! If she knew I was rich she'd be here quick enough! Morgan, she's broken my heart! I never want to see her—even if she turns up in rags and trailing ten children in her wake, *do you hear*?' he'd raged.

'I hear,' he'd said quietly, hoping some day to dissuade him.

But that had been before Morgan knew he was Jack's father. And now Jodie was here, in dazzling scarlet and trailing fire and passion and a steely determination in her wake.

Common sense told him that he should send her away with a photo after a cup of tea. But could he live with himself, knowing that Sam had had the opportunity to enjoy the last year or two of his life in his daughter's loving company?

'God!' he muttered. 'What a choice!'

Hard on himself, as always, he forced himself to go through the motions of making tea, but his fingers were constantly stilled by the strangely haunting image of Jodie's face.

What was it about her? Some element of Sam, his honesty, his goodness? It would have been easier if she'd been an out-and-out cow—selfish, flighty and heartless, as Sam had suggested.

But Morgan's lasting image of her was of her transparent, innocent joy, which had cut through his suspicion and shock like a sword of light.

He stared into space, seeing the blinding smile which had lit up her extraordinary jade eyes till they'd sparkled like gemstones. She'd seemed almost vulnerable in her eagerness to tell him about herself.

Morgan thought of her passion when she'd begged for a crumb, the right to see what her father looked like because she had no photographs of him. Her words had sliced through his heart like a knife through butter. He understood that terrible emptiness of being somehow unfinished because of an unknown parent.

All his life he'd wanted to know who *his* father was. His rootlessness, his avoidance of committal and his dangerous hunger for love had undoubtedly been a consequence of that empty gap in his life. In that instant he had felt a visceral stab of compassion for her. And so he'd weakened.

Of course she was lying about the letters. But it was like the lie of a vulnerable child who can't bear to be in the wrong. A greedy child, perhaps, he reminded himself with a frown, before he became too indulgent. Maybe she'd done some research on the Internet and had discovered that Sam Frazer was one of the most prestigious architects in the country.

He rubbed a thoughtful hand over his stubble. With Sam owning half the village and the lucrative practice, she'd be in line for a huge inheritance. And custody of Jack.

Morgan's hands shook as he filled the kettle. Where would that leave him? Visiting occasionally. Looking on while she brought up his son.

'No!' he muttered vehemently. 'Never in a million years!'

Sam only had a short time to live. Morgan had planned to adopt Jack when the older man died. But if Jodie was on the scene she would be firmly entrenched as Jack's carer by then.

There'd be a legal tussle which could go on for years, with Jack in the middle—and by that time Jodie would to all intents and purposes be a mother figure to Jack. He couldn't take his son away under those circumstances. It would be too cruel.

No! Better if he never let that situation arise. He sucked in a harsh breath. That settled it. He'd keep her at arm's length and respect Sam's explicit wishes. Tea and sympathy, then pack her off home.

CHAPTER THREE

JODIE sat fuming and twiddling her fingers. She flicked through an elaborately illustrated book about buildings in Brazil, which normally would have interested her, but she had one thing only dominating her mind: her father.

She knew she was ready to fall asleep from sheer exhaustion—but before she did she must see him. Over tea—*coffee!*—which would revive her and give her the boost her system needed, she'd ask this man if...

No, she'd demand. She was no collie dog. She would not be ruled by him.

Wearily she hauled herself from the chair and followed the sounds of movement, finding herself in the doorway of an enormous farmhouse kitchen fitted out with limed wood units in the country house style.

Unobserved and unheard in her rubber soles, she temporarily forgot why she'd come because he was wearily dumping leaf tea into a pot like a zombie on sedatives. Intrigued, Jodie counted six spoonfuls before he paused and then uttered a brief expletive.

Each one of his movements was slow and laboured as he emptied the pot and then carefully recounted the correct amount of tea in a voice which betrayed his irritation with himself.

After adding boiling water to the brew, a deep sigh welled up from the depths of his body. His head tipped back in an attitude of despair.

Jodie was fascinated. He seemed more than tired. It was

as if life itself had become untenable. Why? What was going on here?

Not daring to let him know she'd seen him in an unguarded moment, she tiptoed away and made the approach again, ensuring that she made enough noise on her way to the kitchen to serve as a warning.

When she entered, he was back in control of himself again: stiff, erect, and poker-faced.

'I thought I'd see if I could help,' she began crisply. 'And—'

'It's done,' he said, before she could ask for a coffee. 'Now that you're here, we might as well have tea in here instead. Milk or lemon?'

'Whatever.' Jodie was too eaten up with curiosity to pursue her preference and she sat down at the scrubbed pine table expectantly. Tea was a stimulant, anyway. And she needed revitalising before she started making waves. 'Now,' she continued amiably, hoping to disarm him, 'tell me who you are.'

'Morgan Peralta.'

'Unusual name,' she said, encouraging him to open up.

'I have Colombian parents,' he replied grudgingly.

It explained a good deal: his dark good looks, the sense of lurking volcanic passions, the Latin cheekbones and bred-in-the-bone sensuality. He had a magnificent body: just muscled and lean enough for her taste. Beside him, Chas would look a slob. So would most men.

She looked at his hands, always a give-away, and thought that there was something very sensual in the way his slender—almost graceful—fingers dealt with slicing the lemon. He'd be good with women, she mused. Delicate in his touch. Tantalisingly exploring... She blinked, startled by where her thoughts had taken her.

Feeling warm from the heat of the kitchen, Jodie unbuttoned her jacket. She would have removed it but Morgan's hooded gaze had honed in like a guided missile on the tangerine shirt beneath and she felt a sudden frisson of sexual danger as something indefinable sizzled briefly between them.

Stupid. How could he possibly be interested in her? It was her over-developed imagination. Static in the air. Besides, he was hardly going to jump her. Not over tea!

She hid a smile at her caution but decided she'd feel more comfortable if she kept the jacket on. The T-shirt fitted snugly and she didn't want Morgan counting her ribs. Or anything else...

She was astonished to feel a blush creep up her entire body, and she let out a breath she hadn't known she was holding.

Morgan slanted an odd look at her from under his brows then sat opposite her, immediately picking up the teapot and pouring out a thin, almost gold-coloured liquid into their cups and slipping in a slice of lemon. Jodie accepted the offered cup doubtfully. It didn't look like any tea she'd ever seen.

'I'm Jodie,' she offered, anxious to be accepted. 'Jodie Frazer.'

'I know.'

He was close to her father, then. She took a deep breath and plunged in.

'I imagine my father was upset when he didn't hear from me,' she ventured.

'Devastated.' His expression was uncompromisingly hostile.

'That's awful. I wish I'd known.' She leaned forward earnestly. 'But you've heard my explanation. You must understand that I wouldn't want to hurt him for the world.'

She took a sip of the surprisingly refreshing tea and

looked at him over the rim of her cup. He seemed to be having a mental struggle over something. Hopefully she was coaxing him round.

'He's been through a lot recently. I won't let *anyone* disturb his peace of mind,' he stated flatly. 'Your rejection—'

'But I *didn't* reject him!' she cried in frustration.

'He thinks you did.' Stern and forbidding, he leaned forwards. 'I'll find you some snapshots of him to take away. Don't give yourself grief by pursuing this. He won't see you. Accept that and get on with your life.'

'I can't!' she persisted. 'He's only upset because he was hurt when he didn't hear from me. When he knows what happened—'

'He won't hear about it because I'm not telling him your story. Frankly, I just don't believe that you answered him straight away.'

Incensed, she jumped up. 'Then I'll go look for him and tell him myself!'

His arm snaked out to stop her and he rose in one swift and graceful movement, coming to stand menacingly in front of her.

'And I will be forced to prevent you,' he said, very softly.

Jodie squeezed her eyes tightly, to prevent herself from crying in sheer helplessness.

'Please hear me out!' she begged, opening her eyes and staring miserably at his blurred face.

There was a long pause. She stopped breathing. She could hear his breath rasping loudly, feel it hot and quick on her mouth.

'I'll listen,' he muttered. 'But that's all. Sit down. Sell yourself to me if you must.'

She sank gratefully into the seat. A brief reprieve. The

next few minutes were crucial. Feeling oddly hot and flustered, she began to tremble.

'You're…being protective,' she began croakily. 'I understand that. It's good to know someone's been looking out for him. But, like you, I swear I only want what's best for him.'

He grunted and slanted her a cynical glance. 'I wonder. Would you surrender your own needs for his?'

'Can you explain that remark?' she asked in a guarded tone.

'If you really cared for him,' he said quietly, 'you'd do what was in his best interests, not yours.'

She raised one eyebrow. 'And his best interests are…?' He didn't answer and dropped his gaze with a frown. Jodie felt a spurt of hope. 'You're not sure, are you?' she cried shakily. 'He's insisting that he doesn't want to see me— and you're now wondering if he's making a mistake! Morgan, think about this! You can't in all decency stand between us! You'd have it on your conscience all your life if you didn't at least try to persuade him to change his mind! You know that. I can see it in your face. Oh, please give me a chance!'

Morgan drew in a long, hard breath, his eyes betraying the doubts in his mind. Jodie's pulses raced and she twisted her hands together nervously.

'I need some time to think about it,' he growled.

She beamed in delight. 'That's wonderful! Thank you!' she cried passionately.

'I'm only taking time to consider the situation. Nothing's fundamentally changed. Don't build up your hopes,' Morgan warned.

She flung back her head and laughed, her eyes sparkling. 'I'm an optimist. I have to hope! I want to hold my own father in my arms so much that I ache with longing!'

'Then protect yourself from that hope. You could be badly hurt if I decide you must not see him,' he said, his voice low and thick.

Jodie felt a tremor run right through her body. 'It would break my heart,' she breathed.

'Better than you breaking his,' Morgan observed.

'But...why would I?' she asked, bewildered. 'How could I?'

'Do you know anything about him?' he shot.

'No, nothing! That's what's so awful—'

'You know he lives in a large house,' he pointed out cynically.

She drew herself up, insulted by the implication. 'You think I care about his money? That's not why I came! If you can't identify truth and honesty and real affection when you hear it, then I feel sorry for you!'

His eyes flickered. 'You're making it very difficult for me, Jodie,' he said, almost to himself.

She bit her lip, hardly able to bear the suspense which hung in the air between them so tautly she thought it almost crackled with tension. He seemed unable to tear his gaze away from her—and she found herself locked in his thrall.

'Just...what is your connection with him?' she asked, sobered by the power he could wield over her future.

'I'm his right-hand man. He trusts me and my judgement.' The dark eyes continued to bore remorselessly into hers.

She gulped, her head swimming. Tiredness. She had to push this on. 'You could sway him, then?' she said with difficulty.

'If I wanted.'

'Please *want*!' she pleaded.

He jerked back a little, as if startled by what she'd said.

There was a brief, hot melting of that intent gaze and she felt that at last she was getting somewhere.

He wasn't as hostile. A faint warmth was emanating from him, an imperceptible softening of his hard-hewn face as he contemplated her, weighing her up, assessing everything about her.

She flushed, her mouth drying as his thick lashes fluttered and his downward gaze wandered to her bare throat, her breasts, and then to her legs, which she'd hooked over one another. She wanted to tug down the suddenly embarrassing short skirt to hide an inch or two of slender thigh, but that would have drawn attention there.

And now he was studying her parted lips, and she could actually feel them plumping up in some odd biological response. Hastily she sipped her tea, to occupy her wayward mouth and to avoid his scrutiny.

'I stick to the bargain,' he said huskily. 'Try convincing me some more.'

She moistened her lips again before starting. 'I'm twenty-four. I've spent all my working life in an advertising agency where I was on promotions. It was my job to persuade clients in any way I could to take up our ad campaigns—'

'I bet you were very good at your job,' he said, a curl of amusement lifting the corner of his craggy mouth.

'I was!' She furrowed her brow. 'What else? I help two evenings a week at the retirement home nearby—'

'Oh, please!' he mocked. 'You're going too far—'

'It's true!' she said indignantly. 'I'll give you the phone number and you can check!'

'I'll do that.'

'Good—'

'I suppose you're kind to children and animals?' he drawled.

'No, at every opportunity I boil them up in oil—what do you *think?*' she cried crossly. 'I'm just an ordinary sort of person who tries to keep on the straight and narrow and live a decent life—'

'Not that ordinary. You have a boyfriend?'

'Is that relevant?' she asked in surprise.

'Could be,' came the enigmatic answer.

She shrugged. OK, so be it. She'd tell him her bust size and weight if it helped her cause.

'The answer's no. I've just dumped him,' she said with a grimace. 'He was an arrogant controller who'd tried to mould me into his version of the perfect woman!' Her mouth quirked at his raised eyebrow.

'Did he fail?' Morgan asked, clearly doing his best to hide his amusement.

'Dismally. My problem is that I'm highly allergic to thongs!' she said with a giggle.

As she'd expected, he did a double-take, and for a second or two she thought his eyes showed a flicker of genuine interest. Then the impenetrable shutters came down again.

'So when your relationship broke up,' he drawled, 'you decided to give your father in England a whirl, for want of something better?'

'No! It wasn't like that at all!' she said, bristling. 'Hearing from my father was the catalyst for change. My boyfriend's attitude to a reunion with my father was unsympathetic and obstructive. OK, I took my time realising this, but eventually I did—and saw my boyfriend for what he was. A selfish, manipulative, bullying brute!' She pinned Morgan with a determined stare. 'I've spent the last seven years being walked over. I won't be pushed around any more—not by anyone,' she said meaningfully.

'I think you've made that apparent,' he murmured.

Had she gone too far? She looked at him edgily. 'So what's your verdict?'

'The jury's out,' he drawled.

A sudden feeling of hopelessness washed over her. He was playing with her, leading her on. Fatigue and disappointment made her limbs leaden and her brain ragged as she tried to keep up the pressure on him.

'Look. I'm shattered. I haven't the energy to joust with you but I am desperate to see my father,' she said, her voice cracking with emotion. 'If it makes it any easier for you, I totally understand that if he eventually decides that he wants to live his life without me—then that's his choice to make and I will have to accept his decision.'

Morgan nodded in approval. 'Good! That's settled, then,' he murmured with satisfaction.

She saw tension ease from him and felt her own nerves tighten. It looked as if he was going to send her away with a flea in her ear! Annoyed, she fixed him with her brilliant green eyes and grimly set about persuading him to plead on her behalf.

'However,' she said sweetly, 'I'm sure you'll agree that it should be *his* decision, based on personal knowledge of me. It would be wrong if he didn't even see me face-to-face, so that I could explain that there might have been a mix-up with the mail,' she added, being generous about her suspicions concerning Morgan's part in the 'mix-up'.

'He still might not believe you,' he suggested cynically.

'Oh, yes, he would! He'd look into my eyes and find the truth there!' she insisted stubbornly, passion pouring from her blazing eyes. 'You have seen his letter and read his sentiments. He must still care about me deep down! I'm convinced he'll be overjoyed that I've turned up! You may not have read enough of his letter to me to know that he mentioned he'd just moved house—and that he had something special to tell me. I've been consumed with curiosity ever since. You can't deny me the right to see my own father, not when he was initially so anxious that we should be reunited! He must want me, mustn't he?'

Morgan scowled at his tea. His mouth tightened and then he gave a small exhalation of breath. Jodie waited, tense with anticipation.

'Perhaps,' he hedged reluctantly.

Jodie gasped and clasped her hands in delight, drawing his dark, assessing gaze. 'So I'm close to passing muster?' she asked with a relieved laugh, her eyes spangled with deep jade lights.

'You're persuasive,' was all he'd say.

It was enough for her. The moment had come! She jumped up eagerly. 'Let me ask him! Lead me to him! I just can't wait any longer, Morgan. I'll burst if you keep me dangling in suspense!'

He shifted uncomfortably. 'It's...not that simple—'

'Why not?' she cried in exasperation.

He leant back in his chair, studying her expressionlessly. 'He's not here.'

Jodie's jaw dropped in dismay and she gave a little gasp of disappointment.

'Not...*here*! But I imagined...hoped... Oh, when's he coming back?' she wailed.

'Not...today,' he dissembled.

She slumped back into the chair, totally depressed. 'None of this is working out as I expected,' she said morosely. 'This means I'll have to get back into that wretched car, battle my way along the wrong side of the road and search for the hotel.' Her head lolled back and she heaved a heavy sigh. 'It's not a prospect I relish. I feel shattered. I've been living on adrenaline for days. You can't have any idea what this meeting means to me, Morgan!'

'Have a piece of cake,' he suggested gruffly.

'Keep my strength up?' Dejectedly she took the plate and picked at the fruit cake in a desultory fashion as her thoughts came tumbling out. 'It's my fault, I suppose,' she mused. 'I should have waited for a reply to the recorded delivery. But I was mad keen to see him.' She met his gaze, her eyes clouded with sadness.

'Why is it so important to you?' he asked quietly.

'Because he's the only family I've got now. He and my mother separated when I was a year old. Mom and her boyfriend took me to New York and we lost touch with my father. Mom died when I was six—'

'Your mother is *dead*?' he broke in sharply.

'Yes,' she replied, too engrossed in her own problems to pay much attention to his alerted state.

'God!' he groaned. 'Eighteen years ago! If only Sam had known!'

A film of tears washed over her eyes at the implication that her father would have contacted her sooner.

'Mom wasn't much of a mother, but she was better than my foster-parents. All this time I thought I had no living relative in the whole world! W-when my f-father wrote—' She broke off, a lump filling her throat.

'I don't need to hear this,' Morgan rasped.

'You do!' she cried passionately, her eyes glistening with unshed tears. 'I want you to know what this means to me! I discovered that my father was *alive*! It was the most wonderful present I could ever have been given. He was in England, walking, breathing, sleeping… I couldn't think straight. I went around the apartment in a daze, bursting into song…'

Unable to stop herself, she flung her arms in the air in an impassioned gesture as she relived those first joyful hours. His eyes flickered with a strange, glittering light and she faltered, bringing her arms down quickly, lest he think she was mad. But he had to know the intensity of her feelings!

'Morgan,' she explained fervently, 'you had to be there to see me! I danced, I hugged myself breathless, ate a whole tub of ice cream…! Oh,' she cried, husky with the memory, 'I was so happy I felt delirious. I grinned at everyone I met. New York reeled! For days I walked on air—and then every so often I'd burst into tears. I felt so far away from him, you see.'

There was a long silence. Morgan seemed to be finding it difficult to speak. Once again, tension spun a thick blanket between them, crushing the air from her lungs. Jodie clasped her hands anxiously, scanning his face. Her heart turned over. Something was wrong!

Numbed by Morgan's look of pity, she waited, a prey to her imagination. Her father was dead, she thought immediately, her eyes rounding in horror!

'Look…you mustn't get your hopes up. You can't see him now, or in the foreseeable future.'

She blinked, trying to puzzle this out. 'Why?' she asked, her face pale.

The breath caught sharply in her throat. Something akin to anguish had slashed across his well-deep eyes before vanishing again. But it was obvious to Jodie that he was profoundly disturbed about something. She noticed that he'd clenched his jaw hard and balled his hands into fists till the bone shone white through the skin over his knuckles.

Her pulses went into overdrive as fear skittered through her. Her cup clattered to the saucer, freed unwittingly from her jittery fingers. Tea spilled across the blue check tablecloth but neither of them gave the stain more than a cursory glance.

'My father…? He's not…not…?' she whispered desperately, and choked on the terrible lump which blocked her throat.

'No!' Morgan cried quickly, interpreting her distress. 'He's not dead! I didn't mean that!'

In a surprising, reassuring gesture, his hand reached out to hers and held it tightly when she let out a small groan of relief.

'What, then?' she breathed.

'He's unwell—in hospital,' Morgan replied, sounding strained. 'He's been ill for some time—'

Jodie trembled. 'Was…was he ill when he wrote to me?' she asked in a small voice. 'He sounded idyllically happy—'

'He was—but his health was poor even then. That's partly why he contacted you. And now…' His jaw tightened. 'I have to tell you that he's taken a severe turn for the worse—'

'What do you mean?' She stared, aghast, her eyes wide and horrified. 'How much…worse is he?' she croaked. Breaking free, she leapt to her feet in agitation. 'Tell me the truth. I must know!' she demanded hysterically.

His mouth became grim. 'You need to sit down—'

'Answer me! I want to know!' she wailed, ignoring his suggestion.

'Very well. The stark truth. He has pneumonia,' Morgan said quietly. 'He's fighting for his life.'

It was his pained whisper which drained all her body of its strength. The stark gravity of his expression told her—far more than his words—that her father's condition was perhaps more serious than he was letting on.

Stunned by this unexpected development, she swayed as the room whirled around her and a roaring in her ears drowned out anything else he might have said.

With a feeble moan she grabbed weakly at something,

anything, found the chair and collapsed into it, her mind in turmoil.

'No! *No!*' she moaned.

Hot, stinging tears welled from her eyes and poured unchecked down her face. Distraught, shocked beyond belief, she hugged her arms around herself and rocked back and forth, weeping without restraint.

So near and yet so far.

She could have been here months ago! But Chas had told her he couldn't release her from work to go to England. And then there'd been the failure in the mail service—or, worse, Morgan had blocked her letters! And Chas had persuaded her that her father hadn't replied because he'd had second thoughts...

She groaned. All this time she could have been comforting her father, getting to know him, fussing over him... And now he might be close to death.

'Oh, God! My poor father! I—I didn't expect any...anything l-like this!' she mumbled raggedly through her sobs.

The soft folds of a handkerchief touched her hand. She snatched it and pressed the linen against her tear-stained face. He could have caused this situation. She scrubbed her eyes hard and looked at him accusingly.

'I have to ask you this—did...did you hide m-my letters?' she asked bluntly.

'No!' he answered, obviously shocked by the suggestion. 'I couldn't have. I only came to live here a few weeks ago!'

She took a huge, shuddering breath. Her letters had gone astray, then. No wonder Morgan had been so hostile. He'd known that her sick father had written to her, knew how vital it was that she should reply. When no answer had come, Morgan and her father must have hated her for being callous and unfeeling.

She groaned with frustration. But she did care! More than she'd known, more than she could have ever believed! To get so close to being reunited—and then to have that longed-for moment cruelly snatched away—was a worse blow than anything she'd ever known.

This had been her chance to love and be loved unconditionally. To know the purest, most lasting love between a parent and a child.

Her poor father. Dangerously ill…she thought numbly. Her leaden arms dropped and came to rest on the table. She bent her head, too shattered to hold it up any more, and her burning wet cheek found comfort in the soft fabric of her jacket sleeve. Her sobs racked her body till her ribs ached and her throat felt raw.

Dimly, somewhere in the background, she registered an odd crackle, as if someone was brushing a hand across a microphone.

'Excuse me. I have to go!' Morgan muttered.

His chair scraped hastily back and she heard his brisk footsteps crossing the tiled floor rapidly, as though her tears irritated him and he couldn't wait to get out of the room.

Miserably she lifted her head a fraction, suddenly wanting the company of someone, anyone.

'Don't!' she sobbed. But his blurred image was already disappearing through the door.

Her lip trembled uncontrollably. He wasn't giving her the benefit of the doubt. He believed she was a liar and blamed her for upsetting a seriously ill man.

He knew Sam. Cared about him. But she was part of Sam too! She was upset and alone and in a strange country. He *knew* how she felt about seeing her father!

How could he walk out on her? Maybe he was upset himself. But didn't he feel anything for her own grief? She banged her fists on the table. Why were so many men so utterly selfish? *Why* didn't they feel the hurt of others?

A flood of anger and resentment welled up like bitter bile in her mouth and she began to sob as if her heart would break, crying for her father and for herself, hating the cold-hearted Morgan and his lack of humanity.

Her misery intensified. Now she knew where she stood. Entirely alone.

How he'd got out of the kitchen he didn't know. He stuffed the portable baby alarm deeper into his pocket, ravaged by the rawest of emotions.

It had been worse than he'd imagined.

He'd grabbed a bottle from the fridge and picked up the automatic bottle-warmer; grimly he took them to the drawing room, where Jack lay in the rocker-seat uttering plaintive squeaks of protest.

'You pick your moments,' he said quietly. 'Hold on. Just need to plug in this...then we'll undo these straps and you're safe, here with me...'

How safe? came that insistent voice again. When you're tussling with your conscience, toying with the idea that this woman should take her rightful place in this family? When you're close to deliberately handing over your own flesh and blood to a total stranger?

Morgan ground his teeth together, ignoring the maelstrom of his mind, walking up and down with Jack, soothing him with his voice and trying to regain his own equilibrium.

'Hush, little man. Nearly ready,' he muttered. He bent his head and put his cheek to Jack's, desperate for human contact. 'This is tearing me to pieces,' he said bitterly. 'Sam, you, her...'

His brows met in a deep frown as he reined in his ragged thoughts. He didn't want to go through anything like the last few minutes ever again. Jodie's heart-rending sobs had torn through all his defences, getting under his skin more than he could have believed possible.

He should never have asked her in. Damn his sense of morality and fair play! Listening to her had been fatal. She came over as vulnerable, too open and trusting for her own good. Or was she? He'd been fooled before. Badly.

He frowned, feeling keenly his past failure to protect Sam. The repercussions had been disastrous. A shudder of anger and repulsion ran through him. That meant he must do everything in his power to ensure that this woman wouldn't hurt Sam in any way whatsoever.

Jodie was a mass of contradictions: brightly dressed and assertive, yet emotional and sensitive. Morgan grunted. Fascinating she might be, but that could be a deadly combination for a sick man who needed peace and a hassle-free life.

It was essential that he kept a clear head to deal with the threat she posed. Common sense told him to get rid of her. Yet his own innate sense of decency and compassion kept getting in the way.

And, aching with his own anguish about Sam, he'd found himself on the brink of taking that shaking, slender body in his arms and holding her close to show that he shared and sympathised with her grief.

Only his fear for Jack's future had stopped him, urging caution instead of a knee-jerk emotional response.

'All ready now,' he murmured lovingly to the baby. 'There. Worth waiting for, wasn't it? Such big tears...'

His head lifted, his eyes dark with the torment of the past. He'd witnessed hysterical weeping just like Jodie's not long ago, when Teresa had begged him to remain silent about who had fathered her baby. He'd made a promise to a dying woman out of pity, to give her peace of mind. And to protect Sam.

From then on he'd been floundering in an unfamiliar mire of lies and deceit. His mouth tightened in resolve. He'd never go down that road again.

He stared at Jack's small, intent face as he drowsily suckled. Blissful innocence. Heart-wrenching defencelessness... He could never part with this precious gift, this child—*his* child!

'She could take you away from me!' he said to Jack, his eyes blazing and his heart pounding violently in his chest at the very thought. 'I won't ever let that happen!' he vowed fervently.

Whether she was needy or not, he had to persuade her to abandon any ideas of a cosy reunion. But he felt a heel for doing so. Even though he was doing exactly what Sam wanted. The older man had said emphatically—almost hysterically—that he didn't want anything to do with her.

However, Morgan wasn't comfortable with the decision he had now made—even though it meant that his own future with his son would be assured.

The problem was that it would be tough as hell seeing Jodie walk away unsatisfied, knowing how badly she yearned for her father.

He raked a hand through his hair. Curse her for complicating his life!

Jack stopped feeding. With great gentleness Morgan put the baby over his shoulder to burp him. Then he tenderly wiped away the dribble of milk around the petal mouth— and groaned when he incidentally caught a glimpse of his watch as he did so.

'Damn!' he muttered irritably. 'Later than I thought!'

Jodie's arrival had disrupted his plans. The chores would have to wait. Time to leave for the hospital.

On autopilot, he changed Jack's nappy, then found a warm wool hat in the changing bag and carefully pulled it over the thatch of fine black hair before beginning the familiar struggle: getting two small and uncooperative arms into the cosy coat.

And now he had to tell Jodie his decision.

'Hang on a minute,' he said softly, tucking the cooing Jack safely into the rocker chair. 'Back soon.'

He pocketed the alarm and set off for the kitchen, dreading the next few minutes. But he found her sprawled across the table fast asleep, her head on her arms.

He stood there for a moment looking at her, his gaze transfixed by the way her gleaming hair hung around her head like a glossy cap and how it shone with rich red colours in the fluorescent light.

Gently he shook her shoulder. It felt fragile beneath the spread of his fingers and his fingers briefly splayed out, recording the delicate bones beneath the warm flesh. Vulnerable, he thought. Despite her bravado. And a twinge of something inexplicable ground through his stomach before he scowled and paid attention to what he had to do.

'Jodie. Jodie!' he said urgently, determined to get this over and done with.

She muttered, but was too deeply asleep to be roused. Sliding his fingers down the sleeve of her jacket, he found that it was wet with tears. An unwanted rogue sympathy dangerously softened his heart.

Without knowing why, he lifted silken strands of hair and tucked them behind her ear so he could see her face. The huge, soulful eyes were thankfully hidden from view, but the sight of her cutely curling wet lashes touched his emotions.

With a groan, he caught her chin gently in one hand. 'Jodie!'

Her head lolled heavily and he muttered with exasperation, conscious that time was ticking away. She was out like a light.

Well, she couldn't stay there. And he couldn't hang about waiting for her to wake up. Nothing for it, then.

He slid a hand beneath her and lifted. She snuggled with annoying trust in his arms, her head burrowing a little place for itself in his neck—just like Jack did. Her breath came soft and even on his throat. Combined with the feel of her plush curves and the sweet scent of her hair, it was a heady sensation.

An undeniable hunger began to lap at his body. He recognised it as the long-denied desire for the softness of a woman, the sensual pleasure of exploring a woman's body, the release of tightly controlled passions and the tender aftermath.

He scowled. And what had all that cost him in the past?

Angrily he strode out and climbed the stairs. Surrendering anything to a woman had a price. If you made a mistake—and he'd made one too many—you went through hell.

It wasn't particularly surprising that he was reacting to this sexy and appealing woman. He'd been celibate for a long time and every blink of those incredible eyes had sent tingles through him, invigorating each cell in his body. But he could handle that…

Morgan's muscles contracted, proving the opposite. She'd wriggled, and the pressure of her breasts against his chest was fast eroding his resolve. Tight-lipped, he placed her on the four-poster bed in the guest room and eased her arms from around his neck.

For a moment her face lifted and their mouths were close. She sighed, and the urge to kiss those moist, parted lips almost overcame him.

Somehow he drew back and busied himself with briskly hauling the duvet out of the linen press. He hesitated. She'd been travelling for hours. She'd probably sleep through the evening and into the night.

His dark eyes flickered over the thigh boots. Hesitantly he slid his hand over the soft suede and took the zip tab between finger and thumb. In doing so his hand brushed against firm, warm flesh, but he conquered the tremor which slid with a languid warmth through his body and eased the boots off.

Nothing to it. Ignoring the long expanses of shapely leg, he considered the jacket. It had to come off too. Rolling her over on one side and then the other, he finally managed this.

Her arm came up and twined around his neck, pulling his head down to her breast with surprising strength. He found that his face was nestling luxuriantly in the folds of silk, the rise and fall of her perfumed breasts making his head swim. He stayed there for only a split second but it was almost too long.

With ruthless will he extricated himself and hastily covered her with the duvet, bringing it safely up to her chin, as if he knew he had to obliterate all sight, all memory of that delicious, tempting body.

Her cheeks were streaked with tears, her lashes still spiky. In a moment of madness he thought of washing her face with warm water, but he realised he must stay away from this woman and banish her from every part of him.

She was Sam's daughter. Hadn't he caused enough trouble with Sam's mistress already?

He was playing with fire by finding Jodie sexually desirable. Merciless with himself, he drew the curtains around the bed and left her a note in case she woke up, saying he would be out for a couple of hours or so.

And then he showered—cold, invigorating, beneficial—shaved and dressed, collected Jack and headed for the hospital, preparing himself for the harrowing sight of his dearly loved Sam fighting for breath, for life itself.

CHAPTER FOUR

JODIE stirred, her deep, dreamless sleep interrupted by a low rumbling. Groggy and barely conscious, she forced her heavy eyes to open a fraction. Her half-conscious mind took in the swirling greyness above—where she would have expected the darkness of a ceiling—and raw instinct took over.

'Fire!' she yelled, terrified, yet too drugged from the depths of sleep to think straight. 'Help! Fire!'

Her eyes stubbornly refused to focus. A numbing lethargy had taken over her limbs, demanding that she fall asleep again. A nightmare, she told herself hazily.

Smoke surrounded her. Bedding had wrapped itself around her legs, preventing her from escaping. In her dream, or waking, she screamed in panic and forced herself to fight for release, blindly lashing out at everything in her way.

'Help! Help me!' she whimpered as the danger became clear. And then to her utter relief she felt cool air on her face and body as the duvet slid away.

The smoke parted. There was blackness beyond. Paralysed with fear, she blinked in confusion, her eyes thick and heavy, and her tongue cleaving to the roof of her mouth. A shadowy figure moved into sight and she raked in a strangled breath, her eyes wide with horror.

'Hush! It's all right.'

A hand rested comfortingly on her bare shoulder and a light snapped on from somewhere behind her head. She found herself staring into Morgan's liquid dark eyes. They were soft and molten and she felt instantly overwhelmed with relief.

'Fire!' she husked.

'There is…no fire,' he breathed.

'There was…smoke!' she mumbled foggily, trying to make her comatose brain work.

'Uhuh. A…dream,' he said hoarsely.

'No—I heard a rumbling, burning, perhaps…' Her voice faded. There was no smell of smoke, no sign of it. 'I did see smoke!' she insisted, afraid he'd think she was mad. 'I opened my eyes and saw it…'

'You couldn't have,' he interrupted sharply, bending down to pick up the duvet.

She felt its warmth suddenly descending on the bare skin of her pelvis, hips and legs, where previously there had been nothing. Shocked, she realised that she was still wearing her skirt—and that it had ridden up to her waist in her struggles.

She gasped. That meant that when Morgan had first switched on the light… Oh, sweet heaven! Her citrus silk briefs, her bare stomach and thighs and the lace-topped hold-ups would have been exposed to his penetrating gaze!

Furtively she wriggled the skirt down and tentatively moved her hands up her body. Her cheeks flamed when her fingers encountered the soft nakedness of one breast. It seemed her T-shirt had behaved just as recklessly!

Appalled, she cringed beneath the duvet, her apprehensive eyes flicking up to his. He looked as indifferent and as grim-faced as ever, his jaw clenched hard as hewn granite.

He hadn't been interested, she thought, and frowned, shocked by her indignation. Yet she didn't want men to make passes at her as if she were some sex object. She

wanted to be loved for her whole self. So why should she
be annoyed?

'Relax,' Morgan clipped. 'You're safe.'

With difficulty she hauled her mind back. 'But if I didn't
see smoke, what did I see?' she muttered crossly.

'You're in a four-poster bed,' he explained. 'Look up.'

Her sulky gaze followed his. She saw a dove-grey can-
opy above and its swirling pattern—like smoke. Curtains
of the same material had been drawn around the sides. That
was what she'd seen surrounding her in the darkness. She'd
been scared of grey fabric!

'Ohhh!' she groaned. Keeping the duvet safely up to her
neck, she collapsed back on the pillows, deeply embarrassed. 'I feel so stupid. I'm terribly sorry,' she mumbled
in contrition. 'I was deeply asleep. My brain must have
picked up a couple of clues and gone into survival mode.'

'It wasn't your fault. You didn't know where you were,'
he agreed in a faintly slurred voice.

It was then that she registered that he was wearing a
white towelling robe, open at the throat and chest and
loosely tied at the waist. It was short enough to reveal
strong, sinewy legs and a glimpse of muscular thigh.

He'd been in bed. Or in the bath. Were those beads of
sweat on his forehead or dampness? Jodie realised she was
staring and said hurriedly, 'What's the time?' She peered
at her watch on the bedside table and groaned in dismay.
'It's five a.m.! How awful! I woke you!' Her hot, apologetic face lifted earnestly to his.

'I was already awake,' he replied. 'I was doing the washing.'

Her eyes rounded. 'Washing?' and then it dawned on
her. 'That explains it!' she cried. 'The spin cycle—it must
have woken me!'

'Then it's for me to apologise to you,' he said quietly. 'If you're all right now, then—'

'Wait a minute!' Jodie was frowning, trying to piece together what had happened. 'I don't recall going to bed. I'm…I'm still wearing my clothes…but not…all of them… Did I…? Who…?'

She gulped, frightened that so many hours could be a complete blank, her anxious, wide eyes meeting his in a silent question.

'You cried yourself to sleep at the kitchen table.'

She remembered that. Her eyes narrowed at his flat, unemotional delivery. He really didn't give a damn about her!

'It's hardly surprising!' she said feistily. 'And…then?' she queried, feeling herself tense up in anticipation.

He scowled. 'You couldn't stay slumped awkwardly over the table all night…'

His tone was matter-of-fact and curt, but he was strung taut, every muscle in his body straining so much that he shook imperceptibly. Jodie gloomily realised that he must be thoroughly irritated with her. He'd even checked himself in mid-sentence, almost as if he couldn't be bothered to waste his time continuing.

'So?' she prompted with a glower, needing to hear from his own lips what had happened.

'Obvious. I carried you up here,' he clipped.

Like a sack of potatoes, apparently, she thought grumpily. 'Well, thank you,' she muttered, remembering her manners.

He shrugged his wide shoulders as if it were all in a day's work—and an unpleasant job, at that.

'Had to be done.'

The insult to her feminine pride cut her to the quick. But then she found herself consumed with the image of herself, curled up in his arms, the subject of his inscrutable gaze.

At some stage he must have removed her boots. And her jacket. Her tongue flickered across dry lips and they parted as she drew in her breath. Even though he wasn't interested in her as a woman, she found the situation uncomfortably intimate. And alarmingly arousing.

'You—you were very kind to let me stay the night,' she said throatily, frowning at the treacle-like thickness of her speech. She must be more tired than she'd known.

His eyes glittered, then his dark lashes lowered to conceal them. 'I didn't have any choice,' he growled, so quietly that she barely heard at all.

And in the crushing silence that fell she became very aware of everything about him. Suddenly his mouth seemed more carnal, its lines curving with a beautiful sensuality. Her lips parted. He was clean-shaven now, and she found herself aching to touch the smooth lines of his angular jaw.

Her eyes half closed. Not from drowsiness, but from an unstoppable surge of sexual awakening which made her feel she was swimming through warm seas, every part of her body invaded by a lethargic heat.

She'd never felt like this before. Not this desperate, inescapable and reckless need to be touched, to touch…

She swallowed, bewildered and appalled by her uncontrollable lust. It was driving her into danger. This man would take no prisoners.

'Goodnight, then,' she managed, brutally denying her basic instincts.

''Night!' he shot back through his teeth.

He pulled the curtains across and left before she could hold him there any longer. But as he thundered angrily down the stairs he knew with a heart-stopping shock that she had captured a part of him already.

He groaned. Every inch of his body was threatening mutiny. It clamoured to be free of the rigid control he was imposing on it.

The blood was still pumping in his veins, red and hot. The breath had been rasping in his throat so loudly he'd been sure she'd comment on his laboured intake. His eyes could only stare, his lips part in readiness. His hands had almost reached out and touched...

He sucked in a harsh breath, his mind seeing nothing but the sweet curve of her hips, the dark, triangular shadow beneath the tantalisingly fragile scrap of acid-yellow silk. And then that smooth softness of her thighs above the lacy stockings. The incredible swell of her milky-white breast with its dark plum centre, tantalisingly sleepy and un-awoken...

He'd longed to bring it to life. To surround it with his mouth, pulling gently till it peaked hard and sweet while he caressed her fabulous body, feeling its flawless silk against his flesh and bone, crushing her to him till they melted in heat and desire...

That was how he'd felt. His need had been so unexpected and fierce that it had stunned him. And he'd stood there helplessly, a martyr to his lust and shaking with pent-up desire, disgusted that he should feel like this about a total stranger. Sam's daughter. It was a direct betrayal of Sam's trust. Again.

Ruthlessly he'd suppressed his primal urges. And so he'd parried her remarks, calmed her fears, and had somehow walked away without making a total prat of himself.

'Hell!' he muttered.

Every male instinct in his screaming body had demanded that he should put his arms around her, comfort her, allow that to lead to a gentle kiss, and slowly, tenderly make love to her before he lost his reason.

'God!' he breathed, walking unsteadily into the kitchen.

This was an extra complication he could never have fore-seen!

Shaking with the effort of containing every rampaging pagan impulse in his protesting body, he made himself a pot of coffee and concentrated with ferocious intent on the expulsion of the luscious Jodie from his mind.

Jodie lay on the bed horribly wide awake and wishing that the aching emptiness in her body would go. Restless, she slipped out of bed, intending to find her nightdress in the case she'd noticed by the dressing table.

Instead, she paused in front of the mirror and took a good, hard look at herself: a tousled, wide-eyed wanton. She was astonished by the change in her appearance. Where had this pouting-lipped seductive hoyden come from?

'The last thing you need,' she told herself crossly, 'is a selfish, hard-bitten guy who wouldn't know what tender-ness was if it socked him in the eye twice a day!'

Her stomach rumbled suddenly. She needed food. It must be hours and hours since she'd last eaten. Planning on sneaking down to the kitchen, she dived for her case, rum-maging around inside it and bringing out a pair of soft jersey palazzo pants and a warm sweatshirt.

Chas had said she was highly sexed, she mused soberly, changing into the banana-yellow outfit. Although if she was honest it had always been the triumph of hope over expe-rience. Chas had never satisfied her.

Twisting a red and lemon scarf in her hair, she paused, her eyes rounding in alarm. Maybe that was the trouble—she was one of those women who were insatiable, who needed sex like some people needed lunch, and then second helpings, please! The thought was mortifying.

Granted, Morgan was the hunkiest guy she'd ever met, that dark intractable manner only adding to her fatal fascination—but she'd promised herself that she would find someone who was gentle and kind, full of consideration for others. Someone who utterly adored her. Less than that she would not accept. And in any case, she had something more important on her mind.

She sighed heavily, realising she was no nearer to seeing her father. She was even more determined now that she knew he was ill. Morgan *had* to give her the name of the hospital. She'd get it out of him at breakfast time if she had to lick his boots in the process!

Halfway across the landing, she stopped in her tracks. She'd see him sooner than that—Morgan had said he was doing the washing! If she went down now, she'd bump into him! Her face coloured with embarrassment. For a fraction of a second she almost chickened out, and then impatiently brushed away her sense of discomfiture.

She needed food and this was her opportunity to pin him down. *Without fail.*

He was struggling to fold a damp sheet when she padded into the kitchen, her bare feet silent on the terracotta tiles. She took one look at his brooding face and powerful figure and her stomach swooped.

'I'm starving,' she announced as a diversionary tactic for her runaway carnal impulses.

He turned, frowned in the general direction of her searing yellow outfit, and continued battling with the sheet.

'Eggs and bacon in the fridge.'

''Fraid I'm hopeless at cooking,' she admitted. 'I was thinking of toast and coffee, and perhaps a fruit pie or a chocolate cake—'

'In the larder.'

His head jerked abruptly to indicate where. The sheet slipped from his fingers and he glared at it, then her, as if it were her fault.

The old Jodie would have crumpled. This one said drily, 'Here. I'll help you with that.'

They did sides to middle and end to end. The moment she began walking towards him with her end of the sheet she felt the hairs rise on the back of her neck.

'Thanks,' he said curtly, and seemed as anxious as she was to avoid close contact because he virtually snatched the folded sheet from her fingers and spent a while arranging it over a chrome rail attached to the front of the stove.

She let out a shaky breath. It had happened again! Why, she couldn't imagine. Though…he was a hard, moody man, and handsome enough to give women grief. However, she'd had enough of that. For her, men were as passé as thongs. All she had to do now, she thought ruefully, was convince her hormones.

'I couldn't sleep,' she remarked casually, in an effort to break the tense silence.

'So I see.' He yanked at the tie on his robe, knotting it more securely. It was a telling gesture. One of those indicators like…folding one's arms…which made it plain that he was being defensive. Keep out, it said. Don't invade my territory.

She felt deflated. He didn't feel comfortable with her around. He didn't like her, didn't trust her and couldn't bear to be in the same room. And now he was reinforcing her theory by turning his back on her at every opportunity.

Jodie glared at the broad expanse of white towelling. Her wretched sexual hunger interfered briefly and forced her to admire the shapely triangle of his back and the small waist and hips.

And then she pulled herself together. He had his need to be alone, but *she* needed information. Which she'd get, come hell or high water!

Whirling on her small bare feet, she found the bread, the

butter and a large apple pie, and brought them triumphantly to the table.

'I'll help myself to coffee,' she added, pleased with her assertiveness. Wordlessly he handed her a bone china mug and she filled it to the brim. 'I irritate you, don't I?' she said bluntly.

He gave a small and mirthless laugh, finished stacking wet handkerchiefs on top of the chrome lid which covered a hot plate, then hauled an ironing board out of a cupboard.

'You're a complication,' he acknowledged drily.

At least he was honest. She watched him plug in an iron and grab a shirt from a huge basket of ironing, quite dazzled by his domesticity.

'Why are you doing this?' she asked, unable to hold back her curiosity. 'Don't you have a daily help?'

'I *am* the daily help.'

Her eyes widened in surprise. *'You?'* It briefly crossed her mind that Morgan and her father could be lovers, but the idea was so ridiculous and Morgan so utterly male that she dismissed it immediately. 'Where's the toaster?' she said, looking around for one.

'Here.' He took the bread from her, lifted the other chrome lid on the stove and slid the slices between two pieces of mesh shaped like a tennis racket. 'Keep an eye on that. It toasts very quickly.'

She kept lifting the lid and peering at it. The heat coming off the hot plate was intense, and, as he'd said, the toast was done in a matter of seconds. She wasn't sure what impressed her most, the stove—which seemed to be doubling up as an ironing machine and a clothes dryer—or Morgan's domestic talents.

'Is this is your job, then? Washing and ironing and so on?' she fished, lavishly spreading the butter.

He frowned at her from under his lowered brows and

expertly dealt with the collar, cuffs and the front of the shirt.

'No. I do it because someone has to.'

'At five in the morning?' she murmured in amazement, pushing up her sleeves in the warmth of the kitchen. She sat on the edge of the table eating the toast, her legs swinging, scarlet toenails twinkling in the bright light.

Morgan slanted an odd look at her. 'I can't fit it in otherwise,' he said slowly.

'Why don't you employ someone?'

Tight-lipped at her questioning, he pressed fiercely on the shirt, steam rising in clouds. 'The only two possible daily helps who live locally worked here for a few days and then walked out.'

She wasn't surprised. He'd try anyone's patience. Generously sugaring her coffee, she mused that it was his fault if he had to do his own smalls. So she bit back an urge to offer help and bit into the bread instead, munching away and watching him covertly from under her lashes.

Almost immediately she felt that surge of electricity again, a strong current which seemed to pull her towards him. He must have sensed she was watching him because he flicked a glance at her and stopped his manic ironing while their eyes locked.

Jodie felt her mouth drying. She squirmed, caught helplessly in his magnetic field, the remorseless sexual tension boiling up like a seething cauldron inside her.

She seemed to be all heat, her mind consumed by the sight of Morgan, dark, virile, naked beneath the robe…

Swallowing, furious with herself, she slid shakily off the table and moved further away, wandering about at the far end of the kitchen. It wasn't enough. She was reduced to opening and shutting cupboard doors with her free hand in the effort to dissipate the explosive energy building inside her.

And although the temptation was to stay and drink in Morgan's hot sexuality, she knew she must ask what she needed to know and leave, so that she could escape her own frightening desires and retire to the safety of her room.

'My…father…' she began in a terrible croak, and was forced to moisten her lips. She put down the toast in case he saw how much her hands shook and she pushed them into her pockets, determined to see this through. 'I want to know where he is,' she said jerkily, 'and how he is and when I can see him. I want to know all about him—'

'I visited him yesterday while you were asleep,' he broke in obliquely.

Her huge green eyes flinched at the sight of his grim face. It didn't look as if he had good news. She began to tremble.

'Oh! H-how is he?'

'Stable,' he replied, sounding utterly drained.

'What does "stable" actually mean?' she asked anxiously.

'I believe it means he's not getting any worse.' He picked up another shirt and spread out a sleeve on the ironing board, his movements slow and laboured, as if he was walking through a fog. 'They think he'll pull through,' he said huskily, his voice vibrating with emotion.

'Oh, dear God!'

Overwhelmed by relief, Jodie closed her eyes and let out a whimper. The room seemed to spin around and she would have fallen if he hadn't come quickly to her side and steadied her.

His touch brought her sharply back to reality. With intense clarity she could feel the welcome pressure of his hands around her arms, could trace by feel alone each long finger and its soft pad at the tip. The rise and fall of his breath quickened now, and she inhaled the faint warm aura of his body: a clean, indefinable faint fragrance of fresh soap.

She quivered in the thick silence, struggling to understand why he was shaking too. Apparently her father's illness had hit him hard. Sympathetic tears began to trickle down her face again.

'I don't believe this! What a wimp! I don't *want* to cry!' she mumbled crossly, aware that he was looking at her intently. 'But…it was a shock, hearing that my father was on the danger list, Morgan—and now he's going to be all right, I—I—!'

'Of course. You're letting go. I do understand,' he said quietly.

Something in his tone alerted her. 'You're very fond of him, aren't you?' she asked huskily.

'Fond? I love him,' he replied, his breath warm on her lips.

She stared, surprised by his passion and transfixed by the torment in his eyes until she recalled his Latin American background. He would love and hate with a ferocity she could barely imagine.

'If…if he had died,' she said, stumbling over her words as emotion claimed her, 'I—I couldn't have *borne* it.'

'Neither could I,' he said thickly.

She choked on a sob, her lower lip trembling uncontrollably. Pulling her close, he slid his arms around her comfortingly, and then his hands were stroking her hair so tenderly that she could hardly bear the sweetness of his caress.

He really did care for her father, she thought muzzily. Her cheek lay on the soft lapel of his cotton robe; her lips just touched the hot silk of his chest. She could hear his heart beating loudly and suddenly she knew why he'd been short-tempered and curt with her. He'd been desperately worried, perhaps to the exclusion of everything else.

Without realising it, she nuzzled more trustingly in his arms, musing that there was a special link between Morgan and her father which she'd discover soon. In the meantime, she could almost forgive Morgan for his abruptness.

'It's been hard for you too, hasn't it?' she whispered, guiltily enjoying the feel of her mouth against his skin.

'Harder for him,' he growled.

That touched her. She inhaled a raw breath, her emotions stretched too far in compassion for her father, her own relief, and an overwhelming sympathy for Morgan, who was stoically trying not to let his anxiety get the upper hand.

'It's all right now,' she murmured soothingly. 'He's on the mend. It's wonderful news.'

On an impulse, she hugged him, loving the firmness of his body in the circle of her embrace. And then she lifted her head to look at him, her eyes bright with happiness.

'He'll be back here sooner than you know. Won't that be wonderful?'

She felt his muscles relax, felt the huge outrush of air from his lungs. His cheek came down against hers and her arms tightened around him again in sheer relief. Knots in her slender shoulders unwound as she relaxed completely in his arms.

Her father would be well and Morgan had accepted her. There would be no barriers between them now.

She sighed, a gentle joy easing away the remnants of tension. Her body felt warm and molten against his, almost boneless. Suddenly her chin was being tipped up by a questing finger and she smiled up at him, tears still swilling her bright eyes.

Time seemed to stand still. Her breathing was suspended. She was lost, drowning in the dark pools of his liquid eyes, her lips parting of their own volition as his head angled, the light gleaming with an aching beauty on his raw cheek-bones and sinfully smooth jaw.

She knew she should move, say something, even, but speech and conscious thought had deserted her. An irresistible force was weighting her lids and compelling her eyes to close before she understood why.

And then all reality was obliterated because his mouth was on hers, firm yet gentle, his kiss more sweet and tormenting in its restrained passion than any she'd ever known.

Her head tipped back in abandoned pleasure and she wound her arms around his neck with a little whimper of need. Without any thought to what she was doing, she kissed him back, only knowing that she wanted him to stroke her body, to hold her tightly and to kiss her like this for hour after hour till her blind need to be loved had been sated.

But he broke her dream by gently pushing her back, his hands supporting her as he stared, blinking, at her ecstatic face.

'I think,' he said thickly, 'that we're both overreacting to the news about Sam.'

She stared at him blankly, her lungs almost devoid of breath. For a moment his gaze dropped to her parted lips and she thought—crazily hoped—he was going to kiss her again, but he inhaled sharply.

'Yes,' she agreed reluctantly.

He frowned. 'The two of us have been under some strain. Needed someone to hug…'

She released her grip on his robe, pulled herself together and managed a weak smile, thankful that he was defusing the situation.

'You're right! Lucky the vicar wasn't to hand!' she suggested, unnaturally bright. Slipping away and grabbing a piece of stone-cold toast, she waved it airily to give her time to come up with some coherent reply. 'Relief does the oddest things to people!'

She took a bite at the flaccid bread and wished she hadn't, all the time praying he'd agree and not question why she'd fallen so recklessly into his arms. But since he'd grabbed blindly at the nearest source of comfort, he was clearly ready to believe that was what she'd done too.

'Certainly does. I do apologise. I overstepped the mark.'

Back to his abrupt, clipped self, he took up the ironing again with a grim fervour that astonished her.

'That's OK. Understandable in the circumstances,' she said warmly.

She flashed him a smile but he didn't respond. She sighed with disappointment. She'd been mistaken; he didn't want to unbend towards her. That moment of closeness had been purely a reflex action to her father's improvement.

Her teeth dug into her lower lip. It felt awful, being disliked and thought a liar. If only Morgan would trust her! But at least they'd shared a mutual emotion. That was a start.

'The hospital,' she prompted gently. 'I'd like to ring—'

'No!' he broke in roughly. 'Sam is too ill and too frail to cope with you. He has to concentrate on getting better. I will not allow you near him.'

'But...I thought you might have changed your mind—!' she began in horror.

'Then you're wrong. I have some sympathy for you, but my first duty is to him. He's made his wishes about you quite clear.'

'Based purely on an incorrect assumption about me!' she protested.

'So you claim. It doesn't alter the fact, Jodie, that he doesn't want you. Accept this and—'

'No, I won't!'

'Then you leave me no choice.'

Scowling, he switched off the iron and put it and the board away with a clatter. She was speechless at this turn of events. Avoiding her dismayed gaze, he began to prowl up and down the kitchen.

'My advice,' he went on tightly, 'is that you cut your losses and get on with your life, Jodie. There's nothing here for you, and you'll only give yourself grief by fighting for the *impossible*!'

He had thumped his hand down on the counter angrily, his movements faster and his temper closer to exploding as he stalked up and down the floor like a caged animal.

Jodie gulped. His long legs devoured the length of the kitchen as if he was hungry for a fight, and she cringed back against the stove, the chrome bar biting into her back as she arched away from his unreasonable fury.

'I have to try!' she cried bravely.

He stopped dead, the full force of his wrath turned on her. 'Why do you seem determined to pester a desperately sick man?' he thundered.

'My father!' she reminded him hotly.

'Who is in no condition to listen to your excuses—!'

'The truth!' she flared, hands on hips, eyes glittering with combat.

'And who washed his hands of you with the utmost contempt and absolute loathing!' he hurled, white slashes of anger gleaming on his high cheekbones.

Her face paled. 'He doesn't feel that strongly about me…does he?' she moaned, wincing with the pain of what he'd said.

'You drove me to tell you that!' he said in exasperation,

his eyes dark and glittering. He continued his fevered prowling. 'Don't push me any further or you'll regret it! I must protect Sam! He's in no fit state to do so himself!'

'I've *told* you I only want what's best for him!' she protested, frustration making her tearful. She pressed her trembling lips together, her eyes luminous with silent pleading.

'Then go!'

'Not without knowing how he fares! I can't leave. Even if I never see him, I have to know what happens to him—'

'I'll phone you,' he said grimly. 'That's a promise. And now you've taken up enough of my time. I want you out of here—'

'That's rich! I'm his daughter and I have more right to be here than you!' she defended, folding her arms defiantly. 'I'm staying, whatever you say. I will see my father! You can't stop me from enquiring at the hospital about him! If you stand in my way, I'll—I'll call the cops!' she finished wildly.

'Call them!' he snarled, whirling like a cornered tiger. 'They won't be interested. Even if they are, I'll tell them how you broke his heart when you didn't answer his letter, how that had repercussions far beyond anything you could ever imagine—'

'What?' she cried, terrified by his savage fury. Her face went white. 'Morgan! What are you saying?'

He checked himself, his chest heaving in his efforts to contain his anger. 'God!' he muttered, passing a shaking hand through his hair. He looked across at her, his eyes narrowed with pain. 'Forget it!' he ordered.

Jodie stared back, shaking uncontrollably with distress. 'I can't!' she whispered. 'You've said too much.'

His mouth compressed. 'Don't you think I know that? And regret it? Leave it, Jodie! You don't want to know!'

'No,' she mumbled. 'But I must. If I am to understand

the depth of his—and your—hatred for me, I have a right to be told the whole story.'

There was a flash of grudging admiration in his burning eyes and she lifted her chin, determined to show him that she could handle anything he had to reveal to her.

'You insist?' he queried. She nodded and he took several deep breaths. As if drained by anger, he leaned against the counter, his expression far away. 'You weren't to know what damage you'd do, of course,' he said, ominously quiet after his rage. 'When you turned up on the doorstep unexpectedly I did everything I could to put you off—'

'I noticed!' she glowered.

'Jodie,' he said softly, 'at the time I thought you had come here on a casual whim, perhaps eager to cash in on your father's wealth. It was my intention that you'd go away virtually unscathed, accepting that your father wasn't interested in you.'

'Does...does he really hate me?' she asked jerkily.

Morgan's slow nod drew a moan from her. 'I'm sorry you had to know that,' he said roughly. 'For many reasons, I wanted you to leave before you learned the consequences of not replying to Sam's letter. I thought it would be too cruel.' He hauled in a harsh breath. 'But you had to keep at me, didn't you?' he flung. 'Like a dog worrying a bone!'

Her hand had flown to her mouth. '*What?*' she cried in agitation. 'What were the repercussions?!'

Morgan's face twisted in pain. She saw him go pale, saw the torment in his eyes, the contortion of his mouth, and she shrank back, wishing she'd never started this, almost wishing she'd turned around and gone home. She gave a whimper and his eyes flickered, then focused on her as though he'd been miles away.

'What,' she repeated in a strangled whisper, 'were the consequences?'

And he answered, in a pained and inaudible growl, 'The death of the woman he loved.'

CHAPTER FIVE

SHE choked back a sob of horror, frantic to stay in control and to refute his shocking allegation.

'I can't be held responsible for that! It's...' She sucked in a sharp breath. 'It's a wicked thing to say!'

'But true.' He glanced quickly at his watch and she almost exploded with anger.

'How *dare* you? Forget the time!' she yelled. 'This is important! How am I supposed to have killed someone with the Atlantic Ocean between us? You tell me that! I need to know!' she stormed.

'You failed him when he needed you. Sam had fallen in love,' Morgan began. 'He wanted to get in touch with you because he longed to see you before...' Morgan paused, took a steadying breath, avoiding her eyes as if he couldn't bear to look at her. 'Before he got married,' he continued. 'And to do so he needed your mother's address to arrange a divorce.'

'But...my mother was dead!' Jodie protested.

'I know that—now. That information has come a little too late, though,' Morgan replied.

'I still don't understand.'

'I'm getting there. Unfortunately your father chose not to tell his fiancée that he was still married—'

'Why?' she demanded.

He shrugged. 'Your mother could have been anywhere. It could have taken years to trace her. Sam's fiancée was much younger, and—'

'How much younger?' she interrupted.

71

'Nine years older than me,' he replied, his voice tight and stiff. 'Thirty-six.'

'My father must be around sixty!' she said in astonishment. 'Did she love him?' she probed. 'Really love him?'

'How can I answer that?' he hedged. 'Remember, I wasn't around most of the time. All I know is that she wanted to marry him more than anything in the world and he was desperate to make her his wife. Sam feared he'd lose her if she knew there were complications.'

'If she loved him she would have waited!' Jodie said passionately. Morgan just looked at her. 'She didn't love him! *Did she?*'

His lips compressed. 'Possibly not.'

'She was after his money?' Jodie asked indignantly.

'Your father had a lot more than money to offer her,' he answered enigmatically. 'And he was crazy about her. As you can imagine, he became increasingly agitated when there was no reply from you.'

'But…why didn't he write to me again?' she wailed.

'I don't know. Perhaps because he wasn't at all well,' Morgan explained. 'He had a lot on his plate. He and his fiancée were moving house—to here—with all the usual upheavals that entails—choosing carpets, buying antique furniture, paintings, visiting the London silver galleries, rebuilding the kitchen, landscaping the gardens….'

'Good grief! No wonder he was ill! That would have taxed anyone his age!' she exclaimed in concern. 'He should have been taking it easy—'

'I know that,' Morgan said wearily. 'But he was indulgent and could refuse her nothing, particularly as he was keenly aware that his fiancée was afraid she'd end up as a mistress, rather than a wife. Constant delays to setting a wedding date caused endless friction. It wore Sam down and privately he blamed you. One day, he and his fiancée had a blazing row, and when he wouldn't respond to her ultimatum, she stormed out. She'd been drinking and her judgement was impaired by that and by anger...possibly fear, too, that she was being strung along. She drove into the path of an oncoming lorry and...' His voice broke. He bit his lip and turned away.

Jodie stared in horror. The robe stretched taut across his tensed back and she ached to console him. But she'd inadvertently caused the tragedy. She could do nothing. Her fluttering hands fell to her sides and never had she felt so useless in the face of someone's grief.

'Oh, Morgan!' she whispered sadly, and her own voice faltered. What could she say? Words were inadequate. A hug would have been the answer, but that was out of the question.

His head lifted a fraction. 'Your father was taken to hospital in shock. She died a short time later of her injuries,' he said, the low mutter betraying how deeply he'd been affected.

It was extraordinary that Morgan should have cared so much for this woman. But he had, perhaps because she'd brought happiness and love to his friend's life.

Whereas she... Jodie fought back the tears. Everything was horribly clear now. Morgan's utter hostility, her father's rejection of her.

'I'm so sorry. So terribly sorry. Poor woman...my poor father,' she said brokenly. 'No wonder he hates me. And you do, too.' She felt miserable, but at least she knew where she stood. 'Thank you for telling me,' she said, feeling drained. 'It puts me in the picture.'

And despite his antagonism she had to make a gesture, to show how she felt. Impulsively she went to his side, her heart wrenching at his ferocious frown. Tentatively she touched his arm and he started.

'You must have taken the brunt of this dreadful situation,' she observed gently. 'My father ill, his fiancée dead... You must have been the person he turned to, to unload all his grief. Presumably you handled the funeral—'

'Yes,' he agreed tersely. 'Sam couldn't attend.'

'And there would have been the house to organise, my father to visit, chores to be done...so much. You've been through a lot too, haven't you?'

He sawed in a long breath and shook his head slowly. 'I don't know what to make of you, Jodie!' he said in a low tone.

'I am what you see,' she said simply. 'I care very deeply about things. I'm not irresponsible or shallow. I wish I could convince you of my honesty. I swear to you on my father's life that I am *not* lying about sending several letters to him. I don't mind accepting responsibility for all kinds of things, but neglecting to reply to him isn't one of them. Those letters went astray—or were deliberately kept from my father.'

He raised a querying eyebrow. 'Why do you say that?'

'Because I *know* the letters were posted. That means those are the only two possible explanations,' she said quietly. 'I have to say that the woman here wasn't very helpful, and that's putting it mildly. On both occasions when I phoned and told her who I was she told me to take a running jump—'

'A...what?' he exclaimed, grabbing her wrist urgently.

Suddenly she knew there was a chink of light, a chance that he might know who this person was.

'A running jump!' she repeated, her eyes bright and searching. 'Was it the daily help? She sounded young. Very off-hand and dismissive, and she put the phone down on me when I got emotional. Oh, I thought she had a very faint Irish accent, if that helps.' She waited, scanning his face anxiously.

Irish! Morgan groaned and passed a hand over his face. Teresa had never been able to disguise her Dublin background, despite all her expensive elocution lessons. And the expression 'take a running jump' had been peculiar to Teresa. She'd used it often—whenever she lost her temper. That was how they'd lost two good daily helps.

Appalled, he gazed down at Jodie's upturned face and felt like grovelling. 'I think it's possible I've misjudged you,' he said huskily.

Her eyes widened to mossy pools of light and her lips parted as she said breathlessly, 'You know who it was, don't you?'

He felt his heart leap and buck, found himself drawn closer. The satin of her skin beneath his fingers throbbed deeply, and he didn't know whether that was from her pulses or his... He clung on hard to keep his sanity.

'Teresa,' he managed. Common sense told him to remove his hand. Instead, he let his fingers spread out over the fragile bones. She looked puzzled and he expanded. 'Sam's fiancée.'

'But...' Her eyes grew enormous. 'Why wouldn't she want me around?'

That mouth...the soft arch, the hopeful curl at each corner... Morgan slicked his tongue over his lips so he could answer without croaking like an idiot. But the little shudder that ran through her was almost his undoing. He'd taken a step closer before he realised and he had difficulty keeping his mind on his answer.

'Remember, she didn't know why you'd been contacted. Sam's friends...disapproved of Teresa. Perhaps she feared you would too, and might try to influence him adversely. Who knows? As I said, she was desperately eager to get married,' he added, omitting to say why—that she had already been carrying another man's child and time had been running out on her.

She bit her lip. 'It's tragic!' she said passionately. 'I suppose it was she who threw away my letters?'

'Very likely,' he said heavily.

Pain lanced through him. Teresa had caused mayhem. Sam's life, his, Jack's, and now this tender-hearted woman's future had suffered because of Teresa's insecurity and dogged determination to be the wife of a wealthy man.

'There's a terrible irony in this. Without realising it, she prevented her own marriage!' Jodie mused unhappily.

'If she'd known,' Morgan agreed, 'she would have welcomed you with open arms. And...'

He winced, thinking of the repercussions. Only because Teresa had known she was dying had he discovered he was a father. If she had married Sam he would have been in complete ignorance. But he'd held his son in his arms and had fallen hopelessly in love with him.

Because of Teresa, Jodie had been upset unnecessarily by what she'd imagined was Sam's rejection. Consequently Teresa had lost her chance of marriage and she'd brought on her own death. Because of that, Sam had succumbed to shock and then pneumonia, which must have shortened his life expectancy, and the future was a potential mess. He shook his head in disbelief at the cruel quirks of fate.

'If only she had let you come,' he said heavily. 'She would be here today.'

'It sounds as if you were very fond of her,' she said delicately.

He turned away, his shoulders high with the terrible agony of futile wishing. And then a little voice in his head told him that he had benefited by Teresa's death because he knew the joy of fatherhood. He couldn't deal with that.

'I don't want to talk about her,' he jerked out.

'No. I'm sorry. I didn't mean to intrude on your grief,' she said hastily, painfully sweet, heartbreakingly gentle and solicitous of his feelings.

A surge of sympathy for her threatened to overwhelm him. She'd had some tough things to face since arriving here.

'And your own grief?' he asked, facing her again.

She gave a brave smile and he felt more of a heel than ever.

'I feel keenly for my father's unhappiness and for his ill health. I dearly want to do what I can to help him,' she said earnestly. 'If that means walking away, then that's what I'll do. But I think I might have something to offer. He has you, but I'm his flesh and blood, all he has in the world now!'

He stared at her eager face, the love for a father she'd never known glowing in her soft eyes. She was one of those rare women—unselfish to a fault, caring and compassionate, and with a heart that longed to embrace the world. And he'd almost thrown her out!

Sam ought to know his daughter before he died. She deserved that much. And it would bring Sam happiness.

He shut out his own needs, determined now to do what was right. 'Jodie,' he said softly, 'when your father is a little better I will tell him what happened to the letters. We'll take it from there.'

'You mean about his fiancée keeping me away?' she said doubtfully. 'Wouldn't that upset him?'

He gave a rueful smile. 'Leave it to me. I'll make sure he understands why she took such precipitate action. I don't want to lie to him.'

'You're a very honourable man,' she sighed.

He wished that were true. 'I'm afraid he couldn't cope

with seeing you now, Jodie. Are you prepared to bide your time till I can talk to him and break it gently?'

'Anything!' she said fervently, her face wreathed in smiles and her eyes misting with happiness.

Somehow his hands had found their way to her shoulders, and he was frowning because he wanted to cup her face and kiss that tremulous mouth, whisper promises he might regret.

But her innocent, accepting face stared back at him with such joy and hope written there that he found himself saying, 'It might take a while. Why don't you stay here? Make yourself at home.'

She beamed in delight. 'Can I? That would be perfect. I'd be able to hear from you every day how he was, then. And I could help with the washing and keep the house clean—'

'But not cook!'

'Not if you want to live!' she said with a laugh.

He grinned back at her, worryingly elated that she would be here, under the same roof.

There was one problem still nagging at his mind: Jack. He needed time to decide how to handle that. He checked his watch. Jack would surely be waking now. And something still held him back from inviting Jodie up to see him.

'There's something I must do. Will you excuse me for a while?'

He grabbed a bottle from the fridge, concealing it from her, and hurried out before she could comment.

His own subterfuge puzzled him. She was everything Sam would wish for in a daughter: genuinely sweet and honest, courageous and thoughtful. Musing over his secrecy, he entered the nursery and bent over the cot, his love for Jack easing all the anxiety from his face and replacing it with a tender smile.

Whatever Jodie's character, she still remained a threat to Jack's future. OK, he corrected, a threat to the future he'd planned with Jack. Was he being selfish? What would be in Jack's best interests?

He reached down into the cradle and lightly touched the small closed fist. It opened and gripped his finger hard.

Jodie would love Jack, he thought helplessly. And she'd be a wonderful substitute mother to him—a million times better than Teresa, who'd planned on employing two nannies to 'cope with the kid'.

But he'd be a great father! He'd relearnt all the old nursery rhyme books already, studied child development, invested in some books on child health, explored the pros and cons of organic food, environmentally 'kind' nappies...

It was between him and Jodie, then: which of them was best fitted to care for his child? He leaned over and kissed his son's rosy cheek and he knew that his own feelings for Jack were too fierce for him ever to walk away.

Morgan sighed heavily. How the devil could he work for the reunion between Sam and Jodie—and at the same time end up in charge of Jack, who had been registered as Sam's son?

Biting his lip at the impossibility of the dilemma, he heard a sound and jerked his head around, his heart racing. Alarm lanced his eyes before he could control his reaction to seeing Jodie there, her face wreathed in soft smiles.

A sensation like a clap of thunder rolled through him. The decision had been taken out of his hands. She would adore her 'half-brother'. Would want to take him over *now*. Dear God, he thought in anguish. It had come sooner than he'd imagined.

'I didn't mean to disturb you,' she whispered. 'But I was passing and...oh, Morgan, can I come in to see your baby?'

'My…' He swallowed. Of course! She had no reason to think he might be Sam's! But he must tell her. 'I'm not—'

'Oh, please!' she breathed. 'I won't make a sound, I promise.'

He hesitated. What was it called…a lie by omission? Being economical with the truth? Yet this *was* his son. There was no deceit in that. He raised his head and met her pleading eyes.

'It's almost time for him to wake up,' he conceded, unwillingly touched by the radiance of her smile.

She tiptoed to the crib and crouched down, her face awed. 'I knew it was a boy because of the blue everywhere,' she whispered. 'What's his name?'

'Jack Samuel.'

She was too close to him. He could see each one of her long lashes as they fluttered above those amazingly clear green eyes. Her skin was flawless as a baby's itself, her expression too eager and her lips too inviting.

He sat the bottle in the warmer and tried to deal with the conflicting emotions roaring in his head. He wanted her to think his son was the most beautiful, most adorable baby she'd ever seen. And he also wanted her to find babies a total turn-off.

'He's just perfect!' she said shakily, and he detected the suspicion of a tear in the corner of her eye before she brought her hand up and rubbed there, impatiently. 'Oh, look! His lashes are fluttering—aren't they long and black? Like yours. And all that dark, wavy hair… Is he anything like his mother?' she asked with a laugh in his direction.

He frowned, his mouth pinched. 'I can't see likenesses,' he grated.

'I've said something wrong! Is—isn't she…around?' she asked tactfully.

Deceit… It soured everything he did: his love for his

on, his relationship with Sam and now Sam's daughter. But he couldn't bring himself to unburden himself to Jodie, or to say anything which would ultimately result in the surrender of his son.

Jack would be his. Always. His baby's face was imprinted on him like a video screen constantly before his eyes. The little squirming body was as familiar to him as his own. They were one and the same, indivisible.

'No,' he muttered. 'She's not around.'

Her hand enclosed his and when he met her sympathetic eyes he felt like groaning in frustrated anger and telling her that he did not deserve her compassion. She would not look on him so trustingly if she realised what he was hiding from her.

'He's waking!' she cried in delight as Jack uttered a little squawk. 'Oh, his eyes! Black as ink! I thought all babies were blue-eyed?'

'Jack's are. Midnight-blue,' he managed, knowing every shade of those huge bright eyes. 'Indigo-denim in bright sunlight. They look black in the semi-dark.'

He lifted his son out. 'Hello, there,' he said softly, holding him close to his face. His hand cradled the back of the small, warm head. He could feel the curls, flattened by sleep and body-heat to the back of Jack's scalp. 'Look at the sunrise,' he murmured, turning the baby around to see the rays of gold and amber pooling on the nursery floor. 'We'll go out later. We can listen to the birds, see the sheep and hear them bleating...'

He remembered Jodie and glanced at her. His gaze faltered, shaken by the intensity of her emerald eyes.

'I...talk to him,' he said, explaining himself and laying back on the changing mat.

A pain was racking her. It was sweet and hurting at the same time. Morgan had lost his wife—or she'd left him—

and he was devastated. The hurt in his eyes had been so strong when she'd mentioned the baby's mother that it was as if he'd been ripped apart.

What a lot he'd had to suffer, she thought sadly, watching his deft fingers undoing the pearly buttons on Jack's sleepsuit.

She quivered, unbearably touched by his tenderness and the deep love he had for his child. His hands seemed huge, but he manipulated the baby with a sure confidence which suggested he'd been doing this for some time. How long? she wondered.

'How old is he?' she asked longingly, wishing with all her heart that she had a good man in her life and the prospect of a baby of her own.

'Five weeks. He's putting on weight like a Sumo wrestler,' Morgan said, pride in every line of his face. 'And he recognises me. He always calms down if he's crying and I speak to him—or even if I sing. Poor child's clearly tone-deaf.'

She was enchanted by the picture he'd presented. She sat back on her heels and watched the cleansing and changing and hoped he'd ask if she wanted to hold the baby. But he didn't.

So she contented herself with enjoying the sight of Morgan, sitting in a chair and feeding his son, a quiet air of contentment pervading the whole nursery.

'This is a side of you I couldn't have imagined from our first meeting,' she said wryly.

'We are all complex people, Jodie. Multi-faceted, hard, soft, kind, ruthless, depending on the circumstances or the threat to our continued existence.'

'And you were prepared to growl like a bear and yell at any flibbertigibbet who threatened my father's well-being,' she said with a grin.

'I'd defend the people I love with every last breath in my body,' he replied.

'You're very loyal.'

'I love very deeply.'

An older man, a tiny child. The strong caring for the weak. She smiled warmly and was delighted when he smiled back.

'You can be very intimidating! I like you best like this,' she said.

He laughed. 'Me too!' He crossed his long bare legs at the ankles and gazed fondly down at his son.

Jodie's heart lurched and she recognised that she was dangerously on the brink of finding Morgan too appealing for her own good. Looking around, she found something to defuse her sentimental yearning.

'He's a lucky little boy,' she mused, admiring the cheerful trees which had been painted on the walls, with their huge eyes and smiling mouths. 'This is a wonderful nursery!'

Morgan looked pleased. 'I did it,' he said in an off-hand manner which didn't deceive her at all.

'You?' she cried, in amazement. 'But you're a brilliant artist! I especially like the fat robins. And that's the fairy castle of any child's dreams.'

'I enjoyed doing it. Didn't take long,' he mused.

She turned around, seeing that the bright, primary colours of the landscape had been continued across a bank of cupboards, and a bookcase had been disguised as a mountain.

'Are you a professional artist?' she wondered.

'In a way. An architect, like your father,' he replied.

She gave a surprised gasp. 'Morgan, that's what I wanted to be!'

'There's nothing to stop you, if that's what you want to do,' he pointed out.

'No, there isn't!' she cried, her face aglow with the sudden realisation. 'It's been my ambition ever since my teacher said I had talent in that direction.'

'So what did stop you?' he enquired.

'My foster-parents. They needed me to leave school and go to work so I learnt to type instead.'

'How did you feel about that?'

'Sad,' she acknowledged. 'But they were short of money. I felt it was right that I should contribute to the family income.' She smiled. 'I was always drawing as a kiddie. I longed to create something that I could walk past every day of my life,' she said passionately. 'It must be a wonderful feeling to know that a building is your concept, your idea turned into reality.'

He laughed. 'You sound just like your father!' he said in amusement. 'That's how he inspired me. And you're right. It's one hell of a buzz to see your dream, to walk around it and into it, to see it working on a practical scale and filled with people.'

Envious, she brought her knees up to her chin. 'Tell me more about my father and his work,' she begged.

'How about a description of him first?' Morgan lifted an expressive eyebrow and smiled when she nodded eagerly. 'OK. He's sixty, with all his own teeth and a good deal of thick white hair which flops on his forehead and he keeps sweeping back impatiently.' He grinned fondly. 'When he's working it often ends up streaked with the colours he's used.'

Jodie laughed with him at the picture he was painting. 'I can almost see him,' she said softly. 'Is he tall, short?'

Morgan's voice grew quieter than before. 'Tall. He used to have a powerful build but now he's thin and drawn, all cheekbones and jaw. He has your eyes. Less bright, not as clear, but still with the ability to sparkle when he's excited about something. I suppose...I suppose he has a similar character to you.'

'What's that?' she asked warily.

'Honest, good, kind, generous...' He stopped the surprising list of attributes and let his mouth curl wickedly. 'Stubborn, passionate, single-minded and occasionally impossible!' he added.

She giggled. 'There could be fireworks if he and I ever disagree! But...I'm glad to hear he's a good man. Mom never said anything about him, but when I grew older I put two and two together. Knowing what I did of Mom, I assumed that he told her to leave because she was having an affair.'

'I believe that might be true,' he said with great tact. He lifted Jack up a little once or twice and was rewarded with a small belch and a dribble of milk. Jodie then realised why his jumper had been slightly stained at their first meeting. 'Good boy!' he said approvingly, as if, she thought with a smile, the baby had successfully mastered algebra.

'You dote on that baby!' she teased.

He shot her a sharp look from under his brows. 'Yes,' he said, looking defensive.

'Calm down! I approve,' she giggled.

He gave a thin smile. 'I get a bit protective,' he explained a little sheepishly, and hastily changed the subject. 'We were talking about you, though. You said your mother died when you were six?'

'That's right—eighteen years ago. I've wanted to belong to someone ever since,' she confided. She leant forward, once more hoping he'd ask her to hold the baby. Instead, he stood up with Jack tucked in one arm, dealing efficiently with the debris around him. 'Can I help?' she asked.

'No.' He amended that rather curt refusal. 'Thanks. Tell me about your foster-parents.'

Diverted, she made a face. 'They were tough on me. Sometimes I wondered if they only wanted the money I brought into the house. I can't remember either of them ever playing with me or cuddling me. Still,' she said cheerfully, 'they did give me a home, and I learnt to be self-sufficient and how to do chores.'

'But not to cook?' he asked drily, putting a cute little hat on Jack's head.

Jodie jumped to her feet and pre-empted Morgan, handing him the warm jacket he'd set his eyes on. But he wouldn't let her help to put it on the baby.

'My foster-mother taught me basic cooking. I always did our supper when I came in from school. When I left home, fancy cooking was beyond me because I was always scared of ruining expensive ingredients.' She grinned. 'I set the kitchen alight when I was doing a special meal for my boyfriend because I was so desperately anxious to please him. From then my nerves were so bad I seemed hell-bent on cremating everything, including lettuce!'

Morgan laughed long and loud, disconcerting Jodie utterly. The frown had been obliterated and replaced by appealing laughter lines, and the sparkle in his eyes and the dazzling whiteness of his teeth made her chest tighten up as if it were in a vice.

'I'm going to throw on some clothes and then we're going out for a blast of fresh air,' he announced. 'A walk along the footpaths and across the fields. Do you want to come?'

'Oh, yes,' she said happily. 'I'll fetch a jacket from my case.'

'Nothing else you need?' he murmured.

'Maybe a scarf. Why?'

'Sturdy shoes might be an idea, too,' he said drily.

She looked down at her bare feet, her face pink at her forgetfulness. She was too eager. She must throttle back or he'd think she was making a play for him.

'Shoes! Huh! You are so *conventional*!' she said in mock scorn, and ran quickly to her room before he changed his mind, his warm chuckle echoing down the corridor and making her skin tingle.

A little while later she heard him making his way downstairs and whistling up the dog, who had been sitting with resigned patience at the bottom of the stairs waiting for Morgan to reappear.

And she thought fondly of a time when they'd all be living here together: she and her father, Morgan and his baby. She knew that day would come about. Because she wanted it to, so very much.

CHAPTER SIX

THE air was fresh and sharp when they walked down the drive. Morgan had shrugged on a Barbour over jeans and a navy sweatshirt and tucked Jack into a baby pouch, which he'd slung across his chest. He chatted to his son with a natural ease that Jodie admired and envied. Loping by his heels, shadowing his every move, was Satan, totally devoid of a lead or any other restraint.

'Is he all right out here?' she asked doubtfully, when they came to the lane.

'Fine. He's intelligent enough to know that he must stay close to me, in case of a stray car. I'll let him run free when we're in the fields.'

'Unnervingly obedient,' she commented.

He must have noticed—and correctly interpreted—her askance look, because he smiled and said, 'Nothing to do with me. He's not my dog. Sam trained him. He and Sam went to classes and Sam learnt how to be consistent and clear, and not muddle his dog with confusing messages, and Satan responded with his utter devotion.'

Absorbing this, she happily breathed in the wonderful smell of the early morning—damp earth, the faint hint of pine—and thought how glad she was that Morgan wasn't a tyrant.

'And Satan accepted you, it would seem.'

Morgan rubbed the dog's head affectionately. 'Poor old chap. He couldn't understand it when Sam went into hospital. I had to spend some time getting him to trust me. We went for a lot of walks and I hurled a lot of balls before he did.'

More pressures, she thought. Sam, Teresa, Jack…the loss of his wife, coping with a bewildered dog—and now a long-lost daughter turning up.

It pleased her that she could stay and help. Keeping house would be a joy. And perhaps she'd get up the courage to cook something simple and get her confidence back. She beamed, feeling content for the first time in years.

Apart from the liquid sound of birdsong it was silent in the deep-cut lane. Morgan told her that it was an ancient Neolithic trackway, once cobbled with flintstone from quarries on the Downs.

'The area was heavily forested then,' he explained. 'So the tracks to and from settlements ran along the tops of the ridges and only occasionally dropped lower to the wild, muddy parts—perhaps to cross a river. We go over this stile. Satan goes under it.'

He held out his hand to help her over and once she'd dropped to the other side he did not relinquish it. For a short way they walked through the wood, while Morgan pointed out the snowdrops and emerging shoots of daffodils to the totally unaware Jack, with an engaging lack of self-consciousness.

'Why do you talk to him when he doesn't understand what the devil you're talking about?' she asked in amusement.

'So he can learn my voice,' he said, gazing tenderly at his son. 'I don't want him ever to forget it.'

'He's not likely to,' she said softly, loving the velvety tones now he wasn't angry and tense.

'No. It will be part of him. And all his brain cells will be alert and receptive because of the stimulation he receives—sound, sight, touch, smell… I've read a lot about this, you see,' he said earnestly.

'I'm impressed. I know nothing about babies or children,' she said, her face wistful.

'Neither did I. It was something of a crash course.'

'Oh. Yes, of course. How awful.'

'Jack had needs. I had no choice.' Deftly he turned the conversation away from himself. 'You and your boyfriend didn't…uh…consider a family?'

'I'd only have a child if I was married,' she replied firmly. 'And he wasn't interested in marriage or children. But…I'd love to have babies…'

'You will,' he said abruptly. 'When you meet the man you want to spend the rest of your life with.'

Suddenly he fell silent and she was left to wonder. Morgan was so near to her idea of the perfect man that she couldn't imagine herself with anyone else. She tried to block such inappropriate thoughts from her mind but failed miserably.

And she knew with a heart-thumping sadness that Morgan might be pleasant to her but he didn't exactly find her a turn-on. She didn't know what had happened to his wife, but he probably still loved her—and it would take a long time before he got over her.

'I want you to close your eyes,' he said suddenly.

Jodie opened them wider. 'What?' she exclaimed.

'Trust me,' he said with a faint smile. 'Something I want you to see at its best. A surprise. Close them.'

Pretending to grumble, she did so, and his arm came around her waist to guide her along the path. They must look like lovers, she thought, her heart thumping hard.

Beneath her feet she felt the twigs, leaves and mud of the woodland suddenly change to springy turf. 'We're out of the wood,' she declared, when they came to a halt.

There was a long pause. 'Not entirely,' he replied, in a cryptic tone.

'Well, it feels different,' she demurred.

'Yes. It does feel different to what's gone before,' he agreed huskily. 'Wait. Keep your eyes closed.'

It was hard. He was breathing softly beside her, his hand warm and firm, his thigh against hers. The breeze whispered over her face, making her lips tingle. And as his hand moved away to her shoulder she let out an involuntary sigh of disappointment.

'Come forward a little,' he said, loath to release her, longing to watch her expressive face unobserved for a few more moments.

She stood there in her scorchingly bright yellow trousers, red boots and an orange jacket, which she'd teamed with a fuschia-pink scarf and gloves, and the whole ensemble made him want to smile in sheer delight at her outrageously determined cheerfulness.

Her childhood had been hard and almost loveless, and yet she'd emerged as a positive, outward-looking person. He admired her tenacity, her *joie de vivre*, the way her hair curled in little wisps around her forehead, how her cheeks glowed from the walk, the soft lusciousness of her lips...

Something bucked inside him. He thought it wise to let his hand drop. 'Right,' he said, with a stab at briskness. 'Open them.'

The dark brown lashes fluttered and lifted and her gaze was captured immediately by the huge figure outlined on the hill ahead.

'That is incredible!' she breathed. 'What is it? What's it doing up there—can we go up to see it?'

He was pleased at her reaction. He'd hoped she'd be impressed. 'It's the Long Man,' he answered. 'The Giant of Wilmington. We'll go up to see him another day. It's a long hike up and I need to get back in a short while. Here. Let me put my jacket down on the bank and we can admire him in comfort.'

'I'll help,' she said, seeing him struggling to keep Jack upright while attempting to wriggle out of the coat.

She removed his coat for him and they sat side by side on its tartan lining, with Jack sleeping in his arms in blissful peace, rocked by the rhythm of the walk. Her face was rapt as she waited for him to speak and he felt his throat closing up with desire.

It wasn't sexual, but something else. An elusive yearning, a warm contentment, a feeling that this was a companionship he could cherish for the rest of his life.

And that both elated and alarmed him. He had enough going on in his life already, enough of a commitment to Jack and Sam and to the business without adding one more. He had to feel that—when everything righted itself again—he could have personal freedom. He needed to be independent, not to be tied to someone.

And yet…

'I'm admiring,' she said, her white teeth gleaming as she gave a little teasing laugh. 'Do I get a commentary as well?'

'Sure.'

He looked up at the huge outline of a man on the slope of Windover Hill, originally carved out of the chalk some five thousand years earlier. As always, he felt a little shiver of awe and amazement go through him.

'He's the second tallest human figure in the world. Over two hundred feet tall—I forget how much more. Probably Neolithic. No one really knows the truth. But the staves he's holding probably represent a doorway—and it's said he's part of a harvest fertility cult. He represented the midsummer sun god, who brought light, warmth and a full belly; a guardian who made the crops grow.' He gestured with his hand. 'Look. There are Long Barrows on the hill where the people were buried and a prehistoric trackway, the old route taken by travellers from those times to quite recently. Flint mines... A mortuary area for the funeral processions...' He smiled at her entranced face. 'It's a fascinating area. I can't wait to explore it thoroughly.'

'Nor can I! You've picked up a lot of information in the short time you've been here,' she commented. She leant forwards, her knees up to her chin, her expression thoughtful.

'Only because I grabbed a couple of books from Sam's bedside and read to him during the long hours I sat with him,' he replied absently.

'You've been unusually kind to my father,' she declared, turning to face him. The wind blew her hair across her face and the sun warmed the strands to a gleaming copper. 'Without you he might not have survived. You must have improved his chances considerably.' Pushing her hair back, she hesitated, and then reached out to cover his hand where it rested on his knee. 'I'll be forever grateful to you for not abandoning him,' she said quietly.

'I couldn't ever do that.'

Her hair had escaped again and he leaned closer, dangerously close, reclaiming his hand to smooth the shimmering hair on both sides of her head and to arrange it behind her small ears. The skin was warm and silky there, and the feel, the smell of her, was so sweet to him that he had to swallow hard to stop himself from kissing her.

Sexual obsession, he told himself sternly, is for teenagers with exploding testosterone. But a small inner voice protested that there was more to his obsession than raw hunger...

'There is a special bond between you and my father,' she observed, her eyes starry. 'What is it?'

Talk. He had to talk. That would ease the ache in his loins. And the unnerving ache in his heart. Plus the emptiness. The first of those he understood only too well. The latter he could put down to a lack of breakfast. He had no ideas on how to explain the other.

'I owe everything to Sam,' he said simply.

He looked away, out to the ancient hill, and wondered if men and women over the millenia had always experienced conflicting emotions which tormented their sleeping and waking hours.

'I knew it was something like that,' she murmured happily.

His bones strained with the effort of not holding her. Every muscle was ready, tensed and expectant, waiting for the moment when he drew her to him and put that ecstatic face against his. Denying his own body, Morgan breathed long and hard. Never had his arms seemed so empty, their purpose so wasted.

'My mother was his secretary,' he told her, determined to sound, act, *be* normal again. 'She was eighteen when she went for a job at his practice—and she was pregnant.'

'With you?' Jodie surmised.

Nodding, Morgan stroked Jack's squashed cheek with a delicate finger, imagining what it had been like for his mother, alone, in a strange country and unmarried.

'She'd come direct from Bogota, Colombia,' he explained. 'The father—my father—wouldn't marry her.'

'Then you never knew him? I'm sorry, Morgan. You must understand something of the emptiness that I felt, the sense of…of a hole in your life that needs filling.'

He gave a wry smile. 'I do. I wouldn't have asked you in if you hadn't unwittingly touched a raw nerve.'

'I'm glad I did—and that we had something in common. We'd never have known one another otherwise.'

Tension hung perilously in the air. 'No,' he husked.

The threads between them seemed to pull him inexorably towards her but he resisted. She gave a small shudder and drew in a breath through her teeth.

'Cold?' he enquired in concern, reaching out and rubbing her back and shoulders. 'Do you want to walk on?'

'No. I'm all right. Let's stay here for a moment. I want to know more about your mother and my father.'

He let his arm remain casually across her shoulders. Just a friendly gesture. To keep her warm.

'It wasn't a sexual relationship, if that's what's worrying you,' he murmured. 'They became the best of friends. He recognised his own loneliness in her, I think. She was well educated and they enjoyed the same things, the same sense of humour.'

Jodie didn't speak. She was watching Satan rolling on his back in the grass. Morgan continued, wanting to prolong this tantalising intimacy for as long as possible.

'It's odd, how one small thing…a look, an unguarded moment…can change the course of a person's life—'

'Oh, yes!' she said fervently.

He mused that Jodie had come and pleaded to see her father, using the only words which could move him. And so he'd let her in, and now…

Where was he? He frowned. Oh, yes. His mother… 'The interview with Sam didn't go well,' he began, his voice rich with the warmth of memories as he recalled the times he'd begged his mother to tell him the story again and again. 'She was tense and guilty about keeping her pregnancy a secret. Her typing test was a total disaster, though Sam was kind about it, recognising she was nervous. But she broke down in tears because she assumed she'd lost the job. Over coffee in a nearby café, he got the whole story out of her—'

'I assume he employed her on the spot?' broke in Jodie with a broad smile.

'What else would he do? It was typical of Sam,' he said fondly. 'Great benefactor to lame dogs, distressed women and all kinds of lost causes. He took an interest in me when I was born—stood as my godfather—and we became very close.'

She sighed. 'I suppose you replaced me. A kind of sur-rogate son.'

'Do you mind that?' he asked softly.

'No,' she replied. 'He needed someone to love. Everybody does. If it had to be anyone who took my place, I'm glad it was you.'

For a long moment she held his gaze, and then lowered her lashes. He felt honoured by her statement. Touching her cheek with the back of his hand, he met her molten green eyes anew and smiled.

'He would have been a good father to you,' he said gently. 'When my mother died I was eleven and already living with him because Mum had been seriously ill for some time. Sam consoled me, gave me time to grieve and encouraged me to talk about my mother.'

'He sounds a wonderful person,' she mused.

'The best,' he agreed huskily. 'It seemed natural that he should bring me up. I was sent to the best schools, given every chance and encouragement. I was fortunate—and I know it. I bless the day that Sam came into our lives.'

She was looking at him with such open delight that his heart turned over. His breath clogged his lungs as her face seemed to change, his fevered imagination believing that her mouth had intensified its poppy-red hue and had swol-len, demanding his kiss.

Pure wishful thinking. Morgan gritted his teeth, refusing to break the trust she'd placed in him...and wary of the seething emotions filling his heart and mind.

'I'm...' She swallowed and averted her gaze, proving she'd been alarmed by his unwelcome interest. 'I'm really pleased that my father is kind,' she said.

'More than kind. Encouraging. Supportive. He's set standards I can only hope to attain.'

Like honesty, he thought. How badly he'd let Sam down!

'I can imagine you're the apple of his eye,' she murmured. 'He must have been thrilled when you said you wanted to train to be an architect.'

'I even have the career you've always wanted,' Morgan pointed out ruefully.

'I'm definitely going to study,' she said, her eyes shining. 'I'll get there one day.'

'Good. And now we must go,' he said with great reluctance. 'Barges to tote, bales to lift... Here.'

He rose and held out his hand, pulling her to her feet. For a glorious moment she toppled, and laughingly caught at his arms to steady herself. Her glowing, beautiful face swam into vision, the laughter twinkling in her warm eyes. And then she'd exclaimed over her clumsiness and was occupied with helping him into his coat.

Jodie felt deliriously happy. She knew she'd pay for it later, that she'd sober up and realise how crazy she was to let her feelings run away with her, but she wanted this little bit of pleasure to heat her through and through, to wipe away all the pain and misery of the past.

For a short time she could enjoy herself in Morgan's company. Abandoning the nagging little warning in the back of her mind, she began to sing, and he joined in as they strode across fields and stiles, then down a lane through an enchanting village of old flint and Tudor-beamed cottages, twelfth, thirteenth, fifteenth-century, according to Morgan. The houses huddled together in a higgledy-piggledy fashion, their walls leaning in all directions, their gardens sprinkled with the nodding heads of snowdrops and the darker spears of emerging daffodils.

Behind her a hesitant January sun threw its beams on the river, and they paused for a moment while Morgan explained to Jack how to identify ducks and drakes and swans.

'Idiot!' she teased, her eyes warm with affection.

'He needs to hear language! He's going to be a genius,' he informed her with mock hauteur.

'Doesn't take after you, then,' she said rudely.

He was quiet for a moment and began to walk on. 'I wonder who he'll resemble?' he said under his breath.

But his mood had changed. His pace quickened and Jodie had to half-run to keep up. Anxiously she took a quick glance at his face and noted that it was stormy. She'd done it again. Reminded him of his wife.

They continued in silence and misery fell around her like a blanket. That made her feel worse. Maybe his wife had died. It was natural that he should feel his wife's death keenly. But Jodie felt dreadful for resenting the fact that Morgan wanted to cling to the past. Shamed by her selfishness, she strove to cheer him up.

'Right. Check your insurance and make your will. I'm going to cook for you,' she announced as they entered the back lobby, divesting themselves of shoes and coats.

He laughed, and she heaved a sigh of relief. 'A huge breakfast-cum-lunch because we've been up for hours?' he suggested. 'Can you cope with the Aga?'

'What's an Aga?'

'The stove.'

She raised an eyebrow. 'Can it cope with me?'

His eyes twinkled. 'Let me get Jack sorted while you get the food out, then I'll direct you imperiously from a comfortable armchair.'

It was odd, she thought, laying bacon on a rack and sliding it into the roasting oven, that she'd resented domesticity when she'd been with Chas. Yet here she was, eagerly offering her services! It felt different, somehow, though she couldn't identify why.

And his pleasure and praise for the nourishing meal made her glow all over. 'The eggs are a bit crispy,' she pointed out, not wanting to duck her mistakes.

'I like them that way,' he declared, enthusiastically attacking a lamb chop. 'And...to be honest, I probably wouldn't have cared if you'd charred everything. It's a pleasure to be cooked for.'

Jodie smiled, mentally planning on whisking around the house to ensure it was spotless and then conjuring up a simple but sophisticated supper. With wine. Candles... And she'd be wearing something gorgeous and sexy which whispered every time she moved...

She checked herself. Fantasising was OK, providing it didn't try to become reality. She'd better stick to her demure red jersey dress, pasta and electric light.

After they'd chatted and washed up together Morgan left for the office, saying he'd call in on Sam on the way back. It touched her that he took Jack with him.

'No thanks,' he'd said, when she'd tentatively suggested she could babysit. 'He always comes everywhere with me.'

'I understand,' she'd said in secret relief.

Her knowledge of babies was almost nil. Perhaps she ought to get involved with Jack—if she could ever prise him away from Morgan!

Humming to herself, Jodie set to with dusters and polish and a Hoover, enjoying herself enormously.

The house was tastefully furnished but had a cosy, loved feeling, and her father had collected some beautiful antiques; old oak furniture, silver and oil paintings being his particular interest, it seemed.

With the downstairs completed, she started on the large bedroom at the top of the landing. Searching around for somewhere to plug in the Hoover, she noticed that there were a large number of framed photographs on the top of a chest in the far corner.

Most had been knocked over and lay flat, perhaps when a drawer had been opened sharply. One was propped up by the others and she could see that the subject was a woman.

Probably Teresa, thought Jodie. This must be her father's room. And then she saw Morgan's robe on the back of the door—and sticking out of the laundry basket was the sleeve of the stained jumper he'd been wearing.

Her heart thudded. Morgan's room. Therefore... She looked towards the photos. His late wife!

Compelled by curiosity, she crossed to the chest, her feet sinking into the thick cream carpet. With great care, she collected one of the framed photographs and took it to the mullioned window to examine more closely.

Her face fell. 'Oh, she's beautiful!' she said out loud.

Morgan's wife stared back at her with dancing, roguish eyes, her blonde hair enviably long and artlessly framing a perfectly shaped face. She wore an evening dress and it clung to her like a second skin, the deep, revealing cleavage adding to the provocative nature of her pose.

There was no doubt that this was a very sensual woman, with the kind of sophistication Jodie had always envied. She could imagine her with Morgan, teasing him with those seductive eyes, arousing his Latin passions...equalling them...

Feeling sick, Jodie numbly rubbed the duster over the

frame and replaced it with the others, standing them all up
carefully as she dusted each one. There were nearly twenty
in all. Most were of Morgan's wife alone, posing in bikinis,
designer outfits and ballgowns.

One or two showed her with Morgan, several were with
a man who Jodie realised could only be her father.

She paused to study the handsome, laughing man who
clearly had felt great affection for Morgan's wife, and she
decided she liked the look of her father very much.

But Jodie was crushed by the sheer number of photographs. This was like a shrine. It pointed to a deep, all-
consuming love.

She felt sad. For Morgan, for his wife and Jack, and also
for herself. Morgan was one ideal man who'd married his
ideal woman and who wouldn't settle for anyone else, anyone less exotic or beautiful.

Jodie felt a pang of dismay. She'd never match up to
Morgan's wife. She grimaced. Her hair was the wrong colour, she was a good size larger, and she just didn't have
that wicked air of danger about her.

Moodily she finished cleaning the room. She couldn't
stop herself from touching his robe and then burying her
nose in its folds. It smelled of him and she inhaled greedily.

'Oh, God!' she groaned, pulling back sharply in shock.
'I'm falling in love with him!'

CHAPTER SEVEN

MORGAN felt his heart lift as he came nearer to home. And the reason worried him. He was far too happy with Jodie, surprisingly content to be in her company. He liked watching her mobile, joyous face. He liked the sound of her laugh, her eagerness to devour life and her total lack of pretence.

At work he'd been absent-minded, a fact unusual enough to have drawn comment and concern. Later, sitting by Sam's bedside, he'd actually found himself chafing to get away. And so he'd punished his lack of attention by staying longer, even though Sam had been so drugged—after a difficult night—that the older man had barely known anyone was there.

'You fool!' Morgan muttered to himself in astonishment as he turned eagerly into the lane. 'You're actually nervous!'

And so he was. His hands were shaking for absolutely no reason at all. Hastily he checked his appearance, frowning and smoothing down a stray lock of hair—and then uttered a short grunt of annoyance at his action.

When he reached halfway down the drive Satan ran up to the car, barking ecstatically. Morgan parked in front of the house and climbed out, giving Satan a hug and hushing him.

He heard the door open and deliberately kept his head down, his arms around the dog. But his pulses were beating a tattoo everywhere they happened to appear in his body.

'Morgan!' Jodie cried, her voice sounding shaky. 'Thank

heavens! I thought my father had taken a turn for the worse or…or…you'd had an accident!'

Then he looked up. She'd been crying. Her mouth looked crumpled, her eyes pink-rimmed. 'Jodie!' he cried, unfolding his body and surging towards her in sympathy. He checked his watch, groaned, and then his arms were around her before he knew what he was doing. 'I didn't realise—I'm terribly late! I'm sorry. I should have phoned—'

'No, you shouldn't!' she mumbled into his neck. 'I've no right to leap at you with nagging accusations. It's just that I was expecting you, and I waited, and you didn't come, and I hung around and kept going to the window, and you weren't there, and—'

'Hey!' he laughed, raising her face to his. 'You have every right.'

He kissed her forehead. Very good, he told himself. Brotherly. Unfortunately his loins had different ideas. An intoxicating fragrance had wafted into his nostrils and his hands were aching to explore the neat-fitting jersey dress which poured over her beautiful body like red-hot lava. Quickly he detached himself before she noticed his arousal.

'How's my father?' she asked breathily.

Morgan sobered up. 'He's improved a little, they tell me—though he was sedated and I didn't get much sense out of him.'

'As long as he's all right…' she mumbled. 'You'd tell me if they were worried about him, wouldn't you?' she asked, her eyes misty with emotion.

'I would,' he promised. 'Now. I'll get Jack sorted, pour us both a drink. Then I'll change into a sackcloth, roll in ashes, lie at your feet and beg your forgiveness for not phoning you.'

'Excessive,' she chided, all radiant smiles again, as he'd hoped, at his comically humble expression. She made a face. 'You can make yourself useful and fix the fuse box instead.'

It was then that he noticed the house was in darkness. 'Good grief! What happened? When?'

'When I turned on the lights somewhere around three-thirty' she replied. 'There was just enough daylight left for me to search for candles.'

Morgan carried Jack into the hall. 'I'll do the fuses after I've taken him up to the nursery. He should sleep through. Perhaps you'd grab that candelabra and light our way. Your boyfriend didn't teach you about fuses, then?' he enquired, probing.

'I met him when I was seventeen. Chas had strong ideas on what women should do and fuses were men's work,' she said drily.

'You…mentioned thongs,' he said, hating her boyfriend with a deep and abiding passion. She wasn't the thong type.

She shuddered. 'Vile. You don't want to know,' she mumbled.

He was pleased by her evident loathing. He glanced across at her, feasting on the soft glow bestowed on her by the candlelight. And was that a blush on her cheek? And a faint tremble to her mouth?

She'd been scared, alone in this big house. He felt over-come with regrets.

'I'm sorry,' he said abjectly, as they entered the nursery, 'that you've been in the dark all this time.'

She started. 'Do you mean in the dark as in the ex-boyfriend, or as in the light failure?' she asked warily.

'Whatever fits,' he said, hoping to encourage her to open up. He wanted to know everything about her. To listen to her describing her life, her hopes, ambitions…

'It was quite romantic, really,' she mused.

'Being with Chas?' He shot her a dark look from under his brows.

'No! Using candles here! I didn't mind at all, though cooking wasn't too easy. I did worry about what had happened to you and Jack. You'd said eight on the dot, you see, and—'

'I know. I'm an inconsiderate swine,' he said vehemently, divesting the sleeping Jack of his day clothes. 'I had so many things on my mind... Uh-oh. There's a nappy needs changing here.'

He had the dirty nappy half undone when the phone rang and he waited while Jodie answered it.

'For you. Gordon Cook,' she told him, covering the receiver.

'My secretary. Must be urgent. Can you carry on?' he asked.

She was half-appalled, half-delighted. In at the deep end, she thought, grabbing from him the ends he was holding. A *dirty* deep end, she reckoned, gingerly starting to clean the little pink bottom.

'What do I do now?' she hissed, helplessly holding baby wipes.

'Put those and the inner gauze in that carrier bag I put ready. They're for dumping. Wet liner in the nappy bucket for recycling,' he flung rapidly, before continuing with his call.

She managed that, and found some cream and fresh liners and gauzy strips in the changing bag. And then began the struggle. Try as she might, she couldn't work out how everything went together. And when she thought she was almost there, Jack stirred, kicked his legs, and dismantled her beautifully constructed arrangement.

Worse, Morgan was laughing. 'I've got to go,' he chuckled. 'Major disaster area here… No, only Jack needing me. See you next week. Cheers.'

Red-faced, she started again. 'Why don't you use disposables like the rest of the world?' she muttered crossly.

Chuckling, Morgan knelt beside her. 'Precisely for that reason. Environmental conscience. Let me.'

'No—I want to learn!' she protested, disappointed that she couldn't show him what a natural mother she was. 'I only need showing how. It's not rocket science, is it?'

'Like this. Take it round—no, that's too loose…' Gently he guided her fingers, then picked up a sleeping suit decorated with blue rabbits. 'See? Easy when you know how. He can have a bath in the morning. I'll put him to bed now. Pop the clean vest on, then the sleepsuit,' he requested.

'*That* vest?' she cried, aghast. 'With that minute opening? It'll never go over his head!'

'It will. Trust me,' Morgan murmured in amusement.

'Hmm. Well, if you say so. I'll give it a go. Oh, his head's so heavy!' she exclaimed, gingerly lifting it.

Her eyes were huge and terrified with the idea that she could easily harm this child with a clumsy movement. She had a missing motherhood gene, she thought moodily.

'Support his neck,' Morgan advised when the head wobbled in an alarming way. 'His muscles aren't very strong yet.'

The tiny skull lay in the palm of her hand. With the other hand she was supposed to wrestle that vest over the baby's head. It seemed an impossible task even for a rocket scientist, unless he had four hands in total.

Mesmerised, she stared at the beating pulse in the dip at the front of Jack's skull, suddenly horribly aware of the extreme fragility of the tiny baby. This was Morgan's pride and joy, more precious to him than anything in the world.

'I can't do it! You take over!' she cried, panic-stricken.

'But—'

'No! I don't want to! I can't!' she wailed. 'Look at my hands! They're not steady enough. I'll drop him, I know. Take hold of him, Morgan, *please!*' she begged frantically.

'Of course,' he soothed. 'There's no reason why you should do this.' Deftly Morgan dressed his son, his movements so sure and confident that it looked easy. 'Come on, sleepy, you and your rabbits need tucking up.'

He scooped Jack up with enviable confidence and placed him in the crib, securing the blankets around the sleeping child and watching him, a tender smile warming his entire face.

The appalled Jodie remained on the floor, her lower lip trembling annoyingly. She'd failed the test. The little body had seemed frighteningly vulnerable to her lack of expertise and her nerves had ruined her determination to learn.

Her chest tightened with misery. Suddenly it seemed of overwhelming importance that she should be able to look after his child. In the back of her mind she'd seen herself running the house, looking after her father and being a kind of...nanny...to Jack while Morgan went to work.

Just now she'd just proved how useless she'd be. And she dreaded to think how much worse her efforts would have been if Jack had been wide awake, yelling and wriggling.

Her mouth drooped at the corners. Everything had gone downhill since she'd seen that photo of Morgan's wife. Her confidence had begun to desert her. Had her assertiveness been an illusion, then? Was she heading back to dependency and anti-depressants?

She felt sick at the thought.

'Have you eaten?' Morgan asked in a conversational tone, as he selected Jack's clothes for the morning.

She felt sicker. 'I had a sandwich,' she mumbled.

'No humble pie for me to eat, then?'

She wouldn't be cheered up. 'I did a pasta for us with a herb and tomato sauce, but…it's gone rubbery. You could make car tyres out of it,' she said, her face mournful. 'And I burned it whilst trying to keep it hot,' she added honestly.

'Then we'd better start again,' he suggested. 'After all it was my fault I wasn't back at the right time—and I imagine you don't know how to keep things warm in the Aga. I'll give you a lesson.'

She sniffed, finding it hard to cope with his easy-going response. It had been his fault, but irrationally she still felt disappointed in her efforts. She'd wanted to welcome him to a warm house, with delicious smells wafting towards him, which would be mingling alluringly with her new and expensive perfume.

All her painstaking cleaning and cooking, her new dress and carefully made up face had been to no avail. He couldn't see how spotless everything was without electric light, he'd not even noticed how nice she looked, and her scent must have been overpowered by the stink of incinerated pasta!

Her lip trembled. Discovering she had no natural aptitude with babies was the last straw!

'What's upsetting you?' Morgan murmured.

'Nothing.'

Sulky as a stupid child, she jumped up and went out, forgetting the lack of light. When she snapped on the switch outside the door she was met with a resounding nothing in the way of illumination, but pride prevented her from going back and she made her way to the stairs by feel alone.

And failed. Wrapped up in her own misery, she crashed into something hard, doubled up and gave a loud yell of pain.

'Jodie!'

Both light and Morgan appeared in seconds and his arms came securely around her.

'I hit my shin!' she gasped. 'Stupid, *stupid*!'

'Don't cry,' he said gently.

'I'm *not*!' she cried, dashing her fists across her eyes. 'What would I cry for?' she demanded shakily. 'Just because I'm the most cack-handed woman in the world where babies are concerned, just because I totally f-forgot the electricity was off and—and I was too pathetically silly to admit that and g-go back for a candle...'

'Slow down,' he murmured lazily, his blurred face swimming inches away. 'None of this matters. Remember, you've been through a hell of a lot. Take a deep breath... Jodie... *Jodie!* Don't look at me like that,' he muttered thickly.

'Like...what?' she mumbled, trying to focus.

He groaned like someone in despair. She heard the metal base of the candelabra being placed on a table, then felt the soft touch of his tongue on her upper lip, and before she could work out that he'd lapped up a salty tear his mouth was driving into hers, hard, firm, determined and totally abandoned.

'I'm sorry. I must!' he whispered into her hot mouth.

Something terrifying leapt within her, a wild, frantic hunger that fought for freedom, snapping the overstretched thread of restraint and flinging her headlong into a dark, unknown world of flames and heat which licked through her hungry body and turned it into a smouldering furnace.

'Yes!' she moaned.

Her hands reached up fiercely to rake his hair, feeling the silk between her fingers, the warmth of his scalp, as her mouth responded to his dizzying kisses with a ferocity that stunned her.

'God, you're beautiful!' he growled.

'Me?'

'Oh, yes, *yes*!'

She was all force, all need, all desperation. And he was, too, his groans echoing hers, his hands everywhere, like hers, every part of her demanding the relief as his questing fingers cupped, held, kneaded…

Her head rolled back and his mouth descended hotly on her throat, his lips finding the hollow where her pulse beat violently and moistening it with such a delicate sweep of his tongue that she moaned and whimpered as the sweet pain shot through her needy body, contracting her loins and rendering her totally helpless.

'Morgan!' she said on a sigh, and made an inarticulate, incoherent cry of longing when his teeth grazed her lower lip and his tongue tasted its swollen softness.

'Oh, yes!' he rasped.

His deep, shuddering tone made her go limp in his arms and she felt herself being borne backwards by the weight of his body… A welcome pressure, she thought with a groan of pleasure, the full force of his powerful chest and thighs moving her inexorably back and her own weak legs barely able to hold her upright.

And then they both collapsed onto the softness of a bed and she could forget the effort to stay on her feet and give her whole concentration to the wonderful sensation of being pinned helplessly by hot flesh and blood, hard bone and muscle…

Instinctively she arched against him, murmuring her hazy delight when her pelvis slid against his and encountered the hard shaft leaping from his loins.

Her legs wrapped around his body, reckless heels driving into his back and grinding him into her thighs.

'Please!' she whispered, beyond all modesty, all caution or rational thought.

It was as if something snapped in him too. His lips burned intense kisses on every inch of her mouth; his hands cradled her face with a vehemence that exhilarated her.

He shook with desperation and uttered a low, guttural cry, then sat back, the silvery moonlight in the room revealing his eyes to be hot with arousal as he frantically tore off his sweater, swooping down to kiss her senseless and then struggling to undo the buttons of his shirt with hopelessly incapable fingers.

She couldn't wait. She wanted him naked against her. In a quick movement borne of intense need, she sat up and dragged her dress over her head, then put her hands on the front edges of his shirt, ripping them apart.

And she buried her face in his chest, smelling him, kissing, nibbling and tasting. He jerked and gripped her shoulders when her mouth enclosed one taut nipple and, trembling with passion, he pushed her away.

'Too much,' he croaked in torment, catching his breath at the sight of her breasts, swelling luxuriantly above her scarlet silk bra.

'It isn't,' she husked desperately. 'It's not enough—'

Panting, she recognised the sexual greed in his dark eyes and a shiver of anticipated ecstasy rippled through her entire nervous system, intensifying the molten heat between her thighs.

'Touch me,' she whispered, her hands lifting her breasts for his delight.

'My God, Jodie—you...you are...perfect!' His growl was hoarse and thick with desire and she felt her nipples stiffening even more than before, thrusting painfully at the tightly stretched fabric.

One trembling male hand reached out. She watched, hypnotised with expectancy, her eyes drugged and limpid, her breathing harsh and moaning as his finger extended.

There was the briefest of touches through the silk, a faint slide across the taut swelling at the centre of her breast, and she bucked as if he'd sliced her through with a knife.

'Ohhhh!' she groaned. 'Again… So good… Touch me, touch me, Morgan!' she implored.

A thumb this time. She recognised its breadth, its greater heat. She swallowed, almost incapable of bearing the pleasure. Her head rolled back, her lashes fluttered in a plea that he should ease the agony of her other untouched breast.

Gently he slid the straps from her shoulders, his eyes burning into hers, holding her captive. He was too slow, too gentle…the tantalising drift of his fingers on her arms far too delicate. She wanted more. Now.

Her back straightened and the twin globes lifted free. The silk slithered down to her waist and she sat there, waiting, waiting, while he held his breath and the muscles in his chest snatched tightly into spasm then held rigid.

He devoured her with his eyes. His lashes lowered, thick and black against the gleam of his cheeks, and he drew in a short, hard breath that shuddered through him like a wave.

Slowly he shrugged his shoulders out of the shirt. She sighed softly and leaned back in a sinuous movement, raising her arms above her head. Moonlight turned his skin to polished silver, his Latin cheekbones sharply pronounced beneath his liquid tar eyes.

Intent on her, promising everything she longed for, he lifted a muscled arm and flung the shirt behind him. It hit something. Into Jodie's subconscious came the sound of an object slithering and then a crash followed by shattering glass.

Morgan's head jerked around. And he froze.

Jodie could see nothing. When he turned back she saw that a terrible anguish wrecked the beauty of his face, twisting his mouth into an agonised groan. Jodie sensed him retreating into some dark hell of his own, a place which had no corner for her.

Frantic to keep him, she pressed her aching body against his, the rigid peaks of her breasts scraping firmly, insistently, across his straining torso. Her arms twined around his neck and she kissed his tortured mouth.

'Morgan,' she whispered gently, seductively.

But his lips clamped together and she felt his jaw clench hard in denial. Firm hands clasped her arms, pushing her back. Bewildered and angry, she blinked up muzzily at his grim face.

'I can't!' he grated. 'Forgive me. I should never...'

He'd left the bed. Was picking up his shirt, jumper...shoes he'd somehow discarded...

'You can't...*go* like this!' she gasped jerkily, raising herself on her elbows.

He stopped, his back to her. 'I must!' he insisted.

'But...why? You wanted me!' she accused, deeply hurt. And unable to pacify her screaming, demanding body. She'd been so sure of him. And now she felt confused. 'What were you doing, Morgan?' she demanded miserably.

He remained silent, his shoulders in that now familiar rigid hunch. She slid her feet to the floor, intending to get some kind of explanation. And then she found one.

The shirt must have caught one of his wife's photographs which she'd arranged so carefully for him on the chest of drawers. It now lay face down on the floor, the glass smashed to smithereens.

Her stomach sucked in with nausea. Now she understood. He'd been desperate for sex. But smashing his late wife's photo had shamed him. He felt as if he'd betrayed his wife's memory.

Jodie curled up on the bed, her eyes huge as she quietly

drew the covers over her near-naked body. Competition she could cope with. But not a dead woman.

'If you'd keep your back turned for a while,' she said, managing a reasonably normal voice, 'I'll get dressed and you can have your bed back.'

Morgan bit back an urge to tell her why he couldn't make love to her. It had been a mistake to bundle the photos of Teresa on top of the chest. But Sam had said he couldn't bear looking at her and being reminded of her: alive, beautiful, glowing with health.

Morgan had hoped that one day Sam would take them back, for Jack's sake. Jack had a right to see what his own mother had looked like. They must not be lost or thrown away.

But when he'd turned moments ago and found Teresa staring at him with her wicked eyes he'd been reminded of his deceit. And something had clawed at his gut. Pounding relentlessly into his head had come the realisation that he couldn't make love to the open and trusting Jodie under false pretences.

Either he had to tell her the whole truth of the situation or he had to leave her alone. Any kind of relationship based on a pack of lies and half-truths was doomed to fail.

His breath caught in his throat. Astonishingly, he felt that he wanted to build a lasting relationship with a woman he'd barely met, hardly knew. And yet in a strange sense it seemed as if he'd known her all his life.

His hands stilled. *But what of Jack?*

He let the pain scythe through him in punishment for losing sight of his most passionate hope for his son's future.

Jodie—sweet, sexy, all woman—had turned his head. He dared not allow her to get too close. It was one hell of a risk. What if the relationship failed? She'd remain here with Jack, her 'half-brother'. And he'd have no rights to see his on ever again. She'd marry some other guy whom Jack would learn to call Daddy...

God! Why did he want two people who were totally incompatible with his peace of mind?

'I'm dressed now,' she said, behind him.

Numb with anger at himself, he pushed his arms into his shirt. 'I regret what happened—' he began stiffly.

'I understand.'

He whirled, his eyes intensely black. 'No! You don't—'

'Give me some credit!' she flared. 'I know what happens when a man is virile and red-blooded. I'm not some ignorant virgin. I'm familiar enough with the male urges to realise that you needed sex and I was around and willing.'

Touchingly, she lifted her head, as if she had no shame in that self-revealing statement. But it hadn't been the way she'd described: a purely animal desire to satisfy a rampant sex drive. It had been something different, something more profound. Though caution prevented him from saying so.

'But it's too soon, isn't it?' she went on, her voice jerking oddly. 'You can't bring yourself to betray your late wife...because you still l-love her.'

'What?' he muttered, puzzled.

Jodie's eyes looked sad. 'Your wife. I saw you looking at the photos,' she explained. 'She was lovely, Morgan. The kind of woman you—you'd never forget,' she finished, stumbling slightly over her words.

It sliced his heart in two to have Teresa referred to as his wife. As for never forgetting...that was true at least. He'd remember Teresa to his dying day.

'We need to talk,' he said, his mouth tight. 'Come downstairs. I'll fix the fuses and we'll eat some supper. There are some things you need to know.'

But how much should he tell her? He wrestled with his conscience that insisted everything. He couldn't go that far.

They went down the stairs in silence, avoiding contact
avoiding each other's eyes. Which was ridiculous when
they'd been so close a few moments before. He could still
smell the faint fragrance of her skin, feel the firm pressure
of her body...

His teeth clenched together as desire rocketed through
him. In one stupid moment he'd let down his guard and
succumbed to his hunger for her.

He shuddered at his precipitate action. He'd been totally
unprepared. Supposing he'd made love to her? Supposing
she'd become pregnant? What the hell would he have done
then? How would he ever have lived with himself? God
he was a fool!

Jack needed him. Jack would need his support and pres
ence right through his life. How could he have put his son's
future in jeopardy?

The easiest thing would be to ensure she didn't stay long
When the opportunity arose, he must, *must* tell Jodie what
it would mean if she was reunited with her father. The
future for Sam was very bleak, and maybe, like Teresa
she'd hate the prospect of looking after a desperately sick
man.

Then the problem would be resolved. He could keep her
at arm's length and then she'd leave and he and Jack would
continue with their lives in peace.

But... He scowled. He didn't want Jodie to go! Why, he
had no idea; he knew only that she occupied his mind and
body with every breath he took.

Wasn't there a compromise somewhere? When he dwelt
on the possibility of never seeing her again, the anger and
resentment surged up within him, blocking out everything
else. Dear heaven, what was happening to him?

His hands shook as he dealt with the fuse box. The lights
snapped on, illuminating the house, all its surfaces spar

kling where Jodie had obviously wielded a duster with spectacular results.

He didn't look at her when he walked into the kitchen. Instead, he selected a pizza from the freezer and popped it into the roasting oven, then started preparing a salad. She watched him from where she sat at the kitchen table, quietly waiting for him to speak.

Placing the salad and a dressing on the table, he pulled out a chair and sat down heavily.

'First, I want you to know that I have never been married, Jodie,' he said, his voice tight and strained.

She frowned, staring at him with her startled green eyes. 'But...the woman in the photos—'

'Is Teresa. Sam's fiancée.'

She sat back, stunned into silence. He could see her mind working on something which clearly puzzled her. And then she spoke, timidly, jerkily. 'You have loads of framed snapshots of her...I thought she *must* be your—'

'*No!*' It came out as a tortured denial, but that was how he felt.

'Then...why are they in your room?'

Cold inside, he leant his forearms on the table and stared down at the grain of the table, thinking ahead to the moment when he'd have to persuade her to go home. His breath raked painfully in his chest.

'Your father wanted them thrown away,' he said huskily.

'But...he loved her!'

'Yes. That's exactly why—because he...loved her,' he said, forcing out the words against his will. 'When your father heard the news of Teresa's death he went berserk, flinging the photos around like a man demented. He couldn't bear to see her; it was too painful for him. Then he collapsed and I took him to hospital.'

He stirred in his chair, recalling the distaste with which

he'd collected the scattered frames and flung them on the barely used chest in his bedroom.

'So…why are *you* keeping the photos?' she cried tensely.

'For Sam and…' He checked himself, realising he'd been close to involving Jack. Jodie would have demanded an explanation if he had. 'For Sam,' he amended, frantically trying to find a way to finish that sentence. 'And,' he said, relief flooding his face when the answer came, 'my reason was that I knew he'd want them again one day.'

'I see.'

It was a good answer—and perfectly possible. But Jodie knew something wasn't quite right. He was evading her eyes. The story didn't quite match up with what she sensed—or that telling little mistake which he'd hastily corrected.

For Sam and…who? For himself? Had he wanted some of those photos depicting Teresa at her sultriest? Could they still be a kind of shrine—not to his wife—as she knew now—but to the glamorous, utterly desirable Teresa?

Jodie felt her stomach turn. That slip of the tongue had betrayed his real feelings. *For Sam and for me!* She bit her lip as the truth brutally made itself known, and her eyes paled to a silvery hue. Morgan had been wildly infatuated with the stunning and provocative Teresa!

Rooting back in her memory, she now remembered the occasions when there had been some reference to Teresa. Every single time he'd responded with barely concealed grief—and there was only one possible explanation for that. Obsession.

Cold shivers ran down her spine. The situation, if it were true, was appalling. What about the woman who'd mothered his child? Morgan had been in a relationship with Jack's mother—and yet at the very same time he'd coveted his boss's mistress!

Helpless to stop herself shaking, she struggled with her sickening aversion to Morgan's secret passion for her father's lover. It couldn't be true. It must not be. She had believed Morgan to be a man of honour—but where was honour, she thought sadly, where obsession was concerned? It hit you like a blow, wiping out all rational thought, compelling you to behave out of character. She knew that only too well.

She stiffened. Perhaps Morgan was using her now—as he'd used Jack's mother...as a substitute for what he really wanted: someone to ease his frustration for the unattainable Teresa. She winced, unable to bear the degrading humiliation.

'Morgan, there's something I want to say,' she said decisively, her heart lurching with misery. Warily his eyes flicked up then, and met hers in query. 'It's quite simple.'

Her tone hardened with bitterness that she could have been so deceived by a man's coaxing words, the look in his eyes, the tender passion of his touch.

She'd believed he'd felt something special too. But when he'd touched her and looked at her he'd probably been picturing *Teresa's* face, remembering *her* scent, the curves of *her* body—

'You don't know what you've just done!,' she cried angrily, any restraint snapping with those images. 'Oh, you might be hurt. You might be upset. But that doesn't mean you can use me for therapy!' she yelled.

'What the hell do you mean?' he barked, leaping to his feet and glaring down at her white face.

'I mean,' she ground out furiously, 'that I will *not* be used as a sex object ever again! Not by you or by any man!'

'Sex object? And what was I?' he raged. 'Have you miraculously fallen madly in love with me?' Breathing hot and hard, he leant over the table, intimidating her. 'Or did

you feel a need to satisfy some ordinary, basic desires—
the same ones you accuse me of feeling?' he hurled ruthlessly.

'That's unfair!' she cried, colouring up.

'No, it's not! You wanted me as much as I wanted you!'
He drew himself erect, simmering with temper. And something else. A dark, bitter expression permeated his entire
face. 'So, Jodie,' he said in a low and gravelly tone, 'it may
surprise you, but I don't want to be a sex object either. I
don't want a woman to use me as a stud because she misses
rampant sex with her boyfriend—'

'It wasn't that!' she gasped.

Suddenly still, his eyes veiled, he studied her for a long
time. 'What was it, then? An emotional crutch?'

She lowered her head. There was pride, or there was the
truth; there was the counsel of silence...or an attack in the
form of a question.

'Is that what it was for you?' she mumbled evasively.

'Come to your own conclusion,' he snapped.

'I think I have! You wanted me because you're grieving
over Teresa's death. You needed sex and you needed human comfort, the feel of a woman in your arms,' she accused, her voice shaking with pain and resentment. 'Get a
whore for the job!' she flared. 'And keep your hands off
me in future!'

Morgan drew in a long, chest-filling breath. 'And if I
can't?' he said softly.

'You dare come near me again—!' she began, close to
hysterics.

'Stop this, Jodie!' he said curtly. 'We've reached an im-
passe. You obviously can't trust me.'

'No. I can't!'

'In that case there's only one solution. It's time you

moved out. We've just proved that being here together is asking for trouble.'

It was as if the wind had been taken out of her. 'L-leave?' she stumbled.

'It would be best,' he said harshly. 'Why make life hard? If you go, there's no problem. I don't have to control myself.' He shot her a thoughtful, assessing look, as if he had more to say. 'And later, when your father returns here, it would spare you the worst of his illness.'

Jodie stiffened. 'What do you mean?' she asked, puzzled.

His face a cold mask, he leant back against the Aga and folded his arms in an attitude which suggested indifference to her feelings.

'He will never be well again, Jodie. His suffering will increase. Can you take more of the hard, blunt truth?'

Somehow she held herself together. Her eyes were wide and haunted when finally she managed to swallow back the clogging lump in her throat and reply.

'It sounds as if I must,' she said in a small, frightened voice.

'I'll get you a brandy.'

He was gone for a few moments during which she sat there shaking like a leaf. She felt as if she'd been through a sawmill. All her nerves were torn and ragged, her stomach lurching around as waves of nausea hit her.

A brandy balloon was thrust into her trembling hand. 'Drink it.'

When she stared at the glass in her hand, he took it from her nerveless fingers and held it to her lips. 'Drink!' he commanded.

It was hot and fierce and seared rawly through to her stomach. But it did the trick.

Morgan fought to hang on to his objective. Jodie had to go. It was true: he'd been without sex and without a woman's sweetness for too long. He'd misinterpreted his feelings for Jodie and in a short time he would forget all about her.

But Jack would still be there, Jack would be his—if he could only stick to his decision to keep Jodie at a distance—and keep her ignorant of the raw truths which could ruin Jack's life.

But it was hard. He had to give a good performance in the next few minutes, depicting a man with sex on the brain and ice in his heart. That would drive her out.

And yet she was sitting there trembling, eyes great green pools in the ghostly pallor of her face, tragedy etched across her downturned mouth. He reined in all sympathy and harshly jerked out the unvarnished facts.

'Sam was in the Far East working on a project some years ago. They were spraying toxic chemicals nearby. Gradually he began to get headaches, lapses of memory, bouts of sickness and so on. Last summer he had a check-up and they discovered massive damage to the major organs of his body.'

Her hand flew to her mouth as a moan escaped. Like a child, she clenched her fist and bit on it to stop herself from crying out again.

Jack, Morgan kept thinking. I'm doing this for my son.

But it didn't help. He wanted her to think well of him, not to appear an unfeeling monster. He ached to take her in his arms and explain gently. Forgive me, he pleaded silently, turning his back to her. And he occupied his hands by making a coffee, crashing china about unmercifully.

'What...?' Her voice had been just a hoarse croak. He heard her swallow and he gritted his teeth, spooning instant coffee into a mug. 'What treatment is he having?' she asked.

'There is none.'

'Oh, God!'

Sugar, he thought. Three. Anything to stop him turning around and seeing the misery on her face.

'That's why he wrote to me,' she said jerkily.

'Yes. He wanted to see you—and of course he wanted to marry Teresa before he deteriorated further.'

'Tell me what will happen,' she whispered. 'And,' she cried in agitation, her voice rising, 'stop fiddling about with that biscuit tin and darn well face me!'

Perhaps he should. His punishment. He stirred his coffee and glanced across at her, his jaw tight with tension. Tears were swimming in her enormous eyes and her lip trembled.

'I love him too,' he shot tersely.

'Yes. I know.' She bit her lip. 'Tell me.'

'Over a period of time he will become progressively confused, with fewer and fewer lucid moments. His lungs will give out and his heart will be put under excessive stress. He'll be forgetful and difficult, like someone with Alzheimer's. And...I'm told he'll lose control of all his functions.'

She said nothing and it seemed she was in shock. Unable to remain still, he restlessly quartered the room as he spoke in staccato sentences.

'We must do what's best for him. During his last conscious moments I want him to be happy. No stress. I will be plain, Jodie. I find you sexually desirable. But I need to concentrate on Jack, and on Sam.'

'Yes, of course,' she muttered.

'You may decide that you still want to be reunited with your father,' he went on. 'On the other hand, you might not. It would be a short-lived relationship which would give you great pain, and I for one wouldn't blame you for walking away. However, if you do decide to meet him, then I ask you to make things easier for me, for both of us.'

'How?' she whispered.

His strides quickened. 'Stay in a hotel, a flat—whatever you want. I'll pay for it. I just don't want you here. When he's well enough—after a spell in a convalescent home, perhaps—I will tell him about you and arrange for you to visit him here—'

'How long before you'd tell him?'

He shrugged. 'Two, three weeks.' He gripped the edge of a kitchen chair and whirled around, his face grim. 'And you must promise that when he no longer recognises you…'

He paused, overcome with emotion. That would be when he'd need her most.

'What?' she asked in a thin, reedy voice.

He controlled his selfish needs and glared at her ferociously. 'Then I want you to get out of our lives for ever!'

CHAPTER EIGHT

JODIE rose to her feet. And although her legs were shaking, she managed to remain steady by holding fiercely onto the edge of the table, her fingers white with strain.

'Unthinkable!' she snapped. 'Do you really expect me to pick and choose the kind of father I have? To only want a father who is in good health and able to respond to me?'

Morgan seemed disconcerted, his frown bringing his dark brows hard together. 'Just visit him, Jodie. See him when he's awake and settled—'

'*This is my father!* Why should I be sidelined when he needs me most—?'

'Because it will be hell looking after him!' Morgan rasped. 'Because I'm offering you a chance to hold a better memory of him in your mind—'

'Do you think I'm so shallow that I can't see beyond the shell of a person and into the heart and mind and soul? I know what my father's character is—you've told me. I will respect and love him whatever he looks like, however ill he becomes—'

'You can't take on his care,' he insisted grimly. 'And I won't have some ultra-efficient nurse bullying him—'

'Neither will I!' she retorted, horrified that he could even think of that. 'Maybe someone to help with the chores, to do the washing—but not to care for him. That's for the people who love him, who don't flinch at the unpleasantness and the sadness of seeing a loved one slowly declining—'

'You can't put yourself through that, Jodie!' he cried passionately.

'Why not?' she yelled. 'You are!'

'I'm different—'

'No, you're not! Oh, granted, I don't even know him. He's been your substitute father for most of your life, your friend, and the man you admire. But I have a deep and abiding need to know and love and cherish my father—and you can't take that from me!'

Too fraught to know what she was doing, she went to Morgan, catching his wrists in an urgent grip. He had to understand how she felt. She must win him over.

'You forget,' she cried, 'I've been a regular visitor to an old people's home in New York. I've seen things that would make your hair curl. I've watched men and women die and I hope I've made their last few moments easier by my presence, by holding their hands and talking to them till their spirits departed. Yes, it sears the emotions. Yes, it hurts. Yes, I cry when someone I've known has gone. But that's the reality of life and death and love and sorrow, and to know one you must at some time endure the others!'

'Jodie—!' he started hoarsely, his eyes glistening, dark and fevered.

'No, let me finish!' she insisted fervently. 'I don't shrink from what I have to do. It won't be easy. But this is my father we're talking about, and you can't deny me the right to make his life as comfortable as possible! I want his love. I want to love him, Morgan! You, with no father, must feel some pity for me! I have to stay in the house. I will need to be near him. We can work out a rota. You have Jack to think of. Let us share the care between us. *Please!*'

'Hell.'

He wrenched free of her grip and put a hand to his forehead, concealing his eyes. Abruptly he turned away. But she had seen the anguish that racked him and she knew she had hit raw nerves.

'Morgan,' she implored gently. 'Whatever our needs, we have to ignore them for my father's sake. We can do this. More than anything, I'd like my father to be fit and well, but he isn't, so that's what I must accept.'

'You have surprised me,' he said softly.

She blinked. 'Why?'

He came to her, close enough for her to feel the heat of his body. And he seemed less tense than before, his anger abated. She hoped she'd persuaded him. It was so important to her that she stayed, not only for her father's sake but because she wanted to help Morgan break the barriers he'd erected when Teresa had died. He needed to be free so he could meet someone, fall in love...

She frowned, hating that thought, jealousy slicing sharply through her body. And found Morgan's finger smoothing out the furrows on her brow.

'I am impressed by your passion and your devotion,' he said, his deep voice soft and low. 'Not many women would choose such a hard and thankless path. Think carefully about this. You could be surrendering a year of your life in exchange for increasing heartbreak.'

'I would do it for the *rest* of my life if needed!' she cried with all the fervent conviction of her heart.

'I do believe you would.'

Her eyes widened. She found that they were leaning closer to one another, their gazes locked, lips parted. And Morgan was swallowing, as she was, perhaps because he too was overcome with deep emotion.

Her heart clamoured in her breast. Unless she was mistaken, there was more in his eyes than a hunger for sex or comfort. He admired her. Respected her. A wonderful warmth washed through her veins. She smiled shakily.

'Say you agree!' she begged.

His eyes were an irresistible liquid black, drawing her even nearer, the intensity of his gaze making her breath shorten in her throat.

'I must ask you to think about this a little longer. Our passions, our emotions are overstretched, and the situation will get worse. We could both do something we regret. I admit that I have a need to feel a woman's arms around me,' he said huskily. 'I'm warning you for your own good. I've been to hell and back, Jodie. Sometimes I feel I'm still on my way.'

'I know,' she said, longing to ease that hell.

He frowned. 'That's the trouble! You're so damn understanding and compassionate! Having you, a beautiful and achingly desirable woman, around is tempting fate. I can't expect you to spend your time here wondering if I'm going to grab you. I'm not made of stone—and you are...irresistible.'

She blinked. Irresistible! Achingly desirable! 'Am I, Morgan?' she asked, unwittingly alluring.

He licked his lips, the tip of his tongue leaving a glistening sheen on his carnal mouth, and all she could think of was taking his face between her palms and pressing her lips to his—thus forcing him to concentrate on *her* and not Teresa.

'Jodie!' he said sharply, making her jump. 'Nurse your father if you want, spend most of the day here, but don't sleep here. Do you hear that? You *have* to leave!'

She gave him a level glance. 'Why should I? To salve your conscience?'

Morgan winced. 'To prevent a disaster happening,' he bit back.

So, he thought that making love to her would be a disaster! Huh! He wouldn't think that if they did! He'd be overwhelmed, thrilled and besotted with her! she thought indignantly.

Hadn't he almost lost track of reality in her arms? If he hadn't broken that photo, wouldn't they now be snuggling up to one another, glowing and sated in the aftermath of blissful satiation?

Jodie glared, revising her thoughts radically. He couldn't—shouldn't—mourn a dead woman for the rest of his life. He needed someone alive and real to help him forget his mistaken infatuation.

Gradually, over time, he needed to learn what lay beyond sex, what was better than a cold and empty fantasy. He needed to be loved, to find love. Her heart sang. She knew just the woman for the job!

She groaned inwardly, terrified of the emotional risks she was contemplating. This was crazy! He was talking about wanting sex with her for comfort, whereas she was imagining something more profound...

But what did he know? she argued. He was confused, clinging to his shrine to the unattained and unattainable Teresa, consumed with guilt because he hadn't loved Jack's mother as he should have done. But that was in the past.

'Do you *want* me to go?' she purred.

He hesitated, and in that moment she knew the answer. 'I...like having you around,' he said slowly. 'I can hardly deny that, can I? But I'm not blind to the explosive potential of two needy people in close proximity to one another—and I think you should protect yourself from a possibly awkward situation. You don't want a relationship based on sex. We'd quarrel—and our hostility to one another would become obvious. We don't want your father to detect an atmosphere between us.'

'No,' she said. 'For his sake we must be friends. And surely he'd think it odd if I stayed anywhere other than his house? If we're to share the next difficult months then need to get to know you, Morgan. I think you want tha too.'

Morgan opened his mouth to reply and then he let out groan, leaping out of his chair and flinging the oven door open. Smoke billowed out. Jodie went over and they both stood there staring in surprise at the blackened remains of the pizza.

'I don't believe it!' he exclaimed irritably.

'Easy to do.' A smile tipped the corners of her mouth 'What with your cooking and mine, we'll be as skinny as string in no time at all!'

His lips twitched and he gave a rueful grin. 'I've never done that before!'

She laughed, watching him lift out the remains and slam the heavy iron door shut. 'Join the club. I'm an old hand.'

'You're teaching me bad tricks,' he admonished, scrap ing the mess into the bin.

'I've got plenty more up my sleeve.'

He drew away, his mouth pinching in. 'That's what wor ries me. I don't know that I can be what you want, Jodie.'

'You couldn't be my friend?' she asked, disappointed. I was the first essential step to a lasting relationship; any idio knew that.

'That would be the easy part,' he admitted. She beamed and he shook his head in amused exasperation. 'You never give up, do you? I've never met anyone as persuasive.'

'People where I worked used to say I could sell pork pies to vegetarians,' she said, her eyes dancing with hope

Morgan groaned. 'Don't talk about food! I'm starving Look…we need time to think this over. Shall we put a hold on any decisions for the moment and go to the pub first?' he suggested.

A reprieve. Glad that their row had blown over, she nodded. 'And Jack?'

'I can bundle him up and bring him too. There's a children's area—though it'll be fairly quiet at this time of night. What do you say?'

'I say, why not?' she agreed happily.

Things were moving on, she thought, hugging herself in delight. Morgan had admitted they could be good friends. It was a promising start.

From the house it was only a short walk to the pub. When he opened the door she walked in to a cheerful atmosphere full of noise and chatter, which abated when they were noticed and then increased considerably in volume.

'We're being discussed,' he muttered under his breath.

'It's tempting to do something outrageous,' she whispered with a wicked grin.

He looked at her mouth, as if contemplating landing a kiss there. 'I could order champagne and feed you oysters with my teeth.'

She made a face. 'I'd rather have steak pie and chips.'

'The gravy would drip down my chin.'

Jodie raised an eyebrow. 'No problem. There's a bib in your pocket with hedgehogs on it.'

'So there is,' he cried, rummaging for it.

'No! Don't!' she giggled, going pink at the sideways glances from everyone.

'If you insist. Performance over, then. Let's head for the family room,' Morgan proposed.

Family room, she thought sentimentally, and sighed. It was small and empty, but bright with balloons and a colourful rack of children's books and jigsaws. Outside she could see a floodlit garden with a climbing frame and a slide.

Relaxing by the log fire, Jodie enjoyed her experience of

an English pub. She and Morgan chatted all through the meal, though later she couldn't remember what they'd talked about—only that his eyes had never left hers and she'd felt a wild and uncontainable joy.

'Ready to leave?' he asked suddenly.

'Oh, must we go?' She didn't want their companionship to end. Going back would break the spell. 'I like it here. It's cosy.'

'I like it too, but I'm working on baby hours,' he said with a wry smile. 'Jack hauls me out of bed a few times in the night and I need to get some sleep in first.' He stood up. 'OK, force me. One quick half and then we must leave. I'd love to stay longer, but—'

'I understand. We can't have everything we want, can we?'

Morgan froze. Jodie had been on his mind all evening. Jodie and Jack. Something flicked into his mind, a fleeting, crazy thought that flung his resolution into disarray.

'What did you say?' he breathed.

She looked up at him and blinked. 'OK, so it was a trite cliché But it's true. We can never have everything we want.'

His head came up and he stared ahead sightlessly. 'Can't we?' he murmured, a smile curving his masculine mouth.

'You know we can't,' she replied in a sad voice.

But they could. His heart thundered in his chest. 'Two halves of cider coming up,' he said, excitement hurtling through him.

Morgan strode to the bar and waited to be served, his mind whirling with the rapidity of events. All his life he'd had a strength of will that was phenomenal: admired, feared and discussed with awe by friends and colleagues.

With Jodie he could only respond to his basic instincts.

Or perhaps, he mused, some higher command that knew what was right for him.

He liked and admired her. Found himself unable to stop touching her. And she felt the same way about him. All evening they'd talked like old friends. He hadn't imagined the look in her eyes. She was naturally wary, and afraid of being used, but she wasn't the sort of woman to opt for sex without a deeper emotion backing it up.

Could they make a go of a relationship? It was crucial that they did. He licked dry lips, conscious that his lungs were deprived of air. Slowly he brought his breathing under control. He would test the water. Court her. And when the time was right, he'd make love to her. And then he'd propose.

'Yes?'

He stared blankly at the woman behind the bar and then smiled. 'Sorry. Miles away. Two halves of cider, please.'

He opened his wallet and extracted a note, elation rippling through him. He grinned at the woman. 'And one for yourself.'

He could have everything he wanted. Jodie and Jack. He'd found the solution.

His gaze fell on the small packet tucked in the back of his wallet—forgotten since his liaison with Teresa. He stared at it, knowing it gave him the opportunity to make love to Jodie without the danger of a pregnancy.

Dangerous. He was teetering on the brink of a precipice—virtually ready to throw himself over!

Turning, he saw her pensively smiling into space and strode forward, recklessly disregarding caution and more than ready to take the plunge.

They fell into a comfortable routine very quickly—almost like a married couple, Jodie thought happily as she

Hoovered the stairs with loving care.

Since the evening at the pub Morgan had been relaxed and friendly, and despite their worries about her father there had been moments of laughter and a deep contentment that she had never known before.

Morgan concentrated on Jack, she looked after the house, and they both did the shopping and cooking. He'd begun to work in his study, leaving the door open so, he said in a hopeful hint, she could wander in with cups of tea.

Taking him at his word, she brought a pot of tea and chocolate cake one afternoon, pausing to admire the drawing he was finishing.

'That looks like a church!' she exclaimed, placing the tray on his desk.

He swivelled around from the drawing slope. 'It is. Look...I'm really excited about this.'

Encouraged, she came closer. '"St Bartholomew's",' she read. 'You're designing a church?'

He laughed. 'No! Better than that. Converting it. The bishop has decided it's too large for the congregation and most of it is wasted. So I'm dividing it in half.'

He flicked over a sheet. She looked at him and adored him. He was so happy, so absorbed in his work. With a sigh she dragged her gaze from his eager face and tried to make out the drawing.

'Looks like a hotel,' she said, puzzled.

'Close. A hostel—for the homeless.' He put his arm around her shoulders, drawing her even nearer. 'Look, Jodie. It's a brilliant idea. There's a day room, kitchens to cook their meals, and small, individual rooms for thirty people. I've had to tuck them into the church arches, but it works, don't you think?'

She beamed, thrilled with the idea. 'It's wonderful. Oh,

Morgan, you must be so proud to be doing something that's such a benefit to the community!'

He smiled back. 'I am,' he said softly. 'I feel I'm putting something back. I want to see where else this can be done. The only thing stopping this happening all over the country is lack of funding. The bishop wants local firms to contribute—'

'I could help there!' she said with a laugh. 'I sell pork pies to vegetarians, remember?'

'Would you?' He caught her arms, his eyes searching hers as if he hardly dared to believe her commitment. 'Jodie... We could set this up. You could meet the bishop, make contact with the Chamber of Commerce—'

'I'd love to!' she said, dizzy with happiness.

'Jodie.' He kissed her hard. Then drew back. 'Sorry! But...I'm pleased,' he said more soberly.

She forced herself to calm down too. Lifting an eyebrow, she said, 'I hadn't noticed.'

And, nonchalant to a fault, she sauntered over to the tea tray and cut herself a slice of cake. But inside she was fizzing with delight. They were becoming closer than she'd dared to hope. And now she would be working on something that enthused them both.

Later that day they had their usual walk. She skipped along beside him, chattering away, holding his hand and loving its warm, dry enclosure. And a while after he even allowed her to help bath Jack, an honour she valued more than anything.

Under Morgan's guidance she undressed the baby and learnt how to hold him safely, her happiness almost complete.

'It's been a lovely day,' she said softly, when they both tiptoed out of the nursery. 'I've enjoyed every single moment.'

'Coffee?'

She should refuse. Offer a friendly smile and take the newspaper to bed. But she wanted him desperately and the flesh was weak.

'OK,' she said recklessly, hoping her croak sounded vaguely casual.

In the drawing room, softly lit by candles, he poured the coffee and she felt her hunger rising. Her fingers itched to trace his smooth jaw; her mouth quivered in expectation of exploring the golden skin between collar and hairline. And that tempting dark taper of hair in front of his ear...

He stood in front of her, gazing down. The liquid was slopping in the cups he held.

'It's not going to work,' he said thickly, his eyes burning through her fevered body.

'What?' she pretended, her voice hardly hers.

'If you want us to be friends and nothing else then you must go to bed now,' he warned, his deep voice soft as a whisper, flowing over her like liquid velvet.

She couldn't move. Didn't want to. She knew full well what he meant—and what would happen if she remained.

'Trouble is, I'm not sleepy,' she breathed.

He grunted. 'I keep thinking of you and bed—and sleep doesn't figure in the equation at all,' he said huskily.

'We can't fight the inevitable, Morgan,' she murmured.

'I feel I should try.'

'Not on my account.'

He drew in a sharp breath. 'Jodie! This is beyond me! I can't think, can't behave normally when you're around. You're in my head and in my body and I think I'll go mad if I can't touch you!'

In answer, she lifted her face, her lips parted avidly for his kiss. The pain of her passion etched itself in her eyes and through her entire body as she waited for the inevitable

Slowly, without taking his eyes off her, he put down the two cups and knelt in front of her. His fingers lightly smoothed over her hands where they lay on her knees. And then he was pressing his mouth to each palm, first one and then the other, his bone structure infinitely beautiful in the flickering firelight.

Adoring him, she surrendered everything—caution, sense, security, restraint. 'Morgan,' she purred, and slid to the floor, her skirts pooling around her.

'I can't believe I'm doing this!' he said, looking dazed.

'We tried. We did our best to talk ourselves out of it. Who can stop the urging of fate?'

'I don't want you to think that I—'

She stopped him, her finger on his protesting lips. 'No thinking.'

He kissed her fingertip, his eyes burning. 'Hear me out. It's not just sex. Not just comfort.'

Love flowed through her, melting her very bones. 'I know,' she whispered. 'Or I wouldn't be here.'

'No going back this time.'

'No...'

His hand brushed back her hair. His lips touched her forehead, her temple, and the pulse in front of her ear. And she sat there shuddering as if he had spent an hour arousing her instead of a second or two, every part of her alive and humming with electricity, her heart throbbing with happiness.

A finger caressed her mouth. With a groan she took the finger between her teeth and nibbled gently, moaning as her need filled every cell of her body. His mouth came down hard on hers, pushing her back till she lay on the floor, moving like a temptress.

'I want you...' he growled.

She jerked with longing. 'Yes.'

'I shouldn't—'

Impatiently she pushed him away and slid back, a feeling of intense satisfaction rippling through her when he stared at her, appalled, his chest heaving hard.

Lowering her head and flirting with him from beneath her brows, she shimmied out of her dress, exulting in Morgan's inhalation of breath when he realised what she was doing.

'No,' she agreed provocatively. 'You shouldn't. I shouldn't.' She moistened her lips and unhooked her bra. 'Stay!' she ordered when he made an involuntary movement towards her. She smoothed her hands over her breasts, watching his tortured face. He'd never forget her, she thought exultantly, reaching for his hands. 'Touch,' she whispered.

Instead, his tongue slipped wickedly around one turgid nipple, making her buck as the needle spasms flicked like lightning through her body. Her eyes closed as tiny thrills built upon one another, driving her crazy with impatience.

His actions told her that he felt the same. Roughly he stripped off his clothes and slid away her briefs. He was beautiful. His sheer masculinity took her breath away. He wanted her.

Hot-eyed and intent, he let his hands move over her shivering skin—curving around her breasts, enjoying their firmness, finger and thumb tantalising the hot, dark centres.

Her back arched, demanding in the only way she knew how that he satisfied the desperate emptiness within her. She couldn't speak, could barely move her leaden limbs, all her mind obliterated by everything but that one fierce need.

Obeying some deep and primal message, she bent her head and tasted him…heat, silk and throbbing muscle slithering in her warm, moist mouth in a heady combination.

Morgan groaned, close to losing control. He muttered something to her, gently but firmly lifting her away. He wanted this to be for her. To give her something he'd never shared before. His whole self.

'Jodie!' he husked, his eyes brilliantly intense. 'Come here!'

His mouth devoured hers. She felt soft and giving beneath him and he ground his body against hers, letting himself slide against the warm, welcoming tremble of her pelvis.

Their tongues meshed, mimicking what they both desired. A rhythm beat in his pulses, his heart, the movement of their tongues, their hips. He rolled away slightly to allow his hand to explore, hushing her when she jerked and cried out, whimpering and panting as he relentlessly moved a delicate finger across the wet, firm nub between her legs.

Jodie thrashed around, her hair skimming out like burnished gold, her face more beautiful than he could believe possible. He covered it with kisses, suckled her breasts with a tender ferocity, his hands, arms, legs trapping her, forcing her to accept his caresses as the velvet of her skin and the receptive moistness of her body under his fingers built up a friction and a promise that he could no longer refuse.

She seemed possessed. Beneath him her body writhed and lured, the flick of her nipples across his chest infinitely pleasurable. Without inhibition she had parted her legs for him and was intent on slipping her hand to his waiting shaft.

But he stopped her, knowing he couldn't hold back if she did.

'Wait,' he muttered.

'Won't!' she scowled.

'You'll like it better if you do,' he murmured shakily.

Angrily she lurched against his fingers, her eyes dark

with frustration. Her sleek hair whispered over his breast-bone as she leaned forwards and nibbled ruthlessly at his nipple.

She wouldn't wait much longer. Nor could he. Her hands were raking across his back and there was a desperate fury in the sinuous demands of her body. Briefly he reached out, searching for what he needed. Now he was safe—and she too.

'I'm ready for you. Is this what you want?' he whispered.

He allowed himself just to touch the entrance to her body, his hands holding her back. But she flashed him one siren look and jerked her hips in a swift movement, her silky heat enclosing him with a suddenness that left him gasping.

And she groaned with him, a long, urgent release of long-held passion. His bones seemed to melt. Something painful jerked in his heart and he found himself totally unaware of where he was; he felt as if he was floating, slipping slowly and inexorably into paradise.

'Watch me,' she moaned.

He realised his eyes had closed. With difficulty he opened them and saw her fevered face, her gaze intent on the intermingling dark and chestnut coils of hair where their bodies met.

Amazed at what that sight did to him, he found himself thrusting, incapable of restraining himself any longer. And she looked, crying, moaning like him, fiercely intensifying each stroke with the supple thrusts of her own impassioned body.

For a moment he stopped, knowing that the pause would heighten her orgasm. She glared, grabbed his head and kissed him till he felt the pressure of exquisite torture exploding within him.

'Don't stop!' she ordered, her thready voice trembling.

He wanted to make this last. To imprint this moment on her. Hot and hungry, he stemmed his own need and concentrated on kissing her while she did everything she could to entice him onwards.

Sweat slicked on their bodies and she licked at him with her cat-like tongue, causing his skin to shiver and tremble as every nerve responded. He felt the edge of her teeth as frustration drove her to more desperate measures and so he moved again, with the utmost leisure, each gliding movement making him hotter, more swollen, more violently sensitive to her sweetness.

In the back of his dazed mind he was afraid that he would hurt her, but she surged against him and clung with such greed that he banished that fear from his mind, and in a moment of extreme emotion he kissed her tenderly, then increased the tempo of his body.

Jodie whispered with delight, her eyes sparkling as she gazed at him as if... He faltered, then, urged by her frantic writhing, drove firmly into her... As if...she loved him, he thought.

Morgan cried out loud, their rhythm hot and fast, bodies as one, hearts, minds, emotions...who knew? He couldn't think, only his senses were operating, and most of those were focused on the slippery heat in the core of her body.

'Morgan!' she gasped, gripping his shoulders. Her head rolled back, her throat creamy and smooth.

He kissed the pulse there, murmured words...silly words, telling her she was wonderful, beautiful, wicked, luscious...

And then they both shouted, clinging to one another as the violence of their orgasms crashed through them. For the first time he felt the incredible force of her contractions as they squeezed and released the intensely sensitive shaft deep within her. It was a moment of astounding pleasure that almost drove him into orbit as each wave rolled through and around him, the whole of his body seemingly one giant organ of gratification.

It lasted for ever. Hours. Almost as soon as she subsided, with little sighs of deep satisfaction, he was aroused again. Her eyes opened wide in amazement as he began to move. A smile curved her sensual mouth and he smiled back, his eyes glittering with excitement.

This was something else. Something special. He felt like a god. Invincible, all-powerful, able to pleasure his woman. He could no more stop himself from giving himself what he wanted than he could stop breathing.

Gently he hauled her onto his lap. The firm peaks of her breasts swung to him in supplication and he took each in his mouth in turn, savouring the sweetness of them and revelling in what it did to her.

'Ride me,' he muttered.

She stretched her lovely body, and in that moment when she looked at him, her eyes soft and adoring, he felt a crushing sensation in his heart.

'Jodie.' His ragged attempt to articulate his volcanic emotions failed as she slid onto him, her mouth insistent on his.

She swayed, twisting so erotically that he couldn't think at all. There was only the proud carriage of her ribcage, the hollow beneath and the tiny waist, the shine of sweat on her honey skin and the unbelievable fire burning in his loins.

Through half-closed eyes he watched her come, thrilled at her abandon and the wantonness of her frenzied hands as they clutched at his hard, tight buttocks and forced him deeper into her. He slid with agonising exhilaration into that darkness again, where the pleasure was in his head and in his manhood for one magnificent explosion, before rocketing fiercely into every vein and nerve he possessed.

His arms enfolded her lovingly. He held her close to him, her face nuzzled in his neck and his in hers. Inhaling her. His lips pressed to her salty skin, feeling the heat, the satiny fire that quivered and leapt across her entire body as aftershocks trembled through them both.

'Jodie.'

She stirred, but otherwise remained limp in his arms. 'Mmm.'

''Swonderful.' He was slurred. His mouth didn't match up with his brain.

'Mmm.'

Her arms tightened around his neck. Conscious that she might soon be cold, when their heated bodies cooled down, he slid her into his arms and staggered for a moment, then found his balance and strength.

He looked down at her blissful face and knew he was smiling idiotically. 'Bed.'

'Mmm.'

Trustingly she snuggled against his naked chest. He felt like a king. Carrying his precious burden, he made it up the stairs and to his room, his heart thudding so loudly that it alarmed him.

'Shower,' she mumbled.

His loins stirred. 'Shower,' he agreed hoarsely.

He set her on her feet and closed the cabinet door. His shower was vast, the showerhead enormous. Lovingly he supported her wilting body, seeing that she was barely aware of what was happening. She seemed to be where he was—on Cloud Nine, he thought with a smile.

The water cascaded over them and he gently smoothed his gel-soaked palms over her glorious dips and curves. She raised her arms in the air in a sensual stretch and took the gel from the rack. He closed his eyes.

The feel of her fingers exploring each muscle of his shoulders was tantalising in the extreme. Her wet thumb dipped into the hollow of his collarbone. Anticipation set him on fire.

'Oh, Morgan! You're just greedy!' she breathed.

'I can't help it,' he said jerkily. 'I only have to look at you to want you! And this…is more than I can bear!'

Her hands massaged his spine and splayed out to his hips, and he was acutely aware of where he wanted her to touch next. Hungry, he reached out to touch her, but she slapped him down.

'My turn,' she murmured.

And then he rocked on his feet as she knelt, the wet pelt of her hair against his pelvis as she took him in her mouth again, and he felt the pressure increase as her lips slid up and down with a sure skill and sensitivity which came close to driving him insane with ecstasy.

But as she suckled he found it wasn't enough. He wanted to be with her. In her. His hand snapped off the shower. He ignored her protests, wrapped her in an enormous warm bath towel and gently, sensually dried her. Paying close and extended attention to her most erotic areas.

'Bed,' he purred when they were both dry and she was trembling with need.

'Mmm!' she squeaked.

They lay together, looking at one another for a long time. Jodie felt as if her heart had stopped. She loved him. Really loved him.

Gently they explored, learning one another. She felt a great happiness steal over her. Euphoria alternated with elation and then settled on her in a deep serenity. He was smiling, his whole face alight with joy.

She had done it, she thought, hardly daring to believe it. Morgan had come out of mourning. He'd found someone of flesh and bone and their coming together had been little short of miraculous.

Everything between them had resonated with deeper vibrations. This hadn't been pure sex. It had been a celebration of two people passionately involved in one another, two hearts beating as one.

She knew that from the way he looked at her now, in a bemused, dazzled, wonderfully amazed delight.

Their lovemaking was gentle and slow this time. Each movement Morgan made was considered and yet deliciously tentative. They knew one another. Her fingers unerringly descended on a muscle here, a pulse there. His head swooped directly to her breast…to the tiny wet bud between her legs.

Luxuriantly she relaxed every muscle, while the heat of his mouth prepared her. And then with one accord they moved to one another, her heart soaring as he took her beyond any place she'd ever visited, far away to where her love could expand and fill her body and every movement of her hands, every breath she took and every sigh that escaped her bruised mouth.

After, they clung to one another, as if fearful that it had all been a dream. And slowly it became just that: their muscles easing, their heartbeats slowing from their hectic rhythms, their expressions serene and peaceful.

CHAPTER NINE

SHE woke in the night, her hand sleepily reaching out for him. It encountered just the rumpled sheet.

'Morgan?' she mumbled, disorientated.

A kiss brushed her cheek and she saw his dim figure looming over her.

'Baby's awake. Back later.'

'Whosstime?' she mumbled drowsily.

'Three a.m. Go to sleep, sweetheart,' he whispered.

Sweetheart. She sighed with satisfaction and must have dozed, because when she stirred again the room was lighter. Rolling over, she saw Morgan lying beside her, his eyes liquid ink. She smiled and snuggled up.

'Ohh! You're as cold as ice!' she gasped.

'Took a long time to bring up Jack's wind. Another five minutes and he'll be ready for his next feed again!'

Jodie craned her neck. It was five-twenty. 'You must be exhausted,' she sympathised. 'You do need a nanny—'

'No! I look after Jack!' he said forcibly. 'No one else!'

'Then let me warm you. And for heaven's sake, get some sleep now,' she replied, touched by his devotion.

It was wonderful watching him relax in her arms. Slowly the dark lashes fluttered down and his features softened. Her heart turned over when she contemplated the soft arch of his sensual mouth and she couldn't resist touching it with a delicate forefinger.

He murmured in his sleep and nuzzled his face in her neck. She stroked his hair and wondered about the future. Lying there, she pictured herself with Morgan and Jack watching the baby grow into a toddler, a schoolchild, a young adult. Her head swam with the heady delight of being part of a loving family.

Her father would be thrilled, she thought. He patently adored Morgan and nothing would give him greater pleasure than to know that she and Morgan had found happiness together.

She stroked Morgan's hair, imprinting every line, every angle of his face on her memory.

'I love you,' she whispered, kissing his forehead softly.

His eyes snapped open and she jerked back in confusion. Beneath her hand, his shoulder muscles had tensed into a hard knot.

'What was that?' he asked in a low rumble.

She pressed her treacherous lips together, her eyes startled and anxious. Morgan fixed her with his penetrating gaze and heaved himself up on one elbow.

'Cat got your tongue?' he murmured.

She put it out. 'You were supposed to be asleep,' she accused.

'I was.' His eyes twinkled. 'Something filtered through to my subconscious. Something I've been wanting to hear.'

She sat bolt upright. 'What?'

A dazzling smile. A laugh of triumph. An amused shake of his head. 'Oh, Jodie!' he said fondly. 'You don't know how I feel at this moment!' Laughingly he pinned her back on the pillows, kissing her till she could hardly breathe. 'Tell me what you said,' he demanded. And when she remained mute he kissed her again, harder, demanding to know again and again till she surrendered.

'OK, OK!' she complained. 'You're giving me stubble burn!'

Her hand caressed the side of his face, scratching at the bristles. He looked like a sexy gypsy, wild and rough and dangerous—even if she knew he was kind and gentle and thoughtful. Though, she mused, a spark of desire fizzling through her, he could be sexy and wild...

'You're stalling,' he warned, with a ferociously theatrical scowl.

Jodie giggled. 'Just diverted by something.'

'Get back on track,' he growled, pretending to be angry.

'I said,' she breathed, kissing his grumpy mouth till it curved up into a smile again, 'that I love you.'

His eyes closed. He remained as if frozen. She waited, tension stringing out her nerves, robbing her heart of its normal beat. Afraid, she swallowed. Had she spoken too soon?

'Are you sure?' he asked eventually, his voice shaking with emotion.

'I fell in love with you almost at once,' she said simply. 'I didn't believe that could happen, but it did. And, yes, now I'm sure.'

His mouth touched hers tentatively in a delicate kiss. Then his lips brushed her brow. 'Jodie,' he said, very serious, 'I could be rushing you...but I am compelled to speak my feelings—'

'Yes?' She held her breath, waiting for him to declare his love too. She was so certain of it.

'It's only been a short time that we've known one another,' he said huskily. 'But we seem to be in total harmony. I am...so happy when you're around. I can't imagine what it would be like to live apart from you. I want you to be my wife. Marry me, Jodie. Make it soon. Let's be together for the rest of our lives.'

She gave a sob and reached up her arms to him. 'Yes!' she cried, her eyes awash with tears. 'Yes, Morgan!'

His kisses deepened. She felt the tip of his tongue tasting her tears, the warmth of his mouth moving over her face.

Flames leapt through her and she groaned, sliding her body against his for the union which would seal their pact.

And then he was moving away.

'What…? Why…?' she moaned.

'Jack,' he rasped.

'I don't hear him!' she pouted.

'You're not tuned to him,' he replied, dropping a hasty kiss on her nose and flicking off the baby alarm.

Denied and empty, she lay crossly in bed, and then felt selfish and mean for resenting a needy baby even for a few seconds. She leapt up, slipping on her thin cotton robe, and hurried to the nursery, intending to see if she could help in any way.

'Oh, God!' she heard him mutter.

She paused just outside the door, surprised by Morgan's impassioned growl. Her senses might not be tuned to the baby, but they were acute where Morgan was concerned. And he seemed to be in a highly emotional state.

'You're safe!' she heard him say jerkily. 'You're mine!' He let out a loud and protracted sigh, as if every part of his body had been under tension for a long, long time. 'Hold on, sweetpea,' he husked, when Jack whimpered. 'It's coming.' Jodie heard Morgan's bare feet striding hard and fast up and down the room. 'We'll be together. No one will take you from me. Never, never, never!'

Jodie clung to the doorjamb, stunned by what she'd heard. He was talking to Jack now, promising him a rosy future, walks in the snow, swimming lessons, riotous birthday parties…

She gulped. None of these seemed to include her. Confused and muddled, she quietly returned to the bedroom. Six-thirty. Suddenly cold, she showered and scrambled into a pair of yellow jeans and a warm orange jumper.

Her confidence had vanished. She didn't feel so sure of

Morgan. Why had he been so relieved after she'd agreed to marry him? His reaction had been more than male pride, or relief that he hadn't been rejected.

And where did Jack come into this? It didn't make sense that Morgan felt his son was safe now. Who would have taken his baby away from him?

Questions filled her head, making it ache. She went down to the kitchen and made some lemon tea, then put it down, too sick to her stomach to take even that. So she found a pill in the first aid box and took it for her headache.

Fear had suddenly entered her life, spoiling her brief moment of pure joy. There was something dark and threatening lurking in the background, waiting to snatch happiness from her grasp.

And she couldn't, wouldn't interrogate Morgan, for fear that she would arouse a sleeping tiger.

All that day she remained curled up on the sofa with a blinding headache, tended by a concerned and sympathetic Morgan. He was so thoughtful and loving that she could almost believe she must have imagined what she'd heard.

He'd always been over-protective towards Jack. Although she adored him, and dearly wanted to take a larger part in Jack's care, she'd never been allowed to feed him, nor had Morgan ever left her in sole charge of the baby. Perhaps that was just a natural parenting instinct.

She perked up. Perhaps Morgan just felt more secure with the prospect of having a wife. Despite political correctness, it was still unusual for a father to bring up a child alone—especially a tiny baby. Maybe Social Services had expressed doubts as to his ability and he'd felt threatened.

'I'm glad to see you smiling again.' He stood in the doorway, a warm smile lighting his face. And she was sure there was love in his eyes.

'I love you,' she said fervently, ashamed that she'd doubted him for one moment.

'Oh, Jodie!' He came to her, knelt and held her tightly. She could feel him trembling and she hugged him hard. 'We must celebrate our engagement,' he murmured in her ear.

'I could cook!' she suggested, teasing.

'Thanks. I don't want to die yet,' he said drily. 'We should go out. Somewhere special.' He frowned. 'But somewhere we can take Jack—'

'The pub's fine by me,' she said quickly. 'I don't need champagne and waiters with French accents, or designer food sitting on raspberry coulis. All I need is you, Morgan. And Jack too, of course.' She pulled back a little, anxious to reassure him. 'He'll be family, after all.'

His smile touched her heart with its brilliance. 'Yes,' he said throatily. 'He will.' And he enfolded her in his arms again, crushing her to him with such intense passion that she could barely breathe for delight.

Their lovemaking had never been so tender, so sweetly wrung with tremulous emotion. Jodie felt drugged by her feelings, washed by a tide of blissful sensations which made her limbs liquid, her brain dizzy with the intoxication of the deepest love.

She watched him feeding and changing Jack, drowsily amazed at his stamina and energy. No matter how tired he was, how hard a day he'd had—or night—he stayed calm and gentle with his beloved son, and never once did he show impatience or resentment when Jack made his needs known.

Not that the baby cried much. Morgan was always there, interpreting Jack's needs, firmly and competently coping with his son. And she adored Morgan all the more for that, thinking ahead to the time when they would have babies of their own.

Later, when they were settled in their favourite corner of the pub by the fire, Morgan took her hand in his and said gently, 'To us. To our marriage.' He lowered his lashes and said, almost under his breath, 'To the woman I adore best in the world.'

Her heart turned over. 'Oh, Morgan!' she mumbled, tears of happiness shining in her eyes. 'To us,' she responded. 'The man I adore and will love always.'

'We'll go out tomorrow and choose a ring. Name the day. Make arrangements.'

She smiled shyly. 'I'd love that.'

'And there's something else. I kept a piece of news back for you. Sam's going to the nursing home tomorrow. I think perhaps next week—when he's settled in—would be a good time to talk to him about you. I'm sure he'll be eager to meet you when I've told him the kind of person you are.'

'Heavens! Don't do that—he'll run a mile!' she said with a laugh.

'I could make it up,' he offered, his eyes twinkling. 'Tell him you're a slick city girl with a computer for a brain—'

'But kind to ferrets and gerbils—'

'Sure.' He grinned, pretending to shade his eyes when he looked at her. 'And who dresses…' he did a mock wince '…soberly—'

'And who's always calm and collected!' Jodie beamed. She enjoyed his teasing. Chas had teased. But it had been cruel and goading. Morgan did it in a loving way. She gave a contented sigh. 'You've made my day complete,' she said. 'I can't wait to see my father—'

'Jodie…' He hesitated. 'I have something rather difficult to say. It's about Jack.'

She froze. Suddenly Morgan seemed distant and withdrawn, his body language speaking volumes. 'Are you in danger of losing him?' she asked, voicing his fears.

His head jerked up. 'What the hell do you mean?' he demanded roughly.

'I—I don't know, it's just that I wondered...you seemed worried... Jack's so important to you...' Her voice faded under his savage frown. Her hand felt limp and shaky and she put her glass of Château Lafite down hurriedly. Morgan was on the defensive. She'd made a mistake. 'Forget it. A stab in the dark. Silly—'

'OK.' He waved an impatient hand at her incoherent gabble and she subsided, hurt and on edge. She waited while he sat there, chewing over the words he intended to say, alarmed by his tense expression. 'You know I've...looked after Jack ever since he was born.'

She waited again. He seemed stuck, so she decided to encourage him. 'I admire you for that commitment. And you've become welded to him because his mother left—'

'She didn't leave.' His eyes met hers, hard, unfathomable. 'She died.' And before she could express sympathy he went on, his voice rough and grating. 'Jack is Teresa's child.'

'*Teresa's?*' Jodie sat rooted to her chair in shock. 'I thought...' Her brow furrowed deeply as she tried to make sense of what he was saying. 'But...Teresa was my *father's* lover.'

'Yes.' Morgan licked his lips, picked up his wine and put it down again. 'Of course when Sam was taken ill he couldn't take over his role as...' Morgan lifted his glass again and took a long gulp of claret. 'As Jack's father,' he said, oddly hoarse. 'So I took over.'

'Jack...is Sam and Teresa's baby?' she said stupidly.

'He was thrilled to know she was pregnant,' he said, pursuing his own train of thought. But the smile he flashed at her wasn't quite right and there was an odd sharpness to his cheekbones, which were standing high in his strained face. 'I think if it hadn't been for Jack your father might have given up the fight to live long ago,' he finished stiffly.

Her brain didn't seem to be functioning. Why all this should chill her to the bone she didn't know, but she felt shivers running up and down her spine. She stretched out her hands to the fire, glad to be avoiding Morgan's hunted eyes.

What was the matter? Why was he walking on pins? Injecting as much normality into her tone as she could, she said, 'It's a bit of a shock to learn this, Morgan. Why didn't you tell me earlier?'

'Because you might not have stayed. Until I was certain that you would—and that you were committed to Sam—I didn't want your decision to be swayed by an appealing little baby half-brother.'

She turned and fixed him with a worried stare. 'Any more surprises?' she asked shakily, wondering why she didn't entirely accept this reason.

'Teresa is Jack's mother. I swear that is the truth, on Jack's head.'

Again he hadn't answered her question directly. Her heart sank. Was that why Morgan loved the baby so? Did Jack look like Teresa? Was Morgan hoping—longing, maybe—for Jack to grow up reminding him of the woman he'd loved with such an extraordinary passion?

Her breath hissed in. 'Excuse me,' she said. 'Need the Ladies'.'

He caught her hand as she made to leave. 'I want you to know that I did what was best,' he said quietly.

He was a good man. She smiled because she loved him, but she was hurting inside. 'You're taking care of a motherless baby whose father is seriously ill. Anyone would admire you for that,' she told him in a low tone. 'Must dash!'

Her grin faded once she'd reached the safety of the cloakroom. She patted her hot, flushed face with cold water and held her wrists under the tap. In the mirror she saw a woman who'd fallen in love with a man who was still tied to someone else. Tied, too, to that woman's baby.

Of course he loved Jack. Anybody would. She herself adored him, loved his little fingers—builder's hands, Morgan had said outrageously—and his sweetly peaceful face when he slept, the dark mat of hair and his warm, baby smell. And Morgan was a decent, wonderful man to devote himself to the baby.

This was her half-brother. Her hands stilled as a bond sprang up which had not been there before. Awed, she realised that she now had responsibilities, duties towards Jack.

But... Teresa's child!

Jodie groaned and swayed, nausea hitting the pit of her stomach. Her mind whirled, trying to make sense of the new situation.

There was no blood link between Jack and Morgan—only a deep and unbreakable love. Her father was Jack's next of kin.

Numbly she stared at herself in the mirror, her eyes widening as her mind raced on, setting things in place.

Morgan knew that her father only had a short time to live. And he was obviously aware that she would soon be Jack's next of kin. In law, she would be responsible for Jack.

Her hands shook. Morgan had become firmly attached to Jack—almost over-possessive. Was this, perhaps, why Morgan had been so hostile? Why he'd tried to send her away? And why he'd kept Jack's parentage a secret from her until now?

Something else occurred to her. A thought so unspeakable that she pushed it back in horror. 'Please, no!' she whispered, aghast. 'He loves me! He really loves me!'

She would *not* believe that she could be so wrong about someone. Morgan wouldn't have proposed to her just to secure his link with Jack!

'No!' she said fiercely to the doubting woman in the mirror. 'He's kind and he's loving and every part of me knows that!'

Be careful, the eyes of the woman said. Be cautious.

With a wounded cry, Jodie fled, desperately banishing her doubts. Morgan loved her. She would make sure of that.

And later that night she wove a spell over him, teasing, tantalising, luring him with her mind and body and soul, all her intense passions and fears focused on arousing his love.

Once or twice, in the back of her mind, she wondered if he was thinking of Teresa during their most intimate moments. And in those brief seconds she felt her heart would crack in two.

'Love me,' she murmured passionately.

His eyes closed in bliss, Morgan took her lower lip in his mouth, tasting its swollen softness. Jodie's passion more than matched his own, flinging him into the deepest pool of ecstasy he could ever have imagined.

He slid his tongue to her teeth and she immediately allowed him entrance into the dark, warm moistness. Their tongues meshed and fierce stabs of need scythed through his loins.

She felt soft and pliable, her lissom body moving with agonising seductiveness against his, her eyes knowing and excitingly wicked.

He nuzzled her throat and the slender collarbone while

his knee parted her legs and his hands enjoyed the firm lushness of her high, rounded breasts.

He groaned and, dipping his head, he greedily lapped at each thrusting nipple, loving the smell of her, the warmth of her satin skin against his face, the sensual feel of the hard, engorged peak in his mouth as it jerked in response to his impassioned suckling.

'What are you thinking?' she asked in a shaky little voice.

For a moment he couldn't get his head around that. 'Of you!' he croaked.

She seemed to shudder throughout the length of her body and he looked up at her in surprise. Huge tears were seeping from her tightly shut eyes.

'Jodie!' He was holding her, cradling her head against his chest, then kissing and licking away the tears. 'What is it?' he murmured gently.

The enormous liquid green eyes opened. Wet lashes fluttered. 'I'm afraid!' she sobbed.

He drew her close again, stroking her hair. 'Because you think we might not last?' There was the briefest of nods, teardrops wetting his torso. Morgan pushed her back, slid off the bed and came back with a handkerchief. 'Blow,' he instructed. 'Now,' he said when she seemed calmer, 'look at me.' He gazed into those vulnerable eyes and felt his heart cramp. 'For me, marriage is forever. Infidelity is all about opportunity and an attitude of mind. I am a loyal person, Jodie. When I love, I love. I have no intention of ever being anything but devoted to you. If there ever are any hitches in the future then we will work them out, because we are determined that our marriage will last. Trust me. We must not ever separate. Do you believe me when I say that?'

She nodded, though her eyes still looked tragic. 'Yes, I

do. You won't want us to part,' she repeated like an obedient child.

'Come close—'

'No...I feel a bit sick and heady again,' she said in a forlorn tone. 'I'll just curl up and sleep it off.'

'Of course. Anything I can get you?' he asked in concern.

'No,' she mumbled. 'Let me sleep.'

She seemed fine the next day, though more subdued than usual, and she didn't want to put off their trip to London to choose a ring.

Morgan insisted on taking her to an exclusive restaurant for lunch as a treat—an old haunt of his—so that she could wave her left hand about a lot. It was good to hear her laughter when he said this, and he was glad she'd recovered.

Sitting in the restaurant's lounge afterwards feeding Jack, he leant back in the comfortable chair and watched her talking to the waiter who'd brought their coffee. He noticed that she looked the young man in the eye instead of treating him like an object and addressing his stomach. He liked that.

'You're staring,' she said in amusement.

'No. Just blinded by you,' he murmured.

'Oh! Blinded?' She looked pleased.

He decided to tease her. 'Mmm. That flashy egg on the third finger of your left hand is like a car's headlamps on full beam—'

'How dare you?' She made a face and waggled her hand in front of his nose. 'It's not an egg. It's a whacking great diamond and I adore it, so you'd better get used to me flashing it about.'

'Vulgar,' he pretended. Jack burped and refused the rest

of his bottle. 'Right,' Morgan said. 'I'd better find the Mother and Baby room.'

'It's in the Ladies' cloakroom!' she said with a giggle.

He grunted. 'Equality! Where is it when you need it? I can't go into that gold-tapped flouncy-frilled boudoir!'

'How do you know what it's like?' she asked, grinning at the accuracy of his description. 'Anyway, let me change him. I do know how. He's not going to be scarred for life by my ministrations.'

'No. All right.' He watched her slip the baby bag over her shoulder and then carefully take Jack in her arms. 'Don't forget the wipes. And the cream's—'

'In the front pocket; I know. Honestly, Morgan, I can manage! Inspect everything when I come back and give me marks out of ten! And you can get him regressed by a hypnotist when he's twenty-four, and check that the experience wasn't too traumatic!'

He laughed sheepishly. 'Sorry. Cluck, cluck. Mother hen. Go and do your worst, woman!'

Laughing happily, she made her way to the powder room and the baby-changing area in an inner room beyond. It was empty when she began to lay out the little changing mat, but then she heard the click of high heels as a group of women entered the outer room, and after a while the sounds of handbags being emptied and lipstick applied as they chatted.

Absorbed with Jack, securely on the padded table, she didn't pay much attention to the drawling, languid voice which was holding forth. Until she heard Morgan's name.

'…simply amazed to see him, darling!'

'Not really… Damn!' swore a woman with a screeching voice. 'I've forgotten my mascara. Lend me yours, sweetie… No, he often came here with Teresa. It was his favourite dive when he worked in London.'

'Looking gorgeous as ever, isn't he?' This woman was purring.

'Hunky, darling. And a trillion times better than when we last clapped eyes on him. God!' cried the screecher. 'Was he grieving or what? I thought he'd keel over when they lowered poor T into the ground. I was ready to give mouth to mouth. Never got the chance.' The woman tittered.

Jodie felt paralysed. Her hands stilled as the others acknowledged Morgan's despair. She knew she ought to go out, but Jack wasn't finished, and...and she couldn't face them—or Morgan. He'd brought Teresa here! Angrily she glared at her shaking hands. And her eyes fixated on her engagement ring, the reason for their celebration lunch. Why choose this restaurant of all places? she thought miserably.

'What about his current popsie?' asked the languid one.

'Not his type,' replied the screecher loudly. 'He's always gone for blondes. He'll never get over T. He probably needed his bed warmed. Sexy devil! T said his stamina was phenomenal.'

Jodie bit back a cry. Her fingers fumbled with the nappy. Morgan had slept with Teresa! Or not slept, she amended bitterly. And she hastened with her task, intending to stalk out and shock them all.

'Maybe he needs someone to keep house. He can't go on looking after someone else's baby forever, can he?' simpered the purrer.

Jodie snapped the poppers of Jack's vest. Nearly done, she thought frantically...

'Don't be daft, duckie.' Screecher was in full squawk again. 'Remember I had a nice little gossip with T's daily when T was living with Sam Frazer. The daily found T and

Morgan half naked in his bathroom. That's why she was sacked.'

No. No! Jodie's heart bumped painfully. Almost blinded by angry tears, she was finding it almost impossible to do up the small buttons on the little jacket.

'So it's Morgan's kid!' gasped the drawler.

'God, you're quick, Annabel!' retorted the screecher, as Jodie froze, quite incapable of any action whatsoever. She blocked her ears, but the speaker had a loud and raucous voice and it would have carried across a parade ground. 'What do *you* think? A sick, ageing guy or a virile, healthy one? You know T adored Morgan. She wanted it all, didn't she? Money, and a rich lover who was eternally bound to her because she'd produced his son.'

'She got what she wanted,' sighed the more gentle purrer.

'Huh!' barked the screecher. 'Much good it did her!'

A baby wipe dropped from Jodie's fingers. The women's voices faded into the background as the blood rushed to her head and roared loudly in her ears.

She felt so sick she could hardly stand upright. She pressed her hands to her stomach, willing the nausea to vanish. Wave upon wave of it lurched upwards through her body and only her fierce will kept it back.

Teresa's seductive face and body lurched into her mind. No man could have resisted Teresa's advances, least of all one who loved her. Jodie dragged a whisper of air into her choking lungs. Morgan had slept with Teresa. The woman he'd loved. Perhaps still loved.

Jodie remembered his toast on the day he proposed. *To the woman I adore best in the world.* He could have been raising his glass to Teresa.

She tried to search her memory for a time when Morgan had said 'I love you, Jodie'. And failed.

She'd been used. Again. For sex, comfort, and to ensure that Jack was forever his. Jack, beloved, deeply adored Jack, the result of a passionate affair with her father's fiancée.

Suddenly she needed to see Morgan's face, as if she might find some hint of the truth written there. Her hand flattened on the wall, steadying herself, as she finished dressing Jack and packing the baby bag.

Her eyes were pale with anguish but she applied a slick of lipstick, pinched her cheeks and straightened her hunched, miserable body before walking into the outer room.

Conversation stopped. In the deafening silence, Jodie checked her lipstick unnecessarily and flicked back her hair. She saw that her eyes looked like two glowing dark coals in her pale face.

Unable to speak, she looked at the three women with a bright, mocking smile on her lips and felt she'd won a small victory when they hastily glanced away. With the utmost dignity she swept out of the powder room and into the warmth of the crowded restaurant.

Not able to meet Morgan's eyes yet, she gently placed Jack in his arms.

'All in one piece,' she trilled, though she'd been shattered into fragments.

Morgan laughed, pretending to check. Jack cooed and gurgled and gave a gummy grin which made Jodie's heart somersault. No one could doubt that he loved the baby with all his heart.

Because Jack was his. Because Jack was Teresa's.

She shook uncontrollably, and masked this by fussing with the cushions of her chair then vigorously stirring the coffee he'd begun to pour out when he'd seen her walking towards him.

He smiled his heart-destroying smile, and even in the depths of her anger and misery she felt the terrible lurch of her idiotically romantic heart.

'You deserve a prize,' he murmured lazily.

What? she thought furiously. A medal for stupidity? She stared at the dish of bon-bons blankly, marshalling all her self-control.

'I certainly do,' she muttered, taking four, and ate them quickly to conceal her splintered emotions.

They tasted of cotton wool in her dry, parched mouth. Horror sucked at her heart and lungs, accelerating her pulses and robbing her of breath. Oh, dear God, she couldn't bear this!

'I thought we'd go shopping,' Morgan said. 'Buy up Bond Street.'

There was a jagged rip inside her now. She'd felt so close to him. Had trusted and admired him. But to cover up his own guilt he was fooling them all. These people, herself, *and her father*! So much for Morgan's supposed loyalty. How could he live with himself, knowing what he did?

She surveyed him from beneath her brows. 'I hope you mean that,' she said with a calmness that amazed her. 'Because I'm in a spending mood.'

You swine! she thought. Rat! Worm! Cheat, liar... Her face paled. Morgan was betraying his own flesh and blood. A tiny, defenceless baby.

She saw the women come in, and on an impulse she waved to them. Morgan turned around, stiffening. His eyes narrowed and she saw that his hands had clenched. Guilt, she thought dully.

'Do you know those women?' he demanded abruptly.

She continued to smile, despite feeling ice-cold to the

core. 'They were in the cloakroom,' she answered casually, sipping her coffee. 'What gossips!'

He seemed quite incapable of speaking for a moment. Alarm was written all over his face and she continued to play the contented fiancée while her heart shrivelled to dust.

'What...what were they gossiping about?' he enquired.

'You. Morgan,' she said quickly, before he could say anything, 'when we're married...' She paused. He'd visibly relaxed, a huge rush of air escaping his lungs. Oh, it's not over yet! she thought angrily. 'How do you see our lives panning out?'

'I work from home, you study to be an architecht, we both look after your father and also Jack—now that you're a world expert in nappy-changing. We share the cooking. I burn the meal one night, you the next.' His dark eyes glimmered. 'Then,' he murmured, 'we'll take turns to go wild in bed. My turn first.'

She could bear it no longer. Eyes like green glass, she flicked a scornful glance at him. 'Hmm. You're not too good at self-control, are you?'

Morgan stiffened, sensing that this was no tease. He shot a quick look at the group of women at the far end of the restaurant.

'Meaning?' he asked menacingly.

'I *mean*, that you find it hard to keep your hands off any female in the same house. I thought you'd fallen for my abundant charms. It seems I could have been anyone— though preferably blonde—'

'What did they say, Jodie?' he asked, his voice whisper-soft.

She quivered at the granite clench of his jaw, the coldness of his eyes. 'Does it titillate you to keep your liaisons in the family?' she asked frostily. 'To have both my father's fiancée and his daughter in your bed?'

He gave a quick intake of breath. And only she, with her deeper knowledge of him, could tell how overwhelmingly angry he was. To all appearances he was smiling pleasantly and having a casual conversation with her.

'This is not the place to discuss our affairs—'

'Correction. Your affair.'

His mouth compressed. 'Don't judge me yet,' he said with barely a trace of tremor in his voice. 'I'll drive us home. It's not what it seems, Jodie. Don't be upset.'

'Do I look upset?' she said sweetly, producing a saccharine smile.

'Yes. Your skin is taut across your cheekbones, there's a hectic pulse beating in your throat and your eyes are dead. Let's go,' he said curtly.

Hysteria was building up inside her. She needed an outlet. A release of some kind. In silence she slid into the passenger seat of his Mercedes; in silence she endured the journey. Morgan tried to speak to her but she ignored him, and after a while he gave up.

When they got back she poured brandies for them both in the drawing room and then she stood, back to the fireplace, in an attitude of possession. It was deliberate. He would learn that she wasn't to be played around with.

'So. You had an affair with Teresa. Did you father her baby?' she asked, deciding not to beat about the bush.

He let out a short, sharp profanity.

Something terrible happened inside her. Morgan had gone white, his face drained of all colour by the shock of her words. And she took no pleasure in tormenting him. Misery flooded through her, bringing her to the brink of tears.

'Let's get things straight. One thing at a time. Who is his mother?' she flung.

'I told you. He's Teresa's child,' Morgan replied hoarsely.

'And his father?'

Everything depended on his answer. Her life, her future, Jack's, her father's…

'Why don't you look on his birth certificate?' Morgan threw back his head and downed his brandy in one long gulp. Then he looked at her levelly, almost in challenge. 'Your father's name is on that document. He adores Jack. You know that the very existence of the baby has given him delight, hope, something to live for—'

'In that case,' she said, her eyes hollow with despair, 'you are no longer needed. I intend to look after my dying father. It doesn't matter how awful his last days are. I, and I alone, will be with him, because I'm family. I don't care what you do or where you stay—providing you're not in this house…my father's house, I might remind you. Because I will be here. You can visit—he'd expect that— and we will be perfectly civil to one another for my father's sake. And when…when my father dies, I will bring up my half-brother and you will disappear out of our lives for- ever—because you'll only have visited here on sufferance. And without my father there'll be no need for you to come.'

For several seconds he stared at her, the naked horror in his eyes eating like acid into her bruised heart. He tried to speak and couldn't. She knew then for sure that Jack was Morgan's baby and he was facing his worst nightmare.

Time ticked by. She was rooted to the spot by the despair in his face.

Deny it! she begged. Say it *is* my father's baby, that you made a mistake with Teresa and never loved her—say you love me, me, *me*!

He looked diminished. Robbed of energy and life. His whole body was hunched in an attitude of total anguish.

Because she loved him it tore her apart to see him so hurt. But she knew that he'd destroy her if she weakened. He'd insist that she remained with him: first for her father's sake and then for Jack. And she would spend the rest of her days passionately, hopelessly in love with a shell of a man.

'I love you,' he jerked out. 'You love me! We...I thought we'd have our own children together...'

Déjà vu. It was Chas all over again. One more selfish man who thought he had the world and his bit of fluff all sorted: adoring, obedient and pliable—but a tigress in bed.

'It seems I don't love you after all,' she snapped, her eyes flashing sparks. 'Otherwise I'd fall on your neck and say I understood. But I don't actually care. I think I must have been hungry for sex. Chas kept me well topped up in that area,' she said cruelly, hating herself, hating him and what he was doing to her. 'You were right to advise caution. I jumped into your arms when I was vulnerable—for all kinds of reasons. And now I'm jumping out again. I will look after Jack well. He is my half-brother, isn't he?'

No answer. No denial. Perhaps the women were wrong. Morgan surely couldn't give up his baby. He'd say it was his, plead with her for some kind of trade-off, ask for custody...

She passed a hand over her eyes. It didn't matter who had fathered Jack, in a way. She could never trust Morgan again.

He stood there, just breathing. Barely breathing. 'I'll go.' It was a voiceless, silent agreement shaped by an unyielding mouth beneath tragic eyes.

Aching unbearably inside, Morgan turned, faltered, and crouched down in front of the easy chair where Jack had been propped up against protective cushions. Morgan's fin-

gers touched the small hands and were gripped to a series
of coos and gurgles.

He could hear Jodie sobbing. Almost blinded by tears
himself, his throat closed with a huge lump of emotion, he
tortured himself by gazing at his son, loving him through
the pain, marvelling at the perfection of the infinitely loved
little face.

Everything he had feared had come tragically true. He
was losing his dearly beloved child and… He jammed his
teeth together to prevent himself from begging for forgiveness. He must not think. Only act. And close his heart before it broke entirely.

Because he would have to come here to see Sam, to see
Jodie, Jack…

Abruptly he stood up. Reached inside his pocket for his
diary, wrote down his contact number and flung it on the
floor. 'You can reach me there. I'll send someone round to
pick up my stuff.'

And he walked out blindly, stumbling into a table on his
way and reeling as if he were drunk.

Help me to get through this! he implored the fates. Give
me strength! Storming out, on the edge of sanity, he
slammed the front door. Viciously screwed the key in the
lock till the engine of his car roared into life. Scrubbed at
his pathetic red eyes with his handkerchief.

A mistake too far, he thought savagely. No more loving.
Not ever. Wheels screeched on the gravel. One backward
glance in the mirror. Jodie, standing in the doorway, Jack
in her arms.

'Oh, God!' he roared in despair, destroyed by the sight.
And he hurtled down the drive like a man possessed, everything he loved torn brutally from his grasp.

CHAPTER TEN

THE silence was frightening. She was alone. Bereft. Morgan's farewell to his baby had been heartbreaking. She would never forget it for the rest of her life.

She was now beyond tears. Shattered, she slumped into a chair, knowing she must rouse herself and get Jack to bed. Already he was whimpering, as if he'd sensed Morgan's terrible anguish.

Picking him up, she collected the bottle and the baby bag and stomped wearily back to the nursery. Jack was yelling. Upset, her nerves ragged from losing the man she'd loved, she tried to pacify the baby by mimicking Morgan's soothing walk. It didn't work.

Eventually the bottle was ready. She'd never fed Jack before, and it wasn't easy holding him in the crook of her arm while he wriggled and jerked and she tried to take the cap off the teat. Panicking, she wrenched at it.

Both cap and teat came off, ejecting warm milk all over her. Half sobbing with frustration, she gave her skirt a hasty wipe with a muslin square and went down for another bottle.

By the time this one had heated up sufficiently she stank of sour milk and Jack was screaming his head off. He wouldn't take the bottle for a while but eventually he did, gobbling away with awful little jerks and sobs.

Then he stopped feeding, his knees drawing up in agony as he yelled again.

'Come on, sweetheart,' she said, popping him over her shoulder. Awkwardly she put the bottle down on the floor and stood up, pacing the room. Jack stopped crying and she transferred him to the crook of her arm again, ready to feed him. He yelled, so she hoicked him to her shoulder and continued pacing.

It was forty minutes before he burped. Shaking with relief and exhaustion, she sank back into the chair. And kicked over the bottle, the teat spinning into a chair leg and thus becoming dangerously unsterilised.

Jodie felt like screaming. There were no more feeds made up. She'd have to start afresh—and it would be ages before the bottles had cooled.

'I'm sorry, I'm sorry, sweetheart!' she whispered, close to breaking point. 'Oh, hush, please don't cry! I can't bear it if you do!'

'Give him to me.'

She gasped. *'Morgan!'*

He didn't look at her. 'Go and do the bottles. I'll keep him amused.'

She didn't argue. Jack's needs came before hers. She handed the baby over and ran down the stairs, mortified that she'd managed so badly. Morgan appeared, carrying Jack and the baby gym. He obviously didn't trust her, she thought resentfully, waiting for the boiled water to cool.

By a miracle, Jack stopped grizzling and paid attention to the whirring rattle, the musical flower, the mirror and squeaky rabbit. Jodie felt her heart-rate settle down to a mere gallop instead of a thousand beats a minute.

'Did you forget something?' she asked in an unnaturally high voice.

'No.'

'You couldn't bear to leave Jack in my incapable hands,' she muttered bitterly.

'I couldn't bear to leave either of you.'

She whirled, eyes blazing. 'Because I'm your ticket to Jack!'

'No!' he cried, vehement with explosive passion. 'Because I love you. Because I can't live without you. Because I will not let you go without a fight. You are my life. You light my heart. Without you I am nothing.'

'Don't!' she moaned.

'Fill the bottles,' he said gently.

When they were done, she collapsed limply into the big armchair by the Aga. Morgan pulled up a pine chair near her and passed Jack over.

She watched the baby feeding peacefully in her arms and wondered how she could have got into such a state. Because it was important, she thought miserably. She wanted to be good at being a mother.

Morgan watched without comment while she finished the feed, winded and changed Jack. Despite Jack having a dirty nappy, she managed to juggle legs, bottom, wipes, cream and clean nappy with some skill.

Drained, she wordlessly handed him back. But Morgan put the baby on the changing mat beneath the baby gym and, taking Jodie's hand, pushed her back into the chair.

He sat down, his knees inches away. 'I had an affair with Teresa,' he said quietly.

'I don't want to know!' she spat, averting her head.

His hand drew her chin back, forcing her to look at him. 'You'll regret it for the rest of your life if you don't.'

She shrugged. 'Go on if you must,' she said in a hard tone. 'It'll be water off a duck's back.'

'You saw what she was like—'

'Beautiful,' she muttered sullenly.

'Cold and manipulative.'

Jodie's eyes widened. 'What?'

'She fooled everyone. Me included. I fell for the woman

I saw, not the person she was. And soon I disliked her. She was rude to waiters and receptionists and anyone she thought was beneath her. She spent money like water. Made emotional demands on me. I told her we were finished. She decided to spite me and deliberately engineered a meeting with your father, knowing how rich he was—and how highly I esteemed him.'

Morgan leaned forwards, his hands held loosely on his knees. Jodie stared back.

'Your father fell for her,' he went on. 'She knew how to flatter and flirt. I tried to dissuade him and we had our first row ever because he was head-over-heels in love. That very night she moved in with your father—and soon persuaded him to buy a larger and grander house for both of them. I visited less and less—'

'But you saw Teresa alone when you did visit,' she insisted, remembering the story about the daily help finding them together. She held her breath. If Morgan denied that, she'd order him out. It would be the end.

'Once,' he acknowledged. 'I'd done some work in the garden for Sam. I was just coming out of the shower when Teresa walked in virtually naked. I yelled at her to get out.'

'Did anyone see you?' she asked hesitantly.

'I don't think so. Teresa yelled back and ran off, then got into some row with the daily—she went through help like a dose of salts—and the poor woman clearly took exception to Teresa's tantrum and walked out... Just a minute. Jack's dropped off to sleep. Let me settle him upstairs.'

'I'll come,' she said grimly, determined not to let Morgan out of her sight. She waited while he organised the baby alarm and then let herself be led into the master suite. She perched on the edge of a chaise longue. Morgan sat on the floor in front of her.

'It is the truth, Jodie,' he said quietly. 'You either believe me or you don't. I can't prove it. All I ask is for you to consider the kind of man I am, and perhaps your father's opinion of me over the years. And then to weigh that up against Teresa's track record and the kind of friends she went around with. Did you like those women?'

She shuddered. 'No—but I—I daren't risk trusting you!' she whispered.

'No. I see that. Let me finish. You know Teresa was upset when Sam didn't honour his pledge to marry her as soon as possible—particularly as she was pregnant. Sam was over the moon, of course. But when he kept stalling about the wedding she became more than upset—that's when she got herself into a raging fury. After a blazing row she ran out of the house screaming abuse.'

'And she was killed,' Jodie said.

Morgan nodded. He passed a hand over his face. 'It was awful,' he said huskily. 'She'd driven into a tree. Sam went berserk. He blamed himself. I couldn't bear to see him so distraught.'

'And how did you feel about Teresa's death?' she asked shakily.

'I don't know. Angry, sad, annoyed, exasperated—'

'Upset?'

He gave a mirthless laugh. 'Not for her. Not in the way you mean. When I saw her, ruined, dying, my heart bled for her. I would have felt the same for anyone in that position—and I had been close to her, whatever I thought of her morals and values. She told me then that Sam wasn't Jack's father. I realised then why she'd been so utterly appalled when I dumped her—and why she'd found a substitute quickly. In a moment of compassion, because she was near hysterical and about to undergo a Caesarean which would almost certainly end in her death, I agreed that I would never tell a living soul her secret.'

'You are Jack's father,' Jodie choked.

His eyes flickered. 'I can't answer that. I stick by my promise. I can tell you that she was close to term, something she hadn't told Sam, who believed the baby was premature. Do the maths and draw your own conclusions. Teresa and I were lovers, Jodie. But only before your father appeared on the scene. From then on I left her strictly alone. I respected Sam. I wouldn't have poached on his own territory, even if I had loved her.'

'You were devastated by her death,' she said dully.

'By the consequences of her death,' Morgan replied. 'Sam was dangerously ill. I had a baby on my hands. I had to arrange Teresa's funeral and tell lies about how much she would be missed, knowing that my—that Jack,' he corrected, 'would be registered and recognised as Sam's child. And because Sam was so ill—and had been ecstatic about the prospect of a baby, which was all he had left of Teresa—I knew I couldn't break his heart by claiming Jack as my own.' His hand touched hers tentatively. 'What would you have done, Jodie, in my place? How do you choose? The painful, terrible truth, or the silent, protective deceit? I've paced the floor hour after hour, willing some solution to present itself, but to no avail. I kept silent for Sam's sake. It's as simple as that.'

'Sam's or Teresa's?' she asked bitterly.

'It wouldn't have done your father any good to know that she'd deceived him over who'd fathered her baby,' he replied heavily. 'So it was all for his sake, because I knew he was dying.'

'You would have adopted Jack?'

'I would.'

'Then I came along and flung all your plans into disarray!'

He smiled at that. 'You flung me into disarray,' he said drily.

'Until you hit on the perfect solution. If you married me, you'd never lose Jack!' she wailed.

His shock was too profound to be anything other than genuine. 'How can you say that?' he yelled, jumping up angrily. 'I proposed to you because I love you! I'm crazy about you. I think of you all the time. You must know that!'

Her heart thudded. Yes, she did. He loved her. Had never really loved Teresa. She couldn't even imagine them together now. Everything he'd said with such fervour had tallied with the actions of a man who'd placed himself in an impossible position: protecting her father, protecting Teresa for her father's sake and trying to do the best for Jack. She was filled with compassion. He'd never thought of himself. A truly selfless man.

She sighed.

'Jodie,' he said roughly, 'I can see how it looks. Marrying you *is* the solution to all my problems. A wonderful, amazing twist of fate that I hardly believed could have come my way! But if you think I'd ever marry someone for convenience then you don't know me!' he stormed. 'Marriage is too special, too precious to play around with! I wouldn't have anyone as Jack's stepmother just to provide a female body in the house, no matter how sexy or inventive she might be in bed, even though her hair smells of warm silk and her body drives me mad! Even if she makes me feel warm and contented and I feel as if I've found a life-long friend... What are you doing, Jodie?' he scowled savagely.

'Tucking a bit of hair behind your ear,' she answered demurely. 'You're rambling, Morgan. Betraying your feelings. So now I'm going to kiss you... And now I'm going to whisper something in your ear.'

'Jodie…?'

'I love you,' she breathed, nibbling his lobe. 'Now all you have to do is to persuade me very, very thoroughly that you love me too.'

'Uh.' He jerked as she undid a button on his shirt and slid her hand inside to rest on his chest. 'I could shower you with diamonds…' He let out a gasp when she shook her head and slowly undid his belt. 'Buy you a yacht?' he asked shakily. She smiled, flinging the belt to the ground and concentrating on shrugging off his shirt. 'Yellow thigh boots. Ferrets. Steak and kidney pie with rich gravy…'

'Idiot,' she said fondly. And, grabbing his tie, she led him to the bed. 'Just love me,' she husked, opening her arms to welcome him.

Life was perfect, Morgan mused dreamily the next morning, waking with Jodie nestling against him. Soon she would meet up with her father and they'd be living here together, as a family.

But then he frowned, as guilt and regret spoiled the paradise he'd conjured up. He would still be deceiving Sam—and now Jodie would be forced to lie to her own father too, every time they referred to Jack as Sam's baby. Their motives were honourable, but the very act of lying to Sam was souring the idyll, and suddenly Morgan's happiness had a bitter edge to it.

And yet he could do nothing, because of his solemn promise to a dying woman.

It was with mixed feelings that he took Jack along as usual on his visit to Sam that day, and he winced when Sam asked fondly, 'And how's my little boy?'

Morgan handed over Jack and struggled to divert his pain and guilt, gently, slowly telling Sam of the circumstances surrounding Jodie's arrival while the older man listened intently.

Once or twice Morgan's attention wavered, his thoughts and his mind occupied with the conspiracy he and Jodie would be indulging in where Jack's parentage was concerned. With a wry smile, Sam brought Morgan back on track until the story had been completed.

'So Teresa caused this hiatus,' Sam observed after a pause.

'She only destroyed Jodie's letters because she was insecure,' Morgan explained generously. 'She couldn't bear the thought of not marrying you.' He put his hand on Sam's bony shoulder. 'We can't turn back the past. We have all made mistakes. But Jodie desperately wants to see you. She's very special, Sam.'

The older man remained silent for a time and Morgan sat quietly, waiting for his decision. He'd already sung Jodie's praises and it had touched and heartened him to see the tears of pride forming in Sam's eyes.

Jack stirred and cooed happily, flailing his tiny arms about. Morgan gazed at the baby lovingly.

'I'd like to see her too,' Sam said, his voice choked. He took a deep breath and held out Jack, an odd expression of determination on his face. 'Take your son and tell her to come. Bring her to me in the morning.'

'That's wonderful!' Grinning inanely, Morgan leapt to his feet and took Jack eagerly, hugging him close in delight. 'She'll be thrilled! You'll love her!' There was an unusually wistful smile on Sam's face and Morgan hesitated, puzzled by it. 'What's going on? What did I say?' he demanded.

'It's what you didn't say,' Sam said shakily. He drew himself more upright against the pillows. 'You didn't express surprise when I referred to Jack as your son.'

Morgan stared, appalled, incapable of saying anything.

'I imagine,' continued Sam very quietly, 'that this might be one of the mistakes you were talking about.'

The world seemed to lurch, falter, and right itself again. 'Sam!' Morgan floundered hoarsely, knowing he should bluster this out, searching for words which wouldn't come. 'I—I—!'

'Don't deny it!' Sam said fiercely. 'I deserve better than that!'

'Oh, God!' Morgan whispered in horror. 'What have I done?'

With a groan of despair, he sank into the chair again, his head bowed, his free hand covering his face. He'd failed. What would this do to Sam? Jack meant everything to him. And now in a stupid moment of inattention he'd destroyed Sam's happiness, his hopes and his joy of fatherhood.

He knew how deeply a father felt. If Jack were to be torn from *him* he'd be distraught… Fearing for Sam's well-being, Morgan raised his heavy head to stare at the older man with the bleak, tortured eyes of a man in purgatory.

This would be the end to his imagined scenario of a happy family. Sam would never speak to him again and would die with loathing in his heart… Morgan winced from the slice of pain which stabbed him through and through. He loved his substitute father more than he'd ever known.

And now Sam was leaning forwards, tears in his pale eyes… Morgan prepared himself for the inevitable rejection, agonising over the possible consequences for Jodie and her hoped-for reunion. He hung his head again, a broken man, haunted by the thought that he'd probably ensured that Jodie would never meet her father.

And Sam would be left alone, dying by inches, without the care of the people who loved him.

'I can't bear it!' he croaked.

A hand unpicked his fingers, which were digging into his face in brutal punishment. Sam's face loomed close and Morgan jerked his head away, too ashamed to meet the older man's accusing eyes.

'This pains you,' Sam said in a surprisingly gentle voice.

He nodded, the self-castigation unendurable. 'How did you know about Jack?' he managed to rasp in a voice he didn't recognise as his own.

'Observation. I'm an architect. I see things clearly. You look at Jack with a special tenderness and protection. You're besotted with him. When my brain was less fuddled by drugs I realised why that might be so. Morgan!' Sam said unhappily. 'Talk to me! Don't beat yourself up! *Tell me!* Why have you deceived me?'

Wretchedly he dragged together the tattered remnants of his self-control, bracing himself for the ordeal of confirming Sam's suspicions.

'I didn't know until I saw Teresa after her accident. I didn't want to tell you when you were so ill,' he began haltingly. 'I couldn't. Even now…I don't know how—'

'Start at the beginning and continue till you reach the end,' suggested Sam. The startling kindness in the older man's eyes merely served to twist the knife of Morgan's shame. 'Trust me,' Sam added softly. 'I care about you, Morgan, and I can't bear to see you like this. If your motives were right then I will be content. You've given me years of happiness by being my surrogate son. I'm not going to turn away from you now. I believe in you and I think you care for me. Logic tells me there's a rational explanation somewhere.'

The two men stared at one another. Morgan saw compassion in Sam's eyes and felt a little calmer. Falteringly he began to explain the situation. It took a while before the whole story was out. And even then Morgan stuck to the promise he'd made Teresa. He didn't say that Jack was his child. But the truth was glaringly obvious.

'You fool! You utter *fool!*' Sam rebuked huskily.

'I'm sorry! I'd give anything not to have hurt you—'

'So you pussy-footed around, breaking your heart, compromising your own integrity for my protection! I don't blame you. I don't blame Teresa. I understood her very well. I loved her, though I knew her ability to love anyone in return had long been damaged by her past. We're all flawed, Morgan.' Sam sighed. 'What a hell you've been in!'

'I hated deceiving you!' he said vehemently. 'We've always been frank with one another.'

'I would have liked Jack to be my son,' Sam acknowledged. 'But I do have you, and you're very close to my heart. We could say that Jack is my surrogate grandson, couldn't we?'

'Sam…are you sure it's all right? You're not too devastated? Do you feel—?'

'I feel fine. I'm proud of you, of everything you've done to care for me. I owe you a great debt and I haven't lost Jack at all, have I? All I want is your happiness, Morgan. That's the most important thing.'

He embraced Sam, moved by the deep love between them. Both were unable to speak for a moment as emotion claimed them.

Sam swallowed and cleared his throat. 'Just make sure you bring Jodie to me,' he said jerkily.

Still overcome, Morgan rose, a lump in his throat. He felt as if a huge burden had been lifted from his shoulders. His eyes grew bright and his heart raced. 'I'll bring her,' he croaked. Embarrassed, he made a show of adjusting Jack's rucked-up jacket. He found himself grinning with relief and saw that Sam looked more relaxed and happy

than he had for a long time. 'Brace yourself,' he advised
with a fond laugh. 'She's dazzling—in every way!'

Her hand gripping Morgan's tightly, a silent and pale Jodie
walked up the stairs of the nursing home towards her father's room. Pushing the baby buggy beside her, Morgan
squeezed her hand in sympathy.

'I want him to like me,' she said nervously.

'He will, darling. He appreciates the use of colour!'
Morgan joked with a grin, eyeing her tangerine wool dress
and the fuchsia cardigan she was wearing. 'You look wonderful. Here we are. If you look through this small side
window you can see him. It'll give you a chance to prepare
yourself.'

Unable to speak, she nodded. Through the observation
window she saw the painfully thin figure of a tall man,
wrapped in a cheerful tartan rug, sitting in a reclining chair.
Her father.

Tears sprang to her eyes and Morgan's arm came firmly
around her shoulders as her thoughts and emotions churned
chaotically.

'I love him already,' she said in a choked voice. 'Particularly after his reaction to you when he realised you were
Jack's father. I admire him more than I can say. And I
desperately want to make him happy.'

'You will,' Morgan answered. 'Can you see how impatient he is to see you?'

She smiled through her tears. Her father kept glancing
towards the door and then at his watch. He pushed back
the heavy lick of white hair that had fallen onto his forehead and smoothed it with his hand, then checked the way
his open-necked shirt sat, tweaked it, and sat erect.

Her heart went out to him. He was nervous too, anxious
that she should like *him*. Deeply touched, she lost her anx-

iety and headed for the door, giving a discreet tap and hesitantly opening it. She looked up at Morgan uncertainly. He returned her glance with reassuring tenderness, put his hand in the middle of her back and pushed her forward.

'Jodie!' Sam cried, holding open his arms.

In a delirium of delight, she gave a low cry, then ran to her father and gently kissed his wan cheeks. She felt his bony arms around her, heard the breath catch in his throat as he spoke her name again, and buried her face in his neck, too overcome to talk.

'Let me look at you, sweetheart,' he whispered.

Sniffing, she moved back and sank to her knees beside him, scrubbing at her eyes with her handkerchief. 'I can't t-tell you how I feel about seeing you...!' Her voice gave out and Morgan passed her a handkerchief, touching her arm solicitously.

'From what Morgan's told me, I'm sure you will, when you get your second wind,' he teased with a smile.

Jodie laughed, and shot Morgan an amused glance.

'Morgan!' Affectionately Sam held out his hand.

'You're looking well,' Morgan said warmly, clasping it in his.

'I feel wonderful. Hello, Tiddler. Still keeping your father up half the night?' Sam murmured, stroking the baby's sleepy face. He looked up at Morgan with brimming eyes. 'Thank you,' he said passionately, 'thank you for my daughter. For everything.' Earnestly he turned to Jodie. 'This man is like gold. He's the best.'

'I know.' She smiled happily and looked up at Morgan again, her gaze lingering lovingly because he looked as if he might do cartwheels at any moment.

'I thought you might. So when are you two getting hitched?' her father asked with studied casualness.

They both gasped. Morgan began to laugh as Jodie's mouth dropped open. 'How…? Who…?'

'Dozy old man I might be,' he said drily, 'but it doesn't take a psychic to recognise an engagement ring and mutual adoration. Do you two know you hardly take your eyes off each other?'

'No!' Giggling, she kissed him. And, delighted by his chuckle, kissed him again.

'I adore her, Sam,' Morgan said, his hand caressing Jodie's head.

'Of course you do. She's eminently adorable. Takes after me, doesn't she?' her father countered.

'Egocentric, arrogant old man!' muttered Morgan, the twitch of his mouth betraying his amusement.

'Arrogant enough to assume I'll be giving the bride away and not too old that I can't stuff myself into Father of the Bride gear,' he muttered, pretending to grumble. 'And, before you suggest it, I refuse to go down the aisle in a wheelchair.'

Jodie glanced at Morgan in alarm, but he didn't look concerned. 'Then you'd better get off your backside soon and get walking again, you old faker,' he drawled.

Her father laughed. It started as a thin and reedy sound, but gradually became deeper, and she realised the value of healing laughter as the colour came into the sunken cheeks and the thin, pinched mouth filled out.

'Shall we send the wretch away, Father?' she suggested impishly.

'My dearest girl,' he said with a feigned sigh, 'without Morgan and his ridiculous mixture of gentle coaxing and flagrant bullying I wouldn't be alive today. So we'll let him stay and he can continue to gaze at you soppily while you tell me about yourself. To pass the time he can work out a fitness plan for me.'

'I have the very thing,' Morgan said airily. 'Based on a Marine assault course—'

He ducked to avoid the grapes that Sam was lobbing his way and his heart lurched to see the helpless laughter in Sam and Jodie's faces as they exchanged glances.

Sam was on the mend. He knew it would be a brief respite, and that the future was brief, but it would be happy. He and Jodie would see to that. Even now she was plumping up his cushion and deliberately calming down the conversation, talking quietly about her childhood.

Morgan drew up a chair and watched them both in relief. The three people he loved most in this world were in this room and they were happy. That was all he wanted. His hand stole into Jodie's. Their eyes met.

She saw the glisten of tears there and knew she was filling up too. Her father's hand tightened in hers and she heard a sniff from his direction.

'I'm so-o-o ha-appy!' she jerked hopelessly.

The two men laughed fondly, and as they swept her into their embrace she felt a deep sense of serenity. There were three men in her life. And she had more love than she could ever have imagined. She kissed them all: her father, Morgan, Jack. And blissfully settled down to catch up on the past, and to plan the future.

EPILOGUE

To JODIE's profound pleasure, her father lived for nearly three years, his mind wandering only a little towards the end. The doctors had expressed amazement, but Jodie and Morgan knew that it was happiness and the sound of laughter in the house that had kept him alive for longer than expected.

'I still can't believe that he didn't suffer,' she said soberly, when they were reminiscing about him, some six months after his death.

Morgan held her close. 'Nor I, my darling. He loved every day, was grateful for each hour that he was alive.'

'I'm so proud of him. He was a wonderful, adorable man.'

'He was proud of you and your ambition to be an architect.'

'Dadad!' came an imperious little voice.

Morgan's face softened and he picked up his small son, swinging him easily into his arms. 'Come on, sweetheart,' he said softly. 'Shall we go and listen to Mummy reading to Jack?'

Little Tom nodded enthusiastically. 'Baby come,' he said, pointing to Jodie's faintly swelling stomach.

'Baby come,' Morgan repeated tenderly. 'Baby can listen too.'

Jodie took Morgan's hand. Her father's death had left a huge hole in her life. But she had Morgan, and her studies, and their work with the homeless, and she had her beloved babies.

'Coming, Jack! Ready or not!' she called in warning.

There was a familiar squeal as the little scamp raced from the bathroom, where he was supposed to have been doing his teeth—but had probably been lining up his ducks in the sink.

Jodie and Morgan laughed and made their way upstairs to sit together on the bed: Jack all scrubbed, his dark, curly hair temporarily smooth and tidy, little Tom tucked up beside his adored half-brother—who kindly pointed to ducks and jam-eating bears—Morgan, his arm around as many of his loved ones as would reach, and Jodie, dressed in stunning scarlet silk palazzos and a low-cut beaded citrus top, her eyes shining, her heart full of love, as she read to the family she'd always longed for.

'Love you, Mummy,' said Jack when the story had ended. 'Love you, Daddy. 'Night, Tom. 'Night, Baby.'

Morgan grinned. 'Gruesome! It's like the Waltons, isn't it?' he whispered.

Jodie glared. 'Penalty,' she decided.

His eyes lit up. 'Oh, good!' he murmured. 'Bed, Tom.' Morgan kissed their son. 'Bed, Mummy,' he drawled, his eyebrows outdoing Groucho Marx.

Jodie giggled, kissed the boys, hugged them and kissed them again. She tucked under Morgan's arm, where she fitted perfectly, and switched off the light.

And on the landing he kissed her. 'I love you,' he husked.

'Down, boy!' she reproved.

At once the elderly Satan obediently slumped at the bottom of the stairs, grumbling.

Morgan laughed with Jodie as they wandered towards their bedroom. 'It is possible to have everything,' he said, pulling her to him on the high four-poster. 'I have you and the children. It's all I could ever want.'

'You'd go without supper? Hot showers? Races up to the Long Man?' she murmured.

'Shut up and kiss me,' he growled.

She smiled a dreamy smile. Their mouths met and she lost herself in his arms, surrendering to the deepest joy any woman could know: the unshakable love of her family and an enduring, overwhelmingly sweet passion for them all...

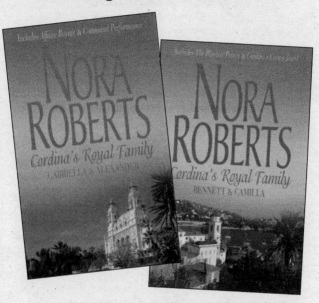

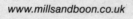